AGAINST THE ODDS

REDLINE SERIES BOOK ONE

N. L. TAYLOR

A&L

Alan and Lane
Media

*For my father, who restored my first car
and taught me that all things were possible with
dedication and hard work.*

Hold fast to dreams
For if dreams die
Life is a broken-winged bird
That cannot fly
—Langston Hughes

PROLOGUE

"Walk with the knowledge that you are never alone."
–Audrey Hepburn

Our Lady of Faith Cemetery, Fall 2013

Jake Masercotti, a broken man before the age of twenty-one, knelt before the granite headstone bearing his mother's name. A cool breeze carrying the promise of winter ruffled his dark hair, stirring the leaves scattered about him—a riot of color against the verdant grass and dark stone markers that encircled him like judges upon high.

His mother loved autumn: the colors, the scents, the possibilities it promised. Like everything about Lilianna Di Silva, her love of fall was infectious, making Jake love it too. But that love came to a violent end when he was twelve. Now, instead of hope and possibility, autumn represented only one thing to him: death.

Jake lifted his head and, with a trembling hand, traced the letters of his mother's name etched into the cold gray stone, his fingertips lingering on the date she died: September 25, 2005.

Eight years.

Eight years since he learned that everything you loved, everything that mattered to you, could be ripped away in a heartbeat. Eight years since he learned that a soul could be broken and never be made whole again.

I

Whoever said there were seven stages of grief was full of shit. For him, there were only two stages: anger and guilt.

He took a deep breath, the acid in his stomach churning. "Hey, Ma. I'm sorry I haven't been here for a couple of weeks. I was—" He stopped short, curling his hands into fists. Even in death, he hated the idea of disappointing her, the one person in the world who'd understood and believed in him. His only champion.

"I was locked up, Ma," he continued. "I messed up. *Again.* I'm sorry. I know I've said that a hundred times before, but I mean it. I do. I...I don't know what's wrong with me. Why I can't do anything right...why I'm such a failure," he choked out.

Jake looked away, disgusted. It wasn't the first time he'd been in trouble with the law, but this recent skirmish was more serious than his usual drunk and disorderly or petty theft charges. This time, he faced assault.

In his defense, Jake didn't start the fight. His little brother's foster father did. He made a crack about their parents during one of Jake's weekly visits with Dario. And while the nasty comment might have held true for their father, it wasn't true for their mother. She was a saint. And there was no way he would let that *stronzo* tarnish her name.

No. Fucking. Way.

So, he beat the crap out of the *coglione*. Right there in the middle of the park for everyone and God to see. At the time, he didn't care. A red haze coated his vision, leaving him with a single goal: putting Bruce in his place. In hindsight, however, Jake knew it was a mistake—one that would cost him. He'd lose his visitations with Dario for sure, and maybe even face serious time in lockup. The lockup didn't scare him. He'd done time in juvie; he knew how the system worked, how to survive. But the time away from Dario? That killed him.

A bleak realization struck. Maybe Dario was better off without him. Jake wasn't exactly the "role model" type—more like the poster boy for bad decisions with his criminal record, tattoos, and anger management issues.

Loneliness swelled inside Jake's chest, making it difficult to breathe. Without Dario, he had no one. He'd be all alone.

He shook his head. Who was he kidding? He already *was* alone. No one, not even his brother, understood the gut-wrenching pain that had branded his heart or about his dark little secret: the corrosive fact that ate away at him day after day, the insidious monster that whispered *your fault* every night before he went to sleep. The sad reality was Jake Masercotti was alone—lost—in a world he couldn't succeed in, couldn't catch a single break in, because he didn't deserve anything good. Not after how he'd failed. Success, joy, family...it was all a lost cause. Hopeless.

He was hopeless.

He reached up and gripped the headstone with white knuckles, choking on a long-buried sob. "God, Ma...I don't want to do this anymore. I don't want to keep screwing up, letting you and Dario down, but I can't help it. And I'm tired...so tired of it all. Maybe you had the right idea. Maybe I should give up too."

He reached into his motorcycle jacket and fumbled for the key that would release him from this prison once and for all. As his fingers pulled the steel blade from his pocket, a desolate wail pierced the air.

Jake's head snapped up. The blade slipped from his fingers and disappeared into the grass as his heart wrenched in two. He clutched at his chest where the soul-deep anguish had sliced through him, its ache embedding itself there, entwining with his own sorrow.

He leaned around the headstone and spotted a girl of maybe seventeen or eighteen kneeling in front of a pair of matching marble gravestones several plots away. Bent over at the waist, she had her arms wrapped around her frame as she rocked in a futile attempt at comfort. Her entire body shook with violent sobs as she murmured a familiar mantra over and over.

"I'm sorry... It was my fault...all my fault. I failed you both."

Jake slumped against the cold granite marker, transfixed by the fragile girl whose emotions mirrored his own. He didn't know how long he sat there like that: watching, listening. It could have been minutes, hours, days. It didn't matter. The only thing that mattered was this girl and the startling awareness that he wasn't alone in his grief and guilt. *She* was there, feeling as he did.

A spark of hope flickered in his chest—a tiny spark, like a flint strike, but for now it was enough. It was enough to know he wasn't alone.

∾

NIKKI ELLIOT LEANED AGAINST HER PARENTS' GRAVES, A LEATHER-BOUND journal clutched in her trembling hands, open to the final page. Her voice shook, wobbling over the words at an agonizing pace, but she kept going, determined to finish reading this entry to her parents.

"*...And I would live for myself and my future, swimming through the oceans of pain, guilt, and sorrow until I found peace. I would thwart the thieves of shadow and sin who'd tried to unravel me, flaunting their failure like a scarlet letter with every breath, every achievement, every moment of my future until my last, dying breath.*"

Nikki puffed out a heavy sigh as she closed the journal.

"So, that's it. That's our story—my version of it, anyway. My therapist asked me to write it to help me open up about that night...to finally put it out there." She ran her hands over the leather journal, a record of the work she and Patty had done to help her come to grips with the loss of her parents. Six months of emotionally fueled sessions and homework assignments that helped bring her healing when she believed there wouldn't be any.

"Patty was happy with it. She even encouraged me to have it published in a compilation of vignettes about grief, but I won't do that. I did this for me, for *us*, no one else. It was the most difficult—most painful—of Patty's assignments, but I'm glad I did it. It was a way for me to finally release the guilt I've carried and to move out of the limbo that's gripped me since you died. And while I have a ways to go in dealing with it *fully*, I've reached a point where I'm ready for what comes next."

She smiled at the thought, knowing her parents—especially her father—would be proud of how far she'd come.

After a few more heartfelt words and a teary goodbye, Nikki stood, clutching at her scarf as a chill autumn wind whipped through the cemetery. Instinctively, she glanced over her shoulder and spotted a pair of familiar black motorcycle boots peeking out from a gravestone down the pathway from her. *He* was there again, as he'd been every Sunday for the last six months. She didn't know his name, what he looked like outside of his boots and his dark hair, who he mourned—anything about the man who came to Our Lady of Faith Cemetery on Sundays. All she knew was that this man, this complete stranger, brought her comfort when no one else could. It was the strangest thing. Though they'd never shared eye contact, much less spoken a word, she knew what he felt. It was instinctual. She knew he carried the pain, the guilt, and the regret that she did. And in knowing that, he'd made her feel like she wasn't alone in her suffering, like there was someone out there who *got it*—who understood what it felt like when their soul was broken.

Part of her wanted to thank him for what he'd done. Today was her last day there for the next year, at least. She'd signed a multiyear contract with Ferrari to compete on their European sports car racing team. This was her last chance to let him know what he'd done for her. But she didn't approach him. That would be beyond creepy, all things considered.

Sighing, Nikki sent the man a smile she hoped he felt and a silent *thank you* she hoped he heard then turned and walked away from the *three* people who'd left indelible marks on her heart and soul and headed toward the future, knowing she was leaving a piece of herself behind with each of them.

4

PART I

*"We must accept finite disappointment
but never lose infinite hope."*
–Martin Luther King Jr.

1

High Plains Raceway, Colorado – Present day

The symphony of four hundred horsepower produced by an orchestra of American craftsmanship thundered through the cockpit of the 1965 Shelby GT 350. The automotive concerto flooded Nikki Elliot's veins with a heart-pumping cocktail of adrenaline and exhilaration, fueling her assault on the track. She and the Shelby were in complete synchronicity as they maneuvered the two-mile course at breakneck speeds with a single goal: winning.

Nikki reveled in the high-octane bliss as she soared down into turn seven, headed for The Funhouse—her favorite series of sweeper turns. But that bliss evaporated when she came up on a familiar '69 L88 Corvette.

"Fan-freaking-tastic," she grumbled into the mic linking her to her oldest brother, Dino, on pit lane.

The worry and frustration in his voice were evident the moment he spoke. "What's wrong? Is something up with the car? Do you need to pit?"

She stifled a groan. Dino always panicked when she came over the radio. Part of her understood. If he'd been in a near-fatal wreck, she would worry too. *Still...* Her wreck was two years and over a season of races ago. There was no need to panic. She had this.

"Relax. It's nothing a passing flag for a certain Corvette driver wouldn't fix," she said, mad-dogging the back end of the Corvette.

Dino rolled off a string of curses. "Worrying about you is my job, Nik.

You're my baby sister, for Chrissake," he snapped. "And why the hell is he in front of you, anyway? I thought Dixon was behind you in qualifying."

Nikki started weaving the Shelby from side to side—a clear signal for the 'Vette to accept defeat. They were eighteen laps into a thirty-lap race. If she took the lead, she'd hold it. Ron Dixon, driver of the L88, was a former stock car champ and a solid driver overall, but she was better. A former European Le Mans Series driver *and* a professional rally driver, Nikki knew the variances of road courses like this one. Out here, she was completely in her element.

She choked back a sharp reply, feeling like she was going to suffocate under Dino's fear and overwhelming need to control *everything*. "I'm behind him because of that issue with the carburetor yesterday. It put me in fifteenth place in qualifying, remember? I'd have caught him sooner, but the flag boys haven't been very forthcoming with my passing flags."

Flag boys. Passing flags.

She gripped the steering wheel tighter.

What a joke.

She didn't belong out here—not at this point in her career. Vintage racing wasn't part of her plan—not for at least another fifteen years. Retired drivers and novices looking to live out racecar driver fantasies raced in vintage series, not someone bound for Formula 1 only two years ago. But an accident at the Classic Twenty-Four Heures du Mans had changed her grand plans—changed everything for her in ways she'd never imagined.

The wreck left Nikki with a severe concussion and back injuries, pulling her out of racing for the rest of that season and much of the next. The grueling recovery cost her nearly a year of track time—a horrific setback that could quickly become a career killer. It was easy for teams to forget drivers when they weren't around; there were plenty of others lined up behind them, vying for a spot on a team. Now she was starting over, scratching and clawing her way back into a sport she was near the top of a short time ago.

The situation wasn't fair—but then, as Nikki knew all too well, neither was life. But you couldn't let that stop you. You had to keep going, no matter the setback. Her father taught her that lesson. He always told her: "No matter what life throws at you, you pick yourself up and keep moving forward. Let nothing stop you from achieving your dreams, *principessa*." And that was exactly what she was doing now: moving forward—even if it felt like she was traveling at a turtle's pace.

She stalked Dixon's rear end through The Funhouse and over Dead Man's Hill, her frustration mounting. Being stuck there—trailing after him like an obstinate sibling when she should have been leading the pack—

killed her. It took several mental countdowns to keep her from blowing track protocols and dusting him, flag or no flag—a move that might give her immediate satisfaction but could cost her in the long run. With Nikki's luck, the officials would kick her off the race, if not the circuit, something she couldn't afford. She was under contract by one of the few sponsors she'd managed to recruit for her Pro Mazda Championship team, to race in the Vintage American Motorsports (VAM) series. If she lost her spot, she'd lose their funding—critical sponsorship dollars she needed to keep her Mazda team afloat.

Nikki let out a whoop when a flagman finally signaled Dixon to move aside and accept his defeat.

"Damn it, Nik! Don't do that! I'll be deaf before I'm thirty!" Dino barked over the sound of their brother, Mike, laughing in the background.

She cringed. "Sorry. I got excited when I saw the passing flag."

"Yeah, I figured that. Just be cool, okay? You know Dixon. The guy hates to lose and has a tendency to ignore the flags, especially when it comes to *you*."

He was right. Dixon hated losing to Nikki—with a passion. Most drivers gunned for her on the vintage circuit. Beating out a former pro would bring them bragging rights they couldn't resist, but Dixon took it to a whole different level. She didn't know what spurned his intense desire to beat her, but whatever it was, it drove him to do things that *should have* gotten him kicked off the track. She supposed it didn't hurt that he was a major contributor to the circuit's financial infrastructure. Losing Ron would mean losing his steady influx of cash—one that Vintage American Motorsports needed to keep the series going.

"Don't worry. I can handle this gearhead," Nikki assured him, sliding the car to the outside of the turn and gunning the accelerator to pass him, only to be blocked by Dixon's 'Vette a half-second later.

"DAMN IT!" She slammed on the brakes and slid behind him.

"*What?* What happened?" Dino yelled. "I can't see from this vantage point!"

She tailed Dixon out of the sweeper turn and onto Highway to Hell—the quarter-mile straightaway that led to the most challenging portion of the course, Jacob's Ladder. The steep incline ended in a hairpin turn, dumping drivers out onto another shorter straightaway with a tricky chicane at the end.

"He swung out and blocked the pass as I was coming up. It's a good thing we installed those rock-solid brakes last week…" She shuddered, not finishing the rest of her thought. She didn't need to. Dino knew what she wasn't saying: without those brakes, she and Dixon would have collided. And a collision like that, at speeds over one hundred miles per hour, would have been devastating. Nikki would know. Her wreck at Le Mans had been at speeds near that.

Dino belted out a chorus of F-bombs as she slid over once more and gunned it, only to have to hit the brakes even harder this time when the Corvette swerved, narrowly missing the passenger door.

Now it was Nikki's turn to swear as the Shelby fishtailed, forcing her to fall back even farther.

"This prick has a death wish. If a wreck doesn't kill him, I will when I finish this race," she muttered.

"Jesus. Where are the track officials? Didn't anyone see that?" Dino paused, barking orders at Mike to go look for someone. "Look, forget the race, Nik. Let him have the win."

Her hackles shot up. "No! I'm not throwing a race because this creep doesn't like to lose."

Nikki didn't have it in her to throw a race—no racecar driver did. But her determination to drive her best—to win—veined deeper than most. As a woman, she'd had to work twice as hard as the men she raced alongside to prove she was a solid driver. And for the last four years, she'd worked even harder to prove to *herself* that she wasn't someone who quit when things got tough.

"Don't be stupid. It's not worth it. It's a vintage heat, not a Formula 1 race. Be smart and let the dick win!" Dino ordered. He had a fuse as long as her pinky—a trait he inherited from their hot-blooded Sicilian father.

She released a slow breath. Did they have to get into this now? Didn't he care she had a race to win?

"I will not take second place to his asshat, Dino. Principle alone dictates that I screw him to the wall," she replied, gathering the reins of her temper and stopping before she said anything else. She needed to stay focused on the race and not justifying her actions to anyone—including her brother. Besides, Dino didn't understand her need to win, so she shouldn't get *too* angry with him, even if she felt like he needed a verbal smackdown. The fact was, unlike her and their father, Dino didn't have racer DNA: the index of primal instinct and raw aggression that fueled drivers at every race, no matter how big or small, to drive hard and win.

"If those are your principles, sis, you are seriously screwed up," he fired back.

Nikki ground her teeth, struggling for patience and understanding—although that grew more difficult with Dino. He'd made it crystal clear since her accident that he hated her career. She wished she could afford to hire someone else to pit for her in the VAM and Mazda series. It would be so much easier if she could—for both of them. Their relationship grew increasingly tenuous with each race, and it worried her. Dino and Mike were the last ties Nikki had to her mother and father. If she didn't have them—

She silenced the thought. Imagining her life without either of her brothers was unthinkable. But she couldn't help but wonder how much more tension her relationship with Dino could take before it snapped.

"I am not screwed up, Dino," she answered. "I'm not the one who's messing up here—Dixon is. Have a little faith. I know what I'm doing." She hoped he took her words to heart and ended the chatter so she could do her job in peace.

"I don't think you do, Nik... You haven't for some time."

Nikki gripped the steering wheel tighter as cold steel shot down her spine.

So much for patience and understanding.

"What the hell does *that* mean?" she bit out before she could stop herself. Dino knew how to push her buttons unlike anyone else.

Silence greeted her. When Dino finally spoke, her chest tightened at the pain in his plea, defusing some of her anger. "Nothing. Forget it. Just, *please*, don't get yourself killed."

Losing Nikki would destroy her brothers, strained relationship or not. Even so, Dino needed to trust her out there and realize that because she'd been in one wreck didn't mean there would be another. And that regardless of the risks, being a race-car driver wasn't simply her career. It was who she was.

"I won't. Trust me. I've got this." She gunned the accelerator until she was centimeters from Dixon's bumper, the desire to pass him building in her veins like a fever.

Rivulets of sweat trickled down her neck, pooling in the hollow of her breasts and lower back as she spent the next two laps drafting him. Colorado in late August was murder, and it was even hotter in the Shelby, which only added fuel to her mounting frustration. But it was the warning flag she received for drafting—of all things—that nearly snapped her temper.

They were going to give *her* a warning? For *drafting*?

Lord.

Why race at all if they weren't *actually* going to race? What was the point of these vintage heats if they weren't going to drive these cars to their full capabilities? Hadn't the US learned anything from the European vintage circuit?

Swearing under her breath, Nikki backed off a fraction, knowing she couldn't take much more. Neither could Dino. He was cursing up a storm on pit lane, yelling to anyone who would listen about Dixon's actions, threatening to sue if anything happened to her.

The lawsuit bit was a total bluff. They couldn't afford a lawyer if they needed one, but the threats he and Mike made to Dixon's personal well-being were rock solid. Nobody messed with their baby sister and got away with it. She hated to think about the kind of trouble her brothers would get into when they caught sight of Dixon in the paddock later—or when she did, for that matter. Nikki had as much hot-blooded Sicilian fire coursing through her veins as they did.

Then, just when she thought she was going to blow her top, she saw Dixon get the passing flag, followed by a warning.

"Finally," she sighed then reported the call to Dino. "If he pulls anything now, it's over for him for the rest of the race—maybe even the season. This is his fourth warning this year. The officials *can't* ignore that, regardless of his money."

"It's about fucking time."

Nikki slid the Shelby over for the third and final time, passing Dixon as they rocketed out onto the straightaway, flipping him the bird.

Dixon returned the rude gesture, but she only caught a fleeting glimpse of it. Free at last to open up the four-hundred-horsepower engine beneath the hood, Nikki hit the accelerator, smiling to herself as the high-octane cocktail of adrenaline and freedom chased away her anger, putting her back in her Zen place: behind the wheel of a racecar with a sea of asphalt spiraling out before her.

"I'M GOING TO DROP OFF THE TRAILER BACK BY THE GARAGE WHEN WE GET home. I'll unload the Shelby later. I need to head into the shop," Dino announced as he turned the Ford Expedition onto Fox Hollow Road, headed for their home in Wood Glenn, California.

Nikki didn't respond. She was too focused on the black Mercedes sedan two car lengths behind them. The vehicle had been with them since they left Sacramento. Before that, a black SUV trailed a few lengths behind them all the way from Colorado. She tried to shake the uneasy feeling the cars brought, but she couldn't. There was something eerily familiar about the scene and the fear slithering down her spine—almost like déjà vu.

She bit back a sharp curse as a sharp pain lanced her skull and a series of images flashed through her mind. In the images, Nikki paced frantically in what looked like an RV—the kind she used to stay in at the racetracks back when she raced for Ferrari. But in the image, she wasn't wearing her black-and-red racing suit. This suit was forest green with white lettering, though she couldn't make out the words. Wherever she'd been, it wasn't a sports car race, which meant it was probably one of the rallies she'd done in Europe two years ago.

Or...

Or maybe it was a memory of the Le Mans Classic, the race that changed everything. The one she couldn't remember.

The concussion she sustained in the accident had left her with retrograde amnesia. As a result, she couldn't remember anything of the race, the accident, or several weeks leading up to the event. Of all of her injuries —and there were many—the amnesia was the most frustrating. Racecar drivers learned something from every race, every accident. Nikki hadn't learned a damn thing from the Le Mans Classic.

She leaned her head against the seat. Could this be a memory of that time? If it was a memory of Le Mans, it was the first she'd recalled since, and a miracle at that. Doctors told her the likelihood of her regaining her memories was slim, especially after this long.

She squeezed her eyes shut as the images began to recede, trying to grab hold of them and make sense of what she saw—what she might have remembered. Where was she in the image? And why did she look so afraid? She was never afraid before a race. Being on the track was her happy place.

A heavy hand landed on her shoulder, jarring her from the puzzle. "Hey, are you listening?" Mike asked.

Her eyes snapped open. "Huh? What?"

"Dino was talking about the plan for when we get home," he said, leaning between the seats. "Whoa... What's wrong? You look pale, *dolcezza*."

Dino glanced at her as he turned the Expedition into their driveway and waited for the automatic gate to open. "He's right. What's up?"

Nikki hesitated. Should she tell them the truth? Tell them what she saw, what she *might have* remembered? She looked at her brothers' strained faces and knew the answer: no. If she told them her memories might be coming back and that, in them, she was afraid, it would only add fuel to their anxiety about her racing again. Besides, it was probably nothing. The worst thing she could have been worried about back then was getting turned down by the GP2 team scouting her at the time.

"I'm fine—just a little tired," she said, only lying a little.

Her head didn't hurt anymore, and she *was* beat. They'd been on the road for two days after five grueling days of racing, trying to get home so Mike could head back to the body shop he and Dino had opened up north, and she and Dino could return to work at Vintage Motors, the Bay Area shop the boys inherited from their parents. Both businesses were thriving but only because Dino and Mike poured their hearts and souls into them, employing some of the best mechanics and restoration specialists in California. Nikki was among those employees. As an amateur driver once more, she didn't earn a living at racing, even with her wins. Everything left over after living expenses went into her Pro Mazda team, leaving her broke most of the time.

"Are you sure? It looks like more than that," Dino pressed, maneuvering the Expedition up the drive leading to the fading farmhouse they called home.

Nikki nodded. "Yeah, I'm sure." She watched the Mercedes continue on past their property, the eerie sense of déjà vu snaking through her again.

Dino glanced over. He started to say something, when his phone chirped. He grabbed it, scowling at the screen as he threw the truck into park.

"What's wrong?" Nikki asked.

He tapped off a rapid-fire text. "Shop stuff," he grumbled then hopped out.

"Did something happen while we were gone? Is everything okay?" Nikki continued, following them to the back where they started unloading their gear.

"Nothing serious...yet," Dino said, avoiding her eyes.

"What do you mean, *yet*?" She grabbed her bag and the trophies from the vintage race and Pro Mazda event she attended a few days before that. The trip to Colorado was a doubleheader. Not that she minded. She was grateful to be back behind the wheel of a car in the Mazda series; she wouldn't catch the eye of potential sports-car or Indy-racing teams and eventually make it to Formula 1 without it. Scouts from those series recruited heavily from the Pro Mazda Series and little else in the US.

Dino and Mike exchanged a look.

Something was definitely up.

Nikki set her things down. "All right. What's going on? You're doing that Jedi-mind-speak thing, and you only do that when something is wrong. Spill it," she demanded, looking from Dino to Mike and back.

Dino ran a hand through his inky hair, exposing the tribal tattoos wrapping his bicep. "I didn't want to get into this now. I planned on talking to you later, when I got back..." He hesitated. "It's...about your racing."

"What about it?" she asked, immediately prickling.

Dino let out a heavy breath, resignation settling on his face. "I can't keep helping you with it, Nik. It's costing me too much."

Guilt soured her stomach. She knew her racing schedule was tough for Dino. Semi-pro drivers and their teams were away from home more than half the year. For a small-business owner like Dino, that was brutal. It's why Nikki was so shocked when he volunteered to take over as lead mechanic after her Mazda team could no longer afford to fund a complete pit crew for this season.

Nikki didn't want Dino to do it, but she had no other choice. She didn't have the money to hire someone to round out the crew herself, and without a lead mechanic, her team would have been forced to withdraw, killing her career for the season, if not altogether.

"I'm sorry. I know it's been hard on the shop not having you around as much, but it isn't for too much longer. The Mazda season ends in November, and I'm sure I'll have an offer from a pro team lined up for next year and be done with the vintage circuit," she said.

Dino folded his arms across his broad chest, his dark eyes flaring. "Unbelievable."

Nikki reared back. "What?"

"You can't see it, can you?"

"See what?"

"That it's not just about the shop. It's also about what your racing is costing *us*." He waved his hand between him and Mike. "Your family."

Nikki shook her head. "I'm sorry. What is it costing you guys besides time?"

"Oh, I don't know. How about our freaking minds?" Dino snarled.

Her brows shot up. "You're *that* worried about another accident? Don't you think that's a little irrational? I mean, come on. The odds of me having another wreck like Le Mans aren't very high."

Dino took a step closer, his lean, muscular frame taut as he loomed over her. "The only one who's being irrational here is *you*. It's not about worrying that you'll wreck again, Nik. It's about knowing that you *will*. It's only a matter of time."

A matter of time...? Didn't he have *any* faith in her?

"Dino," she began, "I'm not the horrible driver you seem to think I am. You're worrying over nothing."

"Bullshit! With the risks you take, another wreck is guaranteed. And the worst part is: You don't see the jeopardy you put yourself in at every event. You're too focused on winning. Nothing else matters to you."

"Uh, the last time I checked, that's what racecar drivers did. They hit the track to win, not pussyfoot around," she said, folding her arms across her chest.

Mike stepped forward, his eyes sympathetic. "This is different from wanting to win, sis. It's like..." He hesitated, glancing at Dino. Mike was never good at being the hard ass, but Dino excelled at it.

"Your judgment, your instinct as a driver, is gone," Dino accused.

Nikki's spine went straight. "That's not true! I know what I'm doing.

I've been racing since I was *five*. Not to mention that this season has been a huge success for me. Several automotive journalists have called it the comeback of the decade."

"I don't care what *journalists* are saying. They don't know you like I do. I've watched you race your entire life. You've been off since—"

"Since when?" she cut in, her temper teetering on the brink of a Mount St. Helens-size explosion. How could they question her instincts as a driver? Hadn't she proven to them, to *everyone*, that she had what it took?

"Since Le Mans," he finished.

"What? That wreck had nothing to do with instinct. The brakes failed. I can't control that."

The hold Dino had on his temper shattered. "Not *failure*, Nik. Brake *fade*! Race officials said the brake failure was due to fucking brake fade! Something *you* should have recognized and pit before it got to that point. You know Le Mans Tigers and their problems with overheating brakes better than anyone, but you were so blinded by your need to win, you ignored the warning signs and nearly got yourself killed. Why can't you see that?"

"I can't see it because it's not true!" she roared back.

"How do you know? You don't remember anything from that day or the weeks leading up to it. You have no idea what was going through your head at that race. There were no in-car video recordings because the camera malfunctioned. And what about your crew chief? He fucking took off after the accident. You haven't seen or heard from him since, which speaks volumes about his confidence in you. Doesn't it? So, really, sis, how can you say for certain you weren't at fault when so much evidence says you were?"

Nikki's breath caught. Dino was right about most of it. The official cause of the wreck had been deemed brake failure due—*likely*—to brake fade. But the key word in that report, the word she clung to like a life raft —and the one that Dino chose to overlook—was *likely*...a far cry from anything conclusive. Without definitive proof, something impossible due to the condition of the car after the wreck, the absence of her memory and in-car video recordings, *and* her crew chief's mysterious disappearance, brake fade remained *one* possibility for the accident. As long as that was the case, she had hope that the brake failure was related to something else —something beyond her control. It might have been only a shred of hope, but she would cling to it until she knew different. She had to. If she accepted what Dino said, that meant—

She silenced that thought. She couldn't go there in front of her brothers.

Nikki gave her head a violent shake, clutching her shred of hope. "I know it's not true because I know myself." The tone of her voice—the uncertainty in it—scared her. "I know I wouldn't take any unnecessary risks. If it was brake fade, I would have pit before it got to failure point."

She thought of her crew chief then. If only she could get in contact with him. He'd be able to clear everything up. She would have communicated any braking problems to him during the race. But as Dino pointed out, Phillipe disappeared right after the accident, and no one had been able to find him since—not the race officials, not her, not even the police. He'd vanished without a trace, taking his knowledge of what led to the accident with him.

"You're wrong, kiddo, and that means you need to quit before it's too late," Dino replied, his handsome features—the ones that reminded her of her father in so many ways—hardening. If only he were more like their dad on the inside. Al Eleuteri wouldn't have doubted his daughter or questioned her abilities, not like this. He would have held on to hope because he believed in her.

"You want me to *quit?*" She gasped.

"Yes." He stepped forward and placed his hands on her shoulders, his voice echoing his worry and frustration. "I can't continue to support you in this. Watching you risk your life race after race is killing me. And then there's the shop. Vintage Motors needs its boss to be there. I can't be away anymore."

Quit racing? It was her whole life. She didn't know what she'd do without it, who she'd be.

Nikki shrugged off his hands and stepped back, determination and anger zipping through her. There was no way in hell she'd walk away—not after everything she'd been through.

"I'm sorry, but I won't quit. I can't. This is my life...I won't give up on it." She grabbed her things and stood tall, looking into her brothers' worried but determined faces, hating that she caused them any sort of pain but also knowing it wouldn't stop her. This was her life to live, not theirs.

"I get that you're worried about me because you love me, *and* that you need to be at the shop. But none of that means *I* have to leave racing," she insisted. "I'll find someone else to round out the Mazda crew and pit for me in the VAM series."

"How will you pay this person—let alone *find* someone willing and able to put in the hours racing requires?" Mike interjected before Dino lost the hold he'd regained on his temper. "You don't have the cash, and the bank won't loan you any. You're too high of a risk. Ask Jack if you don't believe me. He'd say the same thing. And what about the fact that you haven't had any offers from pro teams for next season, despite your success this year? If a team wanted you, they would have come forward by now. And let's be honest, after an accident like yours, it's unlikely that someone will approach you. Not when it looks like it could have been driver error that caused the wreck. I'm sorry, *sorellina*, but Dino's right. It's time to walk away."

Nikki looked at Mike with wide eyes. He of all people should understand what racing meant to her. They'd grown up in competitive go-karting together; he'd seen her love of the sport grow into the passion it was today. Why was he siding with Dino? And why did he think Jack, her long-time manager, would agree? Jack had always supported her career, even now when things seemed bleak.

She blinked back the tears she could feel building behind her eyes. "I don't need to walk away from anything but your irrational fears and this pointless conversation." She gripped her bags tighter, glaring at the two of them. "I may not have had any offers yet, but the season isn't over. There is still a chance a team will come forward. And as for the money"—she wracked her brain for an idea and found one—"I could sell the Modena. That would give me enough cash for this season *and* the next."

Dino blanched. "Are you fucking serious? You can't do that. You love that car. Besides, you'd never be able to sell it in time. It'll take months to sell it at value."

He was right again, and that rankled.

Nikki loved her 360 Modena. The car symbolized a major milestone in her career: her win at the World Rally Championship in 2015—something no one thought their fledgling team would pull off. But Nikki and her navigator proved them all wrong and were rewarded for it...handsomely. The Ferrari team boss gave her and her navigator, Will Daniels, each a Modena as a bonus for winning. And selling it would take months—time she didn't have—if she did so at value, and she would. If Nikki had to sacrifice the Modena, she would get every penny she could out of it.

Swallowing her frustration, she lifted her chin. "You may have a point, but it's not going to stop me, Dino. I don't know how I'll get the money, but I will get it. Unlike the two of you, I refuse to give up."

Dino and Mike studied her for a long minute. When Dino saw that she wasn't backing down, he gave his head a disdainful shake. "Fine. Be selfish—just like you've always been. I don't know why I thought you'd change."

With a sharp nod, Nikki hefted her belongings higher and marched into the house, not bothering to respond to Dino's gibe. A toxic blend of emotions churned inside her as she slammed the front door, closing herself off from her traitorous brothers. Who did they think they were? Did they honestly believe they could order her to *quit*? And what happened to their faith in her? Why had they given up?

Because they're right, whispered an insidious little voice she wanted to ignore but couldn't.

Nikki dropped her bags at her feet and pressed her back to the door. It wasn't the first time this thought had crept through her head. Though like most deep-seated fears, it only surfaced in the dark hours of the night when only silence and shadows were her companions. By morning, she always locked it away deep inside, assuring herself that the Le Mans wreck hadn't been her fault. But her brothers' doubts had opened that carefully constructed door, and now it seemed like she couldn't close it *or* stop the crushing rush of questions and doubt that came with it.

What if they were right? What if Le Mans was her fault? With her memory of the race gone, she only had her gut to go on. And while her gut hadn't failed her in the past, was that enough to go on now? Dino had a point about the brake fade and her knowledge of Sunbeam Tigers. Nikki *did* know Tigers inside and out. She was intimately familiar with the signs of brake fade and when to quit. If that *was* the cause, why didn't she pit? Why did she let it get to failure point? Had she been that desperate to win, that desperate to impress some GP2 team in hopes of getting to Formula 1?

Icicles invaded her chest. She took in a shaky breath. If she caused the accident, then her instincts were nil, as her brothers believed. She pressed her trembling lips together at the thought. It would be one thing to walk away from racing because she'd tried and failed to secure a new ride; it would be another to walk away because she had to admit she wasn't a competent driver.

Dear God...

How could she ever come back from that? How could she ever believe in herself again?

With a deep breath, she pushed off the door and headed for the living room to put her trophies away, her doubts and fears echoing in her head. She opened the glass doors of the trophy case and placed her latest wins next to the dozens of others she'd accrued over the years, wanting to believe they were testimony to her skills as a driver but also wondering, deep down in that dark place inside her, if they represented nothing more than dumb luck.

One of her earliest trophies caught her eye. It was from her first regional quarter midget race when she was five. Memories of that race came flooding back: the excitement, the anticipation, the fear. She'd been so scared that day. But her father, a former professional racecar driver himself, talked her through it, giving her the confidence boost she needed. She smiled at the memory of him throwing her up onto his shoulders after she'd won, shouting, "That's *mi principessa*! You watch! You'll be famous one day, *mi bell'angioletto*! You'll make it!"

Pain ricocheted through her chest. Al Eleuteri had been so much more than her father and coach. He was her friend and biggest champion. Since his death, no one looked at her the way he did: with pride, respect, and pure love.

She closed her eyes as the flood of tears rushed forward, wishing with everything she had that he was there now. He would know what to say to convince her that her brothers, *and* her subconscious, were wrong. But all the wishing in the world couldn't make that happen. Death was permanent. Nikki had to prove to them—and herself—that they were wrong. But how could she do that? If her brothers, Mike especially, doubted her, others might as well. Maybe Mike was right about teams not wanting her because they considered her a risk. Maybe the scouts saw something she couldn't.

She went to the docking station and plugged in her phone. She needed to stop these maudlin thoughts and pull it together. Spiraling into a sea of self-doubt and fear wouldn't get her anywhere she wanted to be.

After scrolling through her playlist, Nikki found the perfect song: Andrea Bocelli's "*Vivo per Lei.*" It was her parents' song and one she knew would make her feel better for the beautiful memories it always stirred. She cranked up the volume and felt the music reverberate through her chest, chasing away the fear and loneliness swamping her.

Lost in the beauty of the classic Italian tenor's voice, she didn't realize she wasn't alone until another voice belted out the refrain in a horrific rendition of the moving piece.

Nikki spun around, clutching her chest. "Damn it, Damon! Don't do that!" she shrieked. "You scared the crap out of me."

Damon leaned against the doorway, laughing. "I know. You should have seen your face. Priceless."

"God, you're a douche."

He smirked. "Yeah, but you love me anyway."

"Whatever," she grumbled, cutting off the music now that he'd ruined it.

She'd known Damon Rossi since they were little, and had even been in love with him at one time. While their romantic relationship had ended, their friendship survived, which was a blessing. Damon stood by her during the most difficult times of her life, helping her and her brothers to pick up the pieces of their shattered family. And he was right: he might be an asshole more often than not, but she did love him—just as she loved Dino and Mike.

"What's up, *bella*? Why are you listening to this old *dago* crap?" he asked, sauntering toward her, his lips pursed.

She gaped at him. "I can't believe you said that. It's so wrong. Even for *you*."

He shrugged. "What? We're Italian. We can say it without it being offensive."

"No, we can't." She rolled her eyes. "Besides, that's my parents' song you're dissing."

Damon swore under his breath. "Sorry. I forgot." He reached over and tugged on her ponytail. "You missing them?"

Nikki nodded. "Something like that."

She wouldn't admit to him, or anyone else, that she had doubts about herself. That would give credence to them, and she refused to go there.

She reached down and grabbed her phone from the docking station. Her shirtsleeve rode up as she did, exposing the black-and-blue handprint Ron left behind when he grabbed her after the race.

"Is that where the son of a bitch grabbed you?" he snarled, glaring at the offending mark.

She stepped back, adjusting her sleeve. "How did you know about that? Did the boys tell you?"

"No. I haven't seen them."

Her eyes narrowed. "Then how did you know?"

He didn't respond. He stood there, staring at her with those crystalline blue eyes—eyes capable of holding so much warmth and so much coldness all at once.

It dawned on her then. The Mercedes. The SUV. Those weren't strangers following her. They were guys from Damon's father's security business—a business rumored to have connections to the Berardi Mafia family. Nikki had no idea if the rumors were true or how much Damon was involved with his father's business, if at all. She never asked. Sometimes it was better *not* to know those sorts of things.

"I can't believe you." She snorted. "You're having me followed?"

"Someone needs to keep you safe. You sure as hell aren't making an effort."

"*Safe?* From what? From whom?" she demanded. This was getting ridiculous. Were all the men in her life paranoid control freaks?

He took a step closer, the muscles along his neck and jaw rigid. "From people like Ron Dixon, for starters. The guy has an anger problem and a hard-on for going after you at the track. I don't trust him."

"Ugh, you're as bad as Dino and Mike." She pulled the elastic from her hair, freeing the long, honey-colored locks from the suddenly too-tight ponytail. "It's a waste of time, Damon. Ron is no *real* threat, and even if he was, I can handle him. In fact, I *did* handle him, so forget it. I don't need your guys following me."

It was true. The MMA and self-defense classes Nikki took at Damon's boxing gym, Undefeated, paid off. She laid Dixon out after he grabbed her in the paddock. Even her brothers were impressed—though not impressed enough *not* to kick him around a little too.

She turned to leave, disgusted by the paranoia spreading like a virus within her family, but Damon latched on to her wrist.

"I don't care if you don't like it. *I* think you need looking after, and as long as I feel that way, I'll do it. Get used to it."

It was an old refrain. Damon, the epitome of a megalomaniac, had his own ideas about *who* Nikki should be and *what* she should be doing—and racing wasn't one of them. It was one of the reasons their romantic relationship ended. Damon wanted Nikki to be someone she wasn't: a pretty little doll he could keep wrapped up on the shelf.

"I don't have to get used to anything!" she snapped. "Using your father's resources to chase after me is stupid. You need to end it. If not for me, do it for yourself. Your dad will go ballistic if he finds out what you're doing."

Vincent Rossi had zero patience. If he found out that Damon was using his business like this, he'd get violent.

"Don't worry about my father," he said. "I'll handle him, *and* I'll handle Dixon too."

Her stomach dropped. Damon's idea of handling Dixon, or people like him, was a shadowy area Nikki never wanted him to explore, least of all for her. She didn't want to think of Damon being involved in anything shady like his father was rumored to be.

She shook her head, eyes wide. "He doesn't need *handling*. Promise me you won't do anything. I don't want you going there, especially for me."

He stared at her, jaw locked, eyes blazing.

"Damon, I mean it. You know how I feel about that stuff."

"*Per l'amor donna di Dio!*" he ground out, moving closer, taking her hand in his. When he spoke, his voice was rough. "Damn it, bella. I'm not trying to be a dick or control you. I'm trying to *protect* you."

Nikki squeezed his hand. "I know you mean well, but I don't need your protection. All I need is your friendship; it's all I've ever needed. Leave Ron Dixon alone, and drop the security detail."

Damon mumbled something under his breath about her and her father, but she didn't catch it. "Fine." He sighed. "I'll leave Dixon alone and call the boys off...for now."

"Thank you." She released his hand and headed toward the stairs. She needed some time and space to deal with her tangle of thoughts and fears.

"You know, this wouldn't be an issue if you'd quit racing. You're putting yourself at risk and your family through hell with this obsession. It's just a sport, for Chrissake," he said.

Nikki stopped short and turned to face him, the threads of her patience snapping. "When are you and my brothers going to get it? It's not an *obsession* or *just a sport*. Racing is my life."

Damon's eyes flared, but before he could respond, Nikki turned on her heel and stormed upstairs to her room, slamming the door behind her.

Her phone buzzed. Leaning against the door, she pulled it out of her back pocket and rolled her eyes. It was a text from a car collector in LA, looking for a Sunbeam Tiger, with his sights set on hers. She didn't blame him. It was in perfect condition and, with its racing history, highly desirable to car collectors. The guy had been pestering her for months to sell it to him, offering her a generous six-figure sum for it. But in Nikki's mind, the car was priceless. It was her father's final gift to her. She couldn't sell it —not without selling a piece of her soul along with it.

She started to text him back with yet another *not interested* when Mike's words echoed in her head: *Where are you going to get the money?*

She gripped the phone tighter, glancing down at the screen. *Six figures*...that would cover her pit crew costs for the rest of the season and well into the next if she needed it.

Her stomach roiled. What was she doing? Was she really entertaining the thought of taking the offer? Of selling her dad's Tiger? She shook her head. No... *No*. She couldn't do that—no matter how desperate things got...right?

She moved to the bed and slumped down next to her nightstand. Mike was right: hiring someone as lead mechanic would take thousands of dollars—money her impoverished bank account didn't have. And if she wanted to continue with this season, she had to find the money and find it fast. With Dino backing out now, she needed to hire someone ASAP. Nikki glanced down at the phone, her heart twisting. There was clearly one way she could get the money fast. But was it worth it, given her darkest fears? Would selling the car be for nothing in the end?

With a world-weary groan, she glanced over at her nightstand and spotted the books she kept stacked there: *The Alchemist*, *Warrior of the Light*, and an old, worn leather journal. These weren't merely her favorite books; they were her inspiration, her source of strength when she needed a boost.

And boy, did she need a boost right now.

Nikki pulled *Warrior of the Light* from the stack and opened to a random page that spoke of believing in yourself and of not giving up, that for every defeat, there was a victory. Staring down at the page, she wanted to believe the words—believe that she would be victorious after so much defeat—but with her faith shaken, it was difficult.

She closed the book and set it back in its place, grabbing the leather-bound journal next. It reminded her of the one she'd used during her grief counseling sessions with Patty. But this wasn't her journal. It was *his*—the man who'd been at Our Lady of Faith every Sunday for the first six months after her parents died. She found the journal over a year ago on the pathway near her parents' graves during a visit. As soon as she opened it, she knew it was his. There were sketches of her profile throughout the journal done from his vantage point several graves behind hers, and then there were the words he'd written: beautiful, moving words, chronicling his observations of her over those six months. She'd read through it hundreds of times since finding it. His words, and the raw emotion behind them, inspired her and gave her strength during the grueling recovery after the accident, just as his presence did those bleak months after her parents died.

Nikki smiled as she ran her fingers over the initials *GDS* then opened to the middle of the book and read a passage from a few weeks before she left for Europe. This one began with one of her favorite biblical quotes:

"She is clothed with strength and dignity." Proverbs 31:25
I see her strength blossom with each passing week. Does she know that it radiates from her like sunlight, spreading to those nearby—even to someone like me, a man who's lived in the dark for so long? Her light, her strength…they are my salvation, giving me the will to go on when I believed I couldn't…

NIKKI CLOSED THE WORN JOURNAL, WISHING HE WERE A PART OF HER LIFE AS more than words on paper. This man, a complete stranger whose face she'd never seen, had touched her heart and soul in ways that no one else ever had, and she'd somehow done the same for him. It didn't seem right that they weren't part of each other's lives—souls bonded through loss, grief, and healing neither expected. Shouldn't people connected on a level that deep be together?

She shook her head with a snort. Who was she kidding? Things like that only happened in Jennifer Aniston movies. Not in real life. In real life, you were left with a worn journal, unspoken gratitude, and a longing you couldn't explain, nothing more. There were just some things you *couldn't* make happen.

Sighing, she ran her hands over the cover before setting the journal back in its place. She might not have been able to find *him*, but if she took his words and her own faith—as shaken as it was—to heart, maybe she could be as strong as he believed her to be and make it in racing after all.

Her father's words echoed in her mind: *No matter what, you pick yourself up and keep moving forward. Let nothing stop you from achieving your dreams...*

He was right. She couldn't let anything stand in her way—not finances, not emotions, nothing. Not if she wanted to make it. And she did. She wanted that more than anything.

Glancing down at the phone again, Nikki made her decision. She tapped off a text, praying it was the right one.

2

Wood Glenn Courthouse, present day

The ticking of the second hand on the clock tolled inside Jake's skull like a death knell. He tilted his head from side to side and tugged at the collar of the shirt that felt too rough against his skin—like sandpaper scoring flesh. He hated wearing a suit and tie. They were too hot, too stiff, too *everything*. He was more of the faded jeans and T-shirt type. But sometimes only a suit could make the right impression. And today was all about that. Dressing like he normally did, revealing the ink snaking up his forearms, wouldn't make the impression he needed.

He fidgeted in his seat.

More minutes that felt like hours dragged by.

Christ, how long was this going to take?

He'd been sitting there for over an hour, waiting for the judge to decide the fate of his family. Sweat gathered under his suit and along his shaky palms. Waiting like this couldn't be a good sign. It shouldn't take *this* long to do a quick review of the application before making a final decision.

He thumped his head against the wall, trying to beat the negative thoughts out of his brain. It wouldn't do him any good to go there. He needed to stay positive, no matter how hard it was, no matter how many times he'd been screwed by the judiciary system in the past. This time would be different. It had to be. He wouldn't get another chance at custody of his brother after today.

His nerves frayed, he started tapping out a rapid tattoo on his knee as he looked up at the clock once more, scowling.

Another minute inched by.

Jake let out a low growl.

Next to him, his buddy Frankie stirred. "Dude, chill. Growling at the clock isn't going to help. She'll be out soon."

Chill. Jake scoffed. Easier said than done—especially for Frankie. He wasn't waiting while a stranger decided whether or not his family would be put back together. Frankie had no idea what this was like. His family was intact. Whole.

He turned and looked at his lifelong friend. "I'll *chill* when Dario's with me. I can't relax until that happens. I've been waiting for this for too long."

Frankie nodded. "I know. I'd feel the same if it was Kassandra or Gabriel, but you've got to be patient. If she sees *anything* that suggests you're unstable, she'll use it against you. I've heard about this judge. She's a real *perra*."

"I know. I know." He groaned, pinching the bridge of his nose.

They'd gone over this a million times while putting together his application—something Jake couldn't have done without him. Frankie was in his second year of law school at Santa Clara University and had been acting as Jake's *unofficial* legal counsel throughout the entire process. He'd hounded his professors, lawyer friends, classmates—anyone—for information that could help Jake's case. He was a godsend and the closest thing Jake could get to an attorney. Attorney's fees were light years from his pay grade. Auto mechanics did all right, but they weren't exactly high rollers.

Frankie was dead on about Jake's attitude; the judge could use it against him if she detected anything other than a calm, stable demeanor. According to Frankie, with Jake's criminal record, the odds of getting custody of Dario were slim. The only thing he had going for him was the fact that his arrests weren't linked to drugs or sexual assault. An open-minded judge *could* take that into consideration, along with everything else he'd done to put his life back together, and grant him custody. If he was lucky, that was. The trouble was, luck never seemed to be on Jake's side.

A few minutes later, the chamber doors opened, and he and Frankie were ushered inside.

The judge, a middle-aged woman with silver-strewn dark hair and cruel, assessing eyes, waved to a pair of chairs before the mahogany desk she stood behind. "Have a seat, Mr. Masercotti. Who have you brought with you today?"

"This is Frank Barrientos, my witness and unofficial legal counsel," Jake explained.

"I see." She tapped her fingers on the case file in front of her. "Well, let's get to it, then, shall we?"

Jake nodded, his stomach twisting into a thousand knots as he sat.

"I've reviewed your application and your file." She sat down, opened said file, and flipped through the pages as she spoke. "I see that you have a number of solid references, that you have been gainfully employed for the last two years at the Tiger's Den, and Formula Performance for two years before that. You've also maintained the same residence for three years." She paused, and Jake could hear a *but* coming. "However, that does not erase your criminal record, both as an adult *and* a juvenile, nor does it erase your familial ties."

He shook his head. "What do you mean *familial ties*? I don't have any family." It wasn't a lie, per se. His mother had died twelve years ago, and while his father wasn't deceased, he was as good as dead in Jake's mind.

The judge leaned forward, eyes narrowed to slits. "Mr. Masercotti, you may have changed your name when you were eighteen, but it doesn't change who your family is. Your father is Carlo Di Silva, correct?"

"Yes, but—"

She cut in before he could finish. "The same Carlo Di Silva who is a high-ranking boss in the Berardi crime family *and* who is currently serving twenty-five years in prison for extortion and drug trafficking. Is that also correct?"

Jake blinked. What did this have to do with *him*? "Okay. Yeah...that's right, but—"

Frankie stepped in. "Your Honor, what does Jake's father have to do with this? Mr. Di Silva's record should have no bearing on Jake's case. He's not the one applying for custody."

The judge leaned back in her chair, folding her arms across her narrow chest. "Mr. Masercotti's family history of criminal involvement establishes a pattern of character, Mr. Barrientos. Statistically speaking, someone who comes from a family involved in organized crime is more likely to become a criminal themselves, which Mr. Masercotti has achieved."

"Your Honor," Jake began, the muscles in his neck and back tensing, "I'll admit I've made mistakes in the past, but I've atoned for those sins. I've changed. If you'll look at the file again, you'll see that."

She shook her head. "I've read the file and noted your volunteer work with the juvenile system and at the local homeless shelter. Nonetheless, your criminal history and your family's legacy of criminal involvement lead me to believe that you would *not* be the kind of parent Dario Di Silva needs."

Panic gripped him like a vise. "You're wrong. Dario does need me. I'm his flesh and blood! His foster family doesn't understand him like I do, Your Honor," he pleaded.

"I agree, Mr. Masercotti. It is often best for children to be placed with blood relatives, unless those relatives are deemed unfit, which I believe to be true in your case. Like all minors, Dario needs a stable, positive environment..."

She went on, but her voice was drowned out by the word *unfit* reverberating in his ears.

He cleared his head in time to hear her deliver the fatal blow.

"And I'm afraid that you've proven yourself to be more like your father than you'd care to see or admit. And I don't believe any child should be exposed to *that*. You're lucky you've had any contact with the boy at all."

The fragile hold on his temper vanished. He knew his record could bite him in the ass. He *knew* there was a good chance that the judge wouldn't look beyond it and see all the positive changes he'd made over the last four years. But his father's reputation? Seriously? *That* was the nail in the coffin?

Hell. No.

Jake jumped out of his chair, pointing his finger at her sharp, angular face. "That's bullshit, lady! I am not my father. I never have been. And as for my criminal behavior, I haven't been in trouble with the law in four years. I've kept my nose clean—done everything I needed to do to turn my life around. And you're telling me it means *nothing*? That the mistakes I made in the past can't be rectified because of who *my father* is? That a person can't be better than those who raised them?"

The judge slammed her hand on the desk. "You will keep yourself in check, or I will revoke your visitation privileges *and* send you back to jail, sir!"

Jake grabbed the edge of the desk, snarling something threatening and nasty at her as Frankie grabbed his arm.

"Calm. Down. If you want to be in Dario's life at all, stop talking."

The mention of Dario's name cleared the red haze coating his vision, replacing his anger with regret. Stepping back, he dropped into his seat, knowing it was over.

He'd failed.

Again.

"I'm sorry. I shouldn't have reacted that way," Jake mumbled, knowing it was too little, too late.

"No, you shouldn't have," the judge remarked, snapping up the folder. "With *all* of this in mind, it is the court's decision that your application for the adoption of Dario Di Silva be denied. His current placement with the

Reynolds family is clearly a more stable environment than you can provide and will remain as such until he is of age. I will, however, continue to allow your bi-weekly visitations, though I am stipulating that they be supervised going forward. You may have turned some things around in your life, Mr. Masercotti, but anger management is clearly not one of them."

With nothing left to say, Jake nodded as he rose from his chair, and left. The midday sun shone brightly as he stepped out of the courthouse, but he didn't notice. His mind was stuck on repeat, replaying a single word: *failure*.

Behind him, Frankie rattled off apologies as they made their way down the steps. When they reached the bottom, Jake stopped and turned, his voice hollow. "Don't apologize, bro. I knew the odds were against me. I thought...maybe this *one* time, I wouldn't fuck up. I guess I was wrong."

"Dude, come on. Don't be like that. You didn't fail. The system did. Don't lose hope," Frankie said, grasping his shoulder.

Jake took a step back. "My father's criminal ties may not have helped the system, but *I'm* the one who failed. If I hadn't lost my temper or fucked up so many times in the past, I wouldn't be standing here today. What happened back there totally fits. I've never succeeded at *anything*, Frankie. Why should today have been any different?" He shrugged, turning and walking away, shoving down the emotions that threatened to burst out of his chest.

"Hey! Where are you going?" Frankie called after him, but Jake waved him off. "At least let me give you a ride home."

"That's okay. I'll walk. Thanks for everything, man. I know you tried," he called over his shoulder, continuing down the street.

AN HOUR LATER, JAKE CLIMBED THE STAIRS TO HIS APARTMENT ON THE SECOND floor to the sounds of children wailing and couples arguing. It was a familiar tune. His complex was overrun with miserable people of all ages. He fit right in.

When he reached his apartment, he stopped cold. The door was ajar. *What the...?*

He pushed the door open with his foot and eased inside, gaping at the scene. The place was cleaned out. His flat-screen TV, docking station, and computer were all missing, as was his vinyl collection. He stared at the spot where his collection of classic rock and Italian records *used to be* and swore.

Fuck. This. Day.

Panic seized him. If they took this stuff, they probably got his camera and his art supplies too. *Shit!* Blood roared in his ears as he darted out of the living room, praying they hadn't taken them. The art and camera equipment were his most valuable possessions. Art—sketching or photography—was the only thing he truly loved doing. It was a passion he and his mother shared and the one thing he'd managed to hold on to after she died.

He charged into the bedroom and tore open the closet. The cylinders where he stored his drawings and paintings were there, but his supplies were gone. He shoved his clothes and extra blankets out of the way, spotting the camera case right where he always hid it, but this time it was open…and it was empty.

Jake staggered back, rage sluicing through his veins. Turning, he beat at the wall until his knuckles bled and the urge to destroy passed. He stumbled away from the destruction, a mess of emotions rattling inside him, and slumped down onto his bed. The ugly mess in his veins took on a dark, familiar form. Curling his hands into tight fists, he focused on the physical pain, trying to tamp down the emotions and the old refrain running in his head:

Loser.

Failure.

Your fault.

Hopeless.

He hadn't felt this kind of desolation in years. Not since the day *she* came into his life—his *angioletto* from Our Lady of Faith. While he hadn't seen her in years, not a day went by when he didn't think of her, wonder where she'd gone. This girl, this *stranger*, changed everything for him that dark day in the cemetery and continued to do so for the six months of Sundays he saw her there afterward. Without knowing it, she helped him heal in ways he never thought possible. She gave him the strength he needed when he feared he had none left; she inspired him to go on, to do better—made him feel whole again. He wanted to thank her, to repay her somehow, but he never had the chance. Like everything else in his life, she'd vanished.

Christ, what he wouldn't give to see her now, to feel her strength.

Jake shook his head. It was too much. It was all too fucking much. He rose on shaky legs. He needed to get out of there—go for a ride, clear the storm gathering inside him before it took hold.

After a quick change out of his only suit into a fitted black T-shirt and Levis, he stormed out of the bedroom, grabbed his keys, motorcycle jacket, and helmet—the thieves had at least left all of *that* behind—and bolted.

A couple of hours later, his customized vintage Harley Sportster skirted along the lush, winding curves of Highway 84. After leaving his apartment, he went by the cemetery to visit his mother. He didn't go there as often as he once did; his schedule was pretty full between work and his volunteer hours. But he felt like he needed to go to regain some of the strength that had leached out of him today.

It didn't work. Seeing his mother's grave, admitting to yet another failure, and *not* seeing his *angioletto* only served to depress him more. So instead of going home, he headed to the Blue Ox—his hideaway of choice —hoping to flush this crap out of his system with a vat of Patron.

Jake liked the Ox, with its rundown façade, squeaky floorboards, and ancient jukebox. Nestled in the wooded hills of Emerald Valley, it was well away from Wood Glenn, making it the perfect place to escape and forget his shit life.

He parked in his usual spot, recognizing the other bikes out front. It looked like the Regulators, a local motorcycle club, were in-house. Bikers from all over the Bay Area went there, but the Regulator MC gathered at the Ox often. Low-key biker bars were rare, and these guys needed low-key. Their reputation would attract law enforcement if they met somewhere on the Peninsula or closer to San Francisco.

Jake strode inside to the sounds of a blues guitar crooning from the jukebox and took a seat at the end of the bar, waving at Tucker Ellis— leader of the Regulators. He was situated at a table in the far corner where he often held court. Candy, the bar's owner, spotted Jake and sauntered over, bar towel in hand.

"Hey there, handsome. What are you doing here tonight? You don't usually come in during the week," she said, grinning. Candy was an attractive woman in her early thirties with a penchant for coloring her hair in violent shades of red and sporting the craziest T-shirts Jake had ever seen. Tonight her shirt was bubblegum pink with an angry-looking unicorn on the front and the phrase *I will cut you* beneath it.

He smiled in return, though it didn't reach his eyes. "I needed to get some air, go for a ride."

"I see." She studied him for a minute. "You okay? You look like someone who watched their puppy get kicked into oncoming traffic and beat the hell out of a wall afterward," she said, glancing from his torn-up hands to his face.

"I'm good. All I need is a couple of shots of tequila and a beer chaser." He was more than ready to get a buzz going.

Candy gave him a final, scrutinizing look. "All right. But if you need anything else, just holler."

Jake nodded but had absolutely no intention of telling her, or anyone, about his life. Why bring anyone else down to his level?

Several shots of tequila and four beers later, he sat at the bar, struggling to keep enough of a buzz going to silence his sorrow and shame. He was about to order another round when a woman's sultry voice whispered in his ear.

"You look like you could use a little distraction, gorgeous."

His hand tensed around his beer. He knew that voice. It belonged to Angela O'Brien, another regular at the Ox. Though in all honesty, she—and the friends who tagged along with her—didn't exactly fit in there. They were more the type to go clubbing in the city, looking for sugar daddies, not slumming it at a biker bar in the middle of BFE.

Stifling a sigh, he turned, gaping at the red dress that left nothing to the imagination. "Hey, Angela. What are you doing here tonight?" he asked, his eyes involuntarily falling to the cleavage spilling out of her dress.

Damn...

Jake gave himself an internal shake. He needed to get a grip. He generally avoided this girl. Jake didn't trust her—there was something in her eyes he didn't like. But before he could throw some cash on the bar and make an exit, Angela leaned forward, giving him an even better view of what her dress barely covered.

"I was driving back from the coast and saw your bike out front. I thought I'd stop in and say hello," she said, placing a hand on his thigh.

Jake bit back a curse as that hand slid inward, making the blood rush to his groin. *Traitorous bastard.*

In all fairness, the traitor hadn't seen any action in months. Jake had hit a dry spell between work and Dario's case. Still, this wasn't the way to break the dry spell. It was not that he was opposed to hooking up at the bar—that was what he typically did—but he didn't mess around with girls like Angela. What he needed to do right now was take control of his libido, remove her hand with a polite *no, thanks*, and get the hell out of there before he made a mistake.

He moved to do that but stopped short as she boldly ran her hand over his length, teasing it with nimble fingers.

Goddamn.

Okay...maybe he should rethink this. He *did* come here looking for a way to take his mind off everything, and the alcohol wasn't cutting it. And if booze wasn't doing it for him, there was only one other thing that would, and right now, only Angela could provide that kind of *service*.

The teasing fingers increased their pressure.

Fuck it.

Jake leaned forward, pressing against her tantalizing hand, all reason and sense vanishing from his brain. "What'd you have in mind?" he asked, his eyes rolling over her curvaceous body. She might be trouble, but at least it was packaged nicely.

Angela grinned as she pressed herself up against his arm, squeezing him.

Holy God...

"Why don't we go in the bathroom, and I'll show you?" she suggested.

Jake slid off his stool and followed her to the bathroom at the back of the bar, catcalls and whistles from the Regulator crew chasing after them. Once inside, he leaned against the back wall and watched as she locked the door behind her and prowled over to him.

"Lean back and relax. I'll take care of you, baby," she purred, unzipping his jeans as she got down on her knees.

Jake tilted his head against the wall, groaning when she went to work. He closed his eyes and lost himself to the mind-numbing sensations, enjoying the bliss it brought—even if it wouldn't last.

3

Sunlight streaming in through the window seared Jake's eyelids, but that wasn't what roused him from sleep. It was the incessant pounding in his skull—or was it out of it? He couldn't tell.

Bang! Bang! Bang!

Cursing, he buried himself under a pillow. The noise wasn't in his head. Some jackass was pounding on a wall, probably the neighbors.

Bang! Bang! Bang!

The pounding continued, but this time a voice followed it. "Dude, I know you're in there. Open up!"

Jake groaned. It was Johnny Lucero, one of two people he considered family, outside of Dario. He peeled open an eyelid, hissing as the sunlight pierced his retina, and looked over at the clock on his night table: it was 7:00 a.m., Saturday morning.

What the hell?

"Come on, Jake. Open the damn door!" Johnny bellowed from the hallway.

Knowing Johnny wouldn't quit, Jake heaved himself out of bed and stumbled out to the living room. His friend was a determined mother-fucker when he wanted something.

Bang! Bang! Bang!

Jake winced at the sound as he reached the door. His head felt like the inside of a bass drum being whaled on by a 350-pound bear.

"I heard you the first time, asshole," he snarled, throwing the dead bolt and wrenching open the door.

"Then why didn't you open up, dickhead?" Johnny replied, striding inside. He grimaced when he got a look at Jake. "What the hell happened to you? You look like shit."

"Good morning to you, too, *sunshine*," Jake grumbled then dragged himself into the kitchen and grabbed a bottle of OJ from the refrigerator. His mouth tasted like a dirty, tequila-soaked carpet. "I was at the Ox last night. I guess I didn't get my beauty sleep." He took a swig and offered some to Johnny.

Johnny shook his head. "No, thanks. You look like you need to pound every drop of it, which means you were up to more than just *being out late.*"

Jake took another long draft as he shuffled over to the old Formica table and sank into a chair. "I may have had some Patron and a few Dos Equis while I was there."

"Yeah...more like a gallon of Patron and a case of Dos Equis—especially if you hooked up with this *puta*." Johnny moved closer and slapped a Post-It note on the table. He sat across from Jake. "I found it on your door this morning."

"Watch the noise, will you?" Jake grimaced, rubbing at his forehead, wishing the goddamn bear would quit it with the epic drum solo. "What's this?"

"Read it. Looks like you've got a fan—or stalker, in her case."

Jake peeled the note off the table and read it. It was from Angela, asking him to call her so they could hook up again.

Shit.

He crumpled the note and threw it on the table. How had she gotten his address? He never gave it out—never brought women back to his place. It was a cardinal rule. If he hooked up with someone, he did so at the Creekside Motel behind the Ox or, if things were desperate, the men's room at the bar. Doing so kept things uncomplicated—something Jake needed since he didn't do relationships. He also didn't want to get a reputation around his apartment complex for bringing home random women in case Social Services decided to ask his neighbors about him. It wouldn't look good if he was labeled a player, and after what happened in the judge's office a couple weeks back, any little slip-up could cost him his visitations with Dario.

Johnny leaned forward, studying him with sympathetic eyes. "What's going on with you? Frankie says you've been partying like this a lot, and now you're hooking up with this *concha*? This isn't like you, man. Is it because of Dario's case?"

"Who are you? Oprah?" Jake glowered. He detested pity, and that was exactly what resonated in Johnny's voice.

Johnny rolled his eyes. "No, dumbass. I'm your friend. You know, someone who gives a shit about you. What's going on? I thought mornings like this were behind you."

"Nothing's *going on*. I needed to blow off some steam last night," Jake said, his stomach burning at the memory of what set him off. When Johnny gave him a look that said, "And..." he released a heavy breath and continued. "It's Dario. I'm worried about him. When he showed up at the pizza place for dinner last night, he had a black eye and a split lip."

"Did he get into a fight at school?"

"That's what he said, but I don't buy it. Dario's not the type of kid to get into trouble like that—especially at school. He's always kept his nose clean in the past. I don't see why he'd start now."

"Okay. If it didn't happen at school, where'd he get the shiner, then? Street fight? We used to get into plenty of those, as I recall."

Jake snorted. "A *street fight*? Dario? Please. The kid's nothing like I was."

Thank Christ.

By the time Jake was Dario's age, he'd done two stints in juvie. Dario had never had so much as a detention.

"All right, then. How do you explain it?" Johnny pressed.

Jake didn't say anything for several beats, trying to rein in his temper. Even thinking about what might have happened made him want to kill something—or someone. "Bruce. The fucker has a short temper, always has," he growled.

Johnny's brows shot up. "His foster father? Seriously? I know you don't like the guy, but beating Dario? I don't know, man. That seems like a stretch, even for that asshole. But even if he did, wouldn't someone at Dario's school or his social worker notice and notify CPS?"

Johnny was wrong about Jake's feelings for Bruce. Jake didn't dislike him. He hated him with an intensity that made the sun feel cold and small. The guy was a grade A douchebag who never showed Jake an ounce of respect or kindness. He always treated him, and his parents' memories, like dirt.

"I hate to think about things being that bad at the Reynolds' place, but it's the only thing that makes sense." Jake ran a hand through his hair. "Dario's been acting *off* for months now—ever since Monica's fifteenth birthday. He's been irritable, secretive, anxious to get home after our visits. Something is going on in that house—something he doesn't want me to know about. And as for the school or the social worker notifying CPS, yeah, they could, and they very well may have. I wouldn't know. They don't have to notify me about it since I don't have custody. And even if CPS was informed, Bruce is slick, and Barbara would back him up, guilty or not. You'd be surprised at what foster parents get away with."

At first, Jake had thought Dario and Monica were dating—that would explain his desire to get home as soon as possible. She wasn't a blood relative, so it wasn't like they *couldn't* date. Monica was an attractive girl with a sweet personality; it wouldn't surprise Jake if Dario had *non-brotherly* feelings toward her. But that didn't explain the irritable behavior...unless they broke up and Dario was upset over it. But why wouldn't he tell Jake about it? They'd always been close. Dario knew he could tell Jake anything —that he would be there for him no matter what. It didn't make sense.

As if he'd read his thoughts, Johnny said, "You think something's up with that little Monica? Maybe they hooked up and things didn't work out?"

"I thought that might be it. But Dario would have come to me about it. He's always confided in me, especially problems of the female variety." Jake shook his head. "This is something else. Something he's afraid to share."

Dario might not have Jake's rebellious tendencies, but he mirrored him in other ways. He was fiercely protective of his older brother. Dario rarely mentioned anything about his home life because he knew it hurt Jake that they weren't living under the same roof.

"Sorry, man. I wish I could help. Maybe he'll open up next time you see him," Johnny offered.

"Maybe..." He clenched his fist. "I hate thinking about him suffering and not being able to do anything about it. It fucks with my head."

"I can see that. It explains your *activities* last night, anyway. But Angela O'Brien? *Really?* That twat gets more action than the Vegas strip. I hope you doubled up on rubbers."

Jake grabbed the bottle of aspirin he kept on the table and shook out the last two tablets. Frankie was right about Jake's partying. There had been many nights like this one lately, and it wasn't good. Drowning out his frustration and failings in booze and pussy never solved anything, but it was hard to resist their numbing lure. They were the only ways he could forget—even if it was just for a few hours—how badly he'd screwed up his life and what little he could do to change it.

"Give me some credit. I didn't have sex with Angela last night," Jake said, swallowing the aspirin. "She gave me head in the bathroom a couple of weeks back. It hasn't happened since and won't. Trust me."

Johnny shook his head. "Blowjobs, sex, same diff. Sticking your dick in *any* part of crazy is never a good idea. If you need sex, get a girlfriend—a nice one, from a good family. Not some skank like Angela at the Ox."

Not this again.

"You know I don't do relationships," Jake began. "And besides, what would be the point of me trying? Nice girls from good families don't go for losers like me. I learned that a long time ago."

"Cut that *loser* bullshit. You've got a hell of a lot more going for you than you realize. If you wanted to, you could have a girl like my Tiff and not the shit you usually hook up with. You deserve better than them, especially that Angela. Someone like—"

Jake held up a hand, putting an end to the lecture. He didn't want to hear it now or ever—something both Frankie and Johnny refused to acknowledge. For some reason, they didn't see him for the disappointment that he was. But then, they didn't know about his dark secret, about his greatest failure. And they wouldn't. He'd never bring that out into the light of day—for anyone.

"Enough. This conversation needs to stop before we both grow a vag," Jake snapped.

"Fine." Johnny rolled his eyes. "Have it your way."

"Good." Jake downed the remainder of the OJ. "Speaking of crazy, what are you doing here this early on a Saturday? It's not even eight o'clock, for fuck's sake."

"Jesus, man. I texted you last night. We're supposed to meet up with Tony Johnson. You agreed to check out his Mustang, remember?"

"I did? Why would I do that? I can't stand that fucktard." Jake tilted his head from side to side, trying to get the kinks out of his neck, hoping the aspirin would kick in soon and kill off the drummer.

"Because it's a favor for Tiffany. She's got a soft spot for that creepy cousin of hers."

Jake remembered now. Johnny's girlfriend, Tiffany, asked if he would help out her cousin, and Jake couldn't say no to Tiff. She was a sweet girl and the best thing that had happened to Johnny outside of graduating from the police academy.

"All right. When are we meeting him?" Jake stood, reaching up and stretching his back. He needed to lay off the booze and hit his weights and run more often. The stiffness in his back and neck were a result of his slacking off on the workouts.

"Soon, which means you need to throw on some clothes so we can meet him out front. I don't think you want him in your apartment."

"Right. Give me five."

Minutes later, Jake strode out of the bedroom, grabbed his wallet off the table by the front door, and stepped out into the early-morning sunlight with Johnny in tow. At least the weather was beautiful—that was some consolation for spending his Saturday morning with a tool.

Jake glanced over his shoulder as they moved toward the stairs. "Dude, the next time Tiffany needs a favor, tell her to leave me out of it if it has anything to do with Tony. He's nothing but trouble."

"I think you've got bigger problems than Tony Johnson. He won't cause you any trouble, but Angela will. You're gonna have to move, dude."

"Yeah, if only I could," Jake grumbled, hating that Johnny was right about Angela. That girl was all kinds of crazy, and now she knew where he lived. This wouldn't end well. Not if she thought she had her hooks in him. But he was stuck in his shithole of an apartment. He'd never find something else he could afford.

"We'll figure something out," Johnny said, trying to be reassuring.

Jake shook his head. Things never went his way—no matter how much he wished they would.

$$\sim$$

NIKKI'S BACK HIT THE MAT WITH A RESOUNDING *SMACK* THAT SHE FELT DEEP IN her bones.

Her trainer, Tsai Thompson, scowled as he loomed over her. "What's up with you? You should have seen that move coming from a mile away," he scolded, his deep voice rumbling through her.

She sat up with a groan. She should have seen the sweeper coming, but her head wasn't in it. She was a million miles away from where she should be, and she would pay for it later.

"Sorry. I've got a lot on my mind today," she said, taking the hand he offered, and stood.

Tsai stood back, his muscled arms crossed over his broad chest. He was a professional MMA fighter and co-owner of Undefeated. He and Damon met in high school and became fast friends through their love of mixed martial arts. When Damon decided to open the gym four years ago, Tsai invested and became a full partner. Gyms were a dime a dozen in the Bay Area, but the risky investment paid off for both of them. Undefeated was one of the most successful MMA gyms in the area, with more than twenty top fighters training there.

"I see that. So, what's up? What's going on in that pretty head of yours that's got you distracted? Is it a guy?" he asked, flashing a crooked smile.

Nikki's heart melted a little. She couldn't help it when it came to Tsai. He was gorgeous with his muscular build and smooth, dark skin. That, combined with his genuine goodness, made him a total knockout. If Nikki dated, she would have gone for Tsai—that was if he were single. Unfortunately for her, he was in a long-term relationship with a wonderful woman he intended to marry.

Nikki snorted. "No, it's not a guy."

She didn't date—at least she hadn't in what felt like forever. Relationships were a hassle with her racing schedule. She learned—the hard and painful way—that men weren't too keen to date a woman who spent two-thirds of the year away at races and remain faithful to her.

"Well, then it must be serious. You don't shake easily."

She pulled off her sparring helmet and wiped the sweat from her brow. To most people, selling a car wasn't a big deal. But Nikki wasn't selling just *any* car today. She was selling her father's Sunbeam Tiger to fund her racing career. For her, it didn't get more serious than that.

"I'm selling my dad's Tiger today," she said in a rush, her chest feeling like a dartboard with every word.

Tsai's eyes widened. "Oh, damn. Why?"

Leaning against a freestanding training bag, Nikki explained. When she finished, Tsai reached over and grabbed her shoulder, a gentle smile on his lips. "That's some heavy stuff, baby girl, but you can handle it. Remember what you learned from *The Alchemist*: there will always be obstacles on your journey to achieving your dream, and it's up to you to find a way around them and continue on your path. I know it's tough. I've been there. But you're strong. You can face this obstacle, no matter how painful, and find your way back to racing. I know you can."

Nikki looked up into his keen brown eyes and couldn't help but smile. Tsai gave her *The Alchemist* to read when they started working out together as part of her physical therapy after the accident. He said she looked like she needed to hear its message, and he'd been right. She did need to hear it then, and it seemed she needed a refresher now. It was one of those books that always gave you what you needed when you needed it, regardless of how many times you'd read it in the past.

"Thanks, Tsai. I needed to hear that."

"Anytime. Now get your head in the game and kick my ass already," he ordered, bouncing on the balls of his feet, itching for a fight.

With a smile she felt for the first time in days, Nikki strapped on her helmet and did her best to do just that.

THE LUSH, WOODED HILLS RUSHED BY AS THE SUNBEAM TIGER SKATED ALONG the winding roads, the roar of its engine echoing through the trees. For Nikki, the only thing that compared to driving the Tiger was being on the track. Just like racing, driving the little Sunbeam gave her a sense of pure freedom—like all of her worries were stripped away, leaving only her, the car, and the open road. It hurt her heart to know that she wouldn't feel this way again in her father's car.

She glanced in her rearview mirror and scowled when she spotted a familiar black Mercedes behind her. It was the same sedan she saw following her when she returned from Colorado—the very same car that had been with her every day since. Clearly, Damon didn't get the message about her not needing a security detail, just like Dino didn't get the message about her *not* quitting racing. Dino made sure to point out to her, at every opportunity, that she wasn't a competent driver and needed to quit for her own safety and for the safety of others. It was taking a toll on her and their relationship, which wasn't helped by the fact that they lived *and* worked together. Escaping Dino, and his opinion, was nearly impossible.

Frustrated and downright pissed at the men in her life—and their refusal to let her live hers—Nikki punched the accelerator as she came out of a turn and hit a length of straight highway. She might not have been able to do much about the situation with her family, but she *could* do something about Damon's boys. If they were going to continue to follow her, she'd make them work for it.

Nikki soared down the straightaway, shifting into fourth gear, the laughter of her friend, Hilda Alcantar, rising over the engine's thunder.

"That's it, girl. Light 'em up!" she shouted.

With an evil grin, Nikki dropped the accelerator, watching the Benz recede into the distance until it was nothing more than a memory.

Making a mental note to discuss the tail with Damon *again*, she turned onto Emerald Valley Road and headed back to town so she could get to the shop in time. Trepidation settled in her stomach like a stone. In all her years, she'd never dreaded going to the shop more than she did today.

"You know I love to go for rides in the Tiger, but can you please explain why we had to get up so damn early to do it?" Hilda asked, breaking through the mess of emotions whirling in Nikki's head. "It's Saturday. Some of us were up late last night and need our beauty sleep."

Nikki rolled her eyes. *Beauty sleep*. As if her best friend needed anything else to make her more attractive. With her wavy mahogany locks, glowing skin, and dark eyes, Hilda was a knockout. The girl could lose sleep for a week and still turn heads wherever she went.

"Sorry, but the buyer said he had to meet me at nine o'clock, and since this is the last time I'll be able to drive the car, I thought you'd like to take the final ride with me," Nikki explained, forcing back the tears that always surfaced when reality struck.

Hilda turned in her seat. "You're really selling it?"

She glanced over and saw the shock on Hilda's face. "Yes. I told you I was."

"I know. I just thought you'd change your mind, that's all. I know what the car means to you…to your family."

Nikki heard what Hilda *didn't* say: that selling the Sunbeam would crush her brothers. And it would. That was why they didn't know about it. "It means everything to us, but I don't have a choice, Hil. I need the money, and this is the only way to get it."

Hilda ran her hands over the dash pad. "Couldn't you sell the Ferrari? I mean, I know you love that car, but this one is on a totally different level of love."

Nikki did love the Modena, but Hilda had a point. She loved the Tiger so much more. It epitomized everything her father stood for: love, hard work, and family. Selling it cut deep, but sometimes life required sacrifices to achieve great things. And if she wanted to achieve greatness in racing, this was a sacrifice she had to make—her brothers had seen to that when they pulled their support.

"I wish I could have sold it over the Tiger, but I don't have time. I need the money *now*. Selling the Modena would have taken weeks, maybe months. It's worth too much, and I'd never sell it under value," Nikki explained, downshifting into a series of turns.

Hilda nodded. "Still, it's a shame you have to do it. Dino and Mike must be devastated."

When Nikki didn't reply, Hilda leaned in closer, eying her over the rims of her aviators.

"They do know, don't they? Please tell me you told them."

Tightening her grip on the wheel, Nikki hit the accelerator harder, pushing the car through the turns. "I haven't said anything, and I won't until the sale is completed."

"*What?* Girl, they're going to lose their shit when they find out you sold it without talking to them first."

"That's why I had to wait until *after* I've done it," she said as they turned onto Highway 84 and headed out of the Glenns, the wooded area that sat above Wood Glenn proper, where they'd grown up. "You know them, Hil. Especially Dino. He would have done *anything* to keep me from selling. I don't have a choice."

Mike and Dino would have tried to talk her out of selling the Tiger at the very least and, at the worst, taken the car away before she could do it —even if it was hers to do with as she pleased. Her father willed it and the family home to her, just as he'd willed his shop and his 1960 XKE to them.

But that wouldn't matter to Dino or Mike. They didn't understand her or what drove her to keep racing, which meant they wouldn't understand how she could come to the difficult but necessary decision to sell the car.

"You're right, but it still feels wrong to keep them in the dark. And it definitely won't be pretty when you tell them it's gone." Hilda paused as a white Mustang fastback went tearing by them in the opposite direction. "If you want me to be there as backup, I will be. I think you're going to need it."

"Thanks," she said, cranking the radio when the Foo Fighters' "Walk" came on—the perfect song for the state of her life. She certainly felt like she was learning things all over again, and she hated that. She hated it almost as much as her mother's old saying, "You live and you learn, sweetie. That's the way life goes." She was so freaking tired of living and learning. For once, she'd just like to *know*.

Minutes later, the white Mustang that flew by earlier pulled up along-side them, the passenger leaning out of the window and shouting over the wind and engines. "Nice car!"

Nikki gave a quick nod and glance at the Mustang. "You too."

"Yeah, the '67's awesome, but yours is amazing," he shouted. When they pulled up to a stoplight, he continued. "So, I've got to ask, with an awesome ride like that, why are you defiling it with that shitty music?"

Nikki scowled and turned to face him. "Do you have something against the Foo Fighters?"

"I'm more of an old-school-rap guy, myself," he said, sliding his sunglasses down and peering at her over the rims. "But I might be persuaded otherwise…if the right person tried."

She rolled her eyes, turning her attention back to the stoplight. If this was his way of trying to pick up girls, he needed a new approach.

"Ah, I see. Well, good luck with that." She chuckled then gunned it when the light turned green.

"What a tool." Hilda laughed as they drove away. "Did he really think he'd get anywhere with that line? And hanging out of the car like that? Is he like sixteen or something?"

Nikki started to answer when the Mustang reached them, and the passenger called out to her again.

"Apparently he did, and he's not ready to give up." She sighed, glancing over at Hilda, who was firing daggers at him.

"Hey, did you hear me?" the passenger yelled when they reached the next light.

"No. Sorry. What did you say?" she called back.

Jesus. Did they have to hit every light?

"I said why'd you rush off? We were getting to know each other."

"I've got somewhere to be, so I can't really hang around and chat,"

Nikki replied, drumming on the steering wheel as she watched the light, refusing to make further eye contact. It would only encourage him.

"Aww, come on. You can make time, sweetheart. A pretty girl like you can afford to be a few minutes late. Especially one who can handle a car like that. In fact, I bet you could get away with anything."

Nikki glanced over at him, an eyebrow raised. He was still hanging out of the car like an overgrown dog. "Uh, thanks. I think."

"You should be thankful. You've got Tony Johnson's personal seal of approval."

Good God…

"Okay," she drawled, wishing the light would turn green already.

"Hey, don't be like that," he said.

"Like what?" She glanced over at him.

Why couldn't he take a hint when it was thrown at him?

"Like a stuck-up bitch."

"What the fuck did you just—" Hilda started to say, but Nikki cut her off.

"I'll handle this," she said, turning and flashing Tony a big smile. "I'm sorry. You're right. I was totally being stuck up. Can I make it up to you later—you know, when I have more time?"

The tool beamed at her, making her skin crawl. "Sounds great. Give me your name and digits."

"Sure thing. I'm Jenny, and you can reach me at 867-5309. Got it?"

"Yeah, cool. My name's Tony, if you didn't catch it earlier. I'll call you later, Jenny, so we can hook up," he said as the blessed light turned green.

Struggling to hold back the laughter, she nodded. "Perfect."

"You better hope you don't see him after he puts two and two together." Hilda cackled as they took off down the street.

"I won't. I'm sure he's got too much pride to go looking for me after falling for that." She chuckled as she sped toward the nearest gas station.

Several minutes later, Nikki was pumping gas into the Tiger at a deserted gas station when the familiar sound of the Mustang's engine roared in behind her. She let out a quiet groan.

Of all the gas stations in Wood Glenn, they had to stop at *this one*.

She peeked behind her as the Mustang came to a stop, hoping Tony had too much pride or that he could laugh off her little joke and not cause a scene. She didn't need any more drama today. She looked at the pump again to make sure she didn't overfill the tank—she didn't trust the automatic shut-off on the pump—and back at the Mustang. Tony was still in the car. From what she could see, it looked like there were two guys with him, and they were speaking animatedly.

Crap.

They were probably explaining to the single-celled organism what she did when she gave him her "name and number." And from the sound of the shouts coming from Tony, he wasn't happy.

Hilda turned in her seat as more yelling came from the car. "I guess he figured it out. Do you need backup?" she asked when the Mustang's passenger door flew open and an angry Tony emerged.

Nikki shook her head. "No. Stay in the car. I can handle him if he tries anything."

"What about the other two?"

"It won't be a problem. Trust me."

"You carrying?"

With a look from Nikki that said, "Duh," Hilda nodded and returned her attention to Tony, who was storming over to her.

"I bet you think you're pretty funny, don't you?" he said, standing too close to the car for her comfort.

"I don't know what you're talking about," she replied, keeping her focus on the pump.

"The fuck you don't!" Tony stepped closer. "You dissed me like the stuck-up little bitch I said you were!"

"Hey, watch it, asshole," Hilda warned from the car.

"Stay out of this, skank," Tony snapped, throwing Hilda a menacing glare.

The muscles along Nikki's shoulders tightened as she released the handle, cutting off the flow of gasoline, and fired a nasty look at Tony. "I'm not a *stuck-up bitch*, and she's no *skank*," she replied coldly, replacing the nozzle and closing her gas cap. She didn't fill the tank completely, but she wanted to get Tony as far as possible from the car before things got out of hand.

Turning to face him, Nikki dropped her arms to her sides, hands in fists as she worked up a rant. "It's not my fault you don't know how to approach women *or* that you're pop-culturally illiterate. That's all on you, buddy!"

Tony's face turned a deep fuchsia. "Nobody, especially some uppity cunt, talks to me that way," he growled, lurching forward to grab her. He never even came close. Thanks to her training with Tsai, Nikki was fast and strong—two things Tony didn't anticipate. With two quick moves, he hit the ground and slid several feet back from the Tiger's rear bumper.

"Back off, asshole," she warned, moving into a fighting stance.

"You're going to pay for that," he promised, lurching to his feet. But before things could go further, a figure appeared behind Tony. In a blur of movement, the figure snatched Tony by the collar and threw him onto the hood of the Mustang.

Nikki winced as Tony's solid body landed on the hood with a resounding *crunch*, slid across it and fell onto the ground, where the figure —a well-built man with dark hair—proceeded to pound him into the next week.

"Holy shit! He's going to kill him if he keeps that up," Hilda yelped from the car.

"Yeah, I think you're right," Nikki breathed, gaping at the stranger's back as he pummeled Tony.

"Uh, Nik...? Maybe we should clear out before things get crazier," Hilda called from the car, pulling Nikki from her stupor.

"Yeah...yeah, you're right. We should probably call the cops too," she suggested, hopping into the Tiger.

"I don't think that's necessary. It looks like the third guy is breaking things up," Hilda said, glancing back.

Nikki nodded. A strange tingling erupted across her neck as she made for a quick exit. As she pulled out into the street, her eyes darted to the rearview mirror, catching a glimpse of the man who'd grabbed Tony. While she only caught a fleeting glance, it was enough. There was something familiar about the man with the dark hair who was being hauled off of Tony, which made no sense. She didn't see his face—only a quick glance of his profile. *Still...* She couldn't shake the feeling that she knew him from somewhere.

Shrugging it off, she tore down the street without another look. They needed to get out of there before things got out of control as Hilda had suggested. Nikki knew volatile guys like that and that it was best to stay away from them—even if something about the stranger called to her deep inside.

~

JAKE WAS GOING TO BREAK THIS MOTHERFUCKER'S FACE. IT WAS AS SIMPLE as that.

With another powerful blow, he felt Tony's nose crack beneath his fist. Blood coated his knuckles in a hot, sticky mess, but he didn't stop. The piece of shit needed to pay for what he did.

"Dude! Snap the fuck out of it!" Johnny's voice ordered as he wrapped his arms around Jake's middle and hauled him off Tony.

Jake struggled against Johnny's hold, but Johnny only held on tighter, dragging him away from a moaning and cursing Tony. "Enough! You're going to kill him! You don't want to go back to jail, do you? Think about Dario."

The mention of Dario's name cleared the haze coating Jake's vision. "Huh? What?" he said, looking down at his shaking, bloody hands.

Jesus.

Johnny released Jake with a shove, placing himself between Jake and Tony. "*What?* Are you kidding? You just beat the crap out of Tony. What the hell?"

"Yeah, what the fuck is your problem, Jake?" Tony winced, pressing his bruised and bloodied body against the Mustang.

Jake blinked and leaned around Johnny, glaring angry death at Tony. "*You're* my problem, asshole! You threatened that girl!"

Tony started to respond, but Johnny cut him off. "Shut the fuck up before you make things worse." Johnny turned back to Jake. "I know he's a piece of shit, but beating him like that? What were you thinking? It's not like you know that girl or her friend. Not that she needed you. She looked like she had it covered."

Jake pulled his gaze from Tony, the rage in his veins still fresh, still potent. "I do know her."

"What?"

He let out a heavy breath. "That girl...it was *her*, Johnny—my angel."

Johnny's eyes widened. "The girl from the cemetery?"

He nodded. "I'd recognize her anywhere."

"Damn. I can't believe it."

"I know...it's...fuck. It's a miracle," Jake breathed, the usual heaviness in his chest lifting.

Johnny winced.

"What?"

"Well, I'm assuming you're going to try to find out who she is," Johnny said, his voice wary.

Hope flared in Jake's chest for the first time in weeks. He'd found his angel, the whole reason he was standing there today and not in the ground next to his mother. His heart started pounding. Of course he was going after her.

"I have to. That girl saved my life. I owe her."

Johnny nodded, his pained expression voicing what Jake hadn't, that he didn't just owe this girl—he needed her...maybe now more than ever. "I know she did. And I'm sure you'll be able to track her down. She drives a Sunbeam Tiger, so Sean probably knows her or at least *of* her. But your little *performance* didn't exactly make a good first impression."

Jake glanced down at his hands and over at Tony, his hope deflating. A moment ago she watched him annihilate someone. That wasn't a bad first impression. It was a horrific one.

Damn it.

How was he going to explain this to her? She'd probably be terrified of him.

He ran his clean hand down his face. Just once, he'd like to not screw anything up. Just. One. Fucking. Time.

Johnny reached out and put a hand on his shoulder. "Don't sweat it. If Sean knows her and you can get in touch, just explain that you were coming to her defense. She'll understand. She might even like it. A lot of chicks go for the whole knight-in-shining-armor bullshit."

"I hope you're right," Jake said, his stomach churning. To find his angel, only to scare her away—

He shook his head, cutting off the thought.

Johnny pulled out his phone. "Come on. Let's get out of here. He'll be fine."

Jake glanced back at Tony, who glared at the two of them through swollen eyes. "You think he'll call the cops? I can't afford an arrest, J."

Johnny gave him a bland look. "Uh, I'm a cop. Remember?"

"I know, but you're also my friend. He could call 911 anyway."

"I don't think he will. I bet he's got a long list of priors. Don't you, Tony?" Johnny said, directing his attention to the tool.

Tony glared at the two of them. "I don't need cops to solve my problems. I can handle my own. And I will handle you, Jake. You're not gettin' away with this shit."

"Whatever." Johnny snorted, brushing off Tony's threat. "Let's get out of here."

"Sounds good." Jake nodded. "But...what about Tiff? Won't she be pissed?" he asked as they made their way down the street.

"Nah. She'll be cool. She knows Tony. This won't surprise her."

Jake let out a heavy breath, wishing things in his life could work out that easily.

4

———

Nikki rolled off a string of curses as she muscled the rebuilt transmission into the custom 1940 Ford coupe—a job that would be easier with a transmission jack, but one wasn't available when she needed it, which figured. This day had been craptastic from the get-go. There were interruptions from other staff from the moment she arrived. Then her manager, Jack Romano, phoned to inform her that Suspension Masters, her biggest sponsor, expected her to not only race the Tiger she wrecked at Le Mans the next year, but also *rebuild* said Tiger if she wanted their continued support—something she would have to do in her spare time between races and her job.

Yep. That was the kind of day she was having, and it was only 7:30 a.m. *Awesome.*

She was tightening the second-to-last bolt on the tranny housing when a pair of work boots appeared next to the car. Blowing an errant hair out of her eye, she started to bark at the owner of the boots to beat feet or risk losing a toe, but he cut her off.

"I need to see you in my office," her brother demanded.

"Can it wait?" She grunted, moving on to the final bolt. "There's a lot of work left, and the car has to be finished today. It's one of West's. He's expecting it tomorrow."

Phillip West was a longtime customer and one of a dozen or so clients who solely requested Nikki to do the work on their vehicles. He was also a *very* patient man. Even though his car was five weeks overdue, he hadn't complained, which made her all the more eager to finish it. She didn't want to push her luck with a loyal customer. Everyone had their limits, and the shop couldn't afford to start losing its clientele—especially ones with deep pockets.

"No, it can't."

Nikki's wrench stilled. The arctic tone in Dino's voice brooked no argument. A knot formed in her stomach. He never interrupted jobs on West's cars; they were sacred.

"Okay," she said, setting down the wrench and sliding out from under the car. She'd tightened enough bolts to hold the transmission in place.

She froze when she caught sight of Dino. Tension radiated from every muscle along his lean frame and rigid jaw. And then there were his eyes. Their usually warm brown depths were as flat as his voice had been.

Icy fingers pricked her spine. She'd only seen Dino like this once before: at her parents' funeral.

The knot in her stomach tightened.

She'd been avoiding him for the last two days in a cowardly attempt at putting off telling him about the Tiger. She knew it was wrong, but she couldn't help it. The idea of hurting Dino and Mike, like she knew the news would, had convinced her to wait. But seeing him now, she knew she'd made a mistake. A big one. He'd found out somehow and *not* from her.

Swallowing the rising tide of regret, Nikki stood, her eyes never leaving his. "Dino, I'm so s—"

"Don't. Not here," he cut in before turning and striding to his office at the back of the shop.

With a silent nod, she followed—all eyes on her as she trailed Dino like a death-row inmate.

When she reached the office, she turned, catching several worried looks from her friends and coworkers. She mustered a small reassuring smile as she closed the door, hoping that she could make Dino understand why she sold the car, but knowing, deep in her heart, that he'd never get it...and quite possibly never forgive her.

~

"He fired you?" Hilda gasped.

Nikki clutched her cell phone with a shaky hand. She was perched on a stack of tires in the field behind the shop where they stored scrap parts destined for the wrecking yard or recycling plant.

"Yep." She sighed, her eyes roving over the makeshift graveyard. It was the first place she thought of after Dino dropped the ax on her and threw her out of the shop. And now that she thought about it, it made perfect sense: like these scrap parts, she, too, had been discarded.

"I get that he's pissed about the Tiger, but *firing* you? That seems extreme."

Nikki couldn't believe it, either. She knew he would be upset about her selling the car—deeply so—but what happened in his office went far beyond even her darkest fears. Dino wasn't *upset* with her or even hurt—he was disgusted. So disgusted that he didn't only fire her from the shop—he fired her from his *life*, cutting her out completely. And it seemed that Mike felt the same way. After Nikki left the garage, she called Mike, hoping to make him understand why she did it, and that he, in turn, could make Dino understand. But that was an epic fail. Like Dino, he refused to listen to her side of things, echoing their older brother's sentiment instead: that Nikki, a selfish, self-centered brat who cared more about her career than her own family, was no longer welcome in their lives. It was a crushing blow and the worst kind of irony. Finding hope for her future for the first time in what felt like forever meant losing two of the most important people in her life.

"He's not just pissed, Hil." Nikki pulled her knees in to her chest in an effort to stop the shaking. "He hates me. I know it. I saw it in his eyes, and I heard it in his voice." Her heart broke at the memory of his words.

"I think you're overreacting. I'm sure he doesn't *hate* you," Hilda assured her.

"Oh, he does. He said he's *washed his hands of me* and that as far as he's concerned, he doesn't have a sister," Nikki said, kicking at an old tire. "If that doesn't scream *hate*, I don't know what does."

"Damn. Someone's been watching too much of The Godfather. I'm surprised you didn't find a severed horse's head in your bed this morning."

Nikki laughed—a sharp, tinny sound that held no joy. "I know, right? Only in my case, it would have been severed fuel lines or a radiator."

"Totally." Hilda paused. When she spoke again, her voice was insistent. "Look, I know you're hurting right now. But trust me, your brothers are wrong here. Going after your dreams doesn't make you selfish."

"I don't know..." She hesitated. "After what Dino and Mike both said, I have to wonder if I did the right thing after all." She let out a shuddering breath as more tears spilled down her cheeks. "I knew I'd have to make sacrifices, but I had no idea it would cost me my family. Maybe...maybe it's not worth—"

"Stop it. Do you want to be a driver in Formula 1?"

"You know I do."

"Is there anything else you want more in the world?" she continued.

"No." Nikki sniffled.

"Okay, then. You did the right thing. Selling the Tiger to keep your dream alive makes you driven, not selfish, Nikki. Anyone who truly knows and loves you would see that. Your dad would have supported your decision, and you know Sean and I both do. Screw your brothers. This crap is all on them and their twisted jealousies over your success—not you. So stop crying, get back on your feet, and keep moving forward like you planned. Remember that quote that Ms. Alvarez used to keep in her office? *Don't let others' opinions drown out your inner voice.*"

"Yeah, I think so."

"Good. Listen to it. Believe it. Your inner voice knows you did the right thing for you and your dreams—as hard as it was. Remember that," Hilda insisted.

"Okay." Nikki wiped the tears from her cheeks with the back of her hand, grateful for her best friend's unflagging support. "And thanks, Hil. I'm glad I've still got you in my corner. I don't know what I'd do without you."

"You'd be forever lost," she said, laughing. "But seriously, I'll always have your back, girl. Now, what's your first move?"

"Well, since I can't go home—Dino's there, moving his stuff out and into his girlfriend's place—I guess I'll head over to Sean's and see if he knows someone I can hire for a lead mechanic on my Mazda and VAM series teams *and* if he knows anyone else who can help with the Le Mans Tiger restoration. I'm going to have to get another job, so I'll need help with the Tiger in the off hours if I'm to get it done by November," she explained, hating the idea of job hunting. It ranked up there with getting her teeth drilled.

"All right. Sounds like a good start. Get to it," Hilda ordered in her no-nonsense tone.

"Yes, ma'am!" Nikki replied through the pain she knew would stay with her no matter what she did or where she went. Like the deaths of her parents, losing her brothers left a hole in her heart she knew would never completely heal.

Dusting off her coveralls, she jumped down from her perch and headed over to the Tiger's Den, the Sunbeam Tiger restoration shop owned by Sean Martin, her father's best friend and someone she considered family. Sean had connections to all kinds of mechanics and specialists across the Bay Area. He'd be able to help her find someone. At least that was what she told herself as she made the short walk to his shop down the cul-de-sac from Dino's. *Something* had to go right that day. It had to.

Jake ran a shaky hand through his hair and frowned. He should have gotten a haircut yesterday. His shaggy mane was out of control, falling into his eyes and dusting the collar of his shirt. Not a good look for a first impression—and he needed to make a good one with his angel when they finally met. He glanced at the scrapes and bruises across his hands as he tried to tame his hair and snorted.

Who was he kidding?

His appearance wouldn't mean shit. She saw him lose it and beat the hell out of someone. More than anything, his temper would ruin things for him. There was a good chance she'd want nothing to do with him after what she witnessed. Jake's heart started to pound. The thought of losing her before he had the chance to repay her—to be a part of her life somehow—sent a wave of panic through his veins.

Dropping his head, he grabbed the edge of the sink in a white-knuckled grasp and let out a long, slow breath. He needed to get this anger under control and not only because he wanted to make the right impression with his angel. He needed to do it for Dario too. If he didn't, he ran the risk of losing it in the wrong place at the wrong time, ending up back in jail...or worse.

He lifted his head and gave himself a long look. He could retry the meditation exercises he learned from Javier, the social worker who ran the homeless shelter where he volunteered on Tuesdays. They had helped in the past, but after the blowup at the courthouse, Jake stopped doing them. He didn't see the point in continuing.

Until now.

After four years of wishing and wondering, he finally found his angel and, in doing so, had regained some of the clarity and purpose that had leached out of him after the failed custody attempt. And this time, he wouldn't let her get away. He couldn't. Not without repaying her for saving his life all those years ago.

With determination and hope coursing through his veins for the first time in what felt like decades, Jake strode out to the living room, grabbed his jacket and keys, and got ready to leave for work. It was still early, only 6:00 a.m., but he wanted to get to the shop in time to talk to Sean about the girl with the Tiger before things got busy. He hoped to have her name and a way to contact her before the day's end.

He reached for the door, when a sharp knock startled him.

Who could that be?

It couldn't be Johnny or Frankie; they both worked early shifts during the week. And it couldn't be Dario, either. He wasn't allowed to come to Jake's place per the visitation agreement—something neither of them ever risked jeopardizing.

Another knock sounded, this one more insistent.

"Okay. Just a sec," he called, tossing his jacket down. Maybe it was Frankie or Johnny after all. They were both as impatient as hell.

Jake opened the door and froze.

Angela O'Brien stood before him, smiling.

Oh fuck.

"Hey there, handsome," she purred, stepping past a speechless Jake and inside the apartment. "Did I catch you at a bad time?"

Shaking off the stupor, he grabbed the door, keeping it partially open. "Uh, yeah. I'm leaving for work. How...did you know where I lived?"

"I have ways of finding people if I need to," she replied, scanning the apartment with assessing eyes.

"I see."

Christ. Johnny was right. This chick was a stalker.

"What can I do for you?" he asked, keeping his tone light as he glanced down at his watch. He needed to leave, or he wasn't going to make it in time to talk with Sean before the other mechanics got there.

Angela turned to face him, her deep-red lips pursed. "For starters, you can explain why you haven't called. I left you messages with my number on your door."

"You did?" Jake lied.

She nodded. "Uh-huh. Several of them."

Several. That was a gross understatement. She had left closer to a dozen over the last couple of days—messages he'd tossed in the trash in hopes that she'd get the hint and leave him alone.

So much for hints.

"Huh, that's strange. I didn't get them."

Angela shrugged as she tugged at the sash of her trench coat. "It doesn't matter. I'm here now." She stepped closer, letting the coat fall open.

"Holy...shit," he hissed, gaping at the tiny red thong Angela wore... and nothing else.

"I was hoping I could persuade you to stay home today." She reached around him and pushed the door closed, her bare breasts brushing against his arm. "I thought you might like this outfit. Why don't you stay and... help me out of it?"

Mustering all the strength he had, Jake took a step back. Crazy or not, Angela was a beautiful and nearly naked woman. Any red-blooded man would be tempted by her offer.

"Sorry, I can't. I have to get to work."

"Are you sure?" she asked, letting the coat fall down around her shoulders, revealing her body in its entirety.

With a long, slow exhale, he nodded and gently pulled the trench coat up and closed. "I'm sure. I can't miss work. I need the money, as you can see."

"All right." She pouted, glancing around. "How about later? I could come back or wait here until you return."

"Yeah...I...don't think so, Ang." Jake turned and grabbed his jacket and keys once more, hating how awkward this was about to get. It was why he liked hooking up at the bar or the motel behind it: boundaries were clear, awkwardness was eliminated, and best of all, no one got hurt.

"The thing is...I don't bring women to my apartment. Ever. It leads to too many complications, and I can't have that right now."

"I see." She moved closer, her eyes narrowed to slits. "So, you'd rather get a quick blowjob at the Ox and be done with it?"

He swallowed audibly. He knew he sounded like a douche, but he couldn't avoid it. He thought he'd been clear with her back at the bar after their first encounter. Apparently, she didn't get *that* message, either.

"Pretty much."

"Are you *actually* turning *me* down?" she asked, pressing herself up against him.

Jake took her by the shoulders and stepped back. "I am. I'm sorry, Angela. Really. I thought I made this clear back at the Ox."

They fell into a staring deadlock for several beats. Jake waited, bracing himself for the slap he could feel coming, but it never did.

"Fine." She stepped around him and yanked the door open. "But just so you know, this isn't over. When I want something, I don't give up until I get it," she vowed, slamming the door shut behind her.

Jake stood in front of the door and waited, her threat echoing in his ears. It was the second one he'd received in two days.

Awesome.

He continued to stand there staring at the peeling yellow paint, not wanting to chance leaving until he knew she was long gone in case she decided to follow him to work. After twenty minutes, he stepped out of his apartment, keeping a watchful eye out as he mounted his bike. Johnny was right again. He needed to move if he wanted to cut Angela out of his life.

"Perfect. Fucking perfect," Jake grumbled as he fired up the Harley and tore out of the driveway.

5

Jake roared into the parking lot of the Tiger's Den an hour later than he'd planned. The only saving grace: he was technically only thirty minutes late to work. While Angela's surprise visit didn't take that long, the horrendous traffic getting across town did.

He parked his bike in his usual spot and sprinted into the shop, fully prepared for Sean's wrath. His boss was a stickler for punctuality.

Eddie Ray, one of the mechanics on staff, poked his head out from an engine compartment. "What's up, Jake? You need something?"

"I'm looking for Sean. Have you seen him?"

"He's out back with Nikki Elliot. She came in earlier looking pretty upset, sayin' she needed his help with something," Eddie explained.

Jake nodded, knowing he'd better make himself busy while he waited. *This could take a while.* While he had never met Nikki or her two older brothers, even though they owned a restoration shop just down the cul-de-sac from the Den, he knew that Sean loved them like they were his own children. There was nothing he wouldn't do for any of them, so if Nikki needed help, he knew to stay away until she left. Sean always put family first. Jake admired and respected that about him.

Forty-five minutes later, Sean strode into the garage as Jake finished up a wiring harness. From the looks of his boss, whatever he and Nikki discussed must have been serious. Tension rippled off him like heat waves as he stomped through the shop and into his office, bellowing at Jake as he went. "Masercotti, get your ass in here!"

All work in the garage stopped.

"Ooh, he sounds pissed," Eddie called from across the shop.

"Yeah. Don't make any sudden moves when you go in there," Carlos Gonzalez, Sean's third mechanic, added.

Jake set the wiring harness down with a sigh. So much for trying to get Sean's help with his angel's identity. He was obviously in a piss-poor mood, which meant Jake couldn't ask him for *anything*. When Sean got worked up, it was best to take whatever he dished out at you then back away slowly and quietly.

"Right," Jake said, nodding at Carlos and Eddie. When he reached the office, he knocked on the open door. "You wanted to see me?"

Sean looked up from his industrial desk. "I need to talk to you about something. Have a seat." He waved at the worn leather chair in front of the desk. "And close the door behind you."

Jake nodded and followed suit. "If this is about my being late, I'm really sorry. I got delayed at home, and traffic was a bitch."

Sean leaned back in his old leather chair, the hinges protesting. "That's not what this is about. But while we're on the subject, what delayed you? You're never late."

Jake rifled through his brain for a way to respond to that question without giving too much away. Telling Sean about his troubles with an unstable female was no way to lead into asking him for the identity of the girl in the Tiger.

"Uh, well...I've been having trouble at my apartment complex lately. I had a break-in a few weeks back, and there was a suspicious person lurking around the property this morning. I didn't want to leave until they took off in case they were up to no good," he explained.

It wasn't a complete lie. He *was* robbed, and Angela was a suspicious person.

"You were *robbed*?" Sean shot upright. "Why didn't you tell me? Did they get much? Do you need anything?"

The concern in Sean's voice and in his expression froze Jake's vocal cords. He never considered telling his boss about what happened. He didn't think he'd care, much less want to help. He was just his boss.

"Are you all right, boy?" Sean pressed when Jake didn't respond.

"Huh? Yeah." Jake shook his head. "I...sorry. They cleaned me out. Took my TV, stereo, camera, computer, everything."

Sean swore. "Sounds like you live in a rough place. Have you considered moving?"

"I have, but the rent anywhere else will be out of my league. I'm pretty much stuck," he said, hating the sheer truth of that statement in more ways than one.

"Rent is sky high around Wood Glenn." Sean paused, studying Jake. "Would you consider renting from me?"

"Rent...from *you*?"

"That's what I said."

Jake considered the offer. He didn't like the idea of renting a room from anyone, let alone his boss. That could get awkward. He also had to think of Child Services. They could see his renting a room as a step backward and rethink his visitations with Dario, and that wasn't worth the risk. Those bi-weekly visits were too important. If he had to slum it in that shit-hole and avoid Angela another way, so be it.

Sean barked out a laugh after Jake explained his situation. "Not a room, son. I meant the apartment above the shop. It's a three-bedroom unit. I was thinking you could live there in exchange for something else."

"What did you have in mind?" Jake asked slowly.

"Nothing crazy," Sean chuckled. "My little Nikki was here this morning. She's looking to hire a mechanic to work on her Mazda Series and VAM pit crews for the remainder of the season *and* someone to help her restore a Le Mans Tiger. I thought you'd be a good fit because of your experience here and with Formula Motors."

Jake gaped at his boss. "You want *me* to work with *Nikki*?"

"I do." Sean arched a brow. "Is...that a bad idea? You do have experience with the Mazda Renesis rotary engines after working at Formula Motors, don't you?"

"I do. But...you're so protective of her. I'm surprised you'd ask *me*."

"Why wouldn't I ask you? You're a good kid with a good head on your shoulders. You've never missed a day of work, you're a top-notch mechanic, and more importantly, you're someone I trust," Sean explained.

Jake gaped at him.

Sean *trusted him*? The guy who'd fucked up his life six ways from Sunday?

That's because he doesn't know your history, an insidious voice whispered.

Jake's stomach churned. The voice had a point. Sean knew nothing of his failures. He only knew the Jake he'd become since finding his angel—the only version of himself he wanted *anyone* to know. If Sean or his buddies ever found out what Jake did—

Jake snapped his thoughts back in line before they went any further down that dark road.

"Look, son, if you're not interested, say so," Sean replied to his continued silence.

"No. No, that's not it. I mean, well, it kind of is," Jake began. "Being on one pit crew involves a lot of traveling. But *two*? It sounds like I'd be gone most of the time, and I can't do that. I have my brother to think about. Not to mention my job here."

"See, that's why I trust you. You put family and responsibilities first—a mark of a good man in my book." Sean grinned as he leaned back in his chair. "And you're right. This job would involve a lot of travel, but I don't think it would interfere with seeing your brother too much. I'm sure you could figure out a way to work around the racing schedule. Besides, it's not long-term. It's only until the end of November. By then, Nikki will have a contract to race professionally next year, and she won't have to worry about hiring her own crew. As for your job here, don't worry about it. You'll work here when you're not traveling or working on the Le Mans Tiger. It would be good money too. Lead mechanics make a good wage."

Lead mechanic?

Damn.

That was an incredible opportunity. The pay for that position plus his work at the Den would help Jake get enough money together to buy back what he'd lost in the robbery a lot sooner than he'd planned and leave him something to put away for Dario's college fund. And if he was careful, he might even be able to put enough a way to actually have a personal savings account—something he'd never had before.

He didn't hesitate. If this work didn't interfere with seeing Dario, then he had to take it. And even if it did interfere *a little*, the job would come to an end soon enough. Opportunities like this didn't come along often, especially for a guy like him.

He sat up straight. "I'll do it. Thanks, Sean. It…it means a lot that you'd offer me this. But what does this have to do with your apartment?"

"*That* has to do with Nikki hiring you to help restore a Le Mans Tiger." His expression darkened. "She needs someone to help her with that, but her finances are tight since her asshole brother fired her this morning."

"Ouch." Jake winced. "Why'd he do it? It seems pretty harsh to fire your own sister."

"I told you: because he's an asshole. I love him, but he's a real piece of shit when it comes to his sister and her choice of profession—always has been, if you ask me." Sean glowered. "Anyway, Nikki doesn't have enough money to pay you for both jobs as a result—at least she won't for long. She'll burn through the cash she got from selling her Tiger quicker than she realizes if she doesn't have another source of income. So I was thinking you could live in the apartment above the shop in exchange for working on the Le Mans Tiger. You'll have to go over to her house to do it, and it'll mean leaving work here a little early, but I won't dock you. When the Tiger is finished, we can sit down and work out your rent for the apartment going forward. I think it's a fair deal."

Fair deal? It was an awesome deal. Sean could easily rent the apartment for more than Jake would make working for Nikki after hours. And paying him for time when he wasn't there? That was too much. Jake didn't take charity.

"I don't know, Sean. I should pay rent, and you should dock my pay if I have to leave early. It doesn't seem fair to you otherwise."

Sean waved off the offer. "Horseshit! I want to do this—for both of you." He got up from his seat, went over to Jake, and placed a hand on his shoulder. "You're both good kids who need a little help making their way, and I'm in a position to do that, so I am. No arguments," Sean insisted when Jake tried to interrupt. "But don't say anything to Nikki about our deal. She'd see it as charity, and like you, she hates that. So, as far as she is concerned, I'm paying you for the off-hours working on the Le Mans car and she's going to pay me back when she can. I won't take her money when she offers it, of course, but she doesn't know that yet."

Jake studied his boss for a long minute. When he saw that Sean was serious and wouldn't take no for an answer, Jake stood. "All right. I won't say a word to Nikki, and I won't forget this, boss. But I will find a way to repay you. No arguments." He gave Sean a pointed look.

"Okay, son. I understand." He led Jake over to the door. "You'll need to meet Nikki tonight at Vintage Motors. She said to be there at eight o'clock. She'll be there finishing up her last job. For now, though, go home and pack. I want you out of that shithole today. I have a bad feeling about that place," he said, handing him a set of car keys. "You can use my Bronco to move your things, but you won't need any furniture, unless you're attached to it. The apartment upstairs is fully furnished."

Jake nodded, swallowing around the lump in his throat. No one outside of Frankie and Johnny had ever done so much for him or believed in him like this. Not since his mother was alive.

He stopped in the doorway, hating the idea of asking Sean for a favor after all this, but he had to know about the girl in the Tiger.

"Before I go, I wanted to ask you something. I ran into a young woman in a Tiger on Saturday. She was around twenty-one or so. It was an early midnight-blue car. Do you by any chance know her? I wanted to find out where she got the bodywork done so we could send our cars there. The Tiger was in amazing shape."

Sean was back behind his desk, shuffling through the mound of paperwork piled there. Organization wasn't his jam. "Sure. That's Nikki—though she doesn't own the Tiger anymore. That's the one she sold to fund her pit crew. You probably saw her on her final run. But I don't know where the bodywork was done. You'd have to ask her that."

Jake gripped the casing so hard his knuckles started to ache. "That was Nikki Elliot?"

Sean arched a brow. "Yes. Why?"

Jake gaped at his boss. His angel was Nikki Elliot? The girl who had *literally* worked down the street from him for the last year and a half?

"You okay, son? You look like you seen a ghost," Sean said, setting down the paperwork.

Jake blinked once, twice. "Yeah…yeah, I'm fine. Just…small world," he stammered, pushing himself off the casing and out into the shop, his mind spinning like the Gravitron.

Not only did he know the name of his angel, but he was going to be working for her.

Holy shit.

How could this be? Things in his life didn't work out like this. *Ever.*

The memory of what went down at the gas station crept through his mind, deflating his elation. Nikki was going to flip her shit when she saw him. She'd never want to work with someone like him—someone capable of such violence.

Unless…

Unless she trusted Sean's judgment when it came to employees. Granted, Sean didn't know about what happened at the gas station, but Jake had a feeling he would back up his actions since he was trying to protect Nikki. And if she trusted Sean as much as he wanted to believe she did, then Nikki might overlook what happened—especially after he explained his side of things.

It was a big *if*, but Jake was going to cling to it with everything he had. He might not deserve it, but he needed her in his life right now just as much as he needed to repay her for saving his all those years ago.

NIKKI DISARMED THE SECURITY SYSTEM AND LET HERSELF INTO THE DESERTED garage. Dino closed the shop promptly at 5:30 every evening to give his mechanics time to be with their families. He adopted the practice from their father, who always put their family first—never missing a family dinner, school play, soccer game, race, anything.

If only Dino practiced what he preached.

After changing into her black Vintage Motors embroidered coveralls and steel-toed boots—standard issue for working in the garage—she headed over to the '40 Ford and got to work. She phoned Dino earlier and told him that she would come in after closing and finish West's car to avoid making things uncomfortable. He argued with her, stating that she was no longer allowed at *his garage*, but after she reminded him that West's contract specified that she *and only she* was to work on his car or it would be voided, Dino caved. The restoration job was over fifteen thousand dollars—money her brother couldn't afford to lose.

Sean phoned an hour later, letting her know that Jake—the mechanic he'd found for her—was running late. Apparently, he'd moved into the apartment above Sean's shop earlier that day and needed more time to get settled. Nikki told Sean it was fine—she'd be at Vintage Motors until at least 9:00, anyway—and for Jake to come over when he finished.

She ended the call and reached for the box of industrial latex mechanics' gloves she wore when working in the shop. Being a mechanic and a racecar driver didn't mean her hands had to suffer. She'd always been told she had beautiful, delicate hands, and she wanted them to stay that way.

Nikki dug inside the box but came up empty.

Cursing the empty box and the headache she felt building behind her eyes, she strode to the storeroom at the rear of the garage and grabbed another box. She was ripping it open when a tingling sensation erupted across her neck, followed by the sound of a wrench hitting the floor.

Her hands stilled.

Someone was in the shop.

She released a long, slow breath. She had no reason to panic. It could be Jake. He was supposed to be there at some point; it was why she'd left the door unlocked.

Another tool hit the ground, raising the hairs along her arms.

On the other hand, it could also be someone else—someone who didn't belong there. It wouldn't be the first time something like that happened. The shop had been robbed several times over the last few years. Wood Glenn had experienced a sharp rise in gang activity several years before, especially in the industrial areas of town like this one. It had inspired Dino to finally invest in a security system—a costly venture but worth every penny. The system and private security squad that accompanied it had prevented two break-ins since he had it installed.

Nikki fisted her hands. She should have locked the door, armed the system, and made Jake phone before coming over. That would have been the smart thing to do. But she didn't think of that until now, of course. She blamed the oversight on the tempest of emotions and endless list of responsibilities churning in her skull.

She set the box down then inched over to the door, keeping her footing light like Tsai taught her. When she reached the door, she peeked around the casing and swore. She couldn't see anyone from her vantage point.

She reached for her phone to call the police but stopped short, remembering that she left it on the tool cart next to the Ford. It was just as well.

The police wouldn't do anything. They were useless in Wood Glenn, especially when it came to crime in *this* area of town.

She would to have to handle this on her own. Hiding back there wasn't the answer. Whoever it was would find her eventually.

Heart pounding, Nikki slipped out of the storeroom and over to the stainless-steel tool chest where Dino kept a shotgun for moments like this. She reached around and pulled the Benelli M2 Tactical shotgun from its mount and crept out into the shop, keeping her back against the outer wall.

When she heard more footsteps and another tool hit the ground, she fell into a crouch behind a '69 Ford Ranger. This couldn't be Sean's guy. Any mechanic worth his salt wouldn't be *that* clumsy in a garage.

Gripping the bumper, she leaned around the rear of the Ranger, spotting the perp. He was crouching down by the rear quarter panel of the Ford. Even in a squatting position, she noted his height and well-built physique. His dark, fitted Henley highlighted a lean, athletic frame that indicated he worked out. *Often.*

Without another thought, she popped out from behind the Ranger, ready to show this idiot that he picked the wrong shop to rob. In three lightning-fast steps, she moved behind him, cocking the shotgun—the pump-action sound echoing across the still garage.

"Get on your knees with your hands in the air!"

"Jesus!" The stranger dropped to his knees, trembling hands thrust into the air.

"Good. Now *slowly* turn around," she continued, the gun rock steady in her hands.

He nodded, his deep voice trembling slightly. "Okay. Just, please. Don't shoot."

"I won't if you—" Nikki started to say but stopped when he shuffled on his knees to face her.

It was the thug from the gas station who'd beat the daylights out of Tony. She recognized his profile.

"What the hell are *you* doing here?" she sneered.

He didn't respond. He merely knelt there, gaping at her with a mixture of fear and something else—something that looked like...awe.

Weird. Did he have a thing for women with guns?

"Hello? Did you hear me?" she pressed.

He shook his head. "S-Sean sent me over. I'm J-Jake...Masercotti. Your new mechanic."

She gaped at him.

This was Jake? The guy Sean raved about this morning?

She narrowed her eyes. "Are you serious?"

"Yes. I can prove it. My ID's in my back pocket."

"All right, but take it out slowly—I won't hesitate to turn your chest into Swiss cheese if you pull anything funny—and set it down in front of you," she ordered, her narrowed eyes tracking every move he made.

Jake nodded and did as ordered. Nikki reached over with her foot and dragged the wallet to her. With methodical movements, she knelt and grabbed the Harley Davidson-embroidered billfold, keeping the shotgun pointed squarely at his chest.

"Look," he began as she opened the wallet. "I get why you're afraid. I should have announced myself when I came in, and after what you saw on Saturday, it's no surprise that you came out with a gun and—"

Her eyes snapped to his. "I'm not afraid. I didn't know who was out here, so I came prepared. If anything, what you did on Saturday shocked me. You could have killed that guy. He may be a dick, but he didn't deserve the beat-down you gave him."

"Okay, so you're not afraid," he said, swallowing audibly as she continued to rummage through his wallet for his ID. "I know what I did was extreme. Believe me. I regret how badly I hurt him, but I did it with good intentions. That guy isn't a just a dick—he's a psycho with a reputation for hurting women. I was trying to protect you, and I got carried away. I'm sorry."

"*Protect* me? Do you have some kind of hero complex? Do you go around defending women at gas stations all over town?"

"No. I didn't want to see *you* get hurt," he replied, sincerity ringing in his voice.

Unimpressed with the pseudo-superhero, she found his driver's license and pulled it from the back of the wallet. He was telling the truth about his identity, and something in her gut said he was telling the truth about the gas station too.

Even so... He had seriously questionable taste in friends. What kind of guy openly *chose* to run around with a psycho?

"Well, thanks for thinking of my well-being—though I didn't need protecting. I can handle my own, Jake." She tucked the ID back in its slot and tossed the wallet at him. "But I'd suggest you get a new class of friends. Running around with a psycho won't do wonders for your reputation."

Jake grimaced. "Tony and I are *not* friends. I detest that guy. I was only there because my buddy's girlfriend asked me to help him with his car. He's her cousin—twice removed," he explained.

Nikki relaxed her stance and lowered the gun, believing him again. But why? She didn't know Jake from Adam. She gripped the barrel of the shotgun. Maybe it was because he'd worked with Sean for the last two years.

Sean was good at reading people; he didn't need to know every facet of a person's life to make a sound judgment call. Or maybe it had something to do with the strange sense of familiarity she felt at the gas station and again tonight—like she knew Jake on a level too deep to fathom considering she'd never seen or spoken to him before. Whatever it was, she felt she could trust him.

"Then if I were you, I'd tell your friend's cousin that Tony is an asshole and doesn't deserve help. Not until he gets a personality adjustment, anyway," Nikki said, turning and setting the gun down on the cart.

"I'll do that."

When she turned back around, he was standing a few feet from her, hands tucked into the pockets of his jeans. Her eyes hadn't deceived her about his build. He was tall and well built, filling out the dark denim and Henley nicely.

She swallowed around the sudden dryness in her throat. "So, you're the mechanic Sean told me about," she said, all business, despite the rush of very *unbusinesslike* thoughts flooding her brain.

"I am." He nodded. "I understand you need someone to work as lead mechanic in both the Pro Mazda and VAM series and help with the restoration of a Tiger."

"That's right. I take it you're interested?" she asked, trying to get her bearings. Nikki was a sucker for tall, dark, and handsome men, and that was Jake—though handsome didn't cut it. *Drop-dead gorgeous* was more like it with his thick, wavy hair, dark eyes, and chiseled jaw. It made her synapses fire like mad. She couldn't remember ever seeing a man this good-looking in person—and that was saying something. She lived with Damon Rossi, a man who defined sexy—or at least he did, until tonight.

Jake smiled, and she could have sworn her heart flipped over and sighed at the boyish charm it brought out. "Absolutely. I'm happy to help you—any way I can."

She cleared her throat, reining in the hormone rush. "Great. Let's meet tomorrow and go over the schedule. I'd do it tonight, but I have to get this car finished, and I don't want to hold you up. I'm sure you've got unpacking to do."

Jake glanced down at his watch and frowned. "I don't think it's a good idea for you to work this late alone—shotgun and all." He tilted his head at the 12-gauge. "Why don't I stay and help you finish up? Whatever it is couldn't take long with the two of us working together, and then we can look at your schedule."

"Really? Are you sure?" she asked, stunned at his generosity. It was getting late, and she knew he had to be up early the next day for work. Sean opened at 7:00 a.m. sharp.

"Absolutely. Let's do this," he said, rolling up his sleeves, revealing a series of tribal-like tattoos snaking up his forearms.

Sweet Jesus...

Her breath stalled at the sight of them. Working in a shop and in racing, she was accustomed to seeing men with tattoos. Over the years, she'd developed an appreciation for them—the artistic ones, at least. And from where she stood, she could see that Jake's were works of art with their intricate swirls, patterns, and lettering.

Nikki gave herself an internal shake. She needed to snap out of it. So what if he was hot and inked with sexy tattoos? He was just another mechanic—like so many she'd worked with before. She needed to focus and get West's job done so she could move on to other things, not drool over Tall, Dark, and Gorgeous.

"All right, then," she said.

The minutes flew by in a seamless blur as they worked. Before she knew it, they were finishing up with the brakes, completing what would have taken her over an hour in thirty minutes.

"Do you need me to get any more brake fluid from the back?" Jake asked as Nikki topped off the master cylinder reservoir.

"No, I'm good," she said, pouring the last of the bottle in, the fish-oil scent of the fluid making her stomach roil. It didn't help her head, either. It started pounding when she was under the car, adjusting the bleeder valves, and now the pain was worse, cutting through her skull like a sharp knife.

Leaning on the fender, she set the brake fluid down and pressed a hand to her temple, trying to massage the ache away. It didn't work. Instead, a blinding, white-hot pain shot through her skull, sending her crumpling to the floor, followed by a series of images flashing in her mind. It was like the day in the car with Mike and Dino, only this time, there were more images—new ones adding to the scene.

"Whoa! Are you all right?" Jake gasped, catching her before she hit the unrelenting floor. She felt him lower the two of them to the ground, his rock-hard arms around her like steel bands.

Nikki didn't respond right away. She was too focused on the images flashing through her mind like a film. In them, she was back in the RV again, pacing like before, but instead of ending there, the scene jumped ahead. She watched herself storm into the bedroom of the trailer, grab her cell phone, then violently punch at the screen to make a call, muttering, "Come on! Come on! Be there! I don't know what to do! I don't know what to do!"

"Hey! Talk to me, angel. Are you all right?" Jake's panicked voice called as the scene faded to black.

Slumping back against his chest, she nodded. "Yeah...yeah, I'm fine. I have a headache and got a little dizzy," she said, not lying entirely. She was a little light-headed, though she suspected that had more to do with the fact that she hadn't eaten since breakfast than the flashback.

With gentleness that stunned her, Jake turned her so she was resting in the crook of his arm. His face was pale beneath naturally tanned skin and etched with worry. "Are you sure? You were pretty out of it. You weren't responsive, and your face got clammy," he said, brushing his hand along her cheek in a featherlight motion.

Nikki didn't say anything at first. The look she saw in his eyes as he stared back at her stole her voice. She saw fear and concern there, but there was something else...something she couldn't put her finger on, but it touched her heart in a way that nothing had for a long time.

She cleared her throat, bringing herself back to the reality where she was lying in Jake's lap—a very fine lap, but one she didn't belong in. "I'm fine. Really. I haven't eaten all day. That's all. I'll grab something when I get home." She sat up and got to her feet. When she swayed a little, Jake steadied her.

"I don't think you should drive home like this. Come to my apartment first, and I'll fix us both something to eat. I'm sure I've got something I could throw together," he offered.

She hesitated. Going over to the apartment with him felt like crossing a line—an intimate one—and doing that with *anyone*, let alone an employee, wasn't a good idea. Her life had enough complications.

On the other hand, he did have a point about her driving. She was in no shape for that at the moment, and Dino didn't keep food in the shop. She didn't have much choice here. Nikki didn't want to call Damon for help—he'd freak out and go all He-Man on her—Sean lived too far to call now, and Hilda was staying with her boy toy in the city that night. It looked like it was Jake's offer or crash at the shop and risk Dino's wrath.

Jake, it was.

"Okay. Give me five minutes to change."

～

"THIS IS WHAT'S UP HERE?" NIKKI BREATHED, GAWKING AT THE BEAUTIFUL space Sean had always referred to as the "old, dusty attic."

This was no old, dusty attic.

The apartment looked like it belonged in *Decor* or *Dwell*. The spacious, open floor plan was warm and sumptuous, filled with dark-wood furnishings and hardwood floors that gleamed beneath luxurious hand knotted rugs. An oversized leather sofa, matching club chairs, an ottoman, and a ginormous flat-screen TV mounted over a gas fireplace added an air of masculinity to the space, creating the perfect bachelor pad.

"I know, right? I couldn't believe it when I saw it," Jake said, striding over to the modern kitchen that overlooked the living area.

Nikki spun around in a slow circle, taking it all in. It made her parents' house—which was hers now, though she still had a hard time thinking of it that way—look downright shabby. "It's...God, it's—"

"Incredible," Jake finished.

"Exactly. I can't believe this was here and empty all this time." She shook her head at the absurdity.

"It looks like all I've got that's edible is peanut butter and jelly. Is that okay?" Jake called from the kitchen.

"Sounds perfect," Nikki said, noticing that there were no moving boxes or other packing materials scattered about the place. "Did you already unpack? I don't see any moving boxes."

He looked up from the counter. "Pretty much. I didn't have a lot to start with. I got robbed a few weeks back. The thieves took all of my electronics, and my other apartment was rented furnished, so I only had my mattress, clothes, and kitchenware to bring."

"I'm so sorry. That's awful."

Jake gave her a crooked smile. "Yeah. They even took my vinyl collection. Can you believe that? Who steals records?"

Her eyes lit up. "You collect records?"

He nodded. "I *had* a bunch of Italian operas, classic rock albums, and my mom's Andrea Bocelli collection—stuff that can't be replaced easily, if at all."

Nikki felt her heart somersault in her chest. She didn't know anyone who collected records, much less the albums he described. "You just described my entire collection," she gushed, beaming like a kid on Christmas. "My mom and dad were huge Bocelli fans. I grew up listening to him. I have all of his albums. He's one of my all-time favorite artists."

He leaned on the counter, his eyes dancing. "Wow. Pretty, smart, and good taste in music. You're too good to be true," he said, a crimson blush staining his cheeks the moment he finished.

She felt her own cheeks flush. He thought she was smart and pretty, *and* he liked her music? He was the one that sounded too good to be true.

"Um, wow. Thanks," she said, feeling epically lame.

That was the best response she could come up with?

"Yeah, well, it's...it's all true," he replied, his voice rougher, deeper than before.

Nikki grinned, turning her flaming face away. She feared what would come out of her mouth if she kept looking at him. Never in her life had she been this awkward around a man.

She scanned the room for something—anything—to distract her from the sex god behind the counter and spotted a pile of photographs lying on the oversized coffee table. Photography didn't interest her in the slightest, but something about these photos called to her.

When she knelt down in front of the table, her eyes rested on the first image: a pathway cutting through the woods. There was something about the light—the way it cascaded through the trees and illuminated a distant area of the path—that tugged at her heartstrings. It made her feel lonely, lost, even. No photograph outside of ones of her family had ever made her feel so much.

She began flipping through the other photographs, most of which were black and white. The subjects were all different, ranging from dramatic cityscapes and natural settings to candid shots of people in varying locales. All of the pieces were stunning, each evoking a different emotion.

"Did you take these?" she asked.

"Take what?" he said, dropping a knife into the sink, and coming over to her.

"These photographs." She cringed when she realized she didn't ask if she could go through them. She'd made herself at home—like it was the most natural thing to do. But it wasn't. Not in the least. "I'm sorry. I should have asked if I could see these."

Jake waved off her apology as he knelt beside her, studying the picture. "It's okay. I don't mind. You can make yourself at home."

She smiled shyly, feeling the sincerity behind his easy words. "So, did you take them?" she pressed.

He nodded, his eyes drifting from the picture to her. Staring into their depths, she couldn't believe how dark they were, like twin pools of obsidian that held all sorts of wonders and mysteries—mysteries part of her suddenly wanted to unlock.

She forced herself to swallow. "Really?"

"Yes. I took most of those a couple of years ago. Why?"

"They're amazing. Do you ever sell any of them?" she asked, sorting through more.

"Uh, no." He snorted.

Nikki turned back to him, brows arched. "Why is that funny?"

He frowned. "Because they're just some pictures I took for fun. No one would want them."

She gaped at him. "Jake, these are *beautiful*. I bet loads of people would want them. I would—especially the black-and-white shots." She held up one of a gnarled old oak tree atop a hill. "The way you accentuated the light and shadows gives me chills just looking at them."

"You really think so?" he said, his voice a soft murmur.

"I do," she replied, stilling when she reached the final picture, though this one wasn't a photograph. It was a black-and-white sketch of a beautiful young woman holding a bouquet of lilies. But it wasn't her beauty that caught Nikki's attention. Part of it was the love the artist captured in her eyes, but the other part—the part that had Nikki's throat constricting and her heart breaking—was the obvious love that went into creating the piece. Every careful stroke, every angle, every shadow had been done with a devoted hand.

She turned to Jake, her heart jumping when she realized he hadn't been staring at the sketch as she had, but at her. "Did...did you do this too?" she asked, her voice barely a whisper.

He nodded, dragging his eyes from her to the picture, a shadow descending over him the moment they hit the canvas. "Yes," he said, his voice grave. "I did that one four years ago."

"Who is she?" Nikki asked, reaching up and placing a hand on his shoulder.

Jake took the picture, his eyes running over the image. "My mother. She died when I was twelve. I didn't have any pictures of her, so I drew this one from memory."

Nikki inhaled sharply, her heart twisting. "I'm so sorry. I know how painful that is."

He set the picture down with care and placed the other pieces in front of it. "Is your mother gone too?" he asked, turning to her.

She nodded. "Both of my parents are. They died when I was seventeen."

"I'm sorry to hear that," he said, taking her hand from his shoulder and encasing it in his.

His hand was warm and strong, and she couldn't help but think how much she liked the feel of it wrapped around hers.

Needing some space before she allowed herself to get caught up in whatever was happening between them, she slid her hand out from his and stood. "You have a lot of talent. Have you ever considered pursuing your art instead of working as a mechanic?"

She felt her cheeks flame an unholy scarlet once more. What was wrong with her tonight? She never acted like this with the other guys at the shop or the track. Why couldn't she act like she did around *them*: all business, nothing personal? Why did she keep prying into his private life?

"I'm sorry...*again*. That was super personal and *none* of my business. I mean, maybe you like being a mechanic. Maybe that's been your dream all along. Maybe art is only a hobby." She snapped her mouth shut, cutting off the rambling, and went over to the breakfast bar, where the sandwiches waited, hating the life-long habit that surfaced whenever she got nervous —though nervous might be an understatement where Jake Masercotti was concerned. *Frazzled* felt more like it.

Jake followed her to the bar. "It's okay. It's nice, actually, having someone show interest in things like that...so few people do." He sat down and pushed a sandwich in front of her. "Honestly, I've never had a dream to pursue. Dreams always seemed like they were for *other* people. Not guys like me. I became a mechanic because working on cars came naturally to me and paid enough to cover the bills, but it's not something I *love*."

Nikki's sandwich froze halfway to her mouth. "You've never had a dream? Something you always wanted to be?"

She couldn't imagine having nothing to reach for.

"Nope." Jake shrugged, taking a bite of his sandwich.

She didn't say anything—just sat there, staring at him. He kept his expression neutral, but the way his jaw worked as he ate suggested there was more going on inside him than he let on. But she didn't pursue it. Things had gotten too personal already. She didn't want to continue down that path—for a lot of reasons.

Instead, she switched up the conversation to something lighter. "So, tell me: what's it like working for Sean? Is he as intense as I imagine?"

The muscles along Jake's jaw relaxed. "Intense would be putting it mildly." He chuckled.

They spent the rest of dinner exchanging stories about Sean, a neutral topic they could talk about with ease, and going over her schedule, lightening the mood as she'd hoped.

After cleaning up the dishes, Jake walked her out to her car. "So, should I meet you at your house tomorrow afternoon at four o'clock?" he asked, opening the driver door when the alarm chirped.

Nikki dropped her purse and duffel bag inside. "Actually, I'll be at the Den tomorrow, so you can follow me home at three-thirty. The clients who request me at Vintage Motors found out I got fired and phoned this afternoon, saying they'd follow me to my next place. Sean said I could use the open work bay he has in the back since my shop at home is currently housing the Le Mans Tiger and all of its parts."

She started to get into the car but stopped. "Oh, and there's something I forgot to mention earlier." She hoped this wouldn't be too awkward for him. "When we're at the races, you'll have to sleep in my RV, where my brother bunked. The crew's rig is small and already full with the few guys we have. But don't worry—your bunk is private."

Jake waved it off. "Sure. No problem."

"Great," she said, turning and getting into the car but stopped short when she heard glass breaking over at Denny's Automotive, the third shop in the cul-de-sac.

She and Jake both whipped around.

"Did you hear that?" she whispered.

He moved closer, his body shielding hers. "It came from Denny's. Around the back, maybe?"

They both fell quiet, their ears tuned to Denny's place. Another crash sounded—this one much louder.

"Shit. Someone's in there, and Denny doesn't have private security," Nikki said, turning and grabbing her purse. "Call 911—tell them...tell them someone's had a heart attack. That should get the EMTs here, and cops usually follow up to make sure things are okay. Meanwhile, I'll head in there and see if I can stop whoever it is."

Jake grabbed her arm in a firm grip that was somehow gentle. "Are you crazy? You can't go in there! You could get hurt."

"Relax. I'm not going in unprepared." She pulled her Sig Sauer P220 from the depths of her purse.

"Jesus Christ. Do you have an Annie Oakley complex?" he hissed.

Nikki pulled her arm free. "First of all, Annie Oakley was awesome." She cocked her gun. "And second, risky or not, I have to go in. Do you smell that?"

"What?" He inhaled deeply. "Fuck. Is that fuel?"

She nodded. "Smells like it. What if they're planning on torching the place once they get what they're after? I can't let that happen."

"Uh, yes, you can. It's too dangerous. Why put yourself at risk?"

She looked at him like he had two heads. "Because Denny's my friend. I won't stand by and watch someone hurt him. It's not right. There are too many bystanders in this world, Jake. I won't be one of them."

Jake's eyes bored into hers. "You're not going to let this go, are you?"

She released the safety. "Nope."

He studied her for another beat, a look of admiration mingled with something else settling over his features. "Fine. But you're not going alone. We're in this together."

Nikki nodded, sensing that he was referring to more than what they were about to do. And that wasn't good. Not at all—because she liked the idea of *more* with Jake.

6

Damon Rossi floored his Mercedes AMG G63, a cocktail of rage and raw horror rushing through his veins. He'd flown out of Undefeated when his emergency notification app reported a fire at one of the shops near Vintage Motors—the same shop Nikki was working at tonight. And as soon as he heard it, he knew she was in danger. He knew the feeling intimately. The girl attracted trouble like light drew moths.

Like father, like daughter.

Terror seized him at the memory of Nikki's father—a man he'd known and admired his entire life—and the horrible, blood-soaked night that set off a chain of events leading him to where he was today: fighting to protect the one person he loved more than anything in this world from the danger she couldn't see.

Damon gripped the steering wheel with white knuckles. *She's all right. She's all right,* he chanted to himself as he drove like a demon across town, cursing the distance between Dino's shop and his gym. Tonight couldn't have anything to do with what happened two years ago. It couldn't. He did everything in his power to make sure she was safe from *that* danger, and her memory—or lack thereof—did the rest.

He slammed on the brakes at a red light. The intersection was too busy to blow through, even at this hour.

Fuck.

His eyes darted around, looking for an opening so he could screw the light and cut across. Where the hell were all these people coming from? It was after 11:00 p.m., for Chrissake! He smacked the steering wheel.

74

Relax. She's fine. Beating the shit out of the Benz won't help, he told himself.

He shook his head, praying that was the case. If she wasn't—his teeth ground together—God help anyone responsible.

Damon saw the flashing red and blue lights before he turned the corner of Restoration Road, the cul-de-sac where Dino's shop resided, and where Nikki was, according to the tracker app on his phone. Whatever went down there tonight had to be bad if the cops *actually* showed. They usually fucked off this area, surrendering it to the gangs and crime families who did business in and around Wood Glenn.

Dumping the Benz on the corner, Damon leaped out of the SUV and sprinted down the street, straight into the melee of police, fire officials, and EMTs.

"*Nikki! Nikki Elliot!*" he shouted over the din.

When there was no response, he grabbed the first person to cross his path. "I'm looking for Nikki Elliot. Have you seen her?" he demanded of the startled EMT.

"Who, sir?" the young woman asked, her skin paling.

Damon released the EMT with a deep breath, grasping for patience. "Nikki. Elliot. Blond hair, beautiful. About this tall." He held a hand up to his shoulder. Nikki was tiny, coming in at only 5'4"—the perfect height for a stainless-steel jockey, and for him at one time.

The woman's eyes lit up with recognition. "Oh, yes. She's over there with her boyfriend, giving her statement to the deputies on scene." She pointed to the heart of the chaos, but Damon couldn't see her.

"Thanks." Damon darted into the crowd, a single word replaying in his head: *boyfriend.* What the hell? Nikki didn't have a boyfriend.

He let that thought go for the moment, calling out to her as he tried to push past the mob gathered there. "Nikki! Nikki, where are you?"

"Damon?" she called from within the throng. "I'm over here!"

Her voice was a beacon. As soon as he heard it, he knew exactly where to go. But it didn't loosen the tightness in his chest. It wasn't until he swept her into his arms and held her that he could breathe again.

"Thank God." He sighed, pressing her to him.

Nikki's small but strong arms came around him. "Hey, it's okay," she said soothingly. "I'm fine."

He stepped back, holding on to her at arm's length so he could see for himself. She smirked up at him with a look of annoyance and begrudging, brotherly love that he'd become accustomed to over the years.

"See?" She dropped her hands to her hips in a familiar move.

He removed one hand but kept the other firmly planted on her shoulder. She would see it as a friendly, if not controlling gesture; for him, it was a way to reassure himself that she was alive and well.

"I see that. *Now.* What the fuck happened? I got a fire alert about Denny's place. And I knew...*knew* you were in trouble," he said, his eyes darting over to Denny's shop and back.

Nikki rolled her eyes. "I wasn't in trouble, and there was no fire—well, not a big one, anyway. Jake and I got in there and stopped the guys before they were able to get too far. They started a small fire in the office, but Jake took care of it."

"*Jake?* Who the hell is he? And why the fuck were you running into a building blind like that?" he snarled, seething at the idea that she'd been in trouble and that someone—someone that *wasn't* him—had stepped in to help her.

"That would be me." A guy around Damon's age and size with some serious ink along his forearms appeared next to Nikki. *Right* next to her—like if he was any closer, they could be conjoined.

Damon glared at the stranger, detesting him on sight.

He slid his gaze back to Nikki, jerking his head in the direction of the tool. "Who's the Sam Crow throwback?"

"Damon!" she shrieked, while Sam Crow flashed him a *what the fuck* look. "Don't be an ass. This is Jake Masercotti. He works for Sean, and he's working for me now, so play nice."

"Whatever. Are you done here?" he asked, ignoring Jake. What kind of name was that anyway? It belonged to guys in westerns or Brat Pack movies, not the Italian kid standing next to Nikki. Was this the assclown the EMT mistook for her boyfriend?

The idea made his stomach burn.

Nikki narrowed her eyes. "Yes. I was getting ready to head home."

"Good. Give me the keys. I'm driving," he ordered, extending his hand.

"Damon, I'm good. I can drive myself home. Besides, you don't want to leave your Benz on the street here at night. It's not safe."

His Benz would be safe out there. All the players in the area knew Damon and what car he drove. They knew not to mess with anything that belonged to him, including Nikki and anyone associated with Vintage Motors and the Tiger's Den.

"It'll be fine. Give me the keys." When she glared at him in return, he leaned in close. "Bella, I... Please, let me drive you home."

Nikki's expression softened when she saw what Damon hadn't said: that he didn't *want* to drive her home—he *needed* to do it. "Okay." She turned to her new employee. "I'll see you at Sean's in the morning."

"Sure. Good night," he said, looking at her in a way that made Damon's teeth grind before turning to him. "Drive safe, man."

"Always do when she's on board," Damon replied, flashing a predatory smile as he pulled Nikki close and steered her away.

On the way over to Nikki's Ferrari, they passed two patrol cars, one of which held the suspects. Damon slowed as they walked by, peering into the back seat of the cruiser. His heart stopped when he caught sight of the tattoos along their bare arms. Even in the darkened police car, he recognized them. These weren't ordinary street thugs. They were Irish mob.

Fucking hell.

She was just like her father: always unwittingly putting herself in the wrong place at the wrong time and with the wrong people—all out of a deep sense of loyalty and friendship. Damon loved and hated those qualities—qualities he feared would eventually, like with her father, get her killed. It was nearly the case two years ago, and now...now it looked like she'd added a new enemy to the list. A list she had no idea existed and one he'd make sure she never discovered. He'd learned, the hard way, that ignorance wasn't only blissful—it could save your life. And he would do anything to save hers: *la bella ragazza del suo cuore*—the beautiful girl of his heart.

7

The roar of Jake's Harley echoed through the hills, mingling with the exotic thrum of the midnight-blue Ferrari in front of him. Nikki Elliot's midnight-blue Ferrari, to be exact.

Nikki Elliot: his angel.

He still couldn't believe he'd found her, even though they'd spent hours together the night before—hours that flew by like seconds where she tangled him further in a web he'd been caught in since he'd first laid eyes on her. The easy way she laughed at his Sean stories, the thoughtful, introspective way she looked at his photographs and inquired about his hopes and dreams, and the way she jumped into unknown danger to save a friend all floored him.

Last night felt like a dream—like someone else's reality. But it wasn't. It was *his* reality. Good fortune had smiled upon him for the first time in over twelve years. But why? He didn't deserve any rewards.

Jake's eyes drifted to the lush wooded area concealing multimillion-dollar homes then returned to the Ferrari in front of him, an idea taking root. The *why* didn't matter. He had a job to do: help his angel until she made it into professional racing. It would be his way of repaying her for saving him that desolate day at Our Lady of Faith. And once she was on her way, he would also move on—hopefully stronger than when he came to her, so he could be there for Dario like an older brother should be and not the piss-poor example he'd been.

It all seemed simple enough and more than fair for a guy like him.

But Jake should have known that it wouldn't be that simple. Nothing ever was.

～

A few minutes later, Jake followed Nikki into a semicircular driveway leading to an older farmhouse surrounded by untouched woods. The property wasn't as grand as the others that dotted the area. Not by half. Even so, as his eyes drifted over the expanse, he couldn't help but feel as if he'd been dropped into one of the Renoir landscapes his mother loved, with the dark greenery of the trees juxtaposed with the vivid cerulean sky and riot of wildflowers. Maybe that was why he felt a sense of calm drape itself across his shoulders as he dismounted his bike. The scene reminded him of his mother, a woman who'd been passionate about art and a talented painter in her own right with works he felt could rival the masters.

After placing his helmet in the saddlebag, Jake watched as Nikki came around to the back of the Ferrari and stopped, her gaze locked on the road and the dark Mercedes that rolled by. Her intense stare trailed after the car until it slipped from sight, her body rigid when she finally turned and approached the house.

"Everything okay?" he asked.

She looked up at him, her hypnotic sea-green eyes troubled even as she told him everything was fine.

"You sure? You looked a little creeped out by the Mercedes. Do you know them or something?"

Nikki headed up the stairs that led to a massive wraparound porch. "Not personally, but I know who they *belong to*, and they shouldn't be here."

Okay...

"What does that mean?" he asked, not liking the sound of it, as he followed her into the house.

"It's nothing. Nothing a chat with Damon won't solve, anyway," she grumbled.

Jake didn't respond to the comment. It looked like Damon was having her followed. It didn't surprise him. He'd pegged the guy as a controlling bastard last night.

God, the arrogance of that prick.

How could Damon believe he could control someone like *her*? It would be like trying to catch lightning in a bottle: destructive. And why would anyone ever want to control or, even worse, *tame* her fierceness? The boldness, the bravery she demonstrated last night when she went busting into

79

Denny's shop was the most incredible, selfless thing he'd ever seen. How could anyone ever want to snuff that out?

After he shrugged off his motorcycle jacket and hung it on the coatrack, they made their way through the house and its attached garage, headed for the workshop. Passing through the house, Jake noted that while it wasn't as modern or well appointed as his new place, he liked this home more. This house, with its worn carpets, dated furniture, and fading paint, welcomed its guests. And he could tell from the myriad of family pictures hung on the walls and scattered across tables and shelves that it was a house filled with love.

Jake had lived in a house like that once, in another life—one filled with hope, possibility, and most of all, love.

"Here it is," Nikki said, flipping on the lights of the workshop, yanking Jake from useless memories that would only serve to cause him pain and guilt.

His eyes surveyed the organized, well-equipped space, complete with a lift, a mechanic's pit, and every tool known to auto repair. The Tiger's body, nothing more than a British-racing-green shell, sat off to the right of the workshop on the lift, while an engine stand was positioned dead center holding a bare engine block.

Jake let out a low whistle.

"I know." Nikki sighed, leaning against a massive tool chest. "It's a ton of work."

"Yeah, it is." He moved into the shop and over to the engine block and ran his hands along the cast-iron heart as he eyed the parts, all laid out, waiting for assembly. "But it's nothing we can't handle," he added, thinking he could tackle almost anything with her by his side.

Nikki walked over to him, her eyes locked onto his in a way that made his heart gallop in his chest. "You're right," she said, pulling her long honey-blond locks into a messy bun. "Let's get started."

They worked for the next few hours, moving through the engine assembly like a well-tuned production line. Jake hadn't worked this closely with a mechanic since his days at Formula Motors, and in the two years he spent there, he'd never worked this smoothly with anyone right out of the gate. It typically took months to build the level of synchronicity he and Nikki now shared, working hip to hip, communicating silently as they anticipated each other's needs. If they kept this up, they'd get the car assembled in no time.

They were installing the heads and lifters when a car pulled up, followed by a voice that grated on Jake's nerves like blades on a chalkboard.

"*Bella?* Where are you? I need to talk to you. Now!"

Oh goody. Damon's here.

Seconds later, Damon's frame filled the doorway of the workshop, blotting out the rosy glow of the sunset drifting in from the yard. Jake looked up in time to see Damon's stony face soften when his eyes landed on Nikki's bowed head, an expression that vanished the moment he caught sight of Jake.

"What the hell is the prospect doing here?" he demanded, striding into the shop like he owned the place.

Prospect? Jesus. What's with the Sons of Anarchy *bullshit?*

Nikki's wrench stilled as her head popped up. "God, Damon. Have a little respect for my friends, will you?" she said, glaring daggers at him.

Jake couldn't help the way his chest expanded at her *friend* reference or the way she dressed Damon down...for *him*.

"*Friend?*" Damon sneered, continuing on like Jake wasn't in the room. "I thought he was an employee."

"You know, you're a real piece of work sometimes." She set her torque wrench down and stepped between Damon and the engine block. "He happens to be both. So, what's up? What's *so* important that you have to interrupt us? We're working on a deadline here."

"Then it's true? You're restoring *that* car?" Damon jabbed a finger in the Tiger's direction.

"Yes."

"Why? You're not planning on racing it, are you?"

"I am. Not that it's any of your business." Nikki folded her small but noticeably cut arms across her chest. "Suspension Masters wants it in the VAM series next season."

An explosion of F-bombs erupted from Damon, drawing Jake's full attention. He didn't like Damon's tone. But it didn't faze Nikki. She didn't even flinch when he continued to rant and rave, waving his hands like an old-school Italian on a tear. She stood strong, feet braced apart, arms crossed, glaring at him with the ferocity Jake admired.

"Are you out of your fucking mind?!" Damon roared.

Jake rolled his eyes. Why was she dating this tool?

"That's enough!" After a tense beat, she flicked a glance back at Jake and gave him an apologetic look. He smiled and went back to the lifters he'd been installing as Nikki dragged Damon to the door. This time when she spoke, she did so in Italian, with Captain Douche responding in kind.

Interesting. She didn't strike him as Italian—not with her California-girl looks and last name. And he didn't think Damon had the patience to learn a second language, much less the intelligence.

"*Yes, I'm racing the Le Mans car next year. It's what I do, remember?*" she hissed, her accent and inflection spot-on.

"But this car? You almost died in it the last time you—"

Jake's head snapped up. *Almost died?*

Sean didn't mention anything about her wrecking the Le Mans car *or* almost dying in it. He gripped the edge of the engine block. The idea of Nikki being in a wreck, let alone almost dying, rocked him to his core.

"That doesn't change anything," Nikki cut in. *"If my sponsor says I'm racing it, then I'm racing it. I don't have a choice if I want their funding. Besides, funding aside, you know I wouldn't let an accident—no matter how serious—stop me from racing. This is my life, remember?"*

"Damn it, bella, why do you insist on putting yourself in harm's way every chance you get?"

"Oh, for fuck's sake, will you quit it with that crap? I've had it with the paranoia! I told you, I'm not risking my life. I'm living it, Damon. Why can't you get that through your thick skull?"

"Because you keep throwing yourself into the line of fire with this." He jerked his head in the direction of the Tiger. *"The racing, Denny's place last night! I swear, keeping you safe is a full-time fucking job!"*

Nikki threw her hands in the air. *"God, you're thick! Keeping me safe is not your job. It's mine. So stop worrying, and STOP having me followed."*

Damon reared back. *"What? I'm not having you followed. I told you I'd call off the tail, and I did."*

"Well, your guys didn't get the message. They've been with me since Colorado."

"They have?" Damon dragged a hand through his hair, looking confused.

It was then that Jake noticed the bandages across his knuckles.

"Yes, they're still—" Nikki stopped short, spotting the bandages too. She grabbed his hand. "What happened?" she demanded, slipping back into English.

Jake suppressed a snarl as he watched Damon's hand close over hers— a reaction he had no right to have but one he couldn't control nonetheless.

"It's nothing." Damon shrugged.

"Uh-uh. Try again."

Damon's jaw tensed. *"Fine.* Dino and I had a disagreement about how he should treat you. He thought he could treat you like shit, and I didn't."

Nikki yanked her hand free and stepped back. "You *hit* him? How could you? That's only going to make things worse."

"How could I? How could I *not?* The son of a bitch broke your heart! Nobody treats you like that!" he roared, taking a step toward her.

Nikki put up a hand and took another step back, forgetting the pallet of parts behind her, and stumbled over the oil pan.

In a lightning-quick movement, Jake slid behind her and caught her before she fell onto the intake manifold.

Damon, who moved equally fast, got there at the same time. "Keep your hands off her, prospect," he warned, grabbing her and pulling her away.

"Damon, stop it! You're acting like an ass," she hissed, wrenching her arm loose.

The arrogant piece of shit didn't listen. He reached for her again. Without a second thought, Jake smacked his hand away, itching to do a lot more. This guy needed a hands-on lesson in respect.

"I believe she told you to stop," Jake replied, his voice deadly calm despite the fever building in his veins.

"What the fuck?" Damon snarled, coming at him.

Nikki jumped in front of Jake and pushed him back, shielding him from Damon. For some guys, like her asshole boyfriend, the move would have been degrading. But Jake didn't see it that way—not even close. The fact that she was willing to defend him was an honor, not an insult. Not to mention a total turn-on.

"*Enough of this!*" she shouted, slapping a hand to Damon's chest and pushing him back. "You need to leave before you say or do something we'll *both* regret."

Damon started to argue, but Nikki held up a palm, silencing him. He stared down at her, unspoken words passing between them, until he stormed out, throwing Jake a threatening sneer as he went.

Nikki huffed out a breath and turned to Jake. "I'm sorry about all of that. Damon is…"

A dickhead. An asshole. A complete douche…

"Intense?" he supplied, not wanting to insult her boyfriend—even if he was all those things and more.

"Yeah." She snorted. "That's one way to put it—a very nice way considering how he treated you. Again, I'm so sorry. I don't know what comes over him sometimes." She reached over and grabbed her discarded torque wrench.

Jake shrugged, watching as she returned to the heads she'd been installing before they were interrupted. "Don't worry about it. I'm sure a lot of boyfriends would react that way if another guy stepped in like I did."

"*Boyfriend?*" Her head snapped up, wrench stilling. "Damon and I aren't together."

"You're not?"

"No," she replied, returning to the heads.

Okay…

"Does he know that?" he asked.

Nikki laughed, a light sound that filled the workshop, brightening her already beautiful face. "Yes, he knows—has since the day we broke up."

Ah. That explained it. Damon, *the ex,* saw him as competition. He wasn't, obviously, but someone like Captain Douche wouldn't see Jake any other way.

"Was your breakup recent?" Jake asked, grabbing a lifter, and returning to his side of the block, where the heads were already installed.

She shook her head. "It was five years ago."

Five years? Damn. And he was still hung up on her?

Wouldn't you be? whispered that nagging little voice in the back of Jake's mind.

It had a point. If he were in Damon's shoes, he'd pine for Nikki too. It would be impossible not to.

"That's a long time to be hung up on someone. Not that I blame him."

Jake wanted to punch himself in the nuts the moment the words left his mouth. He shouldn't—correction: *couldn't*—say things like that to her for a crapload of reasons.

Nikki's hand stilled again, her eyes darting to his. At this rate, the heads would never get finished. "Damon's not hung up on me. He couldn't be. He didn't want me when he had me—a fact he made crystal clear when I caught him sleeping with another girl."

The lifter he held slipped from his hand. "Shit!" He swooped down and grabbed it before it struck the concrete floor. Rising, he gaped at Nikki. "He cheated...on *you?*"

She nodded, returning to the heads.

Jake shook his head. Damon had this woman—this talented, strong, beautiful woman, and he *threw her away?* Controlling wasn't the guy's only problem. He was a fucking idiot on top of it.

"And you're *friends* with him?" he asked, unable to hide his disgust as the idea hit him.

"I know it sounds weird, but when you've been through everything I have in the last four and a half years, you come to realize that anger and grudges are useless. Toxic. Life is too short to waste time on them."

Understanding dawned on him. "He stood by you when your parents died," Jake observed, even more in awe of her strength. What he wouldn't give to be able to let his anger go like that.

"Yes, *and* when I wrecked the Le Mans Tiger. The accident left me with spinal injuries, a serious concussion, amnesia, and a long, grueling recovery my brothers and Sean were not equipped to handle. I needed twenty-four-hour care for several weeks, physical therapy for months, and endless doctor appointments. Damon stepped in and helped me through it all—covering the costs of the medical care that my insurance didn't cover, remodeling the master bathroom so it was accessible for someone in a wheelchair, and making sure I had the best specialists in the area caring for me. I needed someone to help me with all the things we take for granted every day: going to the bathroom, dressing, even eating at one point. He was there through it all."

Jake studied her, vacillating between wanting to break Damon's face and getting down on his knees to thank him. Hearing this, he understood Damon's reaction to Nikki's restoring and racing the Tiger. But unlike Damon, Jake saw that racing was important to her, and he would never get in the way of something like that.

"I guess he's a good guy...underneath it all," Jake admitted.

Nikki laughed. "He is...though that doesn't excuse the douchebaggery he's often capable of, or his obsessive need to control everything, including me. I've told him to knock it off, or he's going to need a new place to call home, but he hasn't gotten the message, obviously."

"He still lives here?" Jake asked, trying not to sound disappointed. He might be grateful to Damon for helping Nikki, but that didn't mean he wanted to see him on the regular.

"He does. It drives Hilda—she's my best friend—nuts. She's hated him since we split up, regardless of how much he's helped me."

Jake liked the sound of this friend.

"But," Nikki went on, "it's time for him to move out. He's crossing too many lines. It's just...I don't have the heart to tell him...not after everything."

"I can see how that would be awkward," he said.

"Until then, I hope it's not going to be a problem having him pop in and out. I'll encourage him to leave us alone, but I can't guarantee anything."

He waved off her concern. "It's not a problem."

It was totally a problem. But Jake would never admit that to her. If Damon, douchebaggery and all, was part of her life, then Jake wouldn't say anything. He respected her too much.

They returned to the engine block and finished up the heads and lifters and got the pushrods in before calling it quits. Nikki insisted he stay for dinner since he'd done the same for her the night before and reheated homemade baked ziti for the two of them. It was the best home-cooked Italian meal he could remember in years. Her friend Hilda joined them midway through dinner and entertained Jake with embarrassing stories about Damon.

He liked her instantly.

Afterward, he helped Nikki with the dishes—a simple act that felt far more intimate and natural than he could have imagined. He'd never experienced anything like that with a woman before... But then, he'd never been friends with a woman, either. And that was what they were: friends. She'd said it earlier in the shop to Damon, but now Jake actually *felt* it. It was foreign territory for him, but he liked it...a little too much. He could feel a spark of something more than friendship kindling, and that couldn't happen. Not with her. Not with anyone.

~

NIKKI LEANED AGAINST THE PORCH RAILING, WAVING AT JAKE AS HE FIRED UP his Harley and took off down the driveway. Watching him drive off, she felt a twinge of something—sadness, longing, maybe? It didn't matter. She shouldn't feel anything watching him leave. Jake was her lead mechanic. Period.

She shook her head. Who was she kidding? He was more than that. He was her friend—had been since he followed her into Denny's and helped stop those thugs from robbing him and destroying the place. Jake hadn't wanted to go in; he wanted to wait for help to come, but he went in anyway—for her. Only a friend would stand by you like that.

*Still...*she shouldn't feel like this as he drove away, even as her friend. This was how you felt when you wanted someone as *more* than that, and she couldn't go there.

She ran her hands over her face, yawning deeply.

"Rough day?" Hilda asked, coming out to the porch.

"Not really. Just tired. I didn't sleep well last night, and I've been running around like crazy trying to get everything done."

"What kept you up? Is it work?"

"No. I had some crazy dreams."

"You mean you had your nightmare again," Hilda corrected.

Nikki turned, dragging her eyes from the point where Jake's bike had disappeared around the bend. "If you want to call it that, then yes. *My nightmare* woke me up in the middle of the night, and I couldn't get back to sleep."

The images Nikki recalled the day she came home from Colorado had been haunting her dreams ever since, and last night the new images joined the party. But unlike during the flashbacks, the emotions she felt in the images during her dreams were amplified tenfold. And when she woke, her brain raced over what it all meant, making sleep impossible.

"Is there anything new? Have you remembered anything else?" Hilda pressed. She was the only person Nikki told about the memories. She didn't tell Damon because she knew he'd freak out, as would Sean, and her brothers were clearly a no-go. Hilda, on the other hand, was her rock. She could tell her anything. Nothing shook her best friend.

"I wish, but no. It's just the same thing over and over again," Nikki said, her stomach twisting at the hint of worry she saw in Hilda's eyes. "What?"

Hilda shook her head, the worry vanishing. "Nothing. I wish you were sleeping better." She flashed Nikki a smile that didn't reach her eyes and swiftly changed the subject. "Did Jake leave already?"

Nikki studied her lifelong friend. "Yeah, he left a few minutes ago. It's late. He has to be at work by seven."

"Ugh. I don't know how you mechanics do it—getting up at zero dark shitty and schlepping off to work like that every single day."

"You get used to it." Nikki shrugged, hoping that she'd adjust to her even earlier schedule; it was a grinder. She had to wake up at 4:00 a.m. to get in her morning run and be out of the house by 5:00 for her workout with Tsai and then be at work by 7:15 so she could put in a full eight hours on her clients' cars before leaving to work on the Tiger.

"I couldn't. I need my full ten hours of sleep, or I'm a complete bitch," Hilda said.

Nikki snorted. "I won't argue with that."

"Anyway." Hilda rolled her eyes. "Tell me about this Jake person you've hired. He seems like a nice guy. Not to mention hot—like panty-incinerating *hot*."

A sharp sting of jealousy shot through Nikki—a feeling she had no right to when it came to Jake. "He's attractive, yes. But there really isn't much to tell. We only met yesterday."

Hilda studied Nikki for a long minute. "Right, but after the looks I saw you *both* shooting each other in the kitchen, I'd say there's a whole lot to tell."

Nikki arched a brow. "*Looks?* What are you talking about?"

"I'm talking about how neither of you could take your eyes off each other. You guys were like magnets the way you were drawn to each other."

"We were not." *Were they?*

"Yes, you totally were, and it's okay. The guy is sex-on-legs, and he seems sweet. It would be insane if you weren't drawn to him. And he to you, for that matter."

Nikki shook her head. "You're wrong. We aren't *drawn* to each other, and even if we were, it wouldn't matter. I can't get involved with him or anyone else."

"Why not?" Hilda demanded, folding her arms across her chest.

She suppressed an eye-roll. She'd been over this with her so many times, but her best friend refused to give up. "Because relationships take time, which I don't have with my schedule—a schedule my track record with men proves is a surefire way to *sabotage* dating of any kind."

Damon wasn't Nikki's only relationship. She'd dated in Europe and in the US since her recovery, but nothing serious ever came of it. Men always let her down. They either hated her crazy schedule or couldn't handle the risks associated with racing. As far as she could tell, relationships were out while she competed, and that was fine. Nikki was young; she had time. Maybe after her career waned—if it ever got off the ground again, that was —she would find someone.

"Okay. Don't have a relationship. Just use him to pop that cherry of yours and find out how great *non*-self-induced orgasms can be. They'd do a world of good for the stress you're under with your crazy-ass schedule and these flashbacks you've been having." Hilda grinned, nudging her with her shoulder. "Come on. Every girl needs a boy toy. Make Jake yours."

"You know that's not me. There has to be an emotional connection before I can sleep with someone. Besides, the self-induced orgasms do the job."

It was an old argument. Hilda was forever trying to do two things: get Nikki to date as many men as possible and lose her virginity. But Nikki couldn't do it. She couldn't separate the pleasures of sex—at least as she imagined them to be—from emotion.

"Okay," her friend conceded. "Then Jake is perfect. He'll be right by your side for the next three months. You can build a connection with him and *then* have great sex. Seems like a no-brainer, especially when I can see that you're into him, whether you'll admit it or not."

Nikki's brows shot up. "There is nothing to *admit*, Hil. I'm not *into him*!"

She wasn't. She just…admired his looks and kind heart. That was all. She definitely wasn't *into* Jake. No way.

"Besides," she continued, working herself up into a rant, "what happens when I go away next year? Do you really think he'll stick around? Because I don't. Why should he when no one else has? Why build something with him when he'll break my heart like the others before?"

Hilda leaned in close. "I know you've been burned by guys and that's made you gun-shy when it comes to dating. I get it. But you need more than work in your life, Nik. You're hyper focused on it, and that's not healthy. It's putting your life out of balance. And not all men are cheating bastards like Damon and Marco."

She cocked her head to the side. "I know that's how you see it, Hil."

"But…" Hilda arched a brow.

Nikki shrugged. "*But* sex, relationships—will to have to wait. That's all there is to it."

"Wait? For what? Someone like *Mystery Man* to come along? Maybe Mystery Man himself?"

She reared back. "What? No. Don't be ridiculous. I'm not *waiting* for him. I don't even know who he is."

"I'm not being ridiculous. I know you, Nikki. I know you've read his journal at least a hundred times since you found it, and that you wish he were in your life. But he's not, and he never will be. He's a ghost—a ghost you need to let go of so you can open yourself up to someone else—someone who's here, like Jake."

Nikki puffed out a breath. She hated to admit it, but Hilda was right—to a degree. She was drawn to the man in the journal—or *Mystery Man*, as Hilda had named him. Who wouldn't be? Not only had he helped pull her from the depths of grief so deep she thought she'd drown in it, he saw her *exactly* how she wanted others to see her: as someone strong and capable. She'd fought her entire life for people, especially in racing, to see her that way. With *Mystery Man*, she didn't have to fight. He saw it without effort, and he respected and admired it. But that didn't mean she wasn't going after Jake, or anyone else, because she was holding out for him.

Did it?

She worried her bottom lip, remembering the desperation with which she'd looked for clues to his identity after she read the journal the first time, and the despair she'd felt when she realized she'd never find him with no name and no idea what he looked like outside of his dark hair and that he wore motorcycle boots.

Nikki shook her head. This was stupid. She might have been sad about not finding *Mystery Man*, but her issues with dating had nothing to do with him. Nikki held on to the journal and took it with her when she traveled because his words gave her strength when she felt weak. The only reason she avoided dating was because it didn't work for her right now, which she explained to Hilda *again*.

Hilda jumped down from the railing. "Fine. If you insist on waiting—for whatever reason—that's up to you. But I wouldn't wait too long. Not with someone like Jake around. I have a good feeling about him in my gut, and you know my gut is *never* wrong. Someone will snatch him up sooner or later, Nik, and it might as well be you."

"I'm sure someone will, but it *won't* be me," she insisted, hating the way her stomach dropped at the thought of Jake with someone else.

∼

DAMON FLICKED OPEN THE SLATS OF THE PLANTATION SHUTTERS COVERING HIS window, glaring. From his vantage point, he had a clear view of the front of the house. And he didn't like what he saw.

That Jake character was standing at the foot of the stairs, staring up at Nikki with a look that made his blood pressure spike. Damon knew that look…knew it well because he'd looked at her the same way countless times—like she was the center of his world.

He slammed the slats closed and stormed away from the windows, snatching his cell off the bed. He knew nothing about this *Jake* guy, and that needed to change. He was going to be sticking around for a while, and based on what Damon witnessed, he wanted to be more than Nikki's mechanic or *friend*, as she called him.

Friend. Ugh.

Damon punched in the pass code and made a call to Nino—the assclown who'd screwed up his instructions to drop the tail from Nikki—hearing Jake's Harley pull away.

Good. Go back to your trailer park and stay there, Sam Crow.

He paced in front of the massive king sleigh bed that dominated his bedroom, surprised by Nino's mistake. He didn't make mistakes like this. Though in all fairness, things had been hectic since their boss cut a deal with the Venezuelan cartel, expanding the smuggling side of the business to South America. The deal secured the family a lot of money, but Damon didn't like it.

The cartels were dangerous. They acted without honor or respect for anything, even their own flesh and blood. In his experience, they wouldn't hesitate to kill off their own children if it meant getting ahead in the war for control over the gun and drug trades. They were such a stark contrast to the family he worked for that it surprised him when their boss okayed the deal.

People could say what they wanted about the Mafia, but at least they took care of their own—for the most part, anyway. A few families were as ruthless as the cartels, but most acted like his: holding those loyal to them and their families in high regard, defending and protecting them to the end.

After what felt like an eternity, Nino answered the phone. "What's good, boss?"

"Finally. What took you so long?" Damon snapped.

"Sorry. I was in the shower. What's up?"

"Did you or did you not stop the tail on Nikki like I asked?"

"Of course I did. I called the boys off right after you told me. They haven't been on her since she got back from Colorado," Nino explained.

Damon gripped the phone tighter. "Are you sure about that? She says she's got a tail," he said, praying that Nino had actually fucked up. If he hadn't, then someone else was following Nikki, and that could only mean one thing: the shit that went down in Europe wasn't over.

"Yeah, I'm sure," Nino began. "Vito and Gianni—the guys I put on it—have been up in Reno the last couple of weeks, handling that shipment of guns for Carlo, remember? You sent them."

He pinched the bridge of his nose. "Are you sure it was only Vito and Gianni you had tailing her? You didn't call Mark or Anthony for it also?"

There was a pause. "Shit. I did, now that you mention it...and I may have overlooked telling them to back off. Organizing the latest shipment to Caracas hasn't been easy, and you know the boss—he likes things done right. No mistakes. I'm sorry, Damon. Really. I'll call them now and make sure they know."

"Do it. I don't want a tail on her. I've got her cell tracked; that should be enough," he said, hoping that was true. "There's more..."

"Yeah, boss?"

"I want you to dig up information on Jake Masercotti. I want to know everything about him, from who the fucker is to what he eats for breakfast in the morning, and I want it yesterday. And keep an ear out for the Irish too. I want to know the minute they decide to make a move against anyone," he barked.

"You got it!" Nino chirped.

"Good."

Damon scowled as he strolled back over to the window and yanked open the slats to scan the road.

Nikki's tail was more than likely Mark and Anthony acting on orders from Nino. It had to be. Nothing from Europe had surfaced since the accident. Why would it start now? Nikki didn't remember anything from that time, and as long as it stayed that way, she was safe.

Damon's stomach churned.

Unless...

What if her memories *were* back? What if she remembered something and told someone? He shook his head, tossing aside that idea. If she remembered anything, she'd tell him first. Wouldn't she?

He leaned against the window casing and watched as she talked with Hilda, remembering her earlier words about his *paranoia* and how frustrated she had been with him recently.

Fuck.

She might not tell him if she thought he'd lose it and go He-Man on her, which he would. But she would tell Hilda. She was Nikki's best friend in every sense. If the memories were coming back, that was who she would go to over him.

He focused his stare on Hilda. She was trustworthy; she'd proven that time and again. But she had a tendency to run her mouth. What if she mentioned it, even casually, to one of her boy toys in the city? If she did, and one of them said something to someone—

Damon shook his head. *Christ.* Maybe Nikki was right when she called him paranoid.

Even so...it might be worth it to have Hilda followed and her boy toys investigated to be on the safe side. If Nikki's memories were returning and the wrong person found out, she was in trouble...

Big, bloody trouble, just like her father.

8

Wearing his black-and-white Lethal Racing team shirt and hat, Jake strode out of the RV he and Nikki shared, making his way across the paddock and over to pit lane. He wanted to run a diagnostic on the engine and check the rear wing before Nikki went out today. She mentioned that the car felt like it needed a little more down force after the practice races yesterday, and Jake wanted to make sure the adjustments had been made so things ran smoothly for her.

It was early still, just after 6:30 a.m., when he rounded the corner and stepped onto pit lane—the central nervous system of the track—already buzzing with energy as crewmembers, media personnel, and drivers milled about. A slight breeze raised goose bumps along his arms as he reached Lethal Racing's pit stall, but he didn't mind. The steel-varnished skies would soon give way to the infamous blistering temps of the Salinas Valley, making them all long for the damp, cool air of the morning.

"Morning, Jake," Nick Alan, crew chief for the team, greeted him. He was studying the data monitors hanging on the left wall. As crew chief, Nick had his hands in every aspect of the team, including the racing data those monitors displayed. After analyzing it, he'd go over it with Will Jennings—chief engineer and owner of the team—and Nikki as a part of their strategy planning for the race.

"Morning," Jake returned, making a beeline for the black-and-white open-wheeled car sitting in the center of the stall.

Unlike the other teams in the series, Lethal Racing was on the small side, with only one car and driver to its name. The other teams were much larger, with two cars running in this series and more in the series below it.

"You're here early. The other mechanics won't be here for another half hour. What's up?" Nick asked, coming over to where Jake inspected the rear wing.

"I wanted to make sure we got this adjusted per Nikki's specs," Jake explained.

Nick patted him on the shoulder. "Excellent. You're a conscientious mechanic, and you listen to Nikki. I like that. It's a refreshing change from that miserable prick of a brother of hers."

Jake looked up from the rear of the car. "Really? Her own brother didn't care if the car ran right and was set up to her specs?"

"Hell no," Nick growled. "He wanted to make sure she was safe, sure, but he couldn't have cared less about how she *performed*. If anything, he wanted Nikki to lose so she'd quit. He hated her career. If you ask me, he was jealous of her success."

Damn.

Jake thought Dino was a hard ass after he heard about him firing her, but *this*? This put him in asshole territory.

"Wow," Jake breathed. "I can't imagine having a brother like that."

"You got siblings?"

He nodded. "A younger brother. I don't see him as often as I'd like, but we're close." Well, at least they had been. Dario continued to hide whatever was causing him stress and getting him beaten up. It drove Jake mad. He wanted to know what was wrong and take care of it.

Nick gave Jake a rough pat on the shoulder. "You're a good man, Jake. Family means something to you. I like that about you too. You're a strong addition to the team, especially for our girl. She needs good, supportive people around her—keeps her grounded and able to concentrate on what counts out here: winning. I'm afraid she doesn't have nearly enough of them."

"What do you mean? The team seems solid and behind her one hundred percent."

"Oh, *we* are. Nikki's the best thing that's happened to Lethal. Without her, Lethal Racing would have closed up last year. We're a family—there's nothing we wouldn't do for her. But it's not enough. She needs someone in her corner on the business end of things too," Nick said.

Jake arched a brow. "She does have someone: her manager, Jack. She raves about him."

"Yeah, she's got him, all right," Nick grumbled.

"You don't sound too happy about it. Did he do something wrong?" he asked, folding his arms across his chest.

Nick ran a hand over his military-grade haircut, his expression wary. "Forget it, son. I shouldn't have said anything. It's nothing."

Bull. Shit.

"Yeah, I don't buy it. Not with that look on your face and the tone of your voice," Jake said. "If someone is hurting Nikki's career, I want to know about it, and I want to help stop it. She's a good person. She doesn't deserve to have someone working against her."

Nick didn't respond right away. He stood there, studying Jake with assessing eyes. Eventually he said, "You care about her, don't you, son?"

Jake blinked. "Um, yeah, sure. I mean, we're friends, if that's what you're getting at."

"*Friends.*" Nick chuckled, flashing Jake a knowing smile. "All right. Then as her *friend*, you've got to swear you won't repeat what I'm going to share with you, especially to Nikki."

Jake didn't like the sound of that or the idea of hiding something from her.

"Why? Why not be straight with her? She has a right to know if someone's hurting her chances."

Nick shook his head. "I agree, but I can't say anything until I have proof. She won't believe me without it because it concerns Jack. She's too close to him. He's an old friend of her father's and is like an uncle to her. She'd see this as some sort of affront and quit the team before the season is up and she has a ride," he explained.

Jake ran a hand along his jaw. He didn't like the idea of keeping something like this from Nikki, but Nick had a point—a good one. "Fine. I won't say anything until *we* have proof," he replied.

"All right." He pulled Jake off to the side of the pit stall. "I've heard from reliable sources that Nikki *has* had sponsorship offers. Several of them, but Jack's turned them away."

"What? Are you sure?"

Nikki worked herself to death to keep things going for her and the team because she didn't have enough sponsorship dollars—all when she didn't have to?

"I know. It shocked me too. And I didn't want to believe it, but I've heard this from several people. And it makes sense. Think about it: How many sponsors does Nikki have versus *other* teams—teams with less-experienced drivers, let's say?"

Jake looked down at his team shirt, where there were three sponsors advertised. He looked up and out the bay door at other crews milling about, noting that their shirts were covered with sponsors—some up to ten. And Nick was right about the other drivers: they weren't half as good as Nikki.

He turned back to Nick. "I see your point. But are you sure it's Jack's fault? Nikki said she might not be getting sponsorship offers because of the wreck at Le Mans."

Nick shook his head. "I know that's what she's afraid of, and honestly, I worried about it in the beginning too. Le Mans was a bad wreck—almost tragic—and with officials unable to completely rule out driver error, it could have worked as a mark against her. But her performance over the last year and a half has proven to the racing community that she's a top-notch driver and that the wreck had nothing to do with her abilities. She's just letting her insecurities get in the way, thinking like that."

What Nick said made sense. Nikki was at the top of the pack in Pro Mazda—a place she wouldn't be in if she weren't highly skilled. "All right. Let's say Jack is doing this. Why don't these sponsors approach Nikki or Will on their own, instead?"

A shadow fell over Nick's face. "They're afraid. According to one source, Jack threatened them if they did. And he's got the unsavory connections to back up those threats."

Jake gaped at Nick. Why would Jack want to hurt Nikki's career? If for nothing else, he benefitted financially when she garnered sponsors.

"I don't get it. Why would Jack want to sabotage her *and* himself in the process?"

Nick shook his head. "I don't know, son. All I know is something fishy is going on with that guy, and I don't like it. Nikki's a good girl and a damn fine driver—the best I've seen in a long time. She doesn't deserve what's happening to her."

"Agreed," Jake said, working to suppress the rage he could feel building in his veins. "So what now? What can I do?"

"Keep this between us, for one. Will knows, but the rest of the team doesn't." He placed a hand on Jake's shoulder and leaned in close. "And look out for anything suspicious. I want to see our girl get her ticket this year and get back to the pros where she belongs. She was born for that. Nothing less will do."

Jake nodded sharply. "Done."

"Good man." Nick smiled. "Now, make sure that car's ready for today. I want us to break a record this weekend."

Jake smiled and got back to work on his inspection, pushing all thoughts of what Nick confided to him away for the time being. Later, when he wasn't absorbed in the work of racing, he'd think more about it and what he could do to help Nikki.

~

AT 9:00 A.M. SHARP, NIKKI STRODE INTO THE PIT STALL, WEARING HER BLACK-and-white racing suit pulled down off her shoulders and tied at the waist, revealing her fire resistant Nomex undershirt, and the brightest smile Jake had ever seen.

"Are we ready to roll, guys?" She beamed.

Jake's heart stumbled in his chest. She'd never looked more beautiful, more radiant, than she did in that moment. The confidence, strength, and fierceness she always carried exuded from her like sunrays. And it hit him like a bolt of lightning in the chest: Nikki was born for this, just like Nick said. Jake hadn't seen it until this moment.

If only he had his Nikon...

He'd love to get a shot of her like that—to capture the pure elation on her face and in her eyes as she stood there with her shoulders back and chin held high. The only thing he had on him was his cell phone, a piss-poor camera in comparison, but...well, it was something.

Jake pulled his cell from his pocket and started taking shots of Nikki and the team.

"Hey there, sweetheart!" Will Jennings smiled, pulling Nikki into a hug. Nick was right about the team too. They were a family, one that he was now a part of.

His chest tightened as he continued to snap photos of them from different angles.

Jake hadn't been part of a family, outside of Dario, since his mother's death. And though he knew he shouldn't, he liked the feeling of being a part of one again.

Nikki returned Will's hug, and the two of them went over to the monitors with Nick, where they examined race data and talked strategy for the upcoming competition. Jake stood at the edge of the pit stall with his phone, watching as they huddled over the computer and a wrinkled track map Nikki produced from her pocket. A sense of pride came over him as he recalled the fragile girl from the cemetery who'd gone there damaged by tragedy and loss. And here she was now, no longer a broken girl but a strong, vital, driven woman going after her dream with everything she had, despite the odds stacked against her.

Jake's conversation with Nick rolled through his mind. Nikki had no idea how bad those odds really were—that someone she trusted was working against her, trying to crush her dreams. But Jake wouldn't let it happen. He would do everything in his power to make sure she made it. He wouldn't fail her like he did Dario or his mother. This time he would succeed.

$\sim$

.

Nikki nodded as she walked out to the grid, her crew chief at her side, giving her last-minute strategy points. She smiled to herself as Nick rolled off reminders one after the other. They weren't necessary. She'd raced at WeatherTech Raceway many times before, but she didn't stop Nick. He knew she had this, but it made him feel better to remind her all the same, especially now, when her chances of getting onto a professional team hinged on her taking first place in the Pro Mazda series.

As of now, Nikki held second place in the series, coming in right behind Nigel Ingleside. Nigel took first in race number one on Saturday, but his fastest lap time—the fastest in the entire series—was only milliseconds ahead of hers. If she could shave off those milliseconds and take first today, she'd knock him out of the top spot and gain a significant lead in the points standing. If she held that lead for the remainder of the season, she stood a good chance of winning the championship and a guaranteed spot on an Indy Lights team next season, putting her career back on track.

"Now, remember what we talked about earlier. There's a massive brake zone right before you hit turn two. Once you're out, get right back on power and don't forget to use all the curbing—apex and exit—in turn three," he reminded her as they reached the car.

Nikki turned, smiling. "Got it, chief."

Nick was a good man and an excellent crew chief. She couldn't ask for better and considered herself blessed to have him in her corner. Skill was only half of what you needed to succeed in racing. You also needed a team that supported you on and off the track. Nikki had both. She had a manager who loved and cared for her and a team that did the same.

"Good. Now get out there and kick ass," Nick ordered.

"She will. She doesn't know any other way," Jake said, coming up behind her with her helmet and HANS device in hand.

She turned and grinned at Jake. His taking Dino's place as lead mechanic had been more of a blessing than she ever imagined. The team felt more cohesive with him there, more relaxed. She hadn't noticed until now how edgy Dino made everyone feel—not just her.

"You know it." She pulled on her balaclava then took the HANS device and helmet Jake offered. After slipping on her racing gloves, she stepped into the cockpit and lowered herself into the tub. Once her legs were wiggled into position, Jake leaned down and belted her in place. Normally, a driver's assistant would do this, but because they were a small team, the lead mechanic had been designated for the job. It worked for their team, as it gave them time to review any mechanical issues to monitor during the race.

Once Nikki was locked and loaded, Jake grabbed the umbrella from the ground next to the car and opened it up, shielding the two of them from the brutal California sun.

"Make sure you let Nick know if there are any issues with down force or if you want the front bar softened for the final races while you're out there today," he said, staring down at her, his team shirt hugging his athletic body in all the right places.

"You got it!" she yelled through the full-face helmet. "And thanks, Jake. You've done an amazing job already, with everything. Seriously."

She meant it. Jake wasn't only the perfect addition to their racing team. He was also the ideal mechanic for the Tiger restoration. In the two weeks they'd been working together, they'd completed and installed the drive-train, including a test run of the motor on a dyno to make sure everything was in tune, and they were now close to wrapping up the suspension. Barring any unforeseen delays, the Tiger would be ready a couple of weeks early.

Jake knelt down and placed a gentle hand on her shoulder. "No need to thank me. It's my pleasure, angel."

Her heart stumbled. *Angel?*

Only one person ever called her that... well, referred to her as *angel* anyway: Mystery Man. She blinked up at Jake. He was wearing that crooked smile of his, the one that brought out the dimple in his left cheek. She'd secretly grown to love that smile.

Staring up at him then, it struck her how alike he and the man in the journal were, and not just because they called her *angel*. There were other things: the way he admired her strength and conviction, the way he sketched on his breaks at the Den when he thought no one was looking, the grief he carried for his mother. She almost wondered—

Nikki shut that idea down before it could finish. It was ridiculous to think that they could be the same person.

God, she was an idiot.

The announcer called for the grid to be cleared. Jake snapped the umbrella shut and leaned down with that crooked smile still adorning his face. "Drive hard, Nikki. And keep it out of the wall—for me."

She nodded as she flipped her visor shut and shoved away the warmth that crept into her cheeks at the tenderness in his plea. It was time to get her head in the racing game and out of the one where she feared she was falling for Jake.

9

Nikki set her shoulders and locked her arms for absolute control over the wheel as she powered up the massive incline, headed for the corkscrew: the most infamous part of the course at WeatherTech Raceway. If things were going to get hairy, it would happen there.

She wound the car through the corkscrew, flicking from one left-hand corner to the next, keeping things light as she came over the crest and down into the ninety-five-foot drop leading to turn nine. Adrenaline rushed through her veins like nitrous oxide as she sailed through corners nine and ten, setting up for turn eleven—the final corner of the course.

A quick glance in the mirror told her Nigel Ingleside was hot on her tail in the Denali car, looking for the first opportunity to pass. She wouldn't give him the chance.

Nikki mashed the brake pedal into the final turn and made the sharp left-hander without a hitch then flattened the accelerator as soon as she exited the apex.

Nailed it!

Grinning, she raced for the finish line, hearing Ingleside's tires screaming behind her as he spun out. Turn eleven was rough. The near ninety-degree angle forced drivers into almost a dead stop to get through it. Take it too fast, and you'd lose it as Ingleside did; take it too slow, and you'd lose too much time.

The high-pitched whine of the rotary engine flooded the cockpit as she soared down the straightaway, her sights locked on the checkered flag waving as she flew across the finish line. Cheers from Nick and the crew burst through the radio connecting her to pit lane.

"Amazing run, sweetheart! Not only did you take first, but it looks like you broke the track record for fastest lap!" Nick said.

"What? Are you serious?" Nikki choked out, slowing down enough to see fans cheering as she took her victory lap.

"I wouldn't joke about that. You did it! You're in the points lead again —this time by a wide margin. Way to go!"

She squealed, pumping her fist into the air, overcome with a mixture of joy, relief, and hope. Breaking a track record could get the attention of major sponsors and lead to offers even greater than Indy Lights, putting her that much closer to Formula 1.

Nikki pulled the car onto pit lane and stopped in front of the podium next to the second- and third-place drivers. The Lethal team swarmed her immediately, and once she was free from the harness, she popped up out of the tub, high-fived her crew, and waved to the ecstatic crowd surrounding them. Nick slapped the team hat on her head as soon as her helmet was off.

"Nice driving, hot-shoe," he said, pulling her into a hug.

Her throat tightened with emotion. She wouldn't be there without any of them.

The rest of the crew swarmed her and patted her on the back, offering more high-fives and a warm hug from Will Jennings. As Will released her, Nikki turned and was swept into the air by a pair of strong arms she'd know anywhere.

"I knew you'd win! You were amazing, angel. I'm so proud of you," Jake's voice rumbled in her ear as he hugged her.

Hearing him call her *angel* made her heart sigh, but the words he whispered at the end brought a new wave of emotion, stealing her voice and flooding her eyes with tears.

I'm so proud of you.

Only her father said things like that to her after a race. Sure, her teams were elated when she won, but no one outside of her dad ever expressed *pride* in what she did or who she was.

Until today.

Jake Masercotti, a man who'd only known her for a mere two weeks, not only believed in her but was also *proud* of her. Just like her father had been. How could that be? How could he care enough to be proud?

Overcome, she pressed her face to the crook of his neck and squeezed him tightly, saying with her arms what she couldn't with words. He returned her embrace, his arms locking around her.

After a minute, he loosened his hold, setting her down. With one hand on her hip, he cupped her face with the other, lifting it to his. When their eyes met, she gasped softly at the riot of emotion on his face, mirroring the tempest swirling inside her.

The moment stretched out between them. The din of celebration and victory faded into the background, leaving only her and Jake. In that quiet moment, Nikki felt something pass between them. Something deeper than she'd ever felt for anyone—scaring and thrilling her all at once.

The announcer's voice broke through the haze, calling all winners to the podium. With what felt like great reluctance, Jake released her and stepped back, clearing the way.

Swiping at her eyes, Nikki turned and headed for the podium and joined the other drivers: Javier Santos from Mexico and Alan Grist from Canada.

Sounds of the cheering crowd and announcers whirled around her as she stood there with her compatriots, trophies held high. While she relished the rush of victory, moments like this saddened her whenever she looked into the crowd and didn't see her dad. He always stood front and center, cheering the loudest, his face shining with pride. It might have embarrassed some kids, but not Nikki. She soaked up his happiness like a sponge, carrying it with her wherever she went.

But today was different. This time when she looked out into the crowd, her eyes instinctively drifted to the left side of the stage. There Jake stood, tall and true, his cheers and whistles carrying over the others, the pride he felt shining from him like the sun. And for the first time in five years, Nikki stood on the podium, gripping her trophy, with only joy in her heart.

~

THE LATE-SUMMER AIR WAS WARM AND LADEN WITH THE SCENTS OF THE approaching fall as she and Jake rounded the corner, headed for Jasper's Roadhouse—a local hot spot for drivers after a race. Mazda Series teams always gathered there for a celebratory dinner and drinks—heavier on the drinks than the dinner for many of those in attendance—at the close of a race weekend.

Nikki kept the conversation light, talking about the next steps in the Le Mans Tiger restoration on the easy, mile-long walk to the roadhouse. She didn't want to get into anything serious and risk bringing up what happened at the track.

Because something had definitely happened.

She could feel something new growing between her and Jake—something more than friendship—and she didn't know how she felt about it.

Part of her was excited and curious: what it was, what it meant, what it could become. But another part, a stronger one, was scared to death. What if something *did* develop between them—something deeper, more intense than friendship? What would happen when a pro team signed her? She'd be gone even more often between that schedule and her commitment to race in the VAM series next year, and this time Jake wouldn't be there with her. Could he have a relationship with her if she was gone two-thirds of the year? No one else she'd dated, seriously or otherwise, had so far. What if Jake ended up being like all the others and broke her heart?

Nikki suppressed a shudder. She didn't think she could survive a heartbreak like that—and it would be a major one if she opened her heart to Jake and he turned around and broke it. He drew her to him in ways she'd never experienced before, and that made allowing *anything* to come of it dangerous.

Jake moved ahead when they reached Jasper's and grabbed the door for her. A thunderous mix of whistles and cheers greeted them as soon as they stepped inside.

"Jesus." Nikki gulped, clutching her chest. She hadn't been expecting *that* warm of a welcome.

"There she is, folks!" Nigel Ingleside called from the bar where he stood. "The fastest woman at WeatherTech Raceway: Nikki Elliot! Get over here, girl, and have a drink to celebrate your amazing race today!"

The crowd erupted into chaos.

A scalding flush swept Nikki's cheeks. She didn't know what to say. She still couldn't believe she'd broken the record. Nikki knew her final lap had been a hot one, but she had no idea it was *that* good.

"Don't just stand there. Go celebrate. You earned it, hot-shoe," Jake whispered in her ear.

She glanced up at him and smiled. "Thanks, Jake." She turned and let the crowd draw her to the bar, where shots of tequila were lined up, waiting.

"I'm not drinking all of these on my own. You've gotta help me, Nigel," Nikki shouted over the noise.

Nigel smiled broadly. "Absolutely. It's an honor to drink with the woman who beat me fair and square this weekend and shattered records on top of that," he said, handing her a glass and grabbing one for himself.

Nikki took the shot, the crowd cheering again, and reached for another. She glanced out across the roadhouse as she lifted the glass to her lips and felt her stomach drop when her eyes landed on Jake. Mandy Geoffrey, one of the Teller Tire girls, had him cornered. Teller Tires sponsored the series and always hired models to walk the event, advertising their products and to pose with winning drivers. The Teller girls didn't usually come to the roadhouse, but Mandy could always be found where drivers and crewmembers mingled.

Jealousy took root in Nikki's gut and spread like a weed as she watched Jake and Mandy laughing and talking. Like all the Teller models, Mandy was stunning, from her long, ultra-shiny locks to her perfect skin and statuesque legs. And standing next to Jake, she looked even more perfect—perfect in a way that Nikki never could. Not that she thought she was ugly or anything. She knew she was attractive, pretty, even, but she wasn't *model pretty* like Mandy. With their dark hair and stunning faces, Jake and Mandy made the picture-perfect couple.

Mandy laughed again at something Jake said, resting her hand on his forearm. Another spike of jealousy surged, but Nikki squelched it. *This is a good thing,* she told herself. She needed to see this—to see Jake with someone else—as a reminder that anything between them other than business and friendship was off limits.

"Are you going to drink that or hold it all night?" Nigel laughed, bumping her shoulder.

Nikki gave herself an internal shake and turned to Nigel. "Drink it," she answered then threw the shot back like a pro.

"Atta girl!" He chuckled then shot his and handed her another.

Forcing herself not to look in Jake and Mandy's direction, Nikki took the shot glass and smiled, fully prepared to have fun—and to drink as much tequila as needed to make sure that happened.

10

The soles of Nikki's sandals slapped the ground, the sound echoing through the dark alley as she ran. She had to get out of there and find somewhere safe to hide. He couldn't find her. If he did—

Images of blood-soaked walls and dismembered bodies rushed through her mind—a gruesome reminder of what would happen if he found her.

Nikki reached the end of the alleyway, her feet losing traction when she rounded the corner. Slipping, she skidded to a halt behind a pair of dumpsters and crouched down low, keeping out of sight. Her heart pounded in her chest, slamming against the cell phone wedged in her bra. She pressed a hand to the spot where the phone sat beneath her sundress, taking several deep breaths in an effort to slow her heart and calm her nerves. Thank God she still had her phone. She'd need it to stay alive.

The sound of heavy boots striking the cobblestone pavement followed by a man's voice firing off directives stilled the air in her lungs.

Damn it.

He was here, and he brought his twisted puppets.

She pulled herself into a tight ball, praying they passed her hiding spot without a second glance. Moments later, two men went charging by, followed by a third a moment after that. Nikki stayed there, crouching in the shadow of the dumpsters until their footsteps faded into the distance. When she thought it was safe, she crept out from behind the dumpster, turned and let out a bloodcurdling scream.

❧

NIKKI JERKED UP IN BED, GASPING FOR AIR. FOR A SPLIT SECOND, SHE WAS STILL in the dream. Then her eyes adjusted, and she realized she was in the bedroom of her Lethal Racing RV, safe.

She ran a shaky hand through her hair, the acid in her stomach roiling. It was just a bad dream—something that normally wouldn't frighten her except that this dream came on the cusp of her *other* dream, the one that replayed the images from her flashbacks.

Nikki shook her head. She shouldn't let this get to her. It was a coincidence that she had a nightmare right after the flashbacks. A nightmare more than likely brought on by the fifth of tequila she'd downed with Nigel at the roadhouse and not her memories. Booze—especially tequila—often gave her acid-trip-like dreams.

A chill swept over her, sending a shudder down her spine. Fear took root in her gut. Coincidental, alcohol-induced dream and all, it still frightened her in a way she couldn't shake…like it was all connected somehow.

Puffing out a breath, she looked down at her sweat-soaked nightshirt and decided she needed a shower. Maybe the water would clear her mind and relax her.

She slipped into the bathroom, where she rinsed off then changed into a fresh tank top and sleep shorts. Knowing sleep would be impossible now, she tiptoed into the heart of the dark, silent RV, headed for the refrigerator to grab a glass of milk. The acid in her stomach continued to churn, and since she didn't have any antacids in the RV, milk would have to suffice.

She was reaching for the fridge when a deep male voice sounded behind her. "It's late. You okay?"

Nikki spun around, letting out an ear-piercing scream as she jumped back, nearly crashing into the table. She didn't hit it, though. Jake got there first, grabbing her before she did.

"Whoa there, angel! It's me," Jake chuckled, pulling her to him.

She slumped against his chest, the air sawing in and out of her lungs. "Holy shit." She panted. "I think I had a heart attack."

"Me too," he breathed. "You scared the crap out of me with that scream. You've got one hell of a set of lungs."

"That'll teach you to sneak up on me, won't it?" She chuckled, straightening and backing out of his arms.

"I guess so. Are you always that easy to scare?" he asked, flipping on the kitchen light.

"Only when—" she started to say but stopped when her eyes landed on him.

He wore nothing but a pair of black sleep pants and that sexy crooked grin of his.

Sweet Jesus...

Standing there, Jake was every girl's panty-incinerating fantasy brought to life.

She gave herself an internal shake, stopping the thoughts swirling through her head before her own panties combusted. "Only when it's completely dark and some guy pops up out of the shadows," she finished as a blinding pain struck her behind the eyes, followed by images from the nightmare flashing through her mind.

"Oh God," she hissed, stumbling toward the table once more.

Jake swore and caught her before she gave herself another concussion. He swept her into his arms as if she weighed nothing, carried her to the overstuffed sofa, and sat her down. "Nikki?" His hands cupped her face. "Nikki, can you hear me? What's wrong? What hurts?"

Eyes closed, she pressed a hand to her forehead and took a deep breath, feeling the pain and images recede. "It's my head," she began. "I felt this sharp, sudden pain, but it's getting better."

"Are you sure? You look pretty pale."

Nikki nodded, opening her eyes. She blinked a few times, and Jake's striking face came into view, etched with worry. "I'm sure. It's almost gone now."

He leaned back, his eyes roving her face with careful precision. "Do you get headaches like this often?"

"No, not really. Not since—"

Not since the flashbacks started.

"Not since when?" he pressed when she remained silent.

Part of her wanted to tell him, more to ease her worried mind than anything else, about the flashbacks. But her other half told her to keep this between her and Hilda until all the pieces were in place. What if she told Jake and he slipped and said something to Sean? If that happened, it would get back to Damon, and she *didn't* want that. He was paranoid enough these days.

"Not since..." She scrambled for a reasonable explanation. "I was recovering from the concussion after Le Mans. I used to get serious headaches, some that would last for days on end." It wasn't a complete lie. She *did* suffer from massive headaches during her recovery—a common side effect of concussions.

His brows drew together. "Okay... Do you need to take something? Is that why you're up at..." He glanced over at the clock on the microwave. "One thirty?"

She nodded. "I woke up with a headache and couldn't go back to sleep. I tried a shower, but that didn't help, so I came out for some milk," she said, impressed at how easily the lies rolled off her tongue.

"I'm sorry to hear that. I hate it when I have trouble sleeping," he said.

"Is that why you're up? I didn't wake you, did I?" she asked, feeling guilty.

Jake shook his head. "No. I was up. Couldn't sleep." He shrugged. "It happens a lot."

"Why?"

His eyes fell to his lap. "I don't know...I guess I have a lot on my mind."

Nikki studied him in the silence that followed, wondering what troubled him to the point of sleeplessness. She didn't push it, though. It didn't look like he wanted to talk about it, and it was none of her business.

"Well, I guess I'll get the milk I came out here for." She moved to stand.

Jake placed a hand on her thigh. A simple gesture but one she felt in every part of her body. "Why don't I get it? You still look pale." He gave her leg a gentle squeeze and stood. "I'll heat it up and put some honey in it. My mom used to do that for me when I woke up in the middle of the night. The honey settles your stomach, and the milk should help you relax enough to get to sleep."

"Um, sure. Thanks," Nikki said then watched as he went to work on the milk-and-honey cocktail, studying the tattoos scattered across his chest and back.

He had a pair of hands gripping a rosary encircled by script between his shoulder blades, some sort of script along his left side, and a lily above his heart. Whoever did them and the ones along his arms was a true artist. And she couldn't help wondering what they meant—what they represented. The tattoos were too beautifully done, too carefully selected to be meaningless. She would know. Her own tattoos along her back, shoulder, hip, and side had been carefully selected for a purpose other than simply marking her body.

"You're awfully quiet over here," he said, coming over and handing her a mug.

"Thanks." She took the mug and sipped the warm mixture. *Yum.* "I was admiring your tattoos. They're beautiful. Who did them?"

Jake sat down on the couch and pulled up a leg, facing her. "Thanks. A friend inked them, but they're my designs."

"Wow. You've got some *serious* talent, Masercotti," she said over the rim of her mug, her eyes falling to the script that wrapped around his left side, and the drool-worthy eight-pack next to it. "Do you mind if I ask what the script says?"

Jake shook his head and leaned over, revealing its entirety. "It's from Corinthians: *Love is patient, love is kind... It always protects, always trusts, always hopes, always perseveres. Love never fails.*"

"It's beautiful. I've always loved that scripture."

"So did my mother," he said, sitting back. "She believed in the power of love—that it could overcome anything."

"Do you believe that too?" Nikki asked, her voice barely above a whisper. The raw emotion on his face and in his voice almost brought her to tears.

His brows fell into a deep frown. "I'd like to, but in my experience, there are some things in life I don't think *anything* can overcome, even love."

The pain and bitterness she heard in his voice struck her heart like a well-aimed arrow. She'd felt pain and bitterness like that herself and knew how powerful they could be...how long they could plague you if you didn't work through them. She'd seen the aftereffects of that in herself and in the pages of the journal she'd found. Mystery Man had also experienced loss—loss that had swamped him with grief and guilt until he'd almost lost all hope.

It hit her again: how much Jake reminded her of the man from the journal. They obviously weren't the same person. The initials on the journal were different from Jake's; she'd checked. Even so...she couldn't help but think of the man behind the pencil and paper when Jake was around. At times, they were like twin souls.

Jake broke the silence between them, pulling Nikki from her sentimental thoughts. "I see you've got some ink of your own," he said, his voice rough.

She took another sip. "I got them a few years ago. I didn't design them." She flashed him a crooked smile. "I don't have your talent. But the person I went to does. He listened to why I wanted the tattoos and came up with the designs." Leaning forward, she pulled the strap of her tank top to the side, revealing one of the tattoos.

Jake leaned in close and examined the delicate forget-me-not etched into her skin. "*La vita e una benedizone,*" he said in perfect Italian. "Life is a blessing." He lifted his piercing gaze to hers. "Why that saying?"

She blinked. "You speak Italian?"

"*Colpevole.*" He gave her a sheepish grin.

"Wow," she drawled, impressed. She didn't know anyone outside of her family who spoke Italian. "Wait." She gasped, realizing something potentially mortifying. "That means you've understood everything Damon's said when he's come into the shop for the last couple of weeks."

"*Mi dispiace.*" He nodded.

Her cheeks flushed scarlet. *Oh God...*

She was beyond mortified. Damon had said some choice things about

Jake, whom she'd defended vehemently. *Too* vehemently, according to Damon, who accused her of having a crush on him.

He cleared his throat. "I...uh...I guess I should have said something sooner." He grinned, trying to look contrite and failing.

She scowled at him. "You totally should have." When he continued to grin at her, she softened. "When did you learn Italian?"

"I grew up speaking it. I was born in Palermo and lived there until I was nine," he explained.

"Really? That's where my father was from," she said, smiling broadly.

"You're Sicilian? With the name *Elliott*, that sunlit hair, and those pretty, aquamarine eyes? No way."

"Half," she corrected, her tummy coiling tight at the compliments. "My mom was Italian, from Varese, near the Swiss border. We're pretty sure she had some Swiss in her background somewhere. I get my Cali looks from her side. As for the name, Elliott isn't my legal name; it's Eleuteri. My father was a Formula 1 driver back in the late '80s. He suggested I change my last name for racing so his fame wouldn't taint the way the racing community treated me," Nikki explained.

"Hold up," Jake said, his eyes bright. "Is your father Aldobrandino Eleuteri?"

She smiled. "Yes. Why? Do you follow racing?"

Jake shook his head. "No, not until I met you. But Dario does. He's a huge fan of open-wheel racing, Formula 1 especially. He's read up on all the famous drivers from back in the day. I think he's even got a poster of your dad. He tends to idolize the Italian-slash-Sicilian drivers more than others."

"That's awesome. He must be envious of you, then—getting to attend all of these races, even if they're semi-pro."

"Are you kidding? The kid's so jealous he's practically green. It's all he can talk about when we go out," he said, smiling proudly, as he always did when he mentioned his younger brother. Nikki could see they were close. She envied them. She and her brothers had been close at one time, too, and she missed the unique camaraderie that only siblings shared.

"When did you lose your accent? My parents never lost theirs," she said, shifting the conversation away from any more talk of siblings. Thinking about her brothers made her feel like bursting into tears or hitting something.

"In high school. I guess it faded after years of only speaking English."

"Too bad. Italian accents are hot." She cringed as soon as the words left her mouth. Why did she say that?

Jake laughed. "Then I guess I'd better get mine back."

Nikki blinked. *Did he mean that?* She gave herself an internal smack.

No. It was harmless flirting. And even if he did mean it, it didn't matter. It wouldn't go anywhere.

"So," he said, breaking the awkward silence. "Why *that* flower and *that* phrase?" He pointed to the tattoo.

The swift change in subject relaxed her, as did his thoughtful expression—one she noticed he typically wore when she spoke, like she had his full, undivided attention.

"To remember exactly *that*," she answered, keeping her response cryptic.

She didn't want to get into the *whole* story behind the tattoos: that they covered scars left from gunshot wounds she sustained the night her parents died. She put the tattoos over them as a symbol of her survival and to remember the sacrifices her parents made to ensure she lived that night.

"Do you have any more?" he asked, not pressing her further on the cryptic remark. She could tell by the look on his face he knew there was more to it and that tonight wasn't the night to go there.

"I have three more like this one—all with different sayings, though—and a vine of them on my back." She finished off her milk, still not feeling sleepy, and slumped back against the couch.

"Not sleepy yet?" he said, spookily responding to her thoughts.

"No. You?"

He shook his head. "Wanna stay up and talk about the craziest tattoos we've seen?"

Smiling, she said, "Sure."

They talked well into the night. At some point, Nikki drifted off, Jake's smooth baritone voice lulling her into a sleep in which she dreamt of him and the man from the journal as if they were one and the same.

THE SOUND OF AC/DC's "MONEY TALKS" ROUSED JAKE FROM THE DEEPEST sleep he could recall in years. He tried to ignore the song, but it persisted, replaying the chorus every few seconds. He let out a slow, lazy breath and decided to give it another ten seconds before he got up and beat the shit out of whatever was trying to drag him from this incredible bed. A warm, soft bed that smelled of star jasmine—a scent he'd known since childhood. His mother loved star jasmine; she had bushes of it all over their yard and in the flower boxes beneath the windows of her art studio.

Wait.

Jasmine? He didn't sleep in sheets that smelled like that. Jake peeled his eyes open, glanced around the room, and saw that he wasn't at home; he was in Nikki's RV, and he wasn't in a bed. He was on the couch in the living area.

How did he end up here?

He wracked his sleep-addled brain. Then, like the rising sun filtering in through the windows, it dawned on him: Warm milk. A discussion of tattoos. Waiting for her to fall into a deeper sleep...

Oh shit.

He didn't. He couldn't have.

Jake glanced down and froze when he spotted a crown of golden hair resting on his chest.

He did.

He fell asleep on the couch, and somehow, he and Nikki had ended up wrapped around one another like a pair of vines...or lovers. That was why this damn couch was so warm and soft and smelled of jasmine: it was *her.*

The previous night came back to him more clearly now: she'd fallen asleep on him while he told her the story of Frankie's first tattoo, and he decided to wait until she was in a deep sleep before he carried her back to her room so as not to wake her. He must have dropped off while waiting.

Damn it. He needed to get out of there before she woke up and things took an awkward, irreversible turn.

Jake started to remove the hand resting on the swell of her hip, but she stirred, her leg sliding farther between his, brushing up against—

White lightning zipped through his veins. He bit down on his lower lip, stifling a groan. If she wasn't careful, she'd wake up to a lot more than just *Jake.*

This was bad. Really bad. He shouldn't be lying here like this. With her. This kind of thing was off limits to him with Nikki. And yet something about it didn't feel wrong. It felt right, natural, even, to be lying there with her—like he was right where he should be, holding her as if she were his.

"Money Talks" started playing again.

It must be Nikki's phone, he thought. Who the hell called *this* early? He glanced over at the clock—it was after 9:00 a.m.

Oops. Not so early after all.

The phone went off again. Nikki stirred, mumbling something about two guys and a journal and them not being the same. Her hand drifted down his chest and across his stomach then latched on to his side.

Good Christ...

Warm breath danced across his skin as she exhaled, sending all the blood to his groin. It was the sweetest kind of torture.

When her leg moved upward again, pressing firmly against a *very* sensitive area, Jake couldn't stop the strangled groan that crept up his throat.

Nikki stilled. He froze. The goddamn phone went off again.

He cringed, bracing himself for the pissed-off hellcat he expected.

"What the...?" she said, lifting her head and turning to Jake.

Eyes the color of the Mediterranean stared at him in confusion. After a second, they cleared and widened, but she didn't move. The hellcat didn't emerge. Instead, she stayed there, pressed up against *every* inch of him, appearing as entranced with him as he was with her. As he stared at her and those hypnotic sea-glass eyes, with the sunlight haloing her golden head, she looked ethereal...like an angel. *His* angel...in his arms.

He swallowed around the dryness gathering in his throat, wanting more than anything in that moment to take her face in his hands and kiss those soft, full lips. Every part of him begged to taste her, to feel her tongue dance with his, to hold her as she melted into his arms, surrendering to his kiss, to him.

Without thinking, he reached up and tucked a strand of hair behind her ear. "Morning, angel," he said, his voice rough with sleep and something else he wasn't ready to admit.

Nikki blinked a few times, pushing herself up onto her forearms, still lying atop him. "How did I...? How did we...? Wait..." She shook her head. "Did you call me *angel*?" she asked, her voice taking on a husky quality he found incredibly sexy.

He cursed himself for saying it out loud. People didn't openly refer to their friends, let alone their bosses, as *angel*. He'd screwed up at the track with that once already, and he couldn't believe he did it *again*. Jake blamed the lust rushing through him. That was a surefire way to addle any man's brain. But he couldn't deny it. He'd look like a bigger ass if he did.

He nodded.

"Why?" she asked.

"Because you remind me of one," he said, internally kicking himself in the ass immediately afterward. What was he doing? He could have come up with something better, something less personal, less flirty for *Chrissake*!

"Oh," she said, her eyes falling to his lips. "That's sweet. You're always so sweet." She dragged her gaze back to his, chewing on her bottom lip.

Sweet? She thought *he* was sweet? How could that be? She should be slapping him for waking up with her like this and flirting with her on top of it. But she wasn't doing any of that. No. She was lying there with an expression that mirrored the thoughts and emotions rushing through him.

He let out a deep groan, his conscience warring not just with his libido but also another part of him, one that had been untouched for years: his heart.

His conscience told him he *needed* to gently remove her from his lap and put as much distance between them as physically possible—like a state or two—apologize, and be done with it, regardless of her reaction. But his heart and his libido didn't want that. Those traitorous bastards wanted to wrap themselves around her, kiss her senseless, and never let her go. And right now, that want overpowered his need like it never had before.

Ignoring all common sense, Jake leaned in, his eyes drifting from hers to those heart-shaped lips and back, ready to screw his conscience to the wall and take what he wanted, whether he deserved it or not.

But he never got the chance. The phone went off like a bomb, shattering the moment.

"My phone!" Nikki gasped, scrambled off Jake, and stumbled toward her bedroom.

Jake puffed out a heavy breath and slumped back against the couch, running a hand over his rushing heart. Jesus, that was close. *Too damn close.* He couldn't believe he almost kissed her! And that she almost let him.

His eyes drifted over to the bedroom, where he could hear her speaking animatedly.

A few minutes later, Nikki emerged, her hair pulled back in a ponytail. She dropped onto one of the barstools in front of the kitchen island where Jake stood, pounding a gallon of OJ in an effort to wash her out of his system.

"You okay?" he asked, tossing the empty jug into the trash and grabbing a bottle of electrolyte water.

She took the water. "Thanks." After taking a deep draft, she set the bottle down. "I'm fine. It was Jack calling to congratulate me."

The muscles along Jake's neck and back tensed at the mention of his name.

"Oh yeah? Did he say anything else?" he asked, keeping his tone light.

She shook her head, her eyes glued to the black granite counter. "Not really. Just that nothing's changed. No new offers of sponsorship or potential rides with a pro team."

Not liking the defeat he could hear in her voice, Jake leaned down to meet her eyes. "No new offers *yet.* You'll get them, Nikki. I'm sure of it. Don't lose hope."

She studied him for a long minute, during which Jake watched as the defeat cleared from her expression and determination took over.

"You're right. Thanks." She got up from the stool and headed toward the bedroom. "We'd better get dressed and packed. We need to get on the road soon." When she reached the door, she turned, frowning at the couch. "And...I'm sorry about falling asleep on you like that and...everything. I don't... know what came over me. I'm not usually like that...like at all."

Jake shoved aside the little stab of disappointment he felt at her embarrassment. Maybe he was wrong. Maybe she didn't want him to kiss her.

"No worries."

She smiled and headed into the bedroom to change, leaving Jake alone with a single thought running through his head: no matter how much he denied it or pushed it away, he wanted Nikki in a way he hadn't wanted anything in a very long time.

11

Sweat trickled down Jake's back as he stood atop the lookout at the turn-six workers' station. The late-September sun made him—and everyone else at Sonoma Raceway—its bitch as it cooked the track, the surrounding areas, and every living thing in sight.

He pulled off his Harley Davidson–issue baseball cap—a Christmas gift from Dario the previous year—and wiped his sweaty brow. He shouldn't complain. He could have been in their garage stall over in the paddock, where many of the other mechanics hung out during the races, or up in the press box above the main grandstands. Those locations offered shade and, in the case of the press box, blessed air conditioning. But he'd chosen to stand out there, in the seventh circle of hell, because it had the best vantage point to watch the race—Nikki specifically.

After spending the last five weeks traveling to different races and test sessions, Jake had fallen in love with watching her drive. He marveled at the way she took charge of the car, sweeping through turns, rocketing down straightaways, or navigating through tricky chicanes. It was an impressive thing to watch and a massive turn-on. Seeing her take total control over a machine with over four hundred horsepower roaring beneath its hood—and have the guts to push that machine to its outermost limits time and again—was as sexy as hell. And here, at the turn-six workers' station, Jake could watch Nikki do all of that across ninety percent of the track. For that privilege alone, he'd endure the blistering sun.

But he wasn't out there to enjoy the view today. He wanted to keep an eye on an additional driver in the circuit, Ron Dixon. Dixon made some veiled threats in the paddock that morning before the qualifying race that Jake didn't like. He managed to keep his cool when it happened...but barely. Nikki held her own against the thug, as she seemed to do in everything, but Jake still didn't like the idea of her driving against a loose cannon like this Dixon prick. Nikki might be a gifted driver, but even a gifted driver could only do so much when someone was gunning for them on the course.

Sean had warned Jake that the Vintage American Motorsport scene was different from the open-wheel circuit. He said that many of the guys in the VAM series treated Nikki poorly out of envy, mainly, but also out of old-fashioned sexism. But Jake didn't take the warning to heart. It was too hard to believe after experiencing the camaraderie and respect drivers and crewmembers in the Mazda Pro Series had for one another. But after Ron's performance earlier that day and the way the flagmen ignored Nikki's right to pass during qualifying, Jake saw that Sean's warnings were true.

Despite the skyrocketing temps, Jake stood out there, slathering on sunscreen and enjoying the sight of Nikki behind the wheel, all the while keeping an eye on the flagmen and Dixon, ready to make a call to the race officials if he saw *anything* that he didn't like. It wasn't much in the way of helping her, but it was all he could do.

Jake turned as the thunderous roar of a pair of cars made their way up the incline and into turn two. He watched as Dixon exited the apex in his '69 L88 Corvette and flattened his accelerator, trying to shake Nikki off his tail in the Shelby.

It didn't work.

Nikki rode the back end of Dixon's Corvette like a prizefighter out for a title, clearly ready and able to pass, but the flagman stationed between turns three and three-A ignored it. He continued to let Ron have his lead when the clear leader was *behind* him, chomping at the bit. Jake rolled off a string of F-bombs, forgetting the radio he wore connected him to Nikki. He wasn't accustomed to communicating with her during the race. In the Mazda Series, he could only listen through his headset as she and Will communicated. But here, it was different. He was the engineer, crew chief, and lead mechanic all in one since Suspension Masters, her sponsor in the VAM series, wouldn't provide her with a pit crew.

"What's up?" Nikki's voice crackled over the radio.

"Nothing," he replied, watching her get denied another pass as she and Dixon rocketed by the workers' station. "Just pissed that you aren't getting your passing flags. You should have dusted that asshat four turns ago in this lap alone."

Nikki chuckled. "Don't let it get to you. This stuff happens all the time. I'll get my turn eventually. In the meantime, relax. I've got this."

Jake smiled into his mic. "I know you do. Go get 'em, hot-shoe."

Nikki chased Dixon's Corvette for another seven laps before she got the OK to pass him coming out of turn eight-A. Jake heard the Shelby's high-powered 289 roar as she swung around the L88 and gunned the accelerator. Dixon looked like he was accepting defeat, but he changed his mind just as the Shelby's front end cleared his front fender. Jake's heart invaded his throat as he watched Dixon jerk his car to the left, forcing Nikki to hit the brakes and swerve to avoid a collision with him and veering off course. Angry, she slid behind him, weaving the Shelby from side to side in a *what the fuck* gesture.

A chorus of F-bombs exploded over the radio that would have burned the ears off a sailor. "I swear to all that is holy, I am going to kill that bastard!"

Jake released the breath he hadn't realized he'd been holding. "Not if I get to him first," he vowed, picturing himself dismembering Dixon's body in the paddock later.

"You won't. I'm too fast." She half chuckled, half snarled over the radio, her cooling temper calming his. "And don't worry. He won't try anything else like that today. He's got too much at stake."

"Okay, angel. Go get him," Jake said, hoping she was right as he radioed track officials to report Dixon.

She wasn't.

Nikki and Dixon played cat and mouse for another full lap before she got the next OK to pass just outside of the infamous Carousel, a decreasing radius turn that dumped out onto an incline. Jake heard the Shelby rev up as she gunned it to pass Dixon coming out of the Carousel. Then, just as before, Dixon swerved over, this time millimeters from clipping the rear quarter panel, forcing Nikki to swerve and hit the brakes to avoid a wreck.

"God damn that SOB!" Max Gunderson, the corner worker stationed at turn six, bit out. "Why does he pull this shit at every race? One of these days, he's going to kill them both."

Jake's head whipped around as he gripped the frayed edges of his temper. "You mean he's done this *before*?"

Max nodded. "He's got a hate-on for her like I've never seen. He's always trying to knock her off course. Can't stand it that she outdrives him."

He'd done this before?

An image of Nikki's Shelby veering off course and crashing flashed through his mind.

His temper boiled over.

Jake glared out across the track, vowing that this would *never* happen again. It couldn't. Dixon would be dead before the day's end.

~

JAKE STORMED INTO THE PADDOCK AFTER THE RACE, HIS FOCUS LOCKING ONTO Nikki, who was climbing out of the Shelby.

"Where the fuck is he?" Jake all but snarled as she pulled off her helmet.

"Who?" she asked, setting her helmet on the driver's seat and shutting the door.

"Dixon."

She turned, her eyes going wide when she saw the rage etched into his face. "I don't know, and I don't think you should go looking for him, either. It's not worth it, Jake."

"He could have seriously hurt you out there, or worse," he snapped, his chest tightening at the thought of how badly it could have gone. "Tell me *that's* not worth beating the shit out of him."

Nikki grabbed Jake's biceps and pulled him in so they were toe to toe. "You need to calm down," she said, her eyes boring into his. The feel of her hands on his bare skin sent a wave of calm through him, easing his temper some. "I know what he did was dangerous and all kinds of wrong," she continued, "but going after him will only cause more—"

"I didn't do anything but drive hard out there. You're the one who shouldn't have passed me, you uppity bitch," Dixon cut in, storming into the garage behind Nikki.

Nikki whipped around faster than Jake had ever seen her move, putting herself firmly between him and Ron. Jake tried to move around her, but when she turned and pleaded with her eyes to stand down, he did.

"Not now, Ron," she warned, moving out of the garage with Dixon in tow.

Dixon didn't listen. Instead, he swung at her, narrowly missing her right cheek when she slid left. Anticipating the move as if this were a familiar dance, he immediately swung at her with his other hand and connected with her chin, knocking her to the ground. She scrambled backward, but he followed even as the garage erupted into shouts for security and for Ron to stop.

Jake's vision went red.

Fuck standing down.

He grabbed Ron as he reached for Nikki, pitched him, and placed himself between them. Jake glanced back at her to make sure she was all right. Blood trickled from her mouth, and her chin was already a violent shade of purple.

He turned back to Ron. He was going to make this asshole bleed before he killed him.

Ron glared angry death at Jake. "You'll pay for that, you no-good thug. You and your little whore!"

"I don't think so, Ron," Jake replied, his voice deadly calm.

"Jake, don't!" Nikki pleaded, but he ignored her.

Tossing his hat to the ground, he dodged Ron's attempt at a sucker punch, then landed a jaw-cracking hit of his own. Dixon stumbled back, shaking his head to clear the stars Jake could imagine dancing before his eyes. The image of Dixon hitting Nikki flashed in his mind: the way she fell, the blood trickling from her mouth, the fear and shock on her face.

He didn't hesitate. He stepped in and struck Ron again, this time knocking him to the ground, where he followed, pounding his fists into him. He wasn't going to stop—not until this fucker wasn't breathing anymore.

Something pulled Jake up and off Ron before he could finish the job. He fought to free himself of the restraints wrapped around him, but they only grew tighter. "That's enough! The police have been notified. You're going to the county lockup for this."

Jake writhed against the security guard's hold.

"Jake, stop! It's over. He's down," Nikki's voice called through the red haze still coating his vision. Jake turned and saw her standing there, chin bruised, eyes wide with shock.

The haze cleared, and Jake stopped struggling.

Nikki looked at the man pinning his arms back. "The police are not arresting this man. He was trying to protect me from that piece of shit." She jabbed a finger in Dixon's direction. "After he attacked me."

"Is that true?" the security guard asked the gathering crowd.

After multiple people confirmed Nikki's story, the guard released Jake. He stumbled toward Nikki and pulled her into his arms, swamped with regret that she saw him lose it again. "I'm sorry. I shouldn't have done that. I was so angry at what he did on the track and then when he hit you I—"

Nikki cut in. "Shh. It's okay. Don't say anything else. I'll go give my statement to the race officials and the *real* cops." She threw a glare in the direction of the security guard. "You go clean up and cool down then come back and do the same. We'll talk later."

Jake pulled back, studying her. Her expression was no longer fearful. Instead, he saw something he never expected: understanding and sympathy.

He nodded. "Okay," he said, knowing it was the best thing to do. If he had to hear her recount what happened, he'd lose his shit all over again and get his ass arrested for sure—two things he didn't want her to see if he could help it.

~

AN HOUR LATER, JAKE WAS PERCHED IN THE GRANDSTANDS OVERLOOKING TURN two, his cell phone pressed to his ear. After he left Nikki to give her report, he went to their RV, showered, gave his report to the police, then decided to call Dario. He'd had to reschedule his visit this week because of the VAM race and a test session with Lethal. They would have two visits during their next scheduled week instead, but he still wanted to call and check in on him.

"So, how did she do today?" Dario asked, thrilled that Jake was working for *the* Nikki Elliot, as Dario called her. The kid knew everything about her career, shaming Jake for not knowing anything about it himself. Jake's only defense was that he hadn't had the extra time to read up on her. Without a computer, he would have to go to the library to do any research, which was closed by the time he got home during the week. Weekends were out because he was usually at a race, as was trying to research on his phone. He couldn't stand reading text or watching videos on such a small screen.

Jake took a beat before responding to keep the rage at what happened earlier tucked away. "She was amazing. It blows me away that someone so small is strong enough and brave enough to do this," he said.

"Nikki's a beast," Dario affirmed. "You should see the footage of her racing in the Dakar rally in 2015. She and her navigator dominated. It's on YouTube. I'll send you the link."

"Cool. I love to watch her drive," Jake replied.

"I bet you *love* to watch her do all kinds of things." Dario laughed.

"What is that supposed to mean?"

"Dude, seriously?"

"Yes, *seriously*. What the hell?"

Dario laughed again. "Uh, you're crazy about her, bro. That's *what*."

Jake's first instinct was to deny it, but he could never lie to Dario. "Is that obvious?" He cringed, hoping it wasn't.

"*Yeah*. I can hear it in your voice now, and I've seen how your face gets when you talk about her. Your eyes get all distant, and you get this stupid grin on your face. It's hilarious. You are *so* whipped, brother."

It was true. Like it or not, Jake was crazy about Nikki. He thought about her constantly, caught himself sketching her in the few moments of downtime he had each day, and even dreamed of her—wicked dreams that made waking up painful, literally and figuratively. He tried pushing her out of his head and heart, but it was impossible. She was there— embedded in him—and there she would remain. It was the worst kind of torture to want someone in every way possible, all the while knowing you couldn't have them.

This must be what it feels like to be a masochist.

"Fine. I'm crazy about her. Happy?" he grumbled.

"Yes and no," Dario began. "Am I happy that you finally found a girl? Hell yes. But I'm not happy that you refuse to do something about it."

"I *can't* do anything. She isn't meant for me. I don't deserve her."

"That's bullshit!" his little brother snapped. "You deserve her and anything else you want to go after."

Jake shook his head. Dario only said that because he didn't know everything about his older brother—about how much he'd messed up his life or about his biggest failure, his greatest sin. And he wouldn't. Jake wouldn't burden him or anyone else with *that* knowledge.

"Anyway," Jake drawled. "How are you? How's school? Home?" he asked, changing the subject to anything but what he did or did not deserve.

Dario wasn't having it. "I know what you're doing, dude. And you don't have to. I'm sixteen. I can handle anything you throw at me."

"That goes both ways," Jake replied, the irony of Dario's statement not lost on him. "I can handle whatever is going on with *you* too—if you'll let me."

There was a long pause, during which Jake hoped Dario would finally come clean about why he was always on edge and getting into fights. He'd had another black eye and split lip during their last visit.

"I know it does," he finally said. "But it's like I told you: I'm good. I can handle my own, bro. Speaking of which, I've gotta jet."

Jake swore silently. His kid brother sounded just like he did, and he hated that. He wanted so much more for him.

"All right, but remember, I'm here if you need me. All I want is for you to be happy and safe," he said, repeating the familiar refrain.

"I know. That's all I want for you too. You deserve it—as much as anyone—whether you believe it or not," Dario replied and ended the call.

Jake hit the end button, but instead of slipping the phone back into his pocket, he opened the photo app and started scrolling through the pictures he'd taken over the last few weeks, most of which were of Nikki. There were countless shots of her racing on the track, hunched over a track map, at Sean's, wrenching on an engine, reading from one of her books...and on and on.

His heart swelled painfully as he scanned through the images. He lied to Dario earlier. He wasn't crazy about Nikki. He was falling for her. Hard.

And there wasn't a damn thing he could do about it...no matter how much he tried.

～

It took an hour for Nikki to give her statement to the race officials and the police. In the end, she didn't press charges. Ron threatened to file charges against Jake if she did, so she dropped it. Jake didn't deserve to go to jail because of that prick. Ron left the race official's tent looking buoyant at getting away with yet another infraction at the track, and Nikki left appearing haggard and worn out. Dealing with Ron was exhausting business, but the fact that she hadn't slept well the night before made it worse. She snorted. That night wasn't her first sleepless night. She hadn't slept well for weeks. The nightmare and the other images from her flashbacks haunted her nightly, keeping her from the sleep she needed to keep performing at the top.

After she wrapped up the Ron situation, Nikki returned to the RV and found it empty. She decided to shower and take some pain reliever for her chin before tracking Jake down. She had a good idea of where he would be. He often went off by himself during downtime at the tracks to call Dario, take photographs, or just get some space. They spent inordinate amounts of time together between Sean's, her workshop, and racing. She'd grown to love it, but she also understood the need for solitude and would sneak off on her own to read from *The Alchemist* or one of her other favorites. Without any word from new sponsors or pro teams, Nikki's confidence waned by the day, and she found herself needing messages of hope and perseverance more and more.

She stopped by the food tent, where they were serving up the end-of-race dinner, and grabbed a box for each of them, filling Jake's with more meat than anything. The man was a carnivore through and through. Boxes of food and bottled water in hand, she headed over to the grandstands overlooking turn two, figuring he'd be perched in one of them. They were quiet, solitary places to think once the crowds cleared out. She used them herself in the early-morning hours before a race to help her get centered before hitting the track.

A few minutes later, Nikki spotted him perched in the uppermost row, a study in solitude as he gazed out across the track. He was looking in the direction of turn eight, so he didn't see her watching him beneath a billboard for Valvoline Oil. She felt like a voyeur standing there in the shadows, but she didn't move.

Even from this distance, Jake's complexities, as much as his devastating good looks, struck her. His personality had so many intricate layers. There were lighter ones, like the tender relationship he had with his younger brother: how he loved and cared for him with the devotion of a parent. Or his love of sketching and photography—things he claimed were *hobbies*, but she knew better. The concentration and focus he had while sketching or the careful eye with which he took photographs suggested these weren't *hobbies*: they were passions—passions, for whatever reason, he refused to admit or explore.

Then there were the darker, painful layers that stood out in stark relief against the others: the grief he carried from his mother's death—something he avoided discussing at great lengths—and the deep-seated anger that fueled his violent reactions toward Tony and Ron. Reactions he claimed came from a need to protect Nikki, but she sensed there was more to it than that. The violence he demonstrated, the anger he so clearly carried, had to have come from something terrible in his past—something that left wounds that continued to fester years after their infliction, poisoning him with toxic rage.

She wanted so badly to peel back each of those layers and explore them, to uncover everything that comprised Jake Masercotti. But she couldn't do that. It would mean getting in too deep, getting too close to him, paving the way for more to happen between them—more than what she already felt growing each day. That was dangerous. If they became more than friends, walking away from him when the time came to return to professional racing—*if it came*—would be more painful than she wanted to think about.

Nikki slumped back against one of the support posts, her eyes riveted to him, as the image of his face when he came storming into the paddock earlier appeared in her mind. His eyes had been filled with so much rage. Her chest tightened at the memory. No one should carry that kind of anger. It was harmful. She would know; she'd carried that kind of rage after her parents died, lashing out at those she loved and even at herself, shouldering the blame for their deaths. If it weren't for Damon getting her to a grief counselor and Mystery Man from the cemetery, she'd still be wrestling with it just like Jake.

She let out a heavy breath. Jake needed help. He needed someone who was willing to step in, to peel back this dark layer and help him face the demons beneath it. Nikki worried her bottom lip. She could do that. She could be that person for him. Not that she imagined herself saving him from his personal demons—her ego wasn't *that* big—but she could help him find a professional who could and be there for him through it all, as Damon had been for her. But could she do that without getting in too deep?

Jake leaned forward, dropping his head into his hands in a gesture that screamed defeat.

A sharp pain sliced through her heart, and she had her answer. She'd be there for him however he needed her. And if that meant putting herself in danger of more heartbreak down the line, she would have to risk it. She couldn't stand by and watch a friend suffer.

Gathering her courage, Nikki pushed off the post and headed for him. She didn't know how she would go about helping him. He didn't say much when it came to his personal life, so getting him to open up would be tough. She would have to tread carefully and take it slow, which meant things wouldn't be solved today. But maybe she could help him start. If not, she'd keep trying until it worked and hope he didn't shut her out in the process.

"There you are," she said when she reached the top of the stands. "I brought you some dinner."

Jake lifted his head and turned to her. She almost dropped the boxes. A riot of emotions crisscrossed his striking face, and the greatest of all wasn't anger, as she might have expected after what happened earlier—it was hopelessness.

"What's wrong?" she asked, dropping onto the bench next to him.

Jake shook his head. "Nothing."

She set the boxes on the bench between them. "Your face says otherwise."

He grabbed the box she placed closest to him and opened it. "It's nothing, really." He stabbed a piece of tri-tip like he was trying to kill the cow all over again.

She reached over and placed a hand over his, stopping his attack on the innocent meal. "Jake, I can see that something is wrong. Talk to me. Maybe I can help."

He looked up through the dark fringe of lashes that rimmed his eyes, his gaze full of misery. "You can't help me with this, Nikki. No one can."

"How do you know unless you try?" she asked. She wanted to chase away the hurt she saw in his eyes.

Jake took a bite of the tri-tip. After a beat, he let out a heavy breath. "It's Dario," he said, his voice deeper, rougher as he dug around in his box for another bite. "I gave him a call since I missed our night this week. I'm worried about him. He's in trouble, and he won't open up about it."

"What kind of trouble?" she asked, heaving a quiet sigh of relief at his decision to talk.

"He's getting into fights. He says it's happening at school, but I know better. He's never been in trouble at school before. He loves it, has tons of friends, top grades…I don't see why he'd ruin that track record now."

"What does your dad say about it? He must have an idea."

Jake was quiet for so long that she didn't think he was going to answer. He never discussed his family outside of his regular dates to hang with Dario. She knew part of it stemmed from his mother's death and the grief he carried, but other parts were a mystery—yet another layer to what comprised his complex persona.

"Dario doesn't live with him. He's in a foster home," he finally said.

Her head snapped up. "What? Is...is your dad gone too?" she asked, her voice cautious. Why didn't he mention this before?

He shook his head. "He's in prison. He's been there since I was a kid."

Nikki blinked. It wasn't the answer she was expecting, and judging by the bitterness in his voice, she knew this was where at least some of his anger originated. "God. I'm sorry to hear that," she said, gauging Jake's reaction before she continued. When he shrugged, she pressed on. "So... if your dad's in prison, why is Dario in foster care? You're an adult and his next of kin. He should be with you."

There was another long pause as Jake chewed another bite, and Nikki feared she'd gone too far. She was about to apologize and tell him to forget it, that she was out of line for prying, when he lifted his face to hers, his eyes teeming not with anger or resentment but guilt.

"I wanted that more than anything, but each time I tried, the courts deemed me unfit to care for him—or anyone, as the last judge put it," he replied, his voice flat.

"What? You? *Unfit*? That's insane."

He shook his head. "No, it's not. After the last hearing, I realized the courts were right. I've made a lot of mistakes in my life. I have a juvie record, some misdemeanors as an adult, and an assault charge from a few years ago. I'm not role-model material, and Dario...he deserves better than that."

Anger shot down her spine. Jake was a good man. She knew this deep in her heart, and yet other people's opinions had made him think otherwise. "So, you made some mistakes. BFD. That doesn't make you unfit, Jake. It makes you human."

He reared back. "*Human?* You don't think an arrest record makes it more than that? Come on. Look at me. Look at my family: we have a history of incarceration. I'd say we're failures, total fuckups, as humans. People like that don't deserve to raise kids," he sneered.

Clearly, some of his anger also came from this situation with his brother. Nikki didn't blame him. She knew what he was going through; she and her brothers went through the same thing when her parents died. The difference with Jake, though, was that he actually believed he wasn't worthy to raise Dario.

"When were these arrests?" she asked, building to something she hoped he took to heart.

Jake shrugged. "Most of the adult stuff goes back six years, but the last one, the assault charge, was four years ago."

"And you haven't been arrested since?"

"No. But it doesn't matter. The record speaks for itself," he said, frustration and defeat ringing in his voice.

Nikki set her box aside and moved closer. "That's bullshit. If anything, your record *highlights* the good man that you are *today*. You turned things around, atoned for your mistakes. You're a better man than you were four years ago. Hell, you're a better role model in some ways than someone who hasn't made mistakes. Anyone could see that."

Jake leaned back, his face skeptical but no longer etched with disbelief. "What makes you an expert on this? Why do you think you know better than the courts about who's fit to be Dario's guardian and who's not?"

"Because I've been there," she said, clarifying when he gave her a *what the hell* look. "The courts did the same thing to Dino when our parents died. He has a record like yours, so when they died, he had to petition for custody of us. The courts denied him, claiming he was unfit because of his past. It didn't matter that he'd kept his record clean for more than two years. The judge only saw the mistakes he'd *made* and not the man he'd *become*: a responsible man who worked hard and loved his family. They misjudged Dino, just as they misjudged you. Unlike Dario though, Mike and I got to choose our foster father. Sean stepped in and filed an emergency petition to take temporary custody of us, and a more official one later, so we didn't have to go into the system."

Jake didn't respond when she finished. He just sat there, staring at her. She shifted on the bench. Was he pissed at her for bringing this up? Did he think she was crazy?

"You mean it, don't you? You really think they misjudged me," he finally said.

She arched a brow. "Of course I do. You shouldn't be judged by the mistakes of the past if you've turned your life around and made the present better. Which you clearly have."

She studied him. When she still saw him warring with disbelief, she said, "I can't be the first person to say this to you. Dario, your friends, Frankie and Johnny, they must have said something similar."

He inhaled deeply. "They have, yes. They've always supported me."

"Then they're good friends," she observed.

"The best."

"Then why don't you believe them? Why don't you see that you deserve better than what you've been dealt?" she asked, hoping she wasn't being too bold.

"Because..." He faltered. "I...guess I never thought about it from your perspective. I've never met anyone else who's been in my shoes before."

Nikki could tell by his voice that he'd only touched on part of the reason behind his disbelief. He was holding back, but for now, this was enough. It was a place to start.

"Jake, have you ever thought about talking to someone about your feelings over losing custody of Dario? It might help you shake some of the anger you've got bottled up inside."

"You mean like a counselor?"

"Yes. I saw one after my parents died, and it helped. A lot."

He shrugged, rooting around in his box again. "I don't know. I don't think I can afford it. That kind of thing is expensive."

"Doesn't Sean provide a health plan for you guys?" she asked, knowing the answer before he said it.

"He does. Why? Do you think that sort of thing is covered?"

She smiled. "It is. I know that for a fact because I helped him select his employee plan when he upgraded it last year." When Jake went quiet again, she said, "Look, I'm not saying you have to get counseling, but I think it would help. What happened today and at the gas station can't keep happening. You have to find a way to release this anger, this rage. It's not good for you, and one of these days, you might go too far."

"I'll think about it," he said as his phone chirped. He grabbed it from the bench where it sat and tapped the screen. When it lit up, she saw an image of her Pro Mazda car soaring across the finish line at the Mazda Raceway event.

"Hey! I didn't know you took that," she said, joy rushing through her that he would at least consider counseling. She made a note to follow up with him about it in a couple of weeks. She wasn't going to let this slide. He needed help before he did something he'd regret.

Jake looked up from the phone. "I've taken a few pictures at the track. They're not very good, being on the phone and all. I could take better shots if I had my Nikon."

"Can I see them?" she asked, her fingers itching to get ahold of the device.

He pinned her with that penetrating stare of his. "Yeah, sure." He opened the app and revealed dozens upon dozens of shots, all of them incredible, even with his cell phone camera.

"Oh...oh, wow! Jake, you are way too modest. These are amazing," she breathed, studying one of her sitting down next to the Shelby. The way the light played with the strands of hair that fell to one side gave the photo an ethereal quality she'd never have seen in herself otherwise.

Jake leaned in and looked at the screen. "That's one of my favorites. You look like an angel sitting there."

Her eyes darted to his, but he didn't notice. He was staring at the screen with a look of such devotion it took her breath away. A heady mix of emotion and lust whirled inside her, and she wanted—more than anything in that moment—to kiss him, to feel him pressed against her.

Nikki shook her head to clear it before she did something stupid. She'd taken enough risks with her heart today. "I can't believe you've never thought about becoming a professional," she said, handing him the phone.

He shrugged. "Taking pictures is something I do for fun. I've never thought about pursuing it. Besides, I don't have the time or the money to do anything about it, even if I wanted to."

He was lying. She could hear it, and she could hear the fear behind it… It was the same kind of fear she felt after her accident more times than she liked to admit: the fear of failing at something you loved.

"Have you ever read *The Alchemist*?" she asked, an idea taking root.

Jake shook his head. "No. Why?"

She smiled knowingly. "It's one of my favorite books. If I gave you a copy, would you read it?"

"Yeah, sure. I like to read when I get the time."

He liked reading? *Lord.* Just what she needed: another reason to be attracted to him.

"Good." She planned on giving him the copy she had in the RV.

They finished their dinner and started going over plans for the Le Mans car, when Nikki's phone rang.

She pulled it out, frowning when she didn't recognize the number. "Hello?"

"Is this Nikki Elliot?" a voice she didn't recognize asked.

"This is she. Who's calling?"

Jake set his dinner aside and focused his attention on her.

"This is Mark Jacobs of Greendale Sunglasses. Do you have a minute? I'd like to talk to you about a sponsorship offer," he explained.

Nikki's heart leaped. "Um, yes, of course," she said, trying to keep the excitement out of her voice. Greendale Sunglasses was one of the most popular brands on the market. A sponsorship offer from them could get her a spot on the pro team before the Mazda Series ended.

"Great. We've been watching your progress this season, and we're impressed. So impressed, in fact, that we have an offer for you," Mark began.

She listened with rapt attention as he went into detail, her heart pounding in her chest. This was the kind of deal she'd been hoping for all season.

"So that's it," Mark said, wrapping it up. "Take a look at the proposal I've emailed you, and go over it with your manager. If you guys like what you see, we can sign the contracts ASAP and get you set up to race with Hastings Motors in the IndyCar Series next year."

"I'll do that. Thank you, Mark. We'll talk soon."

She turned to Jake, speechless.

"Well?" he said when she sat there grinning like an idiot. "What did he say? Good news, I hope?"

Nikki gave her head a shake. "It was the best news," she said, finding her voice at last. "Greendale Sunglasses wants to sponsor me next year and set me up to race with an IndyCar team."

Jake's face lit up. "Are you serious? That's huge!"

"I know, right?" She gasped, taking in her first full breath since the phone call started. "I still have to go over the contracts with Jack, but from the sound of things, this could be it, Jake. This could be my ticket back to the pros and, eventually, a shot at a Formula 1 team."

She still couldn't believe it. Just when she'd started to fear the worst for her career, this happened.

"You mean it *is* your ticket back to the pros," he corrected. "The deal will work out. You're going to make it Nikki. I know it."

The confidence and pride in his voice and on his face made her heart flutter, but it also made her sad. She wished he had that kind of confidence in himself.

They sat in the grandstands, talking about the Greendale offer and racing in the IndyCar Series and eventually moving onto funny stories about Hilda and Jake's buddies, well into the night. It wasn't until Nikki got cold that they finally headed back to the RV.

They walked back in companionable silence, each lost in their own thoughts. "We'd better get some sleep," Jake said, closing and locking the door behind him once they'd reached the coach.

Nikki nodded. "It's late," she agreed, knowing she needed to rest but not wanting to because it meant ending what had turned out to be an amazing evening, and not just because of the Greendale offer.

Jake turned and headed toward the bunks at the other end of the rig, where he slept, but stopped and came back to where she stood in front of the door to her room. With gentle hands, he cupped her face and placed a warm, feathery kiss to her forehead.

"Thanks, angel," he whispered.

"For what?" she asked, blinking up at him, loving his nickname for her.

He gave her a small, boyish grin. "For being my angel and seeing in me the things I can't."

Her heart swelled to near bursting as she gazed up at him. "Always, Jake. Always," she whispered before going into her room and closing the door behind her.

12

J ake closed the book and ran his hands over the worn cover of *The Alchemist*—the book Nikki lent him a few weeks back. It had shocked him when she asked if he would read it. It wasn't the kind of thing women usually asked of him. It had shocked him even more when he agreed to do it.

Jake wasn't lying when he said he enjoyed reading—more like stretching the truth. At one time, he enjoyed reading very much. When he was a kid, he read everything he could get his hands on. He loved reading for the way it transported him to other places, other worlds, made him think about things, and led him to reflect on his own life in ways he might not have otherwise. But that was before everything fell apart. Since then, he avoided reading, books especially. What was the point of doing it if made him reflect on a broken existence with no hope of repair?

But when Nikki asked him to read *The Alchemist*, he'd agreed to do it without hesitation. If this book was her favorite, as she'd claimed, it would be like looking through a window into her mind and heart—places Jake wanted to explore at length—and that was an opportunity he couldn't pass up. Nikki fascinated him like no one ever had before. He wanted to know where her strength and perseverance came from and everything else about her innermost workings—anything there was to know about Nikki Elliot. It might seem silly to some, getting to know a woman he wouldn't see after the year was finished, but not to him. For Jake, knowing her like that would leave him with something to hold on to long after they went their separate ways.

He read *The Alchemist* from cover to cover, including the annotations she'd made throughout the text. And he was right: the fable about the boy on a journey to pursue his dream was like looking through a window into Nikki's heart and mind. He now saw that her strength and perseverance were innate, woven into her DNA, right along with the open-mindedness he'd glimpsed before but hadn't really *seen* until now. The way she tapped into and lived the story's messages came from all of that, leaving Jake more in awe of her than ever.

But that awe came at price, as that window went both ways.

Reading through the pages, even as he tried to keep his mind focused on what it all meant where *Nikki* was concerned, Jake couldn't help but start to reflect on his own life. Santiago's story got under his skin like a splinter, poking at him to read closer, to think deeper as he followed the boy's harrowing journey. In the process, Jake saw much of himself in Santiago's character, in his self-doubt, in his fears of pursuing something he wanted, leaving Jake reeling with emotions and thoughts he didn't want to face but could no longer avoid...thanks to *her*.

His angel was a clever girl.

Nikki saw right through Jake's façade of not having dreams or goals. She saw that he did have them, that he did want more from life than working at something simply because it *paid the bills*, that he had passions he wanted to pursue. More importantly, she saw all of that and cared enough to not only shove it in his face and make him think about it but also give him the tools to help him go after those passions—*if* he chose to.

He slumped back against the couch, clutching the paperback. He'd never thought about going after more in life because it meant finding happiness, and he didn't deserve that. But this book, this goddamned guide to seeking personal fulfillment, said otherwise. It told him to let go of the past, to focus on what he wanted, and to concentrate on what he could do to achieve that. And in doing so, realize the greatest level of happiness.

But how could *he* do that? How could *he* let go of a past in which he'd committed the greatest sin of all? A past filled with actions that had destroyed what was left of his family, affecting not only his life but Dario's as well. It seemed wrong for him to release that and move on.

And yet...

And yet part of him, deep down, thought it might be possible to let go, even a little, of his past and find a measure of happiness.

No one can move on from the sins you've committed. Your past is your present and your future. You don't deserve anything more after what you did to your mother, whispered a familiar voice.

Jake squeezed his eyes shut, his chest tightening with shame. How could he even think of letting go of *any* part of his past? He was a man beyond salvation and true happiness. He looked down in revulsion at the book clutched in his hand and threw it onto the heavy coffee table, making it land with a *thwack!*

The book was full of shit. Personal fulfillment might be meant for some people but not men like him.

You're wrong, whispered a new voice—one he wanted to drown out but for some reason couldn't. *Pay attention to the present, not the past. See who's here and* listen.

Jake leaned forward and dropped his head into his hands with a world-weary groan. *Fuck this book.* He never should have read it. He should have ignored his curiosities about Nikki and refused to do it when she asked. If he had, he wouldn't be sitting here now, torturing himself with ideas and desires he had no business having.

He groaned again.

Refuse Nikki? Yeah, right. Just like Santiago's story, she was under his skin too—only far, far deeper—and there was no getting her out.

He lifted his head and snorted.

Who was he kidding? He could blame that book all he wanted, but it was Nikki who had him thinking about his life, about what he did and didn't deserve, ever since that first night when she found his photographs, and she hadn't stopped since. Not when she did things like give him this book, gush over his photography and drawings, question why he wasn't pursuing art professionally, or when she showed up at his place early one morning before work with a bunch of frames and mats, insisting that he *put his beautiful works of art on display,* or they could *no longer be friends.* She was the catalyst for the war raging inside him now. The book merely fueled the already-smoldering fire—a powerful, dangerous fuel that made him see not only what *was* but what *could be* if he let it: a future in which he wasn't broken by anger and guilt. A future with her by his side, supporting him, loving him in ways he'd never dreamed of...until now.

Damn it.

Why did she have to do this? Why did she have to make him think, make him hope for things he couldn't have? Why couldn't she let him help her and leave *his* life alone?

Because she sees who you are.

A venomous blend of frustration and rage sluiced through his veins. Jake leaped to his feet and began pacing the living room, his eyes riveted to the floor. If he looked up, he'd see the photographs she'd helped him hang or that bloody book. They were all reminders of a life he couldn't have—one she wouldn't want him to have if she knew the truth about him.

Don't be so sure. Listen to the present. See what is and what can be.

He glared at the book on the table. "Shut up!" he snarled at it.

Jake froze mid-step. *Jesus Christ.* Did he seriously yell at a book? He dragged a shaking hand through his unruly mane. He was losing his fucking mind.

Before he fell any further down the rabbit hole, his phone chirped. He stormed over to the island, grabbed it, and punched in the security code. There was a text from Johnny.

R U home?

He tapped off a rapid response.

Y. What's up?

Nada. I'm on my lunch, thought I'd stop by. B there in 5 with Frankie?

Sure. Cool.

Thank Christ.

Jake puffed out a breath and stuffed the phone into his back pocket. He needed a distraction to keep him from soaring over the cuckoo's nest.

Johnny and Frankie arrived minutes later. Jake set down the beer he'd opened and went to the door to let them in, firing another glare at the book that kept calling to him despite his attempts to sweep it from his mind.

"What up, bro?" Johnny said, stepping inside with Frankie right behind him.

"Not too much," Jake said, slapping Frankie on the back. "Were you down the street or something? You got here pretty quick."

Frankie nodded. "We met up at Rosalinda's. We thought we'd take a chance and see if you were home."

Jake led them over to the island. "Rosalinda's? I hope that means you brought some of their *sopes* or *tamales*." His stomach growled at the mere thought of them. Rosalinda's was, hands down, the best Mexican food to be had in all of Wood Glenn. It was a little hole-in-the-wall place, but you couldn't let that stop you from enjoying the incredible food—the sopes and tamales especially.

"Of course we did," Johnny said, pulling three boxes from the plastic bag dangling at his fingertips. "What do you take us for? Cheap asses?"

"Never," Jake said, taking the box Johnny offered. He salivated as the aroma wafted around him, derailing the crazy train in his head.

"Good. 'Cause we brought both," Frankie said, dropping onto the stool and stuffing a whole *sope* into his mouth.

"Fuck yeah! You guys are the best." Jake grinned, ripping into the box and grabbing a tamale straight off. The sopes were incredible, but the *tamales con carnitas* were the shit.

"You know it. Got any more beer?" Frankie nodded at the open bottle on the counter.

"Yeah, sure." Jake grabbed one from the refrigerator and a bottle of water. Johnny was on the clock, so he couldn't partake. A damn shame too. Nothing went better with Rosalinda's than an ice-cold Dos Equis.

They inhaled the food in a matter of minutes, collapsing on the couch afterward in a semi-state of food-coma. Johnny was busting up at a video of an Irishman on a rant on YouTube when Frankie leaned forward and grabbed *The Alchemist* from the coffee table.

"Is this yours?" Frankie asked, examining the cover.

Jake frowned at the book. So much for derailing the crazy train.

"No, it's Nikki's. She lent it to me a few weeks back," he explained.

Frankie nodded. "It looks like she's read it a few times. Why'd she give it to you?"

Why indeed.

Jake shrugged. "It's her favorite. She wanted me to check it out."

"Really?" Frankie beamed. "It's one of my favorites too."

"You read that?" Johnny asked, looking up from the laptop. The computer was Sean's, on loan to Jake. He came across it in the supply closet and asked Sean if he could borrow it since his had been stolen. Sean had no problem with it, especially when Jake explained that he wanted it for research on Nikki's racing career and to upload his photos of her at the track.

"Yup. My mom made me read it back in high school. She swears by the messages in it, says it's never failed her each time she's read it. According to her, it's one of those books that comes to you when you need to hear the messages the most." Frankie shrugged. "I didn't believe her until I read it myself. But she was right. It helped me back in twelfth grade when I was trying to decide what to do after graduation. If it hadn't been for Santiago's story, I don't know if I'd be on the path I'm on today. What did you think of it?"

Jake scowled at the book as Frankie handed it to him. "It's all right, I guess. I didn't really think too much about its message or anything," he lied.

Frankie arched a brow. "Seriously? You're the first person I've heard say that. Most people are deeply affected by that little story."

Jake puffed out a breath and tossed the book on the table. "I guess I'm special, then."

"I guess you are. Here," Johnny said, handing him the computer. "You've got an email from Dario. Thought you might want to see it."

"Thanks." Jake took the computer and set it on the coffee table.

"How's he doing these days? Is he still getting into fights?" Johnny asked, looking at the screen.

Jake nodded, hating the topic but happy to be discussing something other than the book. "Yeah. He's always got scrapes and bruises. He tries to cover them up, but I see them."

Things were getting progressively worse with Dario. He was edgier than ever and was injured more often than not. There were times when Jake wanted to take him by the shoulders and shake the explanation out of him, but he didn't. He would never raise a hand to Dario. His voice was another story, but he couldn't do that, either. Their visits were still supervised, so even raising his voice slightly could get them revoked.

"Looks like he's okay tonight," Johnny noted. "What are those links he sent you? Something about a Le Mans Classic from 2015. What the hell is that, and why does he think you should see it?"

Jake frowned at Johnny. "Dude, do you have any manners? This email is private."

Johnny reared back, feigning indignation. "I happen to have excellent manners. Ask Tiff's mom if you don't believe me. Besides, nothing with Dario is private between us. He's our *hermano* too."

"Johnny's right, man. If something's up, we've got a right to know. I don't hold back where Kassandra and Gabriel are concerned," Frankie added.

"You're right. Sorry," Jake said, feeling like a heel. Frankie and Johnny were his family, and he needed to remember that, even when he felt über protective of Dario. "Le Mans is a town in France where they hold the 24 Heures du Mans endurance race every year, both with modern and vintage cars. Nikki raced in the vintage one a couple years ago," he explained.

"Ah, this is about your little racecar driving angel. Looks like your brother's almost as big a fan as you are. You got a picture of her since we haven't had the privilege of meeting her yet?" Johnny asked, giving Jake's shoulder a nudge.

"I might have one or two," Jake said, shoving him back, a little harder than necessary. He had dozens of them on his phone, but he wasn't going to tell them that. He'd never live it down.

"Well? Let's see one and then check out this YouTube video *manito* sent you," Johnny pressed.

"Fine," Jake grunted, pulling out his phone. He opened the photo app and pulled up a recent picture of her at the awards banquet for the VAM series. His chest tightened the minute she appeared on the screen. She looked stunning in this shot. The candlelight highlighted the ribbons of gold streaming through her honey-colored locks, which were even more vibrant against the black satin of her dress. She'd taken his breath away when he'd first laid eyes on her that night and still did whenever he looked at the photo.

He handed Johnny the phone.

Johnny let out a whistle, his eyes wide. "This...*this* is your little angel?"

"Let me see that," Frankie said, leaning behind Jake. "Daaamn! She's a racecar driver and a mechanic?"

"Yeah. What about it?" Jake glared over his shoulder.

Frankie looked up from the phone. "Nothing. I mean, she doesn't look like either of those things. She's—"

"Model pretty," Johnny finished.

Jake grabbed the phone before his friend could drool on it. "She's not *model pretty*. She's exquisite." He cringed the minute the words left his mouth. He sounded like a whipped bastard.

He groaned internally.

Who was he kidding? He *was* a whipped bastard.

Johnny and Frankie exchanged glances and burst out laughing.

"What's so fucking funny?" Jake demanded.

Frankie slapped him on the shoulder. "It finally happened!" He laughed.

"What the hell does *that* mean?"

Johnny took a deep breath, all humor disappearing from his voice. "*Enamorarse*. You're in love, Jake. And who could blame you? For real."

Johnny's words felt like a dropkick to the gut. Not because it wasn't true, but because it was. Jake was in love with Nikki. There was no escaping it. Even with her scraping at his wounds and forcing him to think about things he'd avoided in the past, he loved her like he'd never loved anyone before or would again. He'd never admit that, though. They'd end up giving him shit every chance they got, encouraging him to pursue the girl he knew he couldn't have, and that would hurt too much.

"What? I'm not in love with her. She's my boss, *my friend*, but that's it," Jake declared, mentally crossing his fingers and toes.

"Bull. Shit," Frankie said. "People don't keep pictures of their boss on their phones, and they don't get that look"—he pointed at Jake's face—"when they talk about someone who's *just a friend*."

Jake waved him off. "Whatever. You two are full of shit." He jammed his phone back in his pocket and reached for the laptop. "Do you want to see the video of her racing or not?"

Frankie started to say something, but Johnny cut him off. "All right, all right. Yes. Play the video. I've got to go, and so does Frankie. Law school papers and crime wait for no one."

Jake clicked on the first link, one that had been posted two years ago—right after the race. A video of the 24 Heures of Le Mans Classic opened with the traditional Le Mans start in which the drivers charged onto the track, leapt into their cars, and took off onto the infamous endurance course.

"Which one is Nikki?" Frankie asked, leaning closer to the screen.

Jake paused the video and found her, darting for the British-racing-green Le Mans Tiger. "That's her," he said, pointing to the tiniest figure on pit lane.

"I can't believe they start the race like that. It looks dangerous," Johnny observed.

Jake shrugged. "It's a tradition, and it's safe enough if you run fast."

He started the video again, and a highlight reel of the race commenced. There was a lot of footage of Nikki battling a Ford GT 40 and a Daytona Coupe for the lead. Nikki's driving, as always, was daring and on point, until about a quarter of the way through the race when she hit the Mulsanne Straight, one of the most notorious strips of raceway in the world.

Jake watched as the Tiger flew through the corner at Tertre Rouge, gained speed as she maneuvered out of the first kink, and gunned it down the remainder of the two-mile straightaway. By his estimate, she had to be traveling over one hundred twenty miles per hour as she reached the second, and sharpest, kink shortly before the infamous Mulsanne corner.

"Dude, why the fuck isn't she braking? She's going to lose control when she hits that turn." Johnny gasped.

"I-I...don't know," Jake stammered.

For some reason, he didn't think about what the videos would show when he'd glanced at Dario's email. He'd purposely avoided watching anything to do with Le Mans. He didn't want the image of Nikki involved in a massive wreck seared onto his brain. He should have reached over and closed the video before he saw something he couldn't *unsee*, but he didn't. He was frozen in his seat, his eyes glued to the screen, his heart crashing against his ribs because he knew what was about to happen.

Frankie and Johnny swore in unison when Nikki veered off course at the apex of the sharp kink, flipped over the tire barrier, and went cartwheeling into a billboard. Flames and smoke poured from the crumpled mass of metal for what felt like an eternity before emergency crews and corner workers reached the scene, swarming the vehicle like ants. Seconds later, they pulled Nikki's limp, unresponsive body from the wreckage and placed her on a stretcher. The video faded to black as EMTs performed CPR and corner workers put out the fire.

No one said anything. They sat there, gaping at the computer screen in a horrified silence. Johnny was the first to speak.

"I...damn...I can't believe she survived that and continues to go out there and race. That is one brave woman," he said, slumping back against the couch.

"Yeah," Frankie agreed. "How do you do it?"

Jake tore his eyes from the computer and looked over at Frankie. "Do what?"

"Watch her go out there and race week after week. Doesn't that scare the shit out of you?"

He shook his head. "Watching Nikki race is like nothing I've ever seen. When she's out there, she's totally in her element, completely comfortable, at peace—fearless. It's amazing to watch."

"Aren't you afraid of something like that happening again and losing her altogether?" Frankie asked, gesturing at the screen.

"No, not really." Jake reached over and closed the link, revealing the email once more. "Nikki's a solid driver; she knows what she's doing."

"Then what happened there?" Johnny pointed to the computer. "Why didn't she slow down? She had to know she was going to wreck if she didn't."

Good question.

Jake and Nikki hadn't spoken about the Le Mans crash at length. She avoided talking about it, so he let it go. He could understand the need to keep some things quiet. But seeing this, he wanted to know what happened. She clearly didn't even *try* to brake along the Mulsanne. That was unlike her. Nikki took risks, but they were calculated risks. What happened at Le Mans was insane.

"I don't know," Jake said, as dumbfounded as they were. "She's never talked about it."

Frankie leaned forward and pointed to the second link. Unlike the first, this one was recent, its publish date only a week ago. "Try the second link. Maybe there's some commentary on that video that explains the crash."

Jake leaned in and clicked the link. Another video opened up, this one called *2015 Le Mans Classic Carnage*. He let out a heavy breath and pressed play. The food in his stomach congealed when a warning about the film containing disturbing footage appeared. He glanced down at the runtime —it was just over a minute. The video must have been of the moments leading up to and during the wreck.

The warning faded, revealing footage from the Le Mans Tiger's in-car camera. Jake reared back. How was that possible? Nick had told him once that the in-car cam malfunctioned at Le Mans. It was one reason why race officials gave no *definitive* cause for the wreck—only a likely one. So where the hell did this footage come from?

Jake tore his focus from the mounting questions to the video. He could hear Nikki's voice, faint but clear enough to make out over the engine, as she communicated with her crew chief on pit lane.

"Everything looks good, Phillipe. No problems with the brakes. They seem to be holding up. I'm going to kick it up a notch through the Mulsanne this lap to make up some of the time we lost earlier," Nikki said, sounding like her usual self: calm, confident, and totally at ease. "I've gotten ahead of the Daytona Coupe, but the GT40 is still eluding me."

There was a pause, during which the only sound was the roar of the Tiger's V8 as she flew through the corner at Tertre Rouge and flattened the accelerator. Nikki's voice came over the video again a second later, but it was different this time. In it, Jake heard something he hadn't heard from her during a race: fear.

"Scratch what I said about the brakes! They're gone, Phillipe! *Gone!*" she all but screamed into the mic.

"Oh fuck," Johnny murmured next to Jake.

Oh fuck was right. She didn't brake because she couldn't. They'd failed without warning.

"I'm going to downshift and see if it will help. I'm at one twenty-five mph."

Jake heard the transmission scream as she downshifted, but it didn't help. He could still see her barreling toward the second kink, her voice panicked as she came over the radio one last time.

"Oh God...how did he know? How did he get to the car?" she cried, screaming as the car flipped over the barrier just before the camera cut off. A black screen appeared then with bold white lettering: *God forgive me... this was no accident.*

Jake gaped at the screen for a moment then made a mad dash for the bathroom. He managed to reach the toilet as Rosalinda's meal made a violent comeback. Stomach empty, he reached up and flushed the toilet, his body shaking from the release.

Johnny and Frankie appeared in the doorway.

"You all right?" Johnny asked, as he wet a cloth and handed it to Jake.

"Yeah."

"Do you know what she meant in the video about some guy finding her or what that slide at the end meant?" Frankie asked, sounding almost as shaken as Jake felt.

"It sounded like she was in trouble, like someone was after her. Whoever posted that video thought the same and may have been involved by the looks of it," Johnny offered.

Jake didn't respond. He just sat there, staring at the white porcelain of the toilet, Nikki's voice stuck on repeat in his mind: "Oh God...how did he know? How did he get to the car?" He didn't know who she was talking about, but one thing was obvious: Johnny was right. Nikki had been in trouble back then and not just any kind of trouble—the kind that got you killed. Questions flooded Jake's mind, one ringing louder than the others: was the responsible party still out there, and were they waiting for another chance?

～

RIVULETS OF SWEAT STREAMED DOWN DAMON'S CHEST AND BACK AS HE delivered punishing kick after kick to the freestanding bag. He'd been working the bag for almost an hour now, but it wasn't enough. His mind raced with a sickening blend of anger and worry. Nino texted earlier to let him know he'd finally gathered all the information Damon asked him to track down weeks ago. The fact that it took this long had Damon's ire up, but the tone in Nino's voice and his insistence on delivering the news in person sent Damon into a fit of worry. Nino never delivered anything in person unless the news was bad. And in this case, that could only mean one thing: Nikki was in trouble.

Again.

Damon whirled around and toppled the bag with a spinning round-house. He was reaching down to pick it up and repeat the move when the gym doors burst open, followed by Nino's booming voice.

"Yo! Boss! I'm here!"

Damon straightened the kick bag and snagged his towel and water bottle from the mat next to him. "My office," he barked, before storming to the back of the gym behind the massive cage where his and Tsai's offices sat.

Nino nodded and followed. When they reached the office, Damon shut the door and closed the blinds. Nino's visit had nothing to do with gym business, so he didn't want any eyes on them. He didn't typically handle *family* business at the gym, but tonight was an exception.

"What'd you find?" Damon dropped into the leather chair behind the formidable steel desk.

Nino opened his briefcase and dropped a heavy file in front of Damon. "Plenty. Let me start, though, by mentioning that I removed the surveillance from Nikki right after we spoke on the phone. Anthony and Mark were following her, as I suspected, which was completely my fault."

A measure of relief eased its way into Damon's chest. "Don't worry about it. As long as they're no longer following her, that's all that matters."

"Great. So, which bit of research do you want to hear about first?" Nino asked, visibly tensing.

"Start with Masercotti. What did you learn?" Damon said, his voice going arctic as he thought about that tatted-up freak.

"Let's see." Nino opened the folder and read through his notes. "He's got a rap sheet: some arrests as a juvenile and some minor shit as an adult, including an assault on his brother's foster father, Bruce Reynolds, four years ago. He's attempted to gain custody of his brother, Dario, but the courts denied him both times. He currently works for Sean Martin at the Tiger's Den and spends time at a biker bar out on Highway 84 called the Blue Ox. When he's not working or at the bar, he volunteers at a local homeless shelter, helps out as a suicide prevention hotline counselor, and—"

Nino stopped short, looking nervous.

"And what? He sounds like a goddamn Boy Scout. What else is there? Does he shelter homeless puppies and kittens too?" Damon sneered, hating this guy even more. Minor arrests aside, Sam Crow was a fucking saint—a fucking saint he was pretty sure Nikki had a crush on. He fisted his hands at the thought, glaring daggers at Nino.

"No. But there is one more thing. His, uh…his name isn't Jake Masercotti—at least not originally. He changed it six years ago. Before that, it was…Giancarlo Di Silva," Nino said, dropping the folder like it was on fire.

"What? Are you sure?" Damon couldn't have heard him correctly. The *Sons* throwback couldn't be Giancarlo Di Silva. If he was, that would make him Carlo Di Silva's son—his boss and the leader of the Berardi crime family.

Nino nodded. "Yeah. I checked it twice. He's one of Carlo's boys."

Blood roared in his ears. Jake Masercotti was one of Carlo Di Silva's estranged sons? What the fuck? How did Nikki get involved with the heir to a Mafia empire? *Sweet mother of God.* After everything Damon did, *sacrificed*, to keep her away from this shit, she kept getting herself in deeper.

Damon took a beat to rein in his frustration. There was an upside to this clusterfuck: the fact that Jake was estranged from his father. He had nothing to do with Carlo or his business. And in terms of the business, he never had, which meant there wouldn't be any connections that could blow back on Nikki.

Carlo, unlike Damon's father, kept his family completely separate from his life in the Mafia. From what Damon understood, the Di Silvas had been close—beyond tight-knit—until Carlo's conviction. A year into his imprisonment, Carlo's wife, Lily, committed suicide. With no surviving relatives to take them, Jake and Dario disappeared into the foster care system and hadn't had any contact with Carlo since.

"Okay. What else. What about Hilda Alcantar's boy toys? Did you get anything there?" he asked, feeling much older than any twenty-five-year-old should.

Nino reopened the folder and pulled out an eight-by-ten of Hilda and a dark-haired companion at a local restaurant. "I looked into all of Alcantar's *friends*. They all turned up clean except for this guy—the one she spends the most time with." He pointed at her companion. "His name is Peter Navé. He's a financial advisor at Brooks & Darmen Investments. On the surface, he looks clean, but he may have some connections to Italy."

"What do you mean?" Damon asked, not liking the sound of this.

"I'm not sure yet, and I don't want to speculate. Not when it concerns Nikki."

"Good idea." Damon's heart sank. If this Navé guy was connected to shady players in Italy, then the shit that went down in Europe might not be over after all.

"Is there anything else?" he asked, his gut filling with dread.

Nino shook his head. "That's it. What are we going to do about Jake?"

"Nothing. Carlo doesn't want him or the younger brother dragged into his business; they're better off as they are. Besides, I'm sure Carlo knows where Jake is and all about the name change, anyway."

"Then if there's nothing else, I'm gonna head out. I've got the next shipment you arranged to prep, so I need to hit the road if I'm going to make it to Reno before dawn."

Damon waved him off. He looked down at the picture of Hilda and Peter Navé, his eyes narrowing to slits as Nino's suspicions echoed in his mind. If this Navé character was connected to the Mafia somehow—

Damon stopped himself. There was no reason to go there until he knew anything about this guy for sure. Still, he needed to talk to Nikki. He needed to know if she'd said anything to Hilda—just in case the Navé thing went south. He glanced at the clock above the door—it was after 11:00. She wouldn't be up, so tonight was out. He opened his calendar app to check her schedule. *Damn it.* She was leaving tomorrow for Lexington, Ohio, at the ass crack of dawn. Her cheap-ass loser manager never booked her on decent flights. They were always redeyes with thirty connections and no perks.

Fuck.

He'd have to wait and call her tomorrow night once she was settled. She'd never answer her phone before then—not when she'd been traveling all day and starting the prep work for the Mazda Pro Series Championship.

Damon leaned back in his chair and ran his hands over his weary face. It seemed like no matter what he did, he couldn't fulfill the promise he made to her father: that he'd keep her as far away from the Mafia as possible. Al Eleuteri knew, more than most, how dangerous the Mafia was, and he didn't want his children anywhere near it. Damon understood. If he'd had a choice, he wouldn't be involved in the life, either. But sometimes choices didn't matter. Sometimes life threw you straight into the fire no matter what you did.

13

Nikki shuffled out the bathroom and over to her bed then slid under the covers with a groan. The time change between the East and West Coasts, combined with grueling testing and qualifying sessions over the last three days and too many sleepless nights to count, had wiped her out. At this rate, she was going to turn into one of the walking dead—brain-sucking ghoul and all.

She closed her eyes with a heavy sigh, listening to the heater kick on. She meant to turn it off before getting into bed, but she wasn't about to get up and do it now. Jake would take care of it when he got back. He was still down in the garage with the car. He'd headed down there right after dinner to run a few more safety checks. It was odd. Jake was always careful—he was the most conscientious mechanic she'd met next to Sean—but he was taking his care of the car several notches higher at this race. She didn't know if it had to do with the championship or something else. He'd been edgy since they left Wood Glenn and overly concerned about the car, its braking system in particular.

Braking system...

Her eyes snapped open.

Oh God.

He must have seen the footage of the Le Mans accident. She knew he'd been reading up on her career; he'd been asking questions about the different types of racing she'd done over the years. He could have easily come across the video footage of the accident on YouTube. She'd watched it herself.

A chill snaked through her at the memory of the footage.

That had to be it. Jake must have seen the highlight reel showing the crash in all its glory, including the shot of the EMTs performing CPR on her lifeless body. No wonder he was so worried about the brakes. He feared there would be a repeat of Le Mans. But why worry about that? If he saw the video, surely he read the articles listed with it. If he did, he'd know that the cause of the crash was likely brake-fade—a Tiger problem and not one for her Mazda series car. It wasn't the theory she liked to go with—it made her look like she was to blame for the accident—but it was the most popular consensus with race officials. She frowned into the darkness. Jake's worry didn't make sense unless...unless he believed it was something else—something beyond her control that caused the brakes to fail. That could explain his concern.

Nikki yawned as her brain sorted through the different scenarios Jake might have thought of for the brake failure. She glanced at the clock on the nightstand—it was after 10:00, early for some but not for her during a race. She needed to put this out of her mind and get some sleep.

She was snuggling down when AC/DC's "Dirty Deeds" came blaring from the shelf next to the bed. She fisted her hands and swore.

Damon.

That was his ringtone. She poked her head out from under the covers and glared at the phone. He'd been blowing up her cell since she left for Ohio, and she'd made a point to ignore him. Honestly, why should she do *him* the courtesy of answering his calls if he couldn't do *her* the courtesy of dropping his surveillance team? That damn black Mercedes followed her wherever she went around town and had even tailed her to the airport a few days back. *Unbelievable.*

The phone stopped ringing. She let out a quiet sigh. Maybe he *finally* got it through his thick, stubborn skull that she wasn't going to answer.

"Dirty Deeds" flooded the room once more.

So much for getting the message.

Snarling like a hellcat on a tear, she threw off the covers and snatched the phone from the table. "What is it, Damon?"

"Why the fuck haven't you been answering your phone or returning my calls?" he demanded.

"Because I didn't *fucking* feel like it!"

"Because you didn't..." He broke off, swearing violently. "Jesus Christ, bella. I don't care if you don't *feel like it*. When I call, you answer or you call me back ASAP. It's as simple as that!"

"Oh, really?" she said, gripping the phone tighter at his high-handed attitude. Why he thought it would work on her was a mystery. It didn't when they were together, and it hadn't in the years since. And yet he *still* pulled this crap. All. The. Damn. Time.

"It's as *simple as that*, huh? Well, tell me, Damon, is it as simple as dropping the freaking surveillance team you've got on my ass?"

"What? You're still being followed?" he replied, his voice quiet.

She exhaled. "Don't play dumb. I'm not one of the *puttanas* you bring home on a Friday night. I know when you're bullshitting me."

Damon rolled off a string of curses in Italian that would have shocked Tony Soprano. "What kind of car is it?"

Nikki rolled her eyes at the ceiling. "It's a black Mercedes S-Class sedan, but I'm sure you already knew that."

He didn't respond to the dig. Instead, he came out of left field with "Have your memories come back? Any of them at all? Have you told anyone?"

"What? What the hell does that have to do with anything?"

"Per l'amor donna di Dio! Just for once, answer the questions! Have your memories come back, and if so, have you told anyone?" he repeated, his voice laced with anger and something else. Something she'd never heard in it before: distress.

She lurched up in bed, cold steel shooting down her spine. "Excuse me? Who do you think you are demanding *anything* of me after the way you've been acting? God, your high-handed ways know no end, and now you're paranoid on top of it. You need help, Damon. For real."

"I'm not *paranoid*. I'm trying to protect you, but you're making it *really* difficult—as usual," he snapped.

"*Protect* me?" *Not this again.* She dragged a hand through her hair, feeling a strange blend of dread and déjà vu slither through her even as she worked up a rant. "*Protect* me from what? From whom? And what in the world could it possibly have to do with my lost memories?"

"That's for me to worry about. All you need to do is answer my questions."

She balled her hands into fists. "If there is something going on that involves me needing protection, I have every right to know!" When he remained silent, she decided she'd had enough. "Forget it. I'm done. If you aren't going to tell me where this is coming from, then I'm not saying anything to you, either. Answering questions goes both ways, buddy. Until you're ready to tell me why you're so goddamn worried about me, we have nothing to say to each other." She ended the call before he could respond and blocked his number for good measure. She didn't have the time or the energy to deal with this. She had bigger things to worry about, like winning the Pro Mazda Championship tomorrow.

She set the phone back on the shelf and collapsed against her pillows, her mind reeling with questions despite her attempts to clear it. Something was obviously worrying Damon, and it somehow involved her and her lost memories. But what? Did he know something about the race and the weeks leading up to it that she didn't?

The memories from the trailer at Le Mans traipsed through her mind. She was so afraid in them. Did he know why? And if he did, why didn't he come clean? Why all the cloak-and-dagger bullshit?

Nikki rolled over onto her side with a growl. None of those questions were going to be answered tonight. She'd get her answers when she returned home or kill Damon in the process. Whatever was going on, she had a right to know...no matter how dangerous he thought it was for her.

~

"Nikki! Nikki, wake up!"

"*No!*" she shrilled, breaking free of the hands that gripped her and scrambling away. Before she could make her escape, a pair of arms wrapped themselves around her, pinning her in place.

"*Whoa!* Nikki! You're dreaming. Wake up, angel! Come on!"

Nikki's eyes flew open at the sound of the voice, deep and riddled with worry. Her eyes darted around the room. She wasn't running for her life or on the street, crouching behind a dumpster. She was in her RV, safe and sound.

She looked down at the arms wrapped around her and spotted familiar tattoos snaking along naturally tanned skin and muscle.

Jake.

She slumped back against him, panting as her racing heart crashed against her ribs.

"Are you okay?" Jake's deep voice rumbled in her ear, his breath dancing along her skin.

"Yeah. It was just a nightmare." She pressed a hand to her chest. It was damp with sweat.

He relaxed his grip and gently turned her to face him. When their eyes met, she saw the worry she heard in his voice reflected there. "That was no nightmare, angel—more like a night terror. The way you were thrashing about and screaming, I was afraid you were going to hurt yourself."

He was right. The nightmare was worse than ever. She took a deep, cleansing breath. This was Damon's fault. His call earlier that night had stirred fears, *irrational fears*, in her that had leached into her sleep, making her dreams more frightening—more lifelike than ever.

Damn him.

"It was pretty scary, but I'm okay." That wasn't exactly true. Fear and adrenaline still raced through her veins like a pair of champ cars, and her mind couldn't shake the terror.

Jake leaned back and arched a brow, knowing full well she was lying out of her ass. "Yeah, I don't buy it. You're pale and shaky, and I bet your heart's going a mile a minute." He ran a hand down her arm. It was a simple gesture, meant for comfort, but she felt it all the way to her toes. "Do you want to tell me about it?"

Her stomach took a nosedive, squelching the warmth his gesture brought. Tell him about the nightmare? No. That would mean having to relive it, and she didn't want to do that. Ever. Like ever and ever. The blood, the gore, and the sheer horror that burned through her like a wildfire as she ran were bad enough in dream form.

Nikki shook her head. "I can't...it's...I can't." She shuddered, hating how afraid she was.

He reached over and took her hand in his. "Okay. Totally understandable. How about some warm milk with honey, then? It would help you relax."

"That sounds great," she said, mustering a fragile smile.

Jake nodded. "Milk and honey coming right up."

She watched as he got up and headed out of the bedroom, thinking how lucky she was to have him there. If it had been Dino or Damon, they would have flipped out and made things worse.

But not Jake. He was a calm and steady presence, offering comfort and solutions not panic and irrational behavior like the other men in her life.

She ran a hand through her hair and found it damp. *Eww.* A shower was definitely in order before she climbed back into bed. She grabbed a new set of pajamas, flew into the bathroom, and rinsed off in a flash. When she emerged minutes later, Jake waited on the edge of the bed, mug in hand.

"Feel better?" he asked.

"Much," she said, taking the mug. "Mmm. That's good. Thank you."

Jake gave her the crooked smile she loved and got up from the bed. "I'll let you get some rest. You've got a race to win tomorrow."

"Okay. Thanks again, for the milk and...for pulling me out of that nightmare. You're like my own personal hero." She wanted to smack herself as soon as the words left her mouth.

Personal hero? Ugh. Lame.

"Anytime, angel," he said, his cheeks tinting with a hint of pink.

He left then, turning off the light and closing the door behind him. Nikki clutched the mug in both hands as she sipped the drink, feeling very small and very alone in the dark room with only her panicked thoughts and deep-seated fears as companions. Shaking, she set the mug on the shelf next to her phone and gathered herself into a ball, feeling ridiculous. She had nothing to fear. It was a nightmare, and now it was over.

Her conversation with Damon echoed in her head, followed by her memories and the brutal nightmare. She clutched her knees to her chest even tighter, the fear that she was somehow in real trouble mounting with every second.

"You're fine...everything is fine. There's nothing to worry about. This is just Damon's stupid paranoia spilling over onto you," she chanted to herself over and over again, rocking back and forth in an attempt at comfort.

It didn't work.

The terror continued to build. Every noise, every shadow was some-thing or someone out to hurt her. A loud *thud* sounded outside her window. The threads of her courage snapped. Without thinking, she leapt off the bed and went running out into the RV, straight for Jake's bunk at the opposite end.

He must have heard her because the curtain tore open before she reached the bunk. "Nikki? What's wrong? Did you have another nightmare?"

"No...I just...I can't shake the...fear. I know it's stupid. I'm an adult, for Chrissake, but I'm so scared. I..." She trailed off, feeling the blush from Hell brand her cheeks.

He reached out and took her hand, entwining her fingers with his. "Hey, it's okay. You don't have to explain. I get it. What can I do?"

She looked down at their entwined hands and felt her heart stumble. "Um...well...I know this is going to sound all kinds of weird, and you'll probably say no because it's totally awkward and we're just friends, but... would you...stay with me? I...I don't want to be alone," she said, the words coming out in a vicious case of verbal diarrhea that continued on in her head after she finished.

How could she ask him that? Idiot! He was totally going to say no. How could he not? How awkward, how *uncomfortable*, would it be for him to share a bed with her? Probably pretty awkward considering they were only friends. And friends of the male-female variety did *not* share beds. Ever.

But Jake didn't do either of those things. He didn't even hesitate when he said, "Sure, angel," silencing the rambling fool in her mind.

Her head snapped up. "Really?"

He squeezed her hand. "*Really.* I'm here if you need me. All you have to do is ask."

She blinked at him, speechless. He meant it. She saw it in his eyes and heard it in his voice. He was there for her, and somehow, she knew he always would be.

Jake gave her a boyish grin as he slid out of his bunk and led her back to her bedroom, not once letting go of her hand until he climbed in behind her.

Once she was settled, he clicked off the light and lay back.

Nikki pulled the covers up to her chin, feeling the shadows and her fears close in around her, even with Jake there. A shudder rolled through her, followed immediately by another.

What was wrong with her? Why couldn't she shake this crap?

"Hey," Jake whispered, reaching over and searching for her hand. When he found it, he took it in his, lacing their fingers together. "It's okay to be scared, but try to relax. I'm here. Nothing is going to hurt you as long as I'm around," he said, spookily responding to her unspoken thoughts.

Her heart rate slowed some at the calm reassurance in his voice. "Do you have nightmare-fighting superpowers I don't know about?" she asked, liking the feel of her hand entwined with his.

"I do. It's one of my many talents," he deadpanned. "Get some sleep. You have a race to win tomorrow. Remember?"

"Okay," she said, closing her eyes. "And Jake?"

"Hmm?"

"Thank you, again. For everything."

"Always, angel. Always."

She squeezed his hand, grateful beyond measure, not just for having him there but also for having him in her life.

14

The distant sounds of engines firing and crews stirring roused Nikki from the deepest sleep she could remember. She didn't want to move, didn't want to think about getting up. All she wanted was to roll over and snuggle down into the bed until her alarm sounded. She shifted, intending to do that, but stopped when she realized that snuggling down into the bed wasn't possible. Not in her position. Not when she wasn't technically *on* the bed.

Oh no. Not again...

Half her body was draped over Jake's chest—a chest she'd admired many times from afar—with no room to spare. There wasn't a centimeter of space between where their bodies met. Even their legs were a tangled mess between the sheets.

Her breath stalled in her chest, while her heart continued to pound out a staccato beat. Waking up with him like this—a tangled mass of arms, legs, and flesh—was how she'd imagined, and had read in countless romance novels, lovers woke.

Lovers.

An unholy blush stained her cheeks that had nothing to do with embarrassment. She and Jake were entwined together like lovers, and she liked it. She liked the feeling of his smooth, firm skin pressed against her, the way his legs tangled with hers, the way his arm wrapped around her waist, pinning her to him. It was comforting and altogether hot.

She released the breath she'd been holding.

Jake shifted slightly, pushing one of his legs farther between hers. A shiver danced across her heated skin as his hand slid from her waist to her hip, gripping her in a possessive gesture. A wave of lust rushed her, and she had to bite down on her lip to stifle the groan she felt clawing at her throat.

She inched her chin upward, stopping when her eyes reached his face. He was in a deep sleep. *Thank God.* Waking up like this a second time would be beyond awkward. But instead of extricating herself right away, she stayed there, deciding to take the opportunity to look at him. The idea immediately sounded creepy in her head, but she didn't move. She was transfixed by what she saw: as he lay there, asleep like this, his face bore the look of a man completely at peace. It was an expression she'd never seen on Jake before. Gone was the quiet intensity that always chased away all possibility of peace.

Nikki swallowed audibly as her eyes continued to rove over his face, her fingers itching to trace the lines of his shadowed jaw and firm lips. An ache formed deep in her core and spread across her body, embedding itself in certain places more than others. She imagined what it would feel like to kiss those lips, to run her hands and tongue over his chest and abs, to feel what it was like to be close to him in that way, to be intimate.

She slammed her eyes shut as a wave of languid heat washed over her already-flushed skin. This was wrong. Bad...so, so bad because it wasn't fair. Nothing was going to happen between them no matter how drawn to him she felt or how hot he made her.

Why not? whispered a nagging voice.

Nikki opened her eyes and let them settle over Jake once more, knowing the answer to that question: fear. She was afraid of getting her heart broken again. But did she really have to fear that from *him*?

The events of last night came back to her in answer: the way he held her after she'd woken from the nightmare; the reassurance he offered her when he saw how frightened she was; the way he agreed without hesitation or question to stay with her and reminded her that fear was natural and not something to be ashamed of. He'd been exactly what she needed last night: a steady force there to support her, to help her, to stand by her as a partner. No other man since her father had done that. Damon, her brothers, and other men she'd dated always tried to take control and fix things *for* her. Jake would never do that. He wasn't like them.

Shame slithered through her, squelching some of the lust. She didn't shy away from things out of fear. She faced her fears head on. And it was time to do that again—time to shove this useless angst aside and go after what she wanted, regardless of the risk. But not *this* instant. She'd do it later when she wasn't sprawled across him or watching him sleep like a creeper.

Nikki let her eyes rove over his sculpted body once more before she untangled her limbs from his. Slowly, so she didn't wake him, she turned onto her back, easing her legs out from his. After what felt like hours, she was nearly free when Jake shifted and rolled over, pinning her to the mattress. Scorched air escaped her lungs as his face nuzzled the crook of her neck and his hand drifted across her midsection, slipping under the tank where it had ridden up during the night. She bit down on her lip when that hand slid over her flushed skin, his fingers brushing against the flesh below her breasts.

Sweet mother of...

Her pulse shot into cardiac territory when his body moved again and he slid his leg between hers, pressing up against the very center of her, mumbling something about an angel and not letting her slip away.

She gasped as a jolt of pleasure shot through her, pinging off every nerve ending.

Jake stilled. She froze. Somewhere out in the paddock, a dog barked.

Slowly, he rose up on his elbow, his hand still pressed to her ribs. Eyes like liquid pools of obsidian gazed at her, confused. "Nikki? What...?" His stare fell to where his hand lodged under her tank top. All confusion fled in an instant.

Dragging in a deep breath, he yanked his hand away and rose up on his powerful arms, hovering over her. "Shit. Oh shit. I am so sorry. I-I don't know what happened. I..." he stammered, his cheeks flushing crimson.

Her heart flipped over in her chest at the sight of him: a riot of conflicting emotions and desires battling against each other. She knew the battle well, and she was done fighting.

Nikki grabbed his arms, loving the way the smooth skin stretched over corded muscle felt beneath her fingers. Swallowing around the sudden dryness in her throat, she shoved any lingering fear or apprehension out of her head and heart and acted.

"Don't be sorry," she whispered in a breathy voice she didn't recognize, sliding her hands up to his biceps. "I'm not." It wasn't exactly how she imagined telling Jake how she felt about him, but sometimes things didn't go as imagined.

Heat flared in Jake's eyes as they widened. "You're not?"

She shook her head and moved her hands to his neck, threading her fingers through the ebony waves at the nape. "No," she said, rising up and doing what she'd wanted to do for weeks.

She brushed her lips over his in a featherlight motion, her heart soaring at the contact. They were as firm as she'd believed and yet soft at the same time. After lingering there, she pulled back, gazing up at the expression of shock and confusion in Jake's eyes as he stared down at her. That confusion faded when what she'd said and done fully registered. She watched in awe as his expression shifted, reflecting the feelings and desires now racing through her veins.

She bit down on her lip. He wanted her just as much as she wanted him.

Jake's eyes flared. A half growl, half moan sounded from deep in his throat, and then in a flash, he was on her. His lips moved over hers once, twice, three times, studying their layout as if he were committing it to memory. Lowering himself down, he pressed his lips to hers a fourth time and ran his tongue over the seam—a gentle inquiry so at odds with the passion she could feel radiating from him like heat from the sun. She felt a shudder roll through him as her lips parted in answer and their tongues met for the first time, falling into an intimate dance. A throaty moan rose from deep within her when he pulled back to suck and nibble on her lower lip.

Jake released her lip, his voice like molten chocolate as he spoke. "I like that sound, angel. No. Scratch that. I fucking love that sound."

Nikki looked up at him through hooded eyes. "Then make me do it again," she said, shocking herself at her boldness.

She'd dated and been in two relationships, but Nikki had never been bold like this before. But Jake differed from the other men she'd known. He wasn't trying to control the moment as they had. He was right there *with* her, alongside her, as they surrendered to and explored the passion between them. It made her feel sexy and daring in a way she never had before. And she liked it. A lot.

His lips quirked up into that crooked smile of his. "As you wish."

Her heart skipped a beat at the *Princess Bride* reference, eliciting another groan from her as she imagined him as Westley's character doing her every bidding.

Jake followed through with his promise, but this time when he kissed her it was bolder, fiercer than before, with an intensity she hadn't expected. Suddenly, what was happening became so much more than kissing.

With his free hand, Jake began to explore her body, running it across the bare skin of her legs, over her hip and up her side, stilling just beneath her breasts, waiting. Her heart swelled with emotion at the care he demonstrated, while the blood in her veins ignited in anticipation. Arching her back with another throaty sound, she gave him her answer. Jake groaned, a rich and decadent noise, as he moved his hand up, his fingers drifting over her breast, his thumb unerringly finding the sensitive tip.

A wave of pleasure darted through her as he teased the area covered only by a thin scrap of cotton. She thrust her head back against the pillow with a gasp, but Jake followed, his mouth nipping and kissing her lips then the delicate skin beneath her jaw and down her neck. Nikki ran her hands through his hair and across his shoulders, digging her fingertips into his flesh when she felt him pull the strap of her tank top down and run his tongue over the swell of her breast.

She couldn't believe what was happening. This was *not* how she'd envisioned her morning, let alone their first kiss, but she wasn't complaining. She could totally get behind waking up like this every day. She let out another cry when her tank slid lower and she felt Jake take a nipple into his mouth, scrambling her senses.

She clutched him to her as he tugged the tank down farther, moving from one breast to the other, feasting on them like a starving man at a banquet.

He lifted his head, his eyes riveted to her bare breasts as she panted, begging him not to stop. "So beautiful..." he murmured, lowering his head once more.

Nikki could feel the tension coiling tight in her core, building higher and higher, until she felt like she was going to explode. She was on the verge of her first non-self-induced orgasm in years when her alarm went off like a bomb, obliterating the moment.

They both froze. A second later, Jake's alarm sounded from his bunk.

Jake lifted his head and reached over to shut off the alarm, burying his head in the valley between her breasts afterward, groaning.

"*Fuucckkk.*"

Nikki ran her hands through his thick waves, loving their silky texture. "I guess we aren't going to get to that." She giggled, shocked at the ease she felt lying there, half naked in his arms.

Jake chuckled against her breasts then lifted his head. "I guess not." He sighed, his eyes dropping down, drifting over her bare chest and back up again. When his eyes met hers the second time, she could feel the heat reflected there. "To be continued, then? A victory celebration?" he said, pulling his lower lip between his teeth.

"Absolutely."

He studied her for another lingering minute before leaning down and placing kisses to her forehead, nose, and then a tender one to her lips. When he rose up this time, he pulled her with him, straightening her tank, then helped her off the bed. He leaned down and kissed her once more before turning and heading out to his bunk to get changed.

A million thoughts whirled through her head as she watched him leave, but she silenced them all, save one: *Don't overthink it. Live and enjoy the present.* And that was exactly what she planned to do. For the first time in her life, she wasn't going to worry about *what might happen* down the road. She was going to live and enjoy the now with Jake.

~

JAKE PULLED THE BEDROOM DOOR CLOSED BEHIND HIM AND SLUMPED AGAINST it, his mind and body rioting against each other.

What the fuck happened? What was he thinking?

You weren't. That's the problem, his subconscious scolded.

And God, if that wasn't the truth. It seemed like wherever Nikki was concerned, Jake was incapable of rational thought. If he were, he would have said no when she asked him to stay with her, or when she'd kissed him, he wouldn't have kissed her back. He would have politely pulled away and hoped it didn't ruin their friendship.

But neither of those things happened. The moment he saw the fear in her eyes last night, he couldn't say no when she asked him to stay with her. He wanted her to feel safe, and if he could help her do that, he would. And this morning, when he tried to leave the bed and she stopped him, telling him with her breathy voice and body that she wanted him, he again couldn't refuse. His control simply didn't exist with her.

He was so screwed.

Cursing his weakness and the dull ache forming in his groin, Jake headed over to the refrigerator for a bottle of the special, hydrating water Nikki always drank. He needed it. His body felt like scorched earth.

He pulled a bottle from the shelf and quaffed half of it in one gulp, his eyes straying to the bedroom door, the last words he'd said to her echoing in his head: "To be continued, then? A victory celebration?" Shit. Why did he say that? That wasn't going to happen. Not today, not ever.

Why not? She cares for you...wants you. Live in the present, whispered the nagging voice he found himself trying to block more and more these days.

Jake leaned on the counter, running his hands through his hair. The voice had a point—about Nikki, anyway. She wanted him just as much as he wanted her. And he knew she cared, cared more for him than anyone outside his small, immediate circle had in years.

He gazed out across the RV as his conscience warred with his desires yet again. His conscience was winning when an idea occurred to him: once she and Jack signed the papers for the Greendale offer, she'd be back in professional racing next season where she belonged. And once that happened, they would go their separate ways, as they were meant to do.

But maybe he could have her *for now*—in the present, like that damn voice kept saying. It was obvious she wanted him, needed him in ways that went beyond friendship. So, shouldn't he give her what she needed?

No matter what it was? Wasn't that why he was here—to help her like she'd helped him in the past?

Jake pushed off the cool granite counter, decision made. He would be whatever Nikki Elliot needed him to be: friend, mechanic, protector, lover. And when she left to hit the professional circuit, she would see that continuing something with him wouldn't work. She'd see that she needed someone else—a man worthy of and deserving of a woman like her—and move on.

Anger, hot and sharp, shot through him at the thought of her being with another man, but he tamped it down. Having anything with Nikki long-term wasn't in the cards for Jake. He knew that. Just like he knew that no matter how much it shredded him when it happened, he would let her go when the time came because he loved her and wanted only the best things in life for his angel…and he wasn't one of them.

15

"Has anyone seen Nikki?" an unfamiliar voice called into the pit stall where Jake and the rest of the crew were finishing up the final safety inspection on Nikki's car.

Jake looked up from the lug nuts he was triple-checking on the rear wheel. "Who's asking?" he asked, eyeing the stranger, who was dressed in a suit that looked like it cost more than Jake made in a month.

He bristled immediately.

With his dark hair slicked back, just beginning to gray at the temples, and dark sunglasses that were of equal expense to the suit, the stranger looked like he belonged on Wall Street, not in a pit stall at the Mid-Ohio Sports Car Course. Professional appearance aside, Jake disliked the man immediately. Maybe because he fidgeted with the gold ring on his pinky or because he looked down his nose at him and the rest of the crew. Whatever it was, Jake didn't like the idea of this guy looking for Nikki. Not at all.

The stranger stepped into the stall and pulled off his glasses, revealing a pair of dark, deep-set eyes that narrowed as they roved over Jake's exposed tattoos. "Yeah, you can tell her—"

"Jack! What are you doing here today?" Nick chirped, striding into the stall with his laptop in hand.

Jack?

This was Jack? The manager allegedly screwing Nikki out of sponsors? Jake's hackles shot up. No wondered he got a bad vibe from him.

Jack turned to Nick and extended a hand. "It's the championship. I wouldn't miss this. Our girl's going to win out there today. Isn't she?" he said, shaking Nick's hand.

"I don't doubt it. She's headed straight for Indy and upward from there." Nick glanced over at Jake. "Have you met our lead mechanic, Jake Masercotti?" He turned to Jake. "Jake, this is Jack Romano, Nikki's manager," he said, firing Jake a knowing look.

Jake studied him before extending his hand.

"Nice to meet you, Jake. Is the car all set?" Jack asked, flashing a set of blindingly white teeth and a smile that didn't reach his eyes.

Jake nodded. "It is. Safe, sound, and ready to win."

"Excellent." Jack turned back to Nick. "So, where is she? I wanted to talk with her about some sponsorship issues."

Nick fired Jake a glance and said, "She's in a drivers' meeting, but it should be wrapping up shortly. What kind of sponsorship issues? Good news, I hope? I wouldn't want her to get any bad news right before she hits the track."

Jack cleared his throat, adjusting the blue silk tie knotted at his throat. "It's not *bad news*, per se. I've been going over the offer she received from Greendale Sunglasses. Apparently they didn't think going through the proper channels to make an offer was necessary," he said, his expression smug. "I warned her that their offer wouldn't be good when she told me about it—they usually aren't when vendors refuse to go through the manager—but I looked over the contract and into the company anyway and found I was right. The money's almost nonexistent, and the company itself is highly unstable right now, so I told them we were passing on it. I wanted to let her know. It won't bother her, I'm sure. She's a tough cookie."

Jake's stomach dropped. Jack passed on the Greendale offer? He couldn't believe it. Nikki had showed Jake the paperwork: it was an amazing deal that would have solidified her career in professional racing. How could Jack do that to her? Or himself? As her manager, he stood to gain a lot from the deal.

"Greendale Sunglasses? Those guys are huge. Why would you think the company is unstable?" Nick asked, setting the laptop down on one of the tables near the monitors.

The muscles in Jack's neck visibly tensed. "I'm the money guy, remember? It's my job to know these things, like it's your job to know the racing things. So, let me worry about all of that," he said, flashing another smile, this one predatory.

Nick raised his hands in front of him. "You're right. Speaking of which, we need to get to work here. Should I tell Nikki you're looking for her when she comes back from the meeting?"

Jack shook his head. "I'll find her before that. Which way is the meeting?"

Nick gestured to the right of the pit stall. "Take a right out of the stall and head toward the front of the track," he said, pointing Jack in the opposite direction of the meeting's location.

"Great. I'll see you all after the race. I'm going to watch it in the press booth. They've got a well-stocked bar up there." He headed out of the stall.

Nick looked over at Jake. "Go meet Nikki at the drivers' meeting and get her back here quickly. I don't want her running into Jack. She's good about compartmentalizing stuff when she's racing, but I still don't want her going into it with this news. That sponsorship with Greendale would have fast-tracked her to Formula 1. I'm sure of it. And now he's ruined it, just like the others," he spat.

Jake set the torque wrench in the tool chest. "I know. She showed me the offer. It was the deal of a lifetime, Nick. Jack's wrong about this. Greendale's brand is everywhere," he said, the acid in his gut bubbling at the thought of Jack hurting Nikki's career.

Nick nodded, his expression lethal. "I'm going to make some calls and see if I can't find out what happened. Maybe this time someone will talk and I'll get the proof I need to get this guy out of her life once and for all."

"Let me know if there's anything I can do," Jake said, heading out to find Nikki at the drivers' meeting.

Jake jogged to the opposite end of the paddock, slowing when he spotted her outside the drivers' tent, speaking animatedly with a group of drivers. He came to a stop several yards away, watching her laugh and joke. She looked radiant, standing there in her racing suit, her golden hair pulled back into the standard-issue braid she wore for racing, smiling at the drivers gathered around her and talking about the upcoming race. Seeing her so happy and full of light made him want to murder Jack Romano. This news would crush her.

Nikki laughed at something Javier Santos said, gripping his arm as she did. Jealousy Jake had no right to rushed through him at the sight. Or did he have the right? After what happened earlier that morning, he very well could. He shook his head. What did she see in him that she didn't see in the guys with her now? Why would she take an interest in someone like Jake and not any of them? They had so much more to offer than he did, and yet it was him she wanted next to her when she was afraid and him she wanted in her bed when she wasn't.

A heavy hand clapped Jake on the back, yanking him from the maudlin thoughts whirling in his head. "She's a wonder, isn't she?" Nigel Ingleside said, appearing next to him.

He tore his gaze from Nikki and met Nigel's eagle-eyed stare. "She is. She's an amazing driver."

Nigel folded his arms across his chest, his eyes darting from Jake to Nikki and back. "You're right—well, half right, anyway."

Jake arched a brow. "Half right?"

"Yeah, half right," he said, his Australian accent gaining strength. "She's also an amazing girl, err, woman. She's been through the wringer, but she never gives up, never loses that optimism and drive. *That* makes her amazing in my book."

Jake's stomach twisted when he thought of how true that was and how much she was still struggling thanks to her louse of a manager. "Mine too, Nigel. Mine too."

Nigel laughed. "I know. I can see it all over your face right now, and I've been seeing it since you started. We all have." Jake started to deny it, but Nigel cut him off. "Don't bother, mate. We know you're a goner for her, and by the looks I've seen her stealing in your direction, she's got it just as bad. A word to the wise, though." He leaned in close.

"Shoot," Jake said, his shoulders tense. How the hell did Nigel or anyone else know how he felt about Nikki? Was he really that obvious?

"Stand by her, but don't stand in her way. Nikki's going to be a world champion one day, and I'd hate to see anyone get in the way of that, even if they didn't mean to," he warned.

Message received, Nigel. Unnecessary but received.

Jake nodded. "Don't worry. I have no intention of getting in her way."

Nigel patted Jake on the shoulder. "Good man. See you out there," he said then trotted off toward the pit stalls.

Jake pushed off the post he'd been leaning against and headed over to Nikki, who was still talking with Javier Santos, Riley Brock, and Daniel Brogan. They all looked vibrant and ready to hit the track—all but Daniel. He appeared withdrawn, pale, even, and wouldn't make eye contact with Nikki even when she patted him on the shoulder and spoke directly to him.

"You okay, Daniel?" Jake heard her ask as he walked up.

Daniel looked everywhere but at her. "Yeah, I'm fine. Ready to get out there," he said, his voice forced.

Nikki gave him a concerned look but shrugged it off, turned, and smiled when she caught sight of Jake. "Hey. What's up?"

"I thought I'd walk you back to the paddock so we can go over the safety inspection," he lied smoothly.

"Oh, okay." She turned to the others. "I'll see you after the race. Good luck out there, guys."

The other drivers wished her the same, all but Daniel, who bolted like a sprinter.

Jake looked down at Nikki as they headed back, the top of her head reaching his shoulder. "Is everything okay with Daniel? He seemed off."

Nikki turned her sea-glass eyes up to his. "He did, didn't he? He was quiet during the drivers' meeting too. It's not like him. Daniel's the comedian of the series, always joking around. It's strange."

"Maybe he's not feeling well," Jake offered, placing a hand at the small of her back to guide her around tubs of bottled water, swearing he could feel the heat from her skin even through the layers of fire retardant gear.

She inhaled sharply at his touch, but she didn't shy away. She moved closer.

"That's probably it." She nodded. "So, how was the safety inspection? Anything I should be aware of?"

He shook his head, his hand anchored to the small of her back. "Everything looks good. I think we've got the wing and front bar adjusted to your specs, but make sure you radio right away if you notice any problems," he said, confident that the car was ready for her.

"I will. Don't worry." She leaned into him.

Jake slid his hand to her waist and pulled her back into him when she started to move away. "I don't worry about you out there, not really. I know you've got this."

They stopped in front of the pit stall. Nikki pulled away but not before grabbing hold of Jake's hand and squeezing it.

"Thanks, Jake."

He watched her approach Will and Nick to review the strategy for the day and go over any final points before the race. Jake kept his distance, giving them their space, deciding to head out of the stall and take some photos of the track and other crews. He had just snapped a shot of the Shaughnessy Irish Whiskey crew as they lowered the body back onto Daniel Brogan's car when he heard shouting erupt from the back of the stall. Jake looked up from the phone and saw Daniel and his crew chief, John O'Malley, going toe-to-toe.

"I don't care what you want!" O'Malley snarled in Daniel's face. "You'll get out there and do as you're told. Do I make myself clear?"

Daniel glared at O'Malley before he nodded and pushed past him, storming out of the stall.

Weird, Jake thought. *What's Daniel's problem today? Doesn't he want to race?*

He turned, shrugging off the strange scene, and continued to snap photos until he got a text from Nick saying it was time to get the car out on grid. He returned to the pit stall a few minutes later and found Jack there, huddled in a corner with Nikki. Anger took root in his gut and spread when he saw the confused, almost defeated look on Nikki's face. Jack was no doubt telling her all about the situation with Greendale Sunglasses.

What the fuck was his problem? Couldn't he have waited until after the goddamn race to tell her?

Nikki glanced over when Jake stepped into the stall and rounded the car to help the crew roll it out to grid. She flashed him a quick smile before turning back to Jack, nodding vehemently at something he said.

Once the car was on grid, Jake jogged back to the stall to grab Nikki's helmet and HANS device. She stood in front of the shelves where they stored her helmet, gloves, and other gear, her gaze distant as she gnawed on her thumbnail.

"Everything okay?" Jake asked, coming up behind her.

"What?" She gasped, spinning around, one hand pressed to her throat.

"Sorry. I didn't mean to scare you."

She huffed out a breath. "No, it was my fault. I was just...thinking and got lost in my thoughts."

"What got you so lost?" he asked, placing a hand on her arm.

"Nothing...nothing new, anyway. Jack told me the Greendale offer was no good." She looked out the stall doors to pit lane, which was bustling with people, her face scrunched up in confusion. "I thought for sure the offer was good, especially with the Indy team already lined up. According to Jack, though, none of that was true. But—" She broke off, shaking her head.

"But what, angel?" he urged, his calm voice at odds with the rage building inside him.

She turned to him, confusion and doubt flowing over her face like water. "But I don't understand why Greendale would lie. Why make me an offer they weren't going to back up? If that kind of thing got out, it could keep them from signing other athletes. It doesn't make any sense. And it makes me wonder if..." She stopped again, worrying her bottom lip.

Jake reached up and tugged her chin, freeing her lip from between her teeth. "Don't do that. You're going to hurt it, and that would be a travesty," he said, his voice dropping several octaves. "Finish the thought. What are you wondering?"

Nikki glanced out at pit lane and back and leaned in close, her voice a strained whisper. "It makes me wonder if something is going on with Jack. He's been different since Le Mans and even more so lately, acting distant, distracted. I'm starting to think maybe my brother got to him. He and Dino were close. What if Dino's convinced him I shouldn't be racing, and he agrees?"

"How close are they?" he asked, thinking this could be a plausible scenario. Most of the men in her immediate circle had control issues. If Jack was like them, it could explain why he was sabotaging things.

"Extremely, especially since the accident."

"And you really think Jack would listen to him about this?"

"He might, yes. Like I said, Jack's been off ever since the accident. Before Le Mans, he was aggressive about bringing in sponsorship dollars and offers from racing teams. But since then, he's cooled off. I mean, he's been there for me and helped me get back in this far, but that's where it's stopped," she said.

It looked like Nick had been wrong when he assumed Nikki was blind to Jack. She had her suspicions but didn't voice them because she wasn't sure and because doing so would hurt. He imagined it had been awful when her brothers turned on her, and now, to have a man she looked at like an uncle to do it too? That had to burn in the worst way. It sickened him to see her going through this and not be able to do a damn thing about it.

Or could he?

Jake was about to mention the conversation he had with Nick when the announcer called for drivers to their cars. "We'll talk about this later." He took her face in his hands and peered down into her eyes. "For now, concentrate on driving hard and taking the win. Don't worry about anything else."

She nodded, the confusion and doubt vanishing and determination and focus taking their place. Jake marveled at the immediate shift, wishing he could tuck his worries and anger away that easily.

"Okay...but there is one more thing I need before we go out there."

He arched a brow. "What's that?"

"This." She leaned in and pressed a kiss to his lips.

His body tightened at the feel of her exquisite lips pressed to his, and before she could slip away, he closed the remaining distance between them and deepened the kiss until they broke apart, breathless.

"Wow," Nikki breathed.

"Yeah." Jake nodded and reached around to grab her gear, willing his heart to slow down. "We'd better get out there before Nick and Will come looking for you." *Or I end up pinning you to that shelf and finishing what we started earlier.*

Nikki smiled, her cheeks flushed. "Right." She grabbed her gloves and headed out. "Let's go."

He exhaled sharply as he watched her saunter out of the garage ahead of him, still shocked by the idea that she wanted him as much as he wanted her, and at how good it felt.

~

JAKE LEANED OUT OVER THE EDGE OF THE PEDESTRIAN BRIDGE THAT SPANNED the finish line, angling the camera to get a shot of Nikki coming over Thunder Valley, the incline that led to the Carousel and the front straight. He wanted a shot of her hitting the Carousel with Javier Santos and Daniel Brogan hot on her tail before she shook them. It would make a great action shot, especially with the way Brogan was driving. He'd been more aggressive today than he had all season, which was even more surprising considering his earlier behavior. Brogan had looked almost scared when Jake saw him with Nikki and later in the stall with his team. But you wouldn't know that now. He was practically riding bitch on Santos, chomping at the bit to pass him.

Jake snapped a dozen pics of the trio battling it out and watched when Brogan finally got his shot and slipped around Santos's car coming out of turn thirteen. The cars screamed as they tore out of the turn and thundered beneath the footbridge and out onto the course, headed for turn one, followed by one of the fastest portions of the track: the front straight. Nikki soared ahead, putting some distance between her and Brogan's car coming out of turn two, but he caught up to her at China Beach, just outside of the Esses.

"Careful, Nik. He's comin' up fast on your eight o'clock. Don't let him get around you, but don't put yourself in the sand, either," Nick warned, his voice crackling over the radio.

Nikki chuckled. "I won't hit the beach today, Nick. Don't worry. I see Brogan. He's coming up too fast for this turn, though. If he doesn't watch it, he's going to—" She broke off as Brogan hit her rear end coming into turn six, breaking the back end of Nikki's car loose.

Jake grabbed the chain-link fencing that ran along the footbridge, the blood roaring in his ears.

"Jesus! Are you all right?" Nick demanded into the radio.

"I'm fine. I've got it, but—"

Brogan swerved sharply left and back to the right, colliding with her rear wheel in what looked like an intentional move. Nikki screamed something unintelligible over the radio as the car flipped up and over Brogan's and crashed into the cement wall in front of the east grandstands.

No!

Jake took off across the footbridge and leaped from the staircase onto the infield. Radio transmissions continued to come from Nick's end on pit lane, but Nikki's was silent. With his eyes locked on her car, Jake charged across the infield, praying to God and anyone else listening that she was alive.

~

NIKKI'S HEAD FELT LIKE IT WAS STUFFED FULL OF COTTON WOOL AND WEIGHED a thousand pounds. She pried open her eyes and spotted the steering wheel of her Mazda series car. What happened? Why did she feel like she'd been asleep?

Her head drooped, and she felt her chin brush her chest. Exhaustion dogged her. If only she could take a nap. That would clear her—

The sound of her name, carried on the wind from a panicked voice, jolted her.

"*Nikki!* Hang on, angel! I'm coming!"

Jake.

Why did he sound so worried?

Clarity struck her like a bolt of lightning: the championship, Brogan hitting her car not once, but twice, the wreck.

Oh shit.

She blinked away the confusion and looked up in time to see Jake leaning over her and pulling off the helmet and HANS device.

"Thank God. Thank God, you're all right," he said, his hands and voice shaking while he worked to free her of the harnesses.

"It's okay, Jake. Slow down. I'm okay," she said, grabbing his hands, stilling their frantic attempt to release her.

He looked up from where her hands covered his, his face sick with worry. "Are you sure? That accident—"

He didn't get to finish the thought. A pair of hands pulled him back. "Don't even think about it, kid. We'll get her out of there," an angry voice barked.

Jake started to argue but stopped when Nikki called out to him. "Jake, stop! They're here to help. Let the guys do their jobs."

"Right. Okay...sorry," she heard him say from somewhere behind her.

The EMTs got her out of the car and loaded her onto a spinal board and into an ambulance with startling speed. Jake was beside her the entire time, holding her hand as the ambulance sped toward the medical center at the track, his face a study in helplessness and fear.

"Hey," she whispered as medics took her vitals. "I'm okay. Don't worry. This is just a precaution."

Jake squeezed her hand. "I know...I know, but...it's a lot."

She nodded. "I get it. I'm sorry," she whispered, wishing he hadn't seen her wreck.

Once they reached the medical center in the heart of the park, things became a blur of doctors, nurses, and Will, Nick, and Jack all demanding answers. After a preliminary examination showed no signs of a concussion

—thank God—and that nothing else was broken, she was told the ambulance would be taking her to the local hospital for a CT scan and possibly an MRI to make sure she didn't have any internal injuries.

"Someone will need to get her something to change into before she heads out," one of the nurses said.

Nikki looked at Jake. "Do you mind grabbing me some clothes from the RV?" she asked.

Jake's brows lowered. "I'm not leaving your side, angel," he said in a voice that brooked no argument.

"I'll go," Will offered, grinning at Jake's hand wrapped firmly around hers. "I've got the keys. I'll grab something and be back in a flash."

Nikki smiled at Will in thanks.

"It looks like you're in good hands," Jack said, coming over and kissing her forehead. "I'll head out and call you tomorrow to check in."

"Thanks, Jack," she said, watching him go.

Nick came over to the other side of the bed, his face grim.

"What is it, Nick? Is it the car? Is it totaled?" she asked, dread creeping in.

Nick shook his head. "I don't know. I haven't spoken to the crew. Will and I wanted to make sure you were okay first."

"Well, I'm fine. So, what's got that scowl on your face?"

"It's Brogan," Nick began.

"What about him?" Jake said, his calm voice laced with barely controlled rage. Nikki squeezed his hand tighter.

"He meant to hit her. I'm sure of it. The move was too calculated."

Jake shot up out of his chair, dropping Nikki's hand. "Are you sure?"

Nikki sat straight up. "Whoa! Stop. Nick, you can't be serious."

He turned to her, pulling his phone out of his pocket. "I'm afraid so, sweetheart. Look." He opened a video file and pressed play. Nikki stared at the screen in horror as she watched Brogan rear-end her then come up alongside her and collide with her rear wheel. Nick was right. The collision looked intentional.

When the video ended, she looked up at Nick with wide, teary eyes. "Why? Why would he do that? Just to win?"

Nick started to answer when shouts erupted from the waiting area. "I need to see her, damn it! Let me through!" Daniel Brogan's voice demanded.

A split second later, he came bursting into the room, his crew chief right behind him, trying to pull him away. "Nikki! I'm so sorry. I—"

"Shut up, Daniel!" O'Malley ordered, pulling a frantic Daniel back.

But Daniel was strong. He broke free and shoved O'Malley backward into a supply cart. "I'm so sorry. I didn't want to do it. I had no choice. Please believe me!" he begged, his eyes wild.

Chaos erupted before Nikki could process what he'd said, let alone respond. Jake snarled something unintelligible as he leaped for Daniel and knocked him into an EKG machine and to the floor, his fists flying.

"Jake, no!" she screamed then jumped off the bed and darted over to where he was beating Daniel into an early grave.

Nick pulled her out of the way before she reached them then latched himself onto Jake and pulled him off Daniel, who wasn't even trying to fight back. He was just lying there, taking the beating like a broken animal.

"Enough, son! Enough!" Nick growled in Jake's ear. But Jake ignored him. He continued to thrash about and nearly broke free but stopped when Nikki scrambled in front of him and grabbed his shoulders.

"Jake! Stop!" she demanded.

He stilled at the sound of her voice, slumping forward onto his knees, head bowed. Nikki pulled him into the circle of her arms and held him.

John O'Malley and two security guards appeared along with two EMTs. The EMTs helped Daniel off the floor and took him to another room, while John turned to Nikki. "I'm sorry about that. The boy's head's not in the right place. What happened out on the course was obviously an accident. He didn't know what he was saying," he said.

Nick stood, glaring angry death at John O'Malley. "I think he knew exactly what he was saying *and* what he was doing out on the track. Don't be surprised if race officials ban him from the series after this."

"We'll see about that," John replied, throwing a menacing glare at Nikki. "Be careful out there, little girl," he warned before turning and storming out.

Jake and Nikki stood, leaning against the bed. "What did he mean by that?" Nikki asked, looking at Nick.

Nick shook his head. "I don't know. We'll let the race officials sort that shit out. For now, worry about getting yourself examined, and I'll find out what's going on with the car," he said before giving her a quick hug and stomping out.

Nikki watched him leave the room, feeling like there was a lot more going on here than met the eye and hating that she had no idea what it was.

~

NIKKI DRAGGED HERSELF INTO THE RV SEVERAL HOURS LATER AND DROPPED down on the couch, feeling like a wrung-out dishrag. After she'd spent hours in the ER, getting poked, prodded, and x-rayed, they finally released her with a clean bill of health and orders to rest up for the next day or two.

"Are you sure you're okay? Nothing hurts?" Jake asked for the hundredth time, grabbing two water bottles from the refrigerator.

"Yes, I'm sure. Don't worry." She pressed her fingers to her temples and began massaging them. "I...I can't get what I saw on the video and what Daniel said in the med center out of my head," she explained, looking up at him. "Do you really think he did it on purpose?"

Jake's jaw hardened to stone. "It looks that way. When I saw it happen, my first thought was that he'd done it deliberately, but I shrugged it off, chalking it up to shock on my part. But seeing the video footage, hearing him in the med center, and the way I told you he behaved in the pit stall before the race, I think it all adds up," he said, leaning up against the granite island.

Nikki's stomach roiled. "But why? It wouldn't have gotten him the ride in Indy Lights. His points standing was too low to qualify even with a win today. Why take me out of the running?"

Jake shook his head. "I don't know. You don't have any enemies around the circuit, and he had nothing to gain. I honestly don't know why he'd do it."

Nikki closed her eyes as a rush of questions swelled. None of this made any sense.

"I'm sorry, angel. I wish there was something else I could say, something I could do," Jake said, coming over and sitting on the couch next to her.

"Me too." She sighed.

Her phone chirped a second later, alerting her to a text. She pulled it from the pocket of her sweats. It was from Nick.

Javier won the race, but Nigel took the ride in Indy Lights. Thought you'd want to know. As for the car, it looks pretty bad. We'll know more soon. Keep your fingers crossed.

Nikki stared down at the screen, her stomach twisting into knots.

"What is it? Is it Nick?" Jake asked.

"Yes," she said, her voice tight. "He, uh...he said that Nigel took the ride in Indy Lights."

"Oh...well, that's good, I guess. He's a good guy," Jake offered.

"He is. He deserved to win it."

"What else did he say?"

She continued to stare down at the phone. "He said the car looks pretty bad and that they'll know more soon."

"If it's totaled, what happens?"

Nikki took a faltering breath, hating the answer. She'd fought so hard to prevent this. "If it's totaled, then I'm done. The team can't afford to replace the car, and I don't have any other offers. So, that's it."

"What? You mean you'd be done with racing...just like that?"

She swallowed around the lump in her throat. "Yes. Unless an offer with another team comes along, I'll be finished," she said, setting aside the phone.

"Jesus. I'm...damn. I don't know what to say other than I'm so sorry." Jake wrapped his hands around hers.

A riot broke out in her head: The flashbacks. The nightmare. The fight with Damon. His worries about her. Jack's news about Greendale. The accident today. Daniel's words. It was too much. She didn't want to think anymore.

She lifted her gaze and met Jake's. "I don't want to think about it, Jake. I don't want to think about anything right now."

Jake stared at her. A look of understanding came over him, his eyes flaring with a heat she could have sworn she could feel. Without saying a word, he leaned in and pressed his lips to hers in a tender kiss, telling her with his actions that he understood what she needed and promised to do everything in his power to chase her thoughts away.

Nikki moaned as he deepened the kiss, all negative thoughts fleeing her brain, leaving only Jake and what it felt like to kiss him, to be in his arms, and how much further she wanted to take this. As if reading her thoughts, Jake pulled her into his lap so she was straddling him, his rock-hard length pressed against the very center of her. Electricity zipped through her veins. She rocked against him in response, loving the sound of his strangled moan when she did.

"I'm going to make you feel so good, you won't think about anything else again," he vowed, trailing kisses over her jaw and down her neck.

"Good." She sighed, burying her hands in his hair.

He chuckled against the space below her ear, his hands sliding upward under her T-shirt to cup her breasts. His nimble fingers swept over the sensitive tips, driving her wild. Without hesitation, she reached down and pulled the shirt over her head and tossed it to the floor. Jake's heated stare fell to the black lace of her bra. Dragging in a shaky breath, he lifted his scorching gaze to hers.

"Are you sure about this?" he asked, his voice deeper and rougher than she'd ever heard it.

She didn't say a word. She simply reached behind her, undid the clasp of her bra, and tossed it on the floor with her shirt.

Jake's eyes dropped to her bare breasts. "Good Christ," he breathed, bringing his eyes back to hers. "Hold on."

Nikki let out a squeak as he pulled her legs around his waist, popped up off the couch and walked the two of them to the bedroom. He set her down on the edge of the bed, stepped back and kicked off his boots, then reached down and pulled off his shirt. She bit down on her lower lip at the sight of his bare, chiseled chest inked with the works of art he'd designed, followed by the tightly rolled stomach and the light dusting of hair that disappeared beneath the dangerously low-slung jeans.

He was magnificent—like Michelangelo's *David* come to life.

He leaned down and tugged at her lower lip, freeing it once more. "Don't hurt that lip of yours, angel. I'm quite fond of it," he said before pressing his mouth to hers in a kiss that started out tender and sweet but quickly progressed to much more.

Without breaking the kiss, he slid his hands down her arms and then under them to lift her up and push her farther onto the bed as he climbed on, his powerful legs straddling her. Nikki's heart thundered in her chest as he eased her back, wedged one of his legs between hers, and settled down next to her. His hands drifted over her breasts, his agile fingers teasing and tantalizing her while his mouth continued its perusal of hers, nibbling, tasting, sucking until she felt like she'd combust.

Her hips began to move of their own volition, rocking against the leg Jake inched higher and higher until it was pressed against the softest, most sensitive part of her. A deep, throaty moan escaped her at the sensation the movement drew forth, making her want more of him pressed against her, inside her. She wanted Jake, every part of him, like she'd never wanted anything or anyone before.

"God, angel. I love the sounds you make," he groaned, trailing kisses across her jaw, along her neck, and dropping to her breasts. She arched her back, crying out as his mouth closed over a nipple, sucking deeply. He ravaged the aching tip, his fingers settling over her other breast, tugging and pulling in tandem with his mouth. Bolts of pleasure shot straight to her core where the ball of tension began to coil.

His mouth shifted to the other breast, where he continued to tug and tease while he slid his hand down her midsection, over her belly button, and lower. She jerked when his fingers slipped under the waistband of her sweats.

Jake's hand stilled, and he lifted his head, his molten stare singeing her. "Is this okay?" He panted.

Her heart melted at the care he took with her—a rarity in her experience. Not that she'd ever been forced to do anything she hadn't wanted to do, but Damon and Marco both never asked, either. If she wanted to stop, she always had to initiate it and felt guilty about it. But not with Jake. She knew that if she changed her mind and wanted to stop, he would without complaint or melodrama.

"Yes," she said, nodding for emphasis as she moved her legs apart for him.

His body trembled as he slipped a hand beneath her waistband, moving lower and lower until it slid over her panties. Jake groaned when she arched her hips against his hand, and he moved his fingers beneath the satin and lace. The first contact of skin against skin made her jump, but it was when he slid a finger inside her that she cried out his name.

"Fuck, angel," he muttered, working a second finger in, "you feel so good."

Her hips punched up as he began to move his fingers, slowly at first, but gained speed when she dug her nails into his shoulders. The tension in her core continued to build. She could feel it coiling tighter and tighter, but just when it was on the verge of snapping, someone started banging on the door.

"What the...?" She panted. *Seriously?*

Jake froze, his hand still nestled between her thighs, listening. The banging came again, this time followed by a voice.

"Nikki? Open up!" Nick's voice called from outside.

"Oh God, it's Nick!" She gasped as Jake pulled his hand free.

"He's probably here about the car," he said, helping her up.

"Just a sec!" she called, looking around for her bra and shirt.

"They're in the front," Jake said, grabbing his shirt.

"Right!" she said, her lust-addled brain finally remembering. She stumbled over to the dresser and grabbed a tank with a built-in bra and tugged it over her head.

After running her hands through her tousled hair, she darted out with Jake in tow. Grabbing the door, she glanced back to make sure he was dressed. Seeing he was, she turned and let Nick inside.

Nick's gaze darted from her to Jake and back, a small, knowing smile playing at his lips.

"Sorry about that. We were...talking," she replied lamely.

"Right," Nick drawled.

"So, what's up? How's the car?" she asked, grabbing her bottle of water from the island and taking a long pull.

Nick let out a heavy breath, and Nikki knew what he had to say wasn't good. "I'm sorry, darlin'. It's...hell, it's too far gone. The frame's shot, as is the engine. There's no repairing it, and you know Lethal can't afford to replace it. I'm afraid this is it for us," he said.

Nikki slumped against the counter, her chest and throat constricting as she tried to suck in a breath. "I see. I'm sorry. I..." She trailed off, not knowing what else to say.

Jake moved behind her and placed a steadying hand at her lower back. "Where's Will?"

"He's still down with the car. He didn't...he didn't have the heart to come up here and tell you," he said, directing his answer to Nikki.

Nick approached and pulled Nikki into his arms, squeezing her tight. "I'm so sorry, sweetheart. You don't deserve this. But don't lose hope." He pulled back and looked into her eyes. She saw that his were rimmed with red and glassy with unshed tears. "You'll find another ride. I know it."

Nikki nodded. "Thanks, Nick. For everything," she said, sniffling back tears.

He squeezed her shoulder, nodded at Jake, and headed out, closing the door softly behind him.

Silence blanketed the RV. It was over. She had no car in the Mazda series, no Indy Lights ride, no other offers from other teams, and no new sponsors to draw in any potential rides. This was the end. All the pain, the sacrifice, the struggle...was all for nothing.

Her body started to shake as wave after wave of anger, despair, and defeat crashed over her, beating her down until she could no longer stand. Her legs wobbled and gave out, but she didn't hit the floor. Jake caught her and hauled her against him. A keening sound bubbled up inside her until it exploded in one long howl, shattering her heart.

16

Nikki yanked on the safety harness, making sure it was secure. She and Jake were wrapping up the Le Mans Tiger's restoration today. Suspension Masters was sending a truck over tomorrow morning to pick it up and haul it out to their headquarters in Colorado. She was scheduled to race it in the VAM series the next season, but for the first time in her life, she felt blasé about it. Hitting the track seemed pointless now that she wasn't a racecar driver—not a professional one, anyway. She hadn't received any offers since returning from the Pro Mazda championship a few days back, and she wasn't expecting any. If they hadn't come in by now, they weren't coming.

Jake ran a rag over the gauges in the dash, polishing the glass. "I think that's everything," he said, kneeling on the floorboards. The vintage racecar didn't have a passenger seat.

Nikki's eyes roved over the steering wheel and dash, in awe of the work they'd put into the car and so quickly. It was shipping out two weeks early, as she'd predicted. "I think you're right. We're done here," she said, patting the steering wheel and backing out of the car.

"When does the VAM series start?" Jake asked as she closed the driver's door.

"In February, down in Florida." The knot she felt in her stomach tightened.

"Ah," he said, closing the passenger door and tossing the rag into the bin next to the workbench. "Well, at least you'll have that until something bigger and better comes along."

Her shoulders dropped. "I don't think bigger and better are in the cards for me."

"Hey." He came up behind her and turned her to face him. "Don't talk like that, angel. Something's going to come along. Don't lose hope."

She looked up at him and shook her head. "Hope? I don't have any hope left, Jake. I did everything I could to make it back into the pros, and I failed. If I haven't gotten an offer at this stage, it's not going to happen. Not for this season. And without Lethal, I won't get the kind of seat-time I need to attract the attention of a pro team for the following season."

A deep frown marred his face. "Stop it. This isn't you. This is just another obstacle, Nikki—one you can find a way around, if you try. Maybe this is your pyramid moment," he offered.

She arched a brow. He was referring to *The Alchemist* and the point in the story where Santiago was literally beaten down at the great pyramids and feared he would never find his treasure.

"You read it?"

Jake nodded. "Every word—including your annotations. I know how much you believe in the story's message, and I know how much faith, strength, and perseverance you have. They're what I admire about you most." He placed his hands on her shoulders. "Don't lose them, angel. Don't give up now when you're almost there."

Her heart pounded at the soul-searing look in his eyes and the plea in his voice.

"I don't want to give up. Believe me, I don't. But it's so hard to have faith now," she said, leaning her forehead against his chest. His arms came around her a second later.

She hadn't been in his arms since the night of the accident at Mid-Ohio. In fact, nothing had happened between them since then. They hadn't seen each other outside of the Den or working on the Le Mans Tiger. Jake gave her the space she needed to manage her grief. But now, feeling his arms around her reminded her of how good it felt to be near him. Not necessarily intimate, but close.

Sensing her thoughts, he said, "Why don't you come with me to see Dario this afternoon? We're meeting up at his favorite pizza place downtown."

Nikki lifted her head and pulled back, touched at his offer. "That's sweet, but I couldn't. That's your time with him. I don't want to take away from it."

He tugged her up against him and locked his arms around her. "You won't take anything away. Besides, I want you to meet him. It would mean a lot to me—to both of us. He's been dying to meet you."

"Really?"

He gave her one of his famous crooked smiles. "Really. I have to warn you, though. He'll probably ask for an autograph or two or ten."

She snorted. "Is he into washed-up drivers?"

Jake reached up and cupped her face with his hands. "Quit it with the negative shit. You're not *washed-up*. Not by a long shot," he said before dipping his head and kissing her tenderly.

Nikki returned the kiss with the first bit of interest she'd felt in days but pulled back, knowing they would need to leave soon. "Well, when you put it that way, okay. No more *negative shit*."

He chuckled. "Come on. I'll drive us," he said as he led her out of the garage and into the house, where he grabbed his motorcycle jacket from the coatrack and her leather jacket as well.

"You're going to drive us? On your Harley?" she asked as he helped her into her jacket.

"Yes. Why?" He slid his jacket on.

"Well...I've...I've never ridden on one," she confessed, following him out the door.

They walked down the porch steps and over to his Sportster. Jake reached down and pulled a second helmet from one of the saddlebags and handed it to her. It was nothing like the helmets she wore for racing. She wouldn't even go so far as to call it a helmet. It was more of a skullcap, but she supposed it was better than nothing.

His eyes took on a mischievous glint. "So, you're a virgin, then?" he asked, watching her plait her hair and strap on the toy helmet.

Her cheeks flushed crimson. "In more ways than one, I guess," she muttered.

Jake's hands stilled on his helmet strap. He cleared his throat. "I see... well, I'm...honored that I'm...your first," he stammered, the flush in his cheeks impossible to miss as he mounted his bike.

Her tummy coiled tight at the double entendre. She climbed on behind him and wrapped her hands around his middle. "You should be," she breathed into his ear as the femme fatale only he could stir in her rose to the surface.

He sucked in a breath as he released the kickstand, then he fired up the Harley. The engine thundered to life with an echoing roar. With a squeak, she tightened her grip, latching onto him like a baby spider monkey. He turned and looked over his shoulder at her, pinning her with a heated stare. "Don't worry, angel. You're safe with me," he said, sliding on his dark sunglasses.

She smiled in return and rested her chin on his shoulder as he took off down the driveway, knowing, deep in her heart, how true that statement was.

~

THEY MET DARIO AT LUCA'S PIZZERIA. SHE SPOTTED HIM THE MINUTE THEY walked in. He looked like an adolescent version of his brother, except for the eyes. Unlike Jake's as-dark-as-night eyes, Dario's were a vibrant shade of green, a startling contrast against his black hair and naturally tanned skin.

Jake introduced her to Dario, who practically leaped out of his chair and proceeded to gush over not only her career but her father's as well. After Jake calmed Dario down, he introduced Nikki to the social worker waiting with him. Nikki bristled when the woman, who didn't look a day over twenty-five, stood and smiled broadly at Jake.

"It's wonderful to see you again," she said, shaking his hand and looking up at him through thick, dark lashes.

"It's nice to see you too." He released her hand and placed his at the small of Nikki's back. "Katelyn, I'd like to introduce you to Nikki Elliot. Nikki, this is Katelyn Jackson. She's the social worker assigned to our case."

Katelyn turned a pair of bright-blue eyes on Nikki. "So, you're the girl Dario's been telling me about. The one Jake works for," she said, emphasizing the last part.

Nikki grinned, pressing herself up against Jake's side in a gesture that made it clear they were more than employer and employee. "That's me," she said, smiling through the desire to reach across the table and bitch slap her.

Katelyn looked at where Nikki and Jake's bodies melded together, her blue eyes hardening to chips of ice. "Well, I'll let you guys sit down and visit." She turned to Jake. "We need to talk about the schedule for December before you go," she said before heading to the front of the restaurant, where she placed herself at a table with a clear view of theirs.

As soon as she was gone, Jake pulled Dario into a giant hug, which Dario returned with equal enthusiasm. It warmed Nikki's heart to see them together, but it hurt a little too. It reminded her of her brothers—brothers she hadn't spoken to in months—and the closeness they'd once shared.

"I missed you," Jake said, releasing Dario, then sat next to Nikki.

"Me too, but I bet you had plenty to distract you," he said, winking at Nikki.

"Watch it," Jake ordered, placing a hand on her knee beneath the table and squeezing.

"I mean no disrespect. I'm only stating the obvious. If I hung out with Nikki Elliot, I'd be distracted too," he replied, wagging his eyebrows.

Sitting there with Jake and Dario that afternoon, laughing, sharing stories about racing and Dario's exploits on the soccer field, and more stories of Jake and his buddies—men Dario thought of as brothers just as Jake did—Nikki saw a side of Jake she'd only glimpsed. The quiet intensity that usually hovered over him vanished. In its place was someone relaxed, carefree—happy. And she wondered, not for the first time, why he struggled with happiness. What did he carry that weighed him down so heavily he couldn't be happy, couldn't do things that fulfilled him? What had happened in his relatively short life to make him closed off to this?

Lunch flew by, and before she knew it, Jake excused himself to go speak with Katelyn about the visitation schedule for December. Once he was out of earshot, Dario leaned forward, resting his elbows on the table.

"I was right," he said, eyeing her.

Nikki arched a brow. "About what?"

"My brother." When she gave him a look that said, "And...," he continued. "He's crazy about you. He has been since you guys started working together."

"Really?" she asked, her heart skipping. She'd been crazy about him then too—even as she tried to deny it.

"Oh yeah. The fact that you're here is proof enough. He's never brought a girl around to meet me. Like ever. You must be special." He pushed his sleeve up, revealing what looked like a black-and-blue handprint around his wrist.

Nikki's eyes widened at the sight, and she remembered Jake telling her about how Dario had been banged up recently. "You know, he's crazy about you too," she said, watching as he realized his mistake and covered up the bruise. She wondered how Katelyn hadn't noticed this or why the school hadn't phoned CPS about it.

"He talks about you all the time, about how proud he is of you...how worried he is about you," she continued, hoping Dario *heard* her.

Dario frowned. "I don't want him worrying about me. I can handle myself."

"I'm sure you can, but take it from me"—she leaned in close—"there's nothing wrong with asking for help when you need it. Don't be afraid to let Jake help you. Please."

"I'll think about it," Dario said as Jake walked up.

"Think about what?" Jake asked.

"About letting her give me driving lessons," he lied smoothly.

Nikki smirked. "Yeah, he's a little on the fence about my offer to take him to the track."

Her phone chirped.

She pulled it out of her purse and frowned at the screen. "I have to take this. It's Jeff from Suspension Masters. He's probably calling about the pick-up time tomorrow."

"Sure. I'll meet you out front," Jake said.

Nikki nodded and hugged Dario goodbye, whispering a final plea for him to talk to Jake, before answering the call.

"Hey, Jeff. What's up?"

Jeff Illingworth greeted her with his usual enthusiasm. "Hey yourself, little girl. How are you? How's my Tiger?"

"We're both ready to race. Is that why you're calling?" she asked, walking past Katelyn, who didn't bother to smile at her now that Jake wasn't by her side.

"Yep! I've got some big news for you," he said.

Nikki closed the door to the pizzeria behind her and moved to a quiet spot a few feet away. "Okay, shoot."

"I've got an invite to join the Goodwood Road Racing Club, which means the Tiger is eligible to race at the Revival next year *and* at the Le Mans Classic," he said, his voice ringing with excitement.

Nikki's stomach dropped. "What?"

"You heard me! We got into Goodwood, and you're going back to Le Mans. Aren't you excited?"

A cold, sickly fear started spreading through her veins. Race at Le Mans? She didn't think she'd be back there this soon, not before her memories were back.

"Nikki? You there?" Jeff asked when she didn't respond.

"Huh? Yeah, yeah I'm here. I'm surprised. That's all. You really think going back to Le Mans is a good idea?"

"Absolutely. It'll be your chance to prove your mettle to the race officials and the European race circuit. Don't you agree?" he said, sounding a little put out.

She gave herself an internal shake. Now was not the time to piss off her one and *only* sponsor to date. The other two pulled their support the minute they learned about the Pro Mazda situation. She needed Jeff on the off chance she got an offer to race with a pro team next season.

"Yes, yes. Of course. Just send me the revised schedule with the added races. I'll be there, and I'll be ready." She prayed the last part was true. Right now, she wasn't feeling at all ready to set foot on the Le Mans course, let alone drive it.

"Great! We'll talk soon. Don't forget, the truck will be there tomorrow at ten o'clock."

"I won't. Don't worry," she said and ended the call.

Nikki slid the phone into her back pocket with a shaky hand. She was returning to Le Mans, where everything had changed in the blink of an eye, to the place she couldn't remember outside of a few flashes of things —flashes that frightened her. Her stomach seized, threatening to force the pizza she'd consumed up and out. She inhaled and exhaled deeply, trying to shake the fear that had somehow gotten a stranglehold on her.

She needed to pull it together. There was no reason to panic. There had to be a simple explanation for her memories—one she needn't fear nor one that should interfere with her racing. She took another deep breath, but this one got stuck as a blinding pain lanced her skull. She pressed her fingertips to her forehead then stumbled down the block and out of sight. She didn't want Katelyn to see this. It could look bad for Jake.

Nikki leaned back against the cold brick façade of the pizzeria, willing the pain to go away, but it didn't. Another blinding ray hit her, this one followed by another flashback. Once again, she was back in the trailer, pacing like a caged animal, but this time, she wasn't alone. Phillipe was there.

"Don't tell me to calm down, Phillipe. I'm in serious trouble here."

"Chérie, you're overreacting. There's no trouble; trust me. Everything is fine," he pleaded. *"Just focus on winning out there. Your team needs you. Tomorrow, we'll go into Paris and have some of those crêpes you love so much to celebrate with Jack. Everything will be fine."*

Nikki watched Phillipe, her MIA crew chief, leave the trailer. Then the memory of her storming into the RV's bedroom replayed, with her grabbing her cell phone and making a call to someone she thought would help her after Phillipe's dismissal.

The flashback ended.

Her eyes snapped open the moment the memory faded, her darkest fears taking shape before her eyes. These memories were definitely of Le Mans, and in them, she believed she was in real trouble. Why Phillipe downplayed it, and what the trouble was, she didn't know. But she could feel in her gut that it was serious. Deadly serious.

JAKE HUGGED DARIO GOODBYE ONE LAST TIME. WHEN HE PULLED BACK, HE said, "Take care of yourself, *fratellino*. If you need anything, you call me. *Capisce?*"

Dario grinned, slapping Jake on the arm. *"Si, capisce.* Okay? Relax." He leaned around and looked down the street. "Now, go find your girl. It looks like she wandered off."

He gave Dario a little salute and turned in the direction he saw Nikki head when she left the restaurant.

Your girl…

He liked the sound of that and the idea that they could have more afternoons like this one…that she really was his girl. In some sense, he supposed she was—at least until she made it back to professional racing. Nikki didn't believe she would at this point, and Jake couldn't help but wonder what would happen between them if that transpired. This arrangement was hinged on her leaving, but if she wasn't, did that mean they'd stay together? He'd made a promise to himself that he'd be there for her however she needed him and for however long she needed. What if that time was indefinite?

An indefinite amount of time with Nikki?

Could he really have that? A strange fluttering rippled through his chest, and he thought maybe he could. If she needed him, if she wanted him like that, he'd be there. It wasn't what he deserved, and honestly, *she* deserved better than him. But if she needed and wanted him, and if their time together was indefinite, he could work at being the man she deserved.

Jake headed down the block, his eyes combing the area for her but not finding her anywhere. *Where was she?* He was nearly to the end of the street when Nikki staggered around the corner, head bowed, nearly running into him.

"Whoa there, angel." He chuckled, grasping her shoulders. "You should really look—" He stopped when she lifted her head. Her eyes were wide, almost wild, and her face was pale and drawn. "What's wrong?"

She shook her head. "Nothing."

Bull. Shit.

He leaned in. "Let's try this again. What's wrong? You look freaked. What happened?"

Nikki swallowed audibly. "I, uh…I talked to Jeff at Suspension Masters. He…he told me I'm scheduled to race in Europe next summer at Goodwood and…Le Mans," she said, her body trembling like a leaf in a storm.

The muscles along Jake's shoulders tensed. "At Le Mans? Really?"

"Yeah," she whispered.

The idea of Nikki returning there to race scared the hell out of him and would until the mystery behind that accident was solved. And it looked like he wasn't alone. She was frightened too. But why? It couldn't be a fear of wrecking again. She faced that every time she raced.

"Okay. And I take it you don't want to do this?" he asked.

She took a step back and leaned up against the building, crossing her arms over her chest. "No. Yes. I…I don't know. There's just…so much going on in my head with what happened last weekend at Mid-Ohio and everything else… I can't think straight."

Jake studied her for a moment. He knew she wasn't telling him the whole story, but for whatever reason, she didn't want to open up. He didn't take it personally; he got it. But that didn't mean he liked it. Something scared her—something bigger than racing at Le Mans. He wanted to know what it was so he could help her, protect her—anything to chase away the fear he saw in her eyes and keep her safe.

"I understand. Let's get you home," he said, taking her quivering hand in his and heading over to where his Harley waited.

Once they mounted up, he took off into traffic, feeling her shudder against his back as he weaved through the streets. She couldn't shake the fear, and it started to worry him. Nikki was the strongest person he knew. If she was this frightened, it had to be serious, but he had no idea how to help her.

An idea occurred to him then. His mother used to go to a place when she was worried or upset. He remembered it vividly. She always brought Jake and little Dario with her when she went, but he hadn't been since before her death, and he wasn't sure he could go now—not without stirring memories he'd buried long ago.

His grip on the throttle tightened when he thought about the last time they'd been there, just after his father's sentencing. His mother took the three of them there right after the hearing to regroup. Like every other time they'd gone, it seemed to work. She was stronger and clearer afterward. It didn't last, though. But then, that was Jake's fault. He drove her to the point where nothing could help her.

A violent shudder rocked Nikki's tiny frame, and he knew what he had to do. He might have driven his mother to the point of no return, but he wouldn't let Nikki go there. He'd do whatever it took to help her—even if that meant opening old wounds and reliving painful memories.

When they rolled up to a stoplight, he reached around and grabbed her waist. "I want to take you somewhere. You down for that?" he asked, glancing back at her.

She lifted her chin from his shoulder. "Sure, I guess. Where to?"

He gave her waist a squeeze. "Somewhere I used to go with my mom. It always made her feel better, and I'm thinking you could use that right now," he said, wishing he could see her eyes through the dark glasses she wore.

"Oh. Um, okay. Sure. Let's go," she said, giving him a fragile smile.

He nodded and turned around just as the light went green, hoping like hell this worked for Nikki and that he could do for her what he didn't for his mother.

17

Nikki watched the scenery fly by in a blur of watercolor earth tones as Jake's Harley skated along the curves of the highway. They were headed in the direction of the coast—not that she cared. She felt honored by this inclusion in Jake's private memories of his mother—something she sensed was sacred to him, as he'd never spoken of her outside of her passing. Could this be a sign that he trusted her? She hoped so. She wanted that—wanted it so badly.

They rode for another twenty minutes before they turned onto the coastal highway. She let her questions and wants go, focusing on the gorgeous scenery spiraling out before her: the rolling hills dotted with coastal redwoods and cypress trees, the rocky cliffs jutting out over long stretches of pristine sands where waves crashed and receded, washing away impurities. Only here, in the Bay Area, could you travel from the city through the mountains and out to the coastline all within an hour.

A few miles down the coast, Jake turned into a deserted parking lot and deposited the bike near a footpath leading down to the beach.

"So, this is it?" she asked, pulling off her helmet and handing it to him.

He gave her a quick nod as he stashed the helmets in the saddlebags on either side of the bike. When he straightened, her heart ached at the tension in his expression. She didn't say anything, though.

Jake took her hand and led her to the narrow footpath, where he guided her down the steep drop that opened up to a ribbon of sand, stretching endlessly in either direction. When they hit the sand, he stopped and turned to her.

"We should take off our shoes here," he said, pulling off his heavy black boots.

She blinked at him. "What? Why? The sand is cold this time of year."

"Nah. It's not that bad. Besides, you can't get your feet wet with your shoes on."

Nikki blanched. "We're putting our feet in the water? It's freezing!" she squeaked. The weather had been warm today, even for November in California, but that didn't mean the water was warm. It couldn't be above sixty degrees.

Jake chuckled, tucking his socks into his boots, then stood. "Yeah, but you'll get used to it. You want this to work, don't you?" he said, extending a hand to her.

She set her boots next to his and took the hand he offered, standing. "Want what to work? You haven't explained what we're doing here or how this is supposed to be helpful."

"Right. Sorry." He led her across the expanse of sand and down to the water's edge, where waves teased the shoreline. "I brought you here because this is where my mom would go whenever she was stressed out, worried, or upset," he began, his face taking on a faraway look, pulling him into another moment in time as he gazed out across the water. "For her, the boundlessness of the ocean was a reminder that there were bigger things out there than her problems."

Looking out across the vastness, Nikki could see how it helped give his mother clarity. But why get in the water?

"Okay…but we don't have to get our feet wet to do that."

"Ah, but there's another step. Part of that reminder came from standing at the water's edge and letting the sea wash over her feet. She felt like the water cleansed her soul like it cleansed the shoreline, taking her worries with it back out to sea," he explained, turning his gaze to hers.

Her breath caught at the pain and guilt reflected in his eyes. She understood those emotions. She knew the burden of carrying guilt and pain on your shoulders, how they weighed you down and wore on your spirit, even years after losing someone. She'd do anything to relieve him of that.

"Did it work for her?" she asked, her voice carrying over the crashing waves.

The muscles along his jaw flexed and strained. "It did. She always felt better after being here, after doing this," he said, averting his eyes.

He wasn't being completely honest. There was more to it, but she didn't want to push him. It was hard enough for him to be here, reliving memories of a woman he loved; she didn't want to make it any more difficult. Dealing with grief was personal and painful and not something someone else could force. You had to open up when you were ready and not before. All Nikki could do was wait and be there for him when he did.

"How about you? Did you do this with her? Did it help you?" she asked, steering the conversation away from his mother.

Jake shrugged. "I was a kid. I didn't really get it then."

Nikki nodded. "Okay. Well, is there something I should do besides stand here? What would she do?"

"You have to stand at the edge of the shoreline and let the water wash over you. While you do that, you're supposed to envision it rinsing away your worries, your fears, anything that's upsetting you," he explained, leading her down to the edge.

The wet sand sent shockwaves through the soles of her feet and up her legs.

"Jesus! This is cold!" she yelped.

Jake laughed. "I know, but it'll get better. Trust me."

She nodded and turned, moving down to the waterline. When he didn't follow, she looked over her shoulder and waved him on.

"Come on. I'm not doing this alone," she called.

He frowned. "We're not here for me. This is all for you, angel."

Nikki rolled her eyes. "Uh-uh. You're not getting off that easily. You need this as much as I do. I know for a fact you haven't even tried to find a therapist or counselor like I suggested weeks ago, so get over here. This can be your therapy as much as it can be mine," she replied, waving him on.

Jake hesitated for a moment, but he finally caved and moved next to her. She smiled up at him then turned her attention to the ocean as the first wave came. Nikki squealed when the cold water washed over her feet, but she didn't move. She stood there and turned her focus to the worries and questions that had been battling in her head ever since the flashbacks began, doing as Jake had directed.

She wasn't sure how long it took, but somewhere around the time she lost feeling in her feet, it happened: Her mind emptied of the worries and fears, and she saw things from a clearer perspective. Nikki saw that while the flashbacks and Damon's crazy paranoia suggested she'd been or might *be* in trouble, it might not be as bad as she'd feared, and that she would have to be patient and wait for more memories to come before she should fret over it. Worry wasn't a wise council. Stressing over what might have been or what might be never served anyone—it certainly wasn't serving her now. And whatever it turned out to be, she could and would handle it, like she'd handled every other tragedy and obstacle before it.

Once her mind cleared and her fears abated, she turned to Jake. He was staring out across the sea, his face a battlefield of emotion. He turned to her a moment later, his expression softening as it roved over her.

"Well? Did it work?" he asked.

"It did. Your mom was right. It brought me the clarity I needed. Thank you. Thank you so much," she said, reaching up and pressing her lips to his.

She didn't intend for the kiss to go anywhere. She meant it as a *thank you*, but Jake had other ideas. When she tried to pull away, he tugged her closer, deepening the kiss. She didn't resist. She couldn't. Jake kissed her like no one ever had—like he was dying of thirst and she was the water his body needed to survive. She loved the way he kissed her, and more than that, she loved him.

A shiver ran through her that had as much to do with the water skating over her calves as it did with the way Jake's hands moved over the curves of her body while his lips tasted hers, consuming her.

Jake pulled back, breathless. "We should get going before you catch cold."

"Yeah. You're right." She panted, wishing they were somewhere warmer where they didn't have to stop. It seemed like something always got in the way of them *fully* exploring the passion kindling between them.

After a final, lingering look, Jake led her back up to where their shoes were stashed. Once they cleaned up, they mounted the bike and headed over the hill toward home, the setting sun lighting their way.

Halfway there, Nikki started regretting her decision to pass on using the bathroom at the beach. The vibrations from the Sportster's V-Twin engine weren't helping, either. Every time Jake accelerated was like a direct hit to her bladder.

She shifted in her seat as he opened up the bike on a brief stretch of straightaway. "You okay, angel?" he called over his shoulder.

"Actually, no. We need to stop at the next gas station. I feel like my bladder's about to explode," she yelled over the wind and engine noise.

Jake's body vibrated with laughter. "All right. We'll stop up around the next bend. There's a gas station there. I can fuel up before we go any farther."

"Thank God!" she breathed.

They pulled into the gas station minutes later, only to find the store and the bathroom were closed. The pumps were still operating, so at least Jake could fuel up. Nikki glanced around the area and spotted a bar up the highway.

She hopped off the bike and handed her helmet to Jake. "I'm going to run up and use the bathroom at that bar over there," she said, pointing to a sign that read The Blue Ox.

Jake blanched. "No. You can't use the bathroom there," he said in a rush.

"What? Of course I can. They have one, right?" She bounced from one foot to the other.

"Yeah, but it's a rough place. Can't you just pop a squat around the back of the building or at least wait until I fuel up?"

She scrunched her face. "No, I can't just *pop a squat*. Not if there is a bathroom right over there. And I can't wait," she said, turning and heading in the direction of the bar. "I'll be fine!"

"No! Wait!" she heard Jake call, but she didn't stop. If she didn't go soon, she was going to have a very embarrassing accident.

She jogged across the highway and up the wooden steps of the semi-dilapidated bar, noting all the motorcycles parked outside. The sounds of a guitar riff pouring from an old jukebox and the scents of stale beer and whiskey greeted her when she stepped inside.

The minute the door swung shut, silence blanketed the bar, and all eyes turned to her, anchoring her to the floor.

Uh...

She cleared her throat, looking around the room for a friendly face. She finally found one behind the bar. It belonged to a gorgeous redhead wearing a neon-green T-shirt.

"Can I help you, sweetheart?" she called from the other end of the bar.

Nikki took a tentative step forward. "I...um...I need to use the restroom. My"—she searched for the right word to describe Jake —"boyfriend is across the street, fueling up his bike."

The bartender cocked her head to the side and moved down the bar. "Okay. Well, the ladies' room is in the back. Help yourself," she said, motioning to the rear of the bar.

"Thank you! You're a lifesaver," Nikki breathed and trotted to the back of the bar, the sounds of gentle laughter following her.

She found the ladies' room right next to the men's at the very end of the hallway. She grimaced as she opened the door, hearing what sounded like a man moaning—and not from pain—in the men's room.

Classy.

Nikki swallowed her disgust and darted into the bathroom. For a hole-in-the-wall bar, the women's bathroom was remarkably clean. Once she finished, she headed back out into the dark hallway toward the din of classic rock, pool balls knocking around a table, arguments over engine modifications, and drunken laughter. She was near the end of the hall when she heard the men's door swing open, followed by the sound of a familiar voice calling out to her.

"Oh my God! Is that Nikki Elliot I see?" the familiar sultry voice beckoned.

Nikki stopped short. *It couldn't be.* She turned and stifled a gasp. It was. Angela O'Brien, the slut she caught Damon having sex with all those years ago, stood there, straightening her dress—if you could call the scrap of fabric a dress—and her disheveled hair.

"A-Angela?" she stammered.

"The one and only," she replied, sauntering up to Nikki.

Nikki glanced around, wondering where Angela had come from. She spotted a door marked *Private* next to the men's room. Maybe she'd been in there?

"Wow. Imagine that. It's been a long time. How are you, Angela?" she asked, forcing herself to stay polite.

Before Angela could answer, the men's room door swung open, and a man appeared, wearing a satisfied grin.

"Thanks, baby," he said, patting Angela on the behind. "Can I buy you a drink? It's the least I could do after that performance."

Nikki stifled her gag reflex, recalling the moaning she'd heard. It looked like Angela hadn't changed since high school.

"I'll be right there. I'm just"—she glanced over at Nikki with a wicked gleam in her eye—"catching up with an old friend."

Old friend? Not in this lifetime.

"Suit yourself," he said and left for the bar.

"That's okay. I need to get going. My boyfriend is waiting for me outside," Nikki said then turned and headed toward the bar.

"Boyfriend? *You?* Well, I hope you've learned a trick or two since Damon. Wouldn't want you to get your heart broken again." Angela snickered.

Anger ricocheted through Nikki's chest, but she forced herself to keep walking. She wouldn't stoop to Angela's level. Her mother had raised her better than that.

When she reached the end of the hall, a woman stepped out, blocking her way. "Where do you think you're going?" she asked, sizing Nikki up with narrowed eyes. "Angela's talking to you. It's not polite to walk away when someone's talking."

It was Katie Johnson, Angela's BFF from high school.

What was this? Old home week?

"Let me pass, Katie. Angela and I are through," Nikki said, noting that the bar had suddenly gone quiet. She looked around and found all eyes focused on her.

Oh, perfect.

"Sorry. I don't think she is." She looked over Nikki's shoulder. "You're not through, are ya, Ang?"

"I don't know. Am I, Nikki?" Angela asked, coming up behind her with a shove.

Nikki stumbled forward but caught herself before she fell. She spun around and planted her feet into a firm stance. "Don't touch me, Angela," she warned.

Angela stepped forward, glaring at her. "Or what? What's Little Miss Stick Up Her Ass going to do? Are you gonna hit me or run out of here in tears like you ran out of Damon's?"

Jesus. What was her problem? This crap happened back in high school. If Nikki could let it go and move on, surely Angela could.

"Neither. I'm going to tell you to leave me alone, and then I'm going to walk out of here," Nikki replied, then stepped around Katie.

She didn't get far.

Angela snarled something nasty then grabbed Nikki by the hair and yanked her backward. Nikki grabbed Angela's hand and spun around, taking a sucker punch to the jaw. She stumbled backward again and bumped into Katie. Katie shoved her back toward Angela, but this time Nikki was ready.

JAKE LOOKED UP AT THE OX FOR THE TENTH TIME SINCE NIKKI HAD DARTED inside. She should have come out by now. What was taking her so long?

He stashed the helmets inside the saddlebags then headed across the highway to the Ox to find her. He hadn't wanted her to go in there for a myriad of reasons: the rough crowd, the seedy undercurrent of the locale, but most of all, the women who frequented the joint. Having Nikki come face-to-face with that side of his past would reveal a part of him he wanted to keep from her. Flaunting his *manwhore status*, as Dario put it, wouldn't make a good impression.

When he reached the door, he heard cheering coming from inside—the kind of cheering that usually preceded a barroom fight.

Shit.

Jake stormed inside. He scanned the front end of the building, not seeing any sign of Nikki.

"Jake? That you?" Cathy called from behind the bar.

He moved toward the bar. "Hey, Cathy. Did you see a young woman come in here? She's about this tall." He held up a hand to his shoulder. "Blond hair, gorgeous eyes?"

Cathy's face lit up with a knowing smile. "Yeah, I did. She said her boyfriend was outside, fueling up, and that she needed the bathroom. I take it you're *him*?"

Jake's chest swelled.

He cleared his throat. "That's right. Where is she?"

Cathy grimaced. "I think she's the one in the back, arguing with your little friend Angela."

The acid in his stomach roiled, burning a hole through the lining. "Fuck. Are you serious?" He started moving toward the crowd.

"Yep. Sorry, sweetheart," Cathy called over the din of catcalls and screeching.

Jake forced his way through the throng of locals and Regulators gathered there. When he broke through the mass, he found Angela and Nikki in the center of the action, wrestling on the ground with Tucker Ellis trying to break them apart.

"Jake!" Tucker called, wedging himself between the girls. "Grab the pretty blond and take her outside. I'll get Angela."

Jake nodded. "Got it!" he said then wrapped his hands around Nikki's middle and pulled her back. When she screamed and writhed against him, he held her tighter. "Angel, it's me. Calm down!"

Nikki stilled at the sound of his voice.

"Let's go," he said and hauled her across the bar and out the doors, into the cool evening air. He wasn't going to stop until they were across the street. He didn't want Angela to see him with Nikki for a lot of reasons, least of all the fight he and Tucker had broken up.

"I can walk on my own," Nikki huffed when he reached the parking lot.

"Fine." He set her down. The doors burst open, and Tucker Ellis appeared with a squirming Angela in his arms.

"Settle down, woman!" Tucker demanded.

"I don't have to do shit, Ellis. You know who my father is! You have no right to treat me this way!" she snarled.

"I have every right if you're going to be picking fights with customers," he barked back, dropping her on her ass.

She glared up at him then swung her gaze to where Jake stood with Nikki, his arm wrapped firmly around her. Her eyes went wide with shock but quickly narrowed to angry slits.

"Are you fucking kidding me?" she demanded, her gazed locked on Jake.

"That's enough," Tucker warned.

Nikki stiffened next to him. "What the hell does she mean?"

Angela barked out a laugh. "Now this is rich. You're with *her*? For real? Little Miss Stick Up Her Ass?"

Jake turned and tried to usher Nikki out of there, but she wouldn't move.

"Do you know her?" Nikki sucked in a breath. "Wait. Were you and that...skank together?" she hissed, her voice feral.

"I'm no skank, am I, Jake? At least you didn't think so when I was sucking you off in the men's room, did you?" Angela growled.

Nikki's eyes cut to Jake, horrified. "What?"

Jake whipped his head around to Angela. "Shut the fuck up, Ang."

Angela reared back. "Wow. That's not how you used to talk to me, but I guess that's thanks to the priss you're running around with these days. Why don't you call me when you want to be with a real woman again, not some dried-up prude," she sneered, pointing at Nikki.

"Just because I won't screw or blow every man in sight doesn't make me a prude!" Nikki snapped.

Angela lurched forward, but Tucker held her back.

"Let go of me!" she demanded, glaring angry death at Nikki. "You better watch your back, bitch! Nobody talks to an O'Brien like that and gets away with it. You have no idea who you're fucking with!"

"Shut up, O'Brien. Your father won't bother. He's done cleaning up your crap," Tucker said and turned to Jake as he stepped in front of Angela. "Get your girl out of here, Jake."

Jake nodded and scooped a fuming Nikki off her feet, making his way across the highway in a flash.

"Hey! What the hell? Put me down!" she cried.

"No. We need to get out of here before someone gets hurt," he ground out, not setting her down until they reached his bike. He gave her a cursory scan for injuries. A measure of relief eased through him; she looked fine aside from her disheveled hair and flushed cheeks. Across the street, Angela and Tucker were roaring at each other in the parking lot.

"Fine!" Nikki clipped, strapping on her helmet. "But answer my question. Were you two together at one point? Was Angela telling the truth about...about the men's room?" she demanded, the revulsion in her voice loud and clear.

Jake grabbed his helmet and strapped it on, noting the fire raging in Nikki's eyes. He had no idea what Angela did to put it there, but he wanted to put it out and forget this ever happened.

"We were never a couple. Did we hook up? Yes. But that's all it ever was—one meaningless hookup," he said, unable to lie to her.

Nikki stared at him, her face paling in the waning light of the sunset. "I see." She swung her leg over the bike like a pro. "Let's go."

"What happened to start the fight?" he asked, as he mounted up and fired the engine.

"It's not worth mentioning," she replied, her voice laced with anger.

Jake looked back at her, noting the set of her jaw as she glared out across the highway at Angela, and he knew he wouldn't get an answer—not tonight, anyway. There had to be a history there to elicit that kind of anger from Nikki, but it didn't matter. For now, he just needed to get her home.

Silence filled the ride back to Wood Glenn, each of them lost to their own thoughts. Nikki had seen a side of Jake's life he never wanted her to see. Not only that, but the barroom fight could have turned out seriously bad if Tucker Ellis hadn't intervened. She could have been arrested or worse. And it would have been his fault for bringing her out there in the first place. Hell, it would have been his fault for being part of her life, period.

He ground his teeth together. He wasn't supposed to be getting Nikki involved in barroom fights and putting her in places like the Ox. But that was exactly what he'd done. Jesus. He'd been kidding himself when he thought he could support her, could be with her...could be anything to her other than poison. He needed to fix this and fix it fast. And there was only one way to do that: end things between them now, before they went further.

They rolled into Nikki's driveway thirty minutes later, Jake's chest heavy with his decision. He pulled the bike in behind her Ferrari and killed the engine then took the helmet she offered and tucked it away. When she started to head toward the porch, he didn't follow.

She turned when she realized he wasn't behind her. "Aren't you coming in?" she asked.

He shook his head. "No. I should, uh...head out."

Nikki's brows drew together, and she came back over to him. "Why? Is it because of what happened at the bar? Because if it is, I'm sorry. I shouldn't have behaved the way I did. It was appalling. And if it's about you and Angela, whatever you two did together is in the past. I don't care. *Really*," she said, emphasizing the last part.

Jake's chest seized at the truth behind her words. After everything she'd seen and heard today, she still wanted him.

Damn. She was way too good for him.

"No, it's not that, not in the way you think, anyway." He took her hands in his. "What happened back there? That kind of shit happens around me all the time. My life is...fuck, it's broken, angel. *I'm* broken, and you and your life aren't, but they will be if things continue as they have between us. I didn't want to see it before. I wanted to believe I could be better for you, be what you needed, but after what happened tonight, I realize I was kidding myself. I can't be better...I can't be the man you need and deserve. And you, angel, you deserve the best."

Nikki's eyes welled with tears. "So, you think it's best if we don't see each other anymore—outside of working at the Den? Is that what you're saying?"

"Yes. It's for your own good. There are things about me that you don't know and I won't share with you—things that make anything between us impossible." He released her hands, holding firm to his decision even as it shredded him.

She studied him for several beats, a resigned expression coming over her. "Fine. If that's what you want, Jake. But whatever *things* you're hiding won't change how *I* see you—as a good, honorable man with so much to offer."

Jake blinked at her. She meant every word. He could see it in her eyes and hear it in her voice. But it didn't change anything. They couldn't be together.

Don't be so sure.

He shoved the annoying voice away and, with a quick nod, turned and mounted the bike. Once his helmet was strapped, he fired the engine and pulled out of her driveway, leaving the only girl he'd ever loved behind, knowing it was the right thing to do...no matter how loudly his heart screamed at him to do otherwise.

18

The next morning dawned bright and early, and like every morning, Nikki went about her routine: go for a run, meet up with Tsai at the gym for her daily ass-whooping, shower, head to the shop. Normally, she enjoyed the routine, even if it meant waking up at zero dark shitty, as Hilda put it. But today was different. Today she was just going through the motions. She couldn't get Jake's tormented words from the night before out of her head: *I'm broken...you will be if we continue.* They haunted her like a mournful melody, shadowing her every thought.

I'm broken.

She shook her head as she flew down the frontage road that led to Restoration Way, the cul-de-sac where she'd spent the better part of her life. Jake wasn't only closed off—he was *broken*, as he'd said, by his mother's death and his father's incarceration. But why? How did it all fit together?

She let the questions go.

This was a mystery she wouldn't be able to solve because Jake didn't want her to...because he didn't believe he deserved to be whole. It shattered her heart to think of him feeling like that: so alone and undeserving. Jake deserved every bit of happiness in the world, but he couldn't see it. That alone cut deeper than the fact that he'd ended things between them.

After pulling the Ferrari to a stop along the fence that ran in front of the Den, she headed inside, dreading to see Jake. Not from anger or hurt, though—his decision to end things had nothing to do with her desirability. He wanted her as much as she wanted him; she knew that deep in her heart. She dreaded today because she didn't want things to be awkward for Sean or the other mechanics. Workplace awkwardness sucked, big time. So, she put on the best impression of a happy face she could muster —without looking like a psycho—and headed inside, determined to keep things casual and light.

The shop bustled with activity as she came through the door. She noted that Jake and another mechanic were putting the engine and drivetrain into an early Tiger at the far end of the shop from the bay where she worked. She waved as she walked by and released a quiet sigh of relief when she reached her spot and got to work on the rear end gear change for a '65 Mustang. The distance would limit their interactions and awkwardness.

Whew.

Sean emerged from his office a couple of hours later, shouting her name. "Nikki! You've got a call on line one. Get in here!" he bellowed across the shop.

Nikki rolled out from under the Mustang. *A call?* Who would call her at the Den? Why didn't they use her cell? She fished the phone from her pocket as she headed over to the office. It was dead.

Ah. It would help if I charged it once in a while.

She caught a glimpse of Jake when she reached the office. He looked wrung out. Dark circles blossomed beneath his eyes, and his face looked pale and drawn. Nikki offered him a small smile as she stepped into Sean's cluttered office.

"Sorry, boss," she said. "I forgot to charge my phone. Did they say who was calling?"

Sean leaned against the desk. "Yeah, some guy named Enzo Santorini. Says he's been trying to track you down through Jack with no luck." He folded his arms across his broad chest. Sean was former navy, and it still showed in his physique.

"*Enzo?* Really?" she squeaked, darting for the phone. She and Enzo had raced for Ferrari together in Europe. He left the team shortly before her accident at Le Mans after a serious accident of his own cut his season short. She hadn't heard from him since she returned to the US.

"Yeah. He sounded anxious, so you better take that," he said, pushing off the desk. "I'll give you some privacy. But please, charge your damn phone. It's no good to you dead."

"Yes, sir," she said, giving him a salute. She grabbed the receiver as the door closed and hit the button for line one. "Enzo? Is that really you?"

"*Tesora!* Of course it's me! How are you, *ragazza*?" he said, his rich Italian voice flowing over her like honey.

"I'm well. How are you? How did you find me?" she asked, thrilled to hear from him.

"*Sto bene, grazie.* I tracked you down through your Lethal Racing crew chief. He gave me your cell number and said to try this one if you didn't answer the cell," he explained, his voice as animated as ever.

She laughed. Nick knew her well. "I'm glad he gave you both numbers. What's up? Did you track me down to catch up or reminisce about old times?"

"*No!*" he practically yelled into the phone. "I called because I've been trying to get a hold of you through your manager, but he said you weren't taking calls or offers."

Her stomach dropped. It was just as she'd feared: Jack *was* trying to sabotage her career. Why would he do that? Had Dino really gotten to him like he'd gotten to Mike? Was it really about protecting her?

"I'm sorry, Enzo, but that's not true. I'm taking calls *and* offers. What's up?"

"What's up is Ferrari wants you as primary driver on their Le Mans prototype team in the IMSA WeatherTech Series this season."

Nikki's jaw dropped. Ferrari wanted her to drive a prototype in the IMSA series? Holy shit.

"Hello? Tesora? Are you there?" Enzo called when she didn't respond.

"Huh? Uh, yeah. I mean, yes, I'm here!" she gasped, her heart racing like a stallion as she brought her brain back online.

"Well? What's your answer? Will you race for Ferrari again, Nikki? The package is good, and because we're backed by the Ferrari factory, you won't need to bring sponsorship, though if you've got it, we'd take it," he said.

She didn't hesitate. "Of course I will! Oh, Enzo, I can't thank you enough, really!" she squeaked.

"*Perfetto!*" he cheered into the phone. "I'll email you a copy of the contract and send one by courier for you to sign. Email me your home address, as I assume you'll be hiring a new manager and will want to handle this yourself for now. It's a one-year deal with an option for you to sign on for more, if *you* choose. Ferrari has been watching you closely this year, and they are excited to have you back. Your season in Pro Mazda was impressive, as was your performance in the VAM series. You're an amazing driver, bella—as you have always been. *Ben tornato!*"

Ferrari had been watching her? She had no idea—no doubt thanks to Jack. The idea of him sabotaging her cut deep, but she pushed it aside for the moment. She didn't want to think about anything negative—not when she was back on the path to Formula 1.

"Thank you, Enzo! Thank you so much!"

When Nikki hung up, she spun Sean's old desk chair around with a squeal, unable to contain her joy, her relief.

Leaping out of the ancient seat, she charged out into the shop. Sean looked up from the seat he was installing in a Mark II Tiger and grinned.

"It must have been good news to put that smile on your face," he said from across the shop.

"It was the *best* news!" she gushed, looking from Sean to Jake, who'd also stopped.

"Well? Don't leave us hanging, girl. What did this Enzo say?" Sean pressed.

A huge smile broke across her face. "He phoned with an offer to race on Ferrari's prototype team in the IMSA WeatherTech Series as primary driver!" she cried.

"Holy shit! That's fantastic! You did it, baby girl! You made it!" Sean yelped, tossing his wrench on the seat and running over to sweep her into a hug.

She returned his hug, squeezing him tight. In all the time she'd been scraping and clawing her way back into racing, he'd never once doubted her. Unlike Dino and Mike, and apparently Jack, Sean had never lost faith in her.

"Thank you, Sean. Thank you for everything!" she said, her voice growing tight.

"I didn't do anything, Nikki. I just wish…" He broke off, unable to say more. He didn't have to, though. She knew what he was thinking: he wished her father was there to see this.

"I know. Me too," she said, releasing him.

As if on instinct, she turned, her eyes seeking Jake. She found him instantly, standing off to the side, his face shining with pride. Tears welled in her eyes at the sight. He was still the only person who looked at her like that. Unable to control herself, she ran over and threw her arms around him.

"I did it, Jake. I made it," she whispered, burying her face in the crook of his neck.

Jake's arms came around her instantly, securing her to him. "I knew you would, angel. I'm so proud of you," he said, holding her tight.

Nikki clung to him for another instant before she pulled away. Jake released her, though she could feel his reluctance to do so. She looked up into his eyes as the moment stretched out, a wealth of unspoken words and wishes passing between them.

The sound of Sean clearing his throat broke the spell. "Let's celebrate tonight! We'll go out to that new steakhouse on Third." He threw an arm around Nikki's shoulders. "Jake, you're going with us. And I won't take no for an answer," he said when Jake started to object, saying it sounded like a family affair. "You're part of this family, too, son."

Jake gaped at Sean for several seconds but finally agreed to go.

The remainder of the day flew by in a flurry of emails from Enzo and a lengthy phone call to Jack, during which Nikki did something she never thought she would do: fire him. He was her father's friend and hers as well, and yet he'd taken it upon himself to make decisions about her life without consulting her. He claimed he was only thinking of her best interests and didn't have the heart to tell her how he really felt about her continuing to race. He refused to take her firing him seriously, claiming he'd always look out for her—that she couldn't get rid of him that easily. She told him she could take care of herself before abruptly ending the call. In the end, Nikki knew she'd done the right thing for herself, despite the pain it brought.

By 5:00, she was dead on her feet and ready for the steak dinner Sean promised. The three of them rode together in Sean's restored 1966 Bronco and dined on prime rib with all the fixings and the best bottle of wine she'd had in years.

Sean dropped them back at the shop sometime after 10:00 and headed to his home in Santa Clara. Nikki's heart warred with itself as she headed over to her car with Jake in tow. The offer from Ferrari both thrilled and saddened her. Racing in the IMSA Series meant she would to be leaving town relatively soon and not returning very often. Her new team was based in Palm Beach, Florida, which meant she'd be spending a fair amount of time there, running test sessions at the Palm Beach International Raceway and meeting with Ferrari. Between the testing sessions, the twelve races in the WeatherTech Series, *and* her commitment to VAM, Nikki would only be in the Bay Area a handful of weeks the next year, leaving her with little to no chance of running into Jake. But maybe that was for the best. Seeing him often would only remind her of what they *could have* had.

Nikki dug her key fob out of her purse, unlocked the Ferrari, and tossed her bag inside along with the leftovers from dinner. Jake hovered near the rear bumper, hands buried in his motorcycle jacket. Standing there, with the moonlight dancing off his ebony waves, he was like something out of a film or romance novel: a tall, dark James Dean come to life.

It hurt to look at him.

"So," she said, leaning against the rear fender. "It looks like this is goodbye. I won't be coming into the shop tomorrow."

"Oh? You finished the Mustang's rear end today?"

"Yep. It was an easy swap, and my last client. It's time to focus on my racing career again. I've got a ton of things to do to prep for the IMSA team, including finding a new manager."

Jake's brows shot up. "New manager? You fired Jack? Why? Was it the sponsor thing?" he asked, coming to stand near her.

"Partly. I found out he told Enzo that I wasn't taking any offers or calls. Luckily, Enzo knew better and tracked me down via Nick," she explained.

"Jesus. I'm so sorry, Nikki. I know that had to have hurt. Jack's family."

Nikki blinked back the rush of tears that came at the thought of how many family members had turned on her like Jack had. "It did hurt, especially when it seems to run in my family: first my brothers, now him. I still can't believe it." She sniffed as a rogue tear escaped.

Jake reached over and caught the tear with his thumb. "When do you leave for Florida?" he asked, his eyes roving over her face.

"In a couple of weeks, according to the itinerary I got from Enzo. I'll be there for most of December to meet with the crew and the business end of the team and for some initial testing. I'll be home for the holidays then return right after New Year's for more test sessions and then the Rolex 24 at Daytona."

"Wow. You're right. This is it." A flash of sadness flickered in his eyes. "What about the VAM series next year? Will you be able to keep that commitment? Who's going to pit crew for you?"

She smiled, remembering how much Jake enjoyed working on the Shelby and watching it race. "It's going to be tight, but I'll manage. I have to. I'm still under contract with them," she began. "Jeff says he has some guys lined up who specialize in racing Tigers to crew for me. What that means, exactly, I don't know. All that matters is he's fronting the money for it this time."

He nodded. "Sounds like you've got it all set then, which is as it should be. You deserve this, Nikki. You deserve to be happy."

"So do you," she said, reaching up and cupping his strong, chiseled jaw, loving the way the five-o'clock shadow felt under her fingertips. "I know you don't believe that, but it's true. You deserve happiness and a life that's full of good things. I wish you could see that."

Disbelief flashed in his expression followed by something else, something she hadn't seen before: a flicker of hope. But before she could say more, he smiled sadly and said, "Me too, angel...me too."

Once again, the moment stretched out between them. But this time, there was no one to interrupt. Standing there, as close as they were, she could feel the heat coming off him like a blast furnace, feel the unspoken connection that ran between them thrum with life. And in that moment, she desperately wanted to kiss him, just one last time before they went their separate ways. One last time, so she could take that kiss and lock it away in her heart, keeping it there forever.

Sensing her unspoken thoughts, as he'd done so many times before, Jake answered her plea. He leaned in and took her mouth, kissing her as if it were the end of days. He drew their bodies together until there wasn't a centimeter of space between them. When she parted her lips and slid her tongue over his, he groaned, turned her and pressed her up against the Ferrari. In his kiss, Nikki could feel everything Jake couldn't say with words: that he wished things were different, that he wished he was a whole man instead of a broken, undeserving boy, that he would miss her terribly...that he loved her more than words could ever say.

Nikki felt all of this as he poured himself and all that he was into the kiss, into her, before he pulled back, breathless.

"You should go, angel. It's...it's time to go."

Nikki nodded, forcing herself not to reach for him, not to beg him to change his mind about them. She couldn't force him to see things differently.

"Right. It's getting late." She climbed into the Ferrari and was about to pull the door shut when Jake appeared, holding it open.

"Wait. I forgot to give you back your copy of *The Alchemist*," he said, his lips still swollen from their kiss.

She smiled up at him even as her heart shattered into a thousand pieces. "Keep it."

He frowned. "Don't you want it back? It's your favorite."

She shook her head. "I have other copies."

"But this one has your notes in it," he insisted.

Nikki reached over and grabbed the door handle, looking into his eyes —eyes that suddenly looked vulnerable, almost desperate. "I know, but I *want* you to keep it—for when you're ready to hear the message," she said before pulling the door closed and backing down the long drive.

Her eyes flicked from the rearview mirror to Jake's shrinking form as she moved farther from him and the places that were like second homes to her. When she reached the end of the drive, she backed out onto the frontage road and took one last look at Jake—a study in loneliness as he stood there in the moonlight—unaware that the familiar black Mercedes was parked only a few feet away.

With a final glance, she waved and drove away, wishing, not for the first time, that he was able to find the hope, the peace, and the happiness he so deserved.

19

Damon threw the burner phone onto the desk. He'd just been informed that he'd be spending the next several weeks, which spanned the holidays, in Caracas—or the seventh circle of Hell, as he thought of it. His boss wanted him there to work out the shipping logistics between them and the Correa Cartel.

Merry fucking Christmas.

Sighing, he reached for his regular cell to call Nino about arranging his travel plans, when Cavo's "Painful Art" blared from it.

Damon blinked at the phone. That was Nikki's ringtone. He hadn't heard from her in almost a week—not since their blow-up while she was in Ohio. Well, that wasn't exactly true. She did send him a text after the wreck, letting him know she was alive. But nothing since. He hadn't been able to reach her by phone—he suspected she'd blocked his number—and he hadn't seen her at home, either.

He shook off the shock and answered the call.

"Bella," he breathed, the relief that she'd reached out almost overwhelming.

"Hi, Damon," she said. "How are you?"

"I'm good. What's up?" he asked. Small talk wasn't his jam.

She chuckled. "You always get right to the point, don't you?"

He couldn't help the grin that spread across his face. She knew him well and wasn't afraid to call him on his shit. "That's me. So, what's going on? Where've you been since you got back?"

"I've been at Hilda's. I needed some time after I got back to sort through some stuff," she began. "I'm calling to apologize for the way I spoke to you back in Ohio, and for texting you about the accident instead of calling. I was rude—on both accounts."

His chest tightened. "You don't have to apologize, bella. I acted like a dick on the phone. And don't worry about the text. I didn't deserve even that much after the way I spoke to you," he said, meaning it.

Damon rarely—no, never—apologized. *Sorry* wasn't part of his vocabulary, generally speaking. But after he heard about Nikki's accident and saw the footage on ESPN, he regretted the way he'd lost his shit with her. The idea that their last conversation could have been filled with anger and ugliness killed him.

Nikki sucked in a breath. "Wow. That...that's sweet, Damon. But you weren't the only one behaving like a dick. I own my fair share of that. So, I'm sorry. And I also wanted you to know that you don't have to worry about my memories or anything else. Everything is fine—good, actually. I got a ride with Ferrari on their sports car racing team. Can you believe it?"

Damon leaned back in his chair. Nikki sounded so Zen about everything. Maybe there was less to worry about than he thought.

"Shit, really?" he asked, his gut tightening with new worries. Sports car racing was the real deal. Those cars were deathtraps, designed to break the fucking sound barrier or close to it.

"Yeah. I'm pretty excited. I'll be leaving for Florida soon for test runs and such."

He fisted his hand, vacillating between happiness and fear. He hated her career for the danger it put her in but wanted her to be happy—and if this did it, he couldn't be too upset. "Cool. I'm happy for you, bella. I know you wanted this."

"Thanks, Damon," she said. "Well, I'll let you get back to work. I've got a bunch of things to take care of before I go. Will you be home later?"

"Absolutely. Will *you* be there?"

"I will. See you then."

Damon blew out a heavy breath. Nikki might have a dangerous career, but it looked like she might be safe from the Europe crap—at least that was what he hoped.

He lifted his phone and dialed Nino. He needed to arrange travel plans for Caracas, then he needed to track down Tsai and let him know he'd be on his own with the gym for the next several weeks.

His eyes drifted to the photo of him and Nikki on his desk while he waited for Nino to pick up. It was a shot of them taken years ago, before everything blew up. He smiled at the image and the two of them: a couple of kids happy and in love. Those were the best times of his life—times he'd give anything to have back.

"Yo, boss! What's doin'?" Nino's voice chirped, saving Damon from a pointless trip down memory lane.

"Get a piece of paper ready. I've got a shitload of work for you," Damon ordered, grateful to have something to focus on other than things he could never have.

PART II

"Being deeply loved by someone gives you strength, while loving someone deeply gives you courage."
–Lao Tzu

"Who so loves, believes the impossible."
–Elizabeth Barrett Browning

20

J ake closed the book and leaned back in the desk chair, staring at the cover of the manual for rising to your destiny, his mind churning. In the two months since Nikki left him standing in the moonlight, he'd had countless days and nights like this: days and nights where he read, thought, wrestled with emotions he'd long since buried, and faced desires he'd denied himself for over a decade.

At first, he fought it. He didn't want to go down this path, didn't want to examine his life. But *The Alchemist* and Nikki's words haunted him day and night, forcing him to finally stop fighting and start thinking—to start living a different life.

Just as his angel had planned.

Since his decision, Jake had read *The Alchemist*, along with Nikki's annotations, several times. Eventually, he moved on to the other works she'd noted in the margins of the worn text: *Warrior of the Light* and *The Four Agreements*—works that all spoke of accepting your failures, of embracing your dreams, of rising up to life's struggles, and of living a life filled with love and happiness. The books challenged him in every way possible, but in that struggle, he found something he never expected: hope.

God, he loved Nikki. She was his anchor, his center, helping him to rebuild his life. It was a process, and a long one at that. Jake still doubted himself and the journey she'd helped him begin, continuing to blame himself for his mother's death, though not entirely anymore—his father owned his share of that tragedy—and doubting he would ever be able to *fully* let that go. And he hadn't sought counseling as Nikki had suggested, either. He wasn't ready for that—not yet. Right now was about taking baby steps—stumbling, bumbling steps that left him feeling bruised and battered but also hopeful.

He pushed his chair back and went into the kitchen to put out the snacks he and Dario would devour during the race. Today marked the start of two things: Nikki's first race in the IMSA series and Dario's first overnight visit with Jake. Katelyn, after observing him with Dario for months, petitioned the judge to increase his visits to weekly ones, reduce the supervised visits to one a month, *and* for him to have overnight visits with Dario every few weeks. In her report, she described Jake as a caring father figure and strong role model. The judge, much to Jake's shock, listened and agreed to the terms Katelyn presented. It was the best news he'd gotten since finding his angel, and he was going to make sure he didn't screw it up.

Dario arrived at 10:00 a.m., courtesy of his foster mother, Barbara Reynolds. She didn't bother to come to the door; she dropped Dario at the gate and took off as soon as Jake stepped out onto the porch. Unlike before, he didn't take her brush-off personally. Thanks to the heavy reading and soul-searching, he saw that the Reynolds' treatment of him was about their own issues and insecurities, not his. The revelation helped him release some of the anger and resentment that dogged him. It felt good, and he wished he could share it with Nikki. They hadn't spoken since the night she left. Not that he'd made an effort to reach out. It would only disrupt her new, busy life. Besides, what would he say to her if he did?

Would it go something like: *Hey, it's Jake. I'm finally getting my shit together; want to meet up?*

No. Too lame.

Maybe something like this: *I miss you like crazy, so please, please take me back.*

Shit, no. Too desperate.

How about: *You're my world, Nikki. I love you—have loved you since you saved my life in the cemetery all those years ago.*

Fuck no. Too stalkerish.

None of that seemed right, even if it was how he felt, so he stayed away, watching her from afar through updates from Sean. Maybe one day, when he came to grips with everything, he'd reach out, but not now. He wasn't ready. He wasn't good enough for her—yet.

"Dude, turn on the TV. I want to see the pre-race interviews. Nikki's slated for a feature at 10:30 a.m.," Dario said, grabbing a soda from the refrigerator and heading to the couch.

"Got it." Jake hit the power button on the remote. He already had the TV set to the network showing the race. "I'm all set, bro."

Dario dropped down on the couch, his face glued to the flat-screen. Jake sat in one of the overstuffed club chairs, feet propped up on a matching leather ottoman. After a series of commercials, the special segment opened up with a series of shots of the Daytona racetrack, followed quickly by a montage of recent and older images of Nikki across her career. Jake recognized the recent shots, catching glimpses of himself in the background with the rest of the Lethal crew. He was doing fine during the opening segment, but when she appeared on screen, live and in person, his pulse launched, forcing him upright in his chair, eyes fixed to the television.

She looked more radiant than ever, standing next to the Ferrari Prototype car, smiling and speaking animatedly. She talked about being thrilled to be back in professional racing after her hiatus, and how the face of auto racing had evolved since she began her journey at the age of five in go-karting and Quarter Midget. Jake didn't think he took more than a handful of breaths during the thirty-minute segment. When it was over, he slumped back in his chair, winded.

Dario looked over and frowned. "You still haven't contacted her, have you?" he asked, his tone bordering on scolding.

Jake rubbed a hand unconsciously over his heart. "No."

Dario leaned forward, resting his elbows on his knees. "Why not? It's obvious you're in love with her. Why not call her and tell her?"

"*Because* I love her. I'm not in a position to start a relationship with her, Dario. I'm a fucked-up mess, and until that changes, I can't be anything for Nikki but trouble. It wouldn't be fair to her. She deserves better," he explained.

"You're wrong." Dario held up a hand when Jake started to object. "I get it. I know you've been through hell since Mom died and that you're carrying some serious baggage about Dad, but you've also got a lot going for you. It's not just your baggage you'd bring to the relationship. You'd be bringing good things too."

Jake shook his head. "It wouldn't be right to burden her with my shit, not when she has so much going on."

Dario stood and moved over to the framed photos on the far wall. Jake had added to the collection displayed there since Nikki left. One of the new additions was a shot of the entire Lethal Racing team taken at Mid-Ohio after the final qualifying race. Everyone smiled at the camera, their faces filled with hope—everyone but Nikki. She only had eyes for Jake in the shot, smiling up at him with a look of adoration that took his breath away every time he looked at it.

"She wouldn't see it as a burden. That girl loves you. Look." He jabbed a finger at the team photo. "That's what love looks like, Jake, and it's not something you want to throw away because you're afraid. If you don't tell her how you feel, you're going to lose her for good. Someone will come along and snatch her up, and you'll be left on the sidelines, alone. Is that what you want?"

The idea of Nikki with another man was like a hot poker to the balls. He stared at the photograph, his hands curling into tight fists. A message from *Warrior of the Light* drifted through his mind. It spoke of knowing your faults but also knowing your strengths and not being afraid to go after the love you wanted because without it, you were nothing.

He let out a heavy breath and turned to his little brother. "When did you get so knowledgeable about life and love?"

Dario strode over to him and patted him on the shoulder. "It's a gift," he quipped, turning and grabbing the chips and salsa from the counter. "Seriously, though, I do a lot of reading. Monica's got me reading that book I've seen you with: *The Alchemist*. It's all about that shit." He dropped back down on the couch.

Jake's brows shot up. "*You're* reading *The Alchemist*?" he said, almost choking.

"Don't look so surprised, bro. You know I like to read." Dario stuffed a chip in his mouth. "I'm surprised you haven't taken the book to heart and done something about Nikki by now. You've read it enough. I thought you were smarter than that."

"I guess I'm not...but—" He broke off with a snort. "Maybe you're right. Maybe I should go after her," he finished, shocked at the admission and the idea taking root in his gut. Maybe he should tell her how he felt, beg her to take him back. There were still things Nikki didn't know about him, dark things. But deep down, Jake knew she wouldn't hold them against him—she'd said as much the night he ended things between them. He hadn't been ready to *hear* it then, but now...maybe he was ready.

Dario's head snapped to Jake. "Really?"

Jake nodded, still stunned. "Yeah, really." He held up a hand when Dario let out whoop. "I said maybe I should, not that I *would* do it for sure," he amended.

"You know what? That's good enough for me. It's a start, bro. It's a start."

~

"Yo! Jake! Open up!" Johnny's voice called from the porch.

"Just a sec!" Jake shouted, his eyes fixed to the screen as Nikki's teammate, Anton Dubois, pit for a driver change. It was the last one of the race, with Nikki jumping in to hopefully lead the team to a podium victory.

"I'll get it. I know you want to watch your girl," Dario said, rising from the couch, and opened the door for Johnny.

"Hey! *Manito!* What's up?" Johnny said, pulling Dario into a hug.

"Not too much, man. Just watching Nikki's debut race with Jake."

Johnny walked in and stood next to the chair Jake was anchored to as he watched the driver change, catching only a glimpse of Nikki's eyes through her helmet when she leaped off the guard wall and slid into the prototype Ferrari. Once she took off, he stood and greeted his best friend.

"What's up, bro?" Jake said, slapping Johnny on the back.

"*Nada.* Thought I'd stop by on my lunch and hang with you guys, catch some of the race," he said, heading to the kitchen for a bottle of water.

"Cool. We've got plenty of food. Help yourself." Jake waved to the brunch spread they'd put together.

Johnny grinned and dove in, eyeing Jake as he mounded food on his plate. "You look beat. Did you get any sleep last night?"

Jake shrugged. "A few hours. This is a twenty-four-hour endurance race. I didn't want to miss too much of it."

Johnny flashed him a knowing smile. "You mean you didn't want to miss seeing your girl out there or in interviews. Right?"

Running a hand over his rough jaw, Jake laughed. He had to be the most transparent motherfucker he'd ever known. "Pretty much, yeah," he said, heading back to the living room.

Johnny sat down next to Dario. "He's thinking about gettin' her back," Dario announced.

"Really?" Johnny arched a brow in Jake's direction. "Is that so?"

"Yep." Jake nodded.

"Well, you'd better get on that shit. A girl like that's got to have all kinds of men sniffing around her. Don't wait too long."

Jake rolled his eyes. "Don't worry. I won't." He'd thought of little else since yesterday, but he wasn't sure how to go about approaching her.

"So, is she winning?" Johnny asked, pulling Jake from his thoughts.

"Yup," Dario said. "Her team is in the lead in their class. Nikki and her boys make a powerhouse team. They're the fastest bunch out there."

"Sweet," Johnny said, sitting back.

Thirty minutes later, Nikki was holding both leads with a half hour left in the race, when Johnny called from the hallway.

"Jake, can I see you for a sec?"

"Yeah, sure." He tore his eyes from the screen, and headed back. "What's up?" he said, meeting Johnny in the hallway.

"I was going to ask you the same thing." He pushed the door to one of the bedrooms open, revealing something Jake didn't want anyone to see.

"Why the hell did you go in there?" he demanded, storming inside to make sure nothing had been disturbed. A whiteboard hung on a wall covered with photographs and notes. The other walls were littered with newspaper articles written primarily in Italian, save for the few articles he'd found on Nikki's crash at Le Mans and some about her personal life while living in Europe.

"I wanted to get *The Four Agreements.* You said I could borrow it, remember? I thought I'd grab it since you were so focused on the race. What the hell is all this shit?" he asked, waving at the room.

"If I tell you, you have to swear not to repeat any of this," Jake said, his tone deadly serious.

Johnny's expression flicked to cop mode. "Done. What's going on?"

"Do you remember the videos we saw of Nikki's crash on YouTube?" Jake asked.

"Yeah. I don't think I'll ever be able to forget them. So, what about 'em?"

"So...that video taken from inside the car shouldn't exist," he began. "Nikki's crew chief on Lethal told me that the in-car camera malfunctioned at Le Mans. It's the primary reason race officials never determined an *official* cause for the accident, only a likely one."

Johnny ran a hand over his jaw. "Okay, that *is* suspicious. But what does it mean? Why did the officials think the camera was broken? And since it clearly wasn't—not after what we saw—what happened to the footage after the race? Who took it? Why? And why is it surfacing now?"

Jake folded his arms across his chest. They were all excellent questions, all leading to frightening possibilities he didn't like thinking about.

"I think her crew chief was behind it. He's the one who would have access to the footage. He could have taken the footage and told the officials there wasn't any. There would be no way to prove him wrong—not after the car was totaled and the camera inside destroyed. Why he did it and why it resurfaced *now* remains a mystery," Jake explained.

"Could we track him down?" Johnny asked.

Jake shook his head. "I tried. He disappeared after the race and hasn't been seen since. No one's been able to find him: race officials or the cops."

"Damn... Sounds like a man on the run."

"Exactly," Jake agreed. "And it made me wonder if Nikki got mixed up in something bad, something that her crew chief was connected to somehow, and that's why she thought someone had gotten to the car *and* how and why key evidence disappeared."

"You might be right. So, did you do any more digging? What do you think she got mixed up in?" he said, waving Jake on.

Jake moved to the whiteboard. "I did. I found out she was dating this guy." He pointed to a picture of Marco Luccianno. "His dad's a Mafia boss," he said, indicating Gianni Luccianno's picture next to it.

Johnny's eyes bulged. "Oh shit. You think she saw something she shouldn't while they were together?"

Jake nodded, his expression grim. "It's a possibility." He moved over to a gruesome photograph that showed dismembered bodies at the Roman Forum. "I started researching news articles in Rome during the time she was there just before Le Mans, looking for anything that could be mob related. That's when I found this," he said, pointing to the grisly image. "Someone took out several major players in the Falco crime family two weeks before the race—the same family Luccianno's father heads."

Johnny moved closer, studying the picture. "And you think she may have seen this or something linked to it?"

"Maybe. There are no other records of major Mafia activity during this time, outside of this event. I'm thinking she either saw this or overheard something related to it. Either way, someone would definitely want to eliminate her if she could connect them to this."

"I don't know," Johnny said, shaking his head. "You don't think you're reaching a bit? I'm not saying she couldn't have seen or overheard something, but why *this*? It could be any number of things—things that didn't show up in the media."

"I wish I was, Johnny, but no."

"Why? Did Nikki say anything about *this* event specifically?"

Jake let out a heavy breath. "No. I don't think she remembers it, not consciously, anyway. She told me once that the head injury she suffered at Le Mans caused some amnesia. I think she's blocked out the accident and what led up to it. Except in her dreams."

"*Dreams?*" Johnny asked, turning away from the wall of violence.

"Yes. When we stayed at the track, I noticed she didn't sleep well. She tossed and turned and whimpered all the time. Then, one night, she had this explosive night terror. It was so bad I ended up staying with her because she was too afraid to be alone." The memory of that night and the morning that followed rushed through his veins, scorching his blood. "I think she was reliving whatever she witnessed or overheard in the dream. I read that memories can come back like that: in flashes, dreams. And whatever she was remembering was horrific. I've never seen her so scared."

Johnny nodded. "You might be on to something—though I still think it's a stretch." He ran a hand over his duty belt. "Even so, it's worth checking out. You need to tell her about this."

"I know. I thought about telling her ex, Damon, since she and I haven't been in contact. He keeps a close eye on her and may be able to fill in the blanks since he was there for her recovery. But I've decided to approach her myself, instead," Jake said, seeing this as a way of making initial contact with her without sounding like the hard-up, desperate jackass he was.

"Good. Do it soon. If she knows anything about this or anything like it, they might try something again. In fact, I'm surprised they haven't. Crime families don't leave loose ends," Johnny said.

"I know. I thought of that, and the only thing I can come up with is that maybe they've left her alone because of the amnesia. If her memories are gone, there's no need to kill her and run the risk of exposure."

"True, but it's been my experience that these mob guys don't take chances like that. The Irish mob, for example, takes out anyone they even remotely suspect has evidence against them, risky or not. They're scary as fuck."

Jake's stomach soured at the thought of Nikki being caught up in any of this. Johnny was right: the mob didn't dick around. She could be in danger now and didn't know it. He'd call her first thing on Friday. She'd be in town by then. Sean had conveniently posted her schedule on the calendar in the shop.

Johnny left shortly thereafter, leaving Jake and Dario to finish up the race. As he watched Nikki make her final laps around the track, Jake's mind flitted from what he'd discussed with Johnny to seeing Nikki sooner rather than later.

Both scared the daylights out of him.

∿

"How are you on fuel, Nikki?" Enzo's voice crackled over the radio.

"We're close, but it's enough. No need to pit," she replied, soaring past a Porsche 911 RSR. They'd taken fuel and tires at the end of Jose's last stint. They should be able to make it with only thirty minutes remaining.

"Roger that," Enzo said. "Keep your lead, Nikki."

"I'm trying." She locked her biceps as she maneuvered through The Bus Stop, Daytona's infamous chicane.

Her team held the lead, but Reinhardt Engel in the Black Hawk Audi prototype was right behind them in lap times. It was going to be a close race and the most challenging one of her career to date. The countless test sessions in which she got reacquainted with handling a car with over six hundred horsepower had helped prepare her and the team for today, but they were still nothing like being in the actual race. In a race, the adrenaline kicked in like a nitrous oxide boost to the bloodstream, fueling drivers, pushing them to be more and more aggressive as they strove to outdrive every other person on the course. You couldn't replicate that in practice sessions or test runs. Just like you couldn't replicate the fervor that came from making every move, every second, count. It was exhilarating and stressful all at once. But as tough as it was both physically and emotionally, Nikki loved every minute of it.

As the clock ticked down, she fought through the corners, braking later and later, tracking out closer and closer to the barriers lining the track, clinging to the lead in the last precious minutes of the race.

"You've almost got it. Just hang on," Enzo's voice crackled over the radio.

Nikki growled her response, her arms locked for total control of the car as she flattened the accelerator and rocketed down the final straight, sprinting across the finish line and taking the checkered flag. Her ears rang with the sounds of Enzo cheering across the radio, and her team's shouts and screams echoing in the background.

"You did it! You did it!" Enzo screamed over and over again as Nikki slowed the car, seeing the cheering crowd along the track and infield.

They'd won. They'd won the Rolex 24 Hours of Daytona.

Holy shit!

Her eyes welled with emotion as she whooped and hollered into the mic while she waved to the crowd from the cockpit: tens of thousands of people all cheering for her and her team, wild with excitement as she made the victory lap.

"Amazing drive, Nikki! You killed it out there, hot-shoe!" Jose Borja, one of her teammates, shouted into the radio.

"It was a team effort, Jose. I just finished what we all built today," she managed around the lump in her throat as she finished the victory lap and pulled the car into the pits, where the other class winners would line up beside her.

Rivers of fans and crew members streamed toward her, swarming the car. Before she could do anything, the car door opened and her crew was there, helping her out of the harnesses. Once they removed her helmet and HANS device, Enzo pulled her into a tight embrace.

"You were amazing, tesoro!" he cheered.

She returned his hug. "It was a team effort, Enzo. We did this together."

Enzo pulled back, his eyes brimming with excitement. "I know, but without you, we'd never have taken the podium, let alone an overall win. Not in the first race out."

Nikki smiled as her team and crew engulfed her. Once the hugs and high-fives were done, she and her teammates jogged to the podium and took their place in the center, the cheers of the crowd swelling around them. Nikki smiled as one of the trophy girls handed them two first-place trophies: one for their class and one for overall. She turned to the roaring crowd and held one of the glass symbols of their victory over her head, cheering wildly.

Her heart twisted in her chest when she looked out into the crowd and didn't see the one person she wanted to share this moment with the most: Jake. They hadn't spoken a word to each other in over two months, but she still thought of him every morning and again every night. And she wondered then, as she stood before the crowd, was he watching her now? Did he think about her? Did he ache inside from the sheer absence of her as she did for him?

Nikki shook off the questions and maudlin thoughts that would serve no purpose. It was time to celebrate, she thought as Jose Borja grabbed a bottle of champagne and sprayed her. She squealed in delight, choosing to enjoy the moment and her first victory in the series and not dwell on the fact that even as she reveled in the win with her team, crew, and thousands of fans, she'd never felt more alone.

21

Damon pulled off his hat and wiped the sweat from his brow, scowling out across the opening in the dense Venezuelan jungle. It was hotter than Hades out here in the middle of BFE, and if there was one thing he hated, it was intense heat.

He'd been in Caracas for weeks, but the trip and the time were worth it. Visiting the Correa Cartel bosses in person and working out the logistics of their shipments would pay off in the long run. The work they'd done these last six weeks would pave the way for smoother transactions and less stress in the future for Carlo and the family back home. That would translate to less stress for Damon and his guys and more time for him to devote to figuring out what the fuck was going on with Nikki.

The theme from *Scarface* chimed in his pocket.

He pulled his phone out. "Rossi," he snapped, wiping more sweat from his brow.

"Hey, boss!" Nino shouted.

Damon rolled his eyes. How the fuck was this guy so cheerful all the damn time? "What is it, Nino? I'm busy."

"I was calling about that thing with the Irish you wanted me to keep an eye out for and about Alcantar's boy toy," he explained.

Damon stilled. "All right. Start with the boy toy. Is the fucker dirty?"

"It's a possibility. A strong one. One of his cousins works for Gianni Luccianno's son Marco, and he's been seen visiting with Navé recently as well as contacting him by phone."

Damon swore.

Gianni Luccianno was the underboss of the Falco crime family based in Rome. The Falcos had little to do with the Mafia families in the US—most of their business was concentrated in Europe—but occasionally they did business stateside with the Berardi family, or at least they had. The families weren't on good terms these days. Nikki dated Marco for a short time while she was racing in Europe, but the relationship ended—for reasons unknown to Damon—a few weeks before the accident at Le Mans. An accident he later surmised had been orchestrated by someone on Marco's crew.

Shortly after Nikki returned to the US to continue her recovery, Damon received an anonymous email stating that as long as her memories remained gone, she'd live. Damon had already suspected foul play was involved in the accident. Nikki tried to contact him right before the race, but the call went to voicemail. In her message, she mentioned something about needing him and being afraid, but she didn't elaborate. After receiving the email, his fears were confirmed, and he immediately had its origin traced. The email had come from a small café in a village outside of Rome. Further investigation and several thousand Euros later, Damon learned that the message was sent from a computer owned by one of the guys on Marco's payroll.

Damon had no idea why Marco put a hit on Nikki; her memories of that time were gone, and he couldn't get anything out of Marco's guy without rousing suspicion within the Falcos or his family, so he dropped it. Not that it really mattered. At the time, Damon knew what he needed to keep Nikki safe, and that had been enough...until now.

Now he needed to know everything about her lost memories. It was too big of a coincidence that a cousin of one of Marco's guys was dating Nikki's best friend. Way too big.

He ran a shaky hand over his face. "Okay. What about the Irish? Any good news there?"

"Sorry, boss, but no. I've heard grumblings about them taking revenge on someone for getting a couple of their key guys popped for attempted arson and burglary back in September."

September...

Damon rolled off a slew of F-bombs. "Did you find out who the target is?" His pulse skyrocketed. Those had to be the guys Nikki got busted at Denny's place.

Jesus Christ, could shit get any more complicated with her?

"No. And apparently, this isn't going to be their first attempt, either. They tried to take the person out back in November, but the attempt failed. The person's still breathing, and they're not happy about it."

Shit.

That was Nikki he was referring to. It had to be. The botched hit fit the timeframe for her accident at Mid-Ohio, the one his gut had told him was a hit after he found out who'd caused it: the kid who drove for Shaughnessy Irish Whiskey—a business owned and run by the Irish mob based in San Francisco…the same Irish mob family that was trying to expand into Wood Glenn and whose boys he'd seen in the back of the police cruiser that night at Denny's.

He'd been hoping his gut was wrong, that it was a coincidence, but he should have known better. Coincidences didn't exist when you were dealing with the underbelly of society.

"All right. Put the tail back on Nikki. But make sure you mix the cars up this time. It can't be the same guys every day, or she'll notice. And make sure you tell them to intervene if it even *looks* like she might be in trouble. You got that?" Damon barked.

"Yeah, sure, boss. But why? Is she the target?" Nino asked, his voice dropping to a whisper.

If anyone else had asked him, he would have lied. Damon trusted few; Nino was counted among that number. He'd saved Damon's ass on more than one occasion in the past. He was good people.

"I think she might be, but keep that shit to yourself. Tell the boys to keep their eyes on Nikki and to make sure if they go into a situation, they go in hot. Got it?"

"Jesus," Nino muttered. "You got it, boss. Don't worry. We'll look out for your girl."

Your girl.

If only that were still true…but it wasn't and never would be again. He'd made a promise to Nikki's father shortly before he died, and he didn't welch on promises or bets, no matter what.

"Good. I'll see you in a few days." Damon ended the call.

He needed to find out if Nikki's memories were back and if she'd said anything to Hilda. If they were and she'd spoken to her about it, then it was possible that Hilda could have said something to Peter, not realizing the danger she was putting Nikki and herself in. Hilda cared about Nikki like a sister. She might have confided in this Navé guy if they were as close as Nino suspected because she was worried about Nikki and needed someone to talk to about it. And if that was the case and he reported it back to Marco—

He cut off the thought before it could surface and dialed Nikki's cell, hoping it was charged. She'd fallen into the habit again of not charging it, making it impossible to get ahold of her. He wanted to let her know his return date and set up a time for them to meet. She'd assured him everything was fine where her memories were concerned, but he didn't buy it. Not now.

Her cell went straight to voicemail.

Of course.

He glared out across the clearing to where his guys and the Correa crew were loading kilos of the finest South American cocaine into crates marked *Humanitarian Relief.* A ghost of a smile graced his lips as the irony of that hit him. He supposed in some ways, the drugs were a relief of sorts to those who used them. He wouldn't know. Drugs were never his thing. All he cared about was getting the shipment finished and off to its destination. When that happened, he'd be heading back to Wood Glenn, where he could figure out what the fuck was going on with Nikki's memories and try to straighten out the Irish issue. It wouldn't be easy. Nikki thought he was paranoid and wasn't going to fess up easily. And the relationship between the Irish and the Berardi family was tenuous at best, especially for him. His one-night stand with Angela O'Brien years back saw to that. She hated him, which meant her hotheaded father, head of the SF Irish mob, hated him too.

Fixing this would take time and hell of a lot of creativity to pull off without too much bloodshed. And it couldn't happen soon enough.

22

Nikki dropped the heavy suitcase on her bed and ripped open the zipper. She'd flown home the Friday after the race, and even with a direct flight, the trip took more than half the day.

She was pulling out a stack of clothes headed for the closet when her bedroom door burst open.

"You're back!" Hilda squealed, pulling Nikki into one of her infamous bear hugs.

"Hey, Hil! How'd you know? I got here like fifteen minutes ago," she squeaked as Hilda continued to squeeze the life out of her.

"I was driving home and saw the gate open. It's been shut tight since you left." She released Nikki and dropped onto the bed, peering into the suitcase. "Did you bring me anything?"

"I was in Florida, not Paris. There's nothing to bring back but oranges and bug bites from vampire mosquitos," Nikki lied. She always brought Hilda something from her travels, just as Hilda did for her.

Hilda's lip popped out in an epic pout. "Really? You were gone all that time and *nothing*? Not even a stuffed Miami Dolphin?"

Nikki chuckled. "I'm kidding. Of course I brought you something. It's under my books." She pointed to the small stack of books that traveled with her everywhere.

"Yay!" Hilda clapped, pulled out the books, and found a small bag containing a shot glass that read Palm Beach beneath a cartoon palm tree. "Awesome sauce! This will go perfect with my collection."

"I thought so," Nikki said. She always brought Hilda a shot glass when she traveled, among other things. Hilda had a massive collection of them from all over the world.

"Hey, did you lose the journal?" Hilda asked as Nikki continued to unpack.

"No. It's on the nightstand, where it always is," she said, glancing over her shoulder.

Hilda's brows shot up. "You didn't bring it with you? You always do."

It was true. Nikki usually brought the journal with her on extended trips along with a copy of *The Alchemist* and *Warrior of the Light*. They were the books that brought her comfort and strength when she felt hers waning, especially the journal. But she didn't bring the journal this time and hadn't taken it with her for several months now. Not since Jake started traveling with her. His appearance in her life had made bringing the journal unnecessary. Like Mystery Man, he gave her the strength and comfort she needed when she felt low.

But when she started traveling for Ferrari, she'd left it behind for a different reason. After things ended with Jake, she decided she needed to break her dependence on *both* of them. Nikki needed to learn that she could pull strength and comfort from herself, and if she needed reminders, she could turn to the powerful messages in her other books to help guide her, and not Jake or Mystery Man.

"I decided to leave it at home," she said.

"Really? I thought it helped you when you needed a boost," Hilda commented, her eyes tracking Nikki around the room.

Nikki shrugged. "It did, but I realized that I don't need someone else to give me a boost. I can find strength on my own."

"Wow. Good for you. It's about time too." She tilted her head to study her. "So, tell me: why do you look so sad? I mean, for a girl who's had a personal breakthrough and hit a major career milestone, you look awfully down."

After dropping her T-shirts into the hamper, Nikki turned to Hilda. "It's Jake. I miss him."

Hilda rolled her eyes. "Of course you do. You love him. So why don't you go tell him that?" she said in that matter-of-fact way only Hilda could pull off without sounding like a bitch.

Nikki reared back. "I can't. *He's* the one who broke things off. He needs to come to me when he's ready, not the other way around."

"Why?" she countered, continuing on when Nikki gave her a *what the hell* look. "Did it ever occur to you that he needs *you* to make the first move? If he feels as broken as you described, he needs you to show him that you love him and will help him get to a place of healing. You understand that loving someone means standing by them no matter what, but

Jake doesn't understand that because he's never had it. You need to shove that shit in his face, girl. You need to fight for him—for both of you."

Nikki considered her friend's advice. Hilda did have a point. Jake wasn't able to see that love could help him heal and that he deserved to heal in the first place. And maybe *shoving it in his face,* as Hilda put it, would work.

"But what if it doesn't work?" she asked Hilda. "What if he rejects me? What if he's moved on?"

"He's not with anyone. The guy's miserable."

"How do you know?"

"I went by the shop a couple of weeks back. Sean called and said you left some tools at his place. I went by to grab them and bring them back here so you wouldn't have to worry about it. While I was there, I saw Jake. He was friendly enough, but I could tell that he was struggling with something, especially when he asked about you. Sean confirmed my suspicions when he walked me out and told me that Jake had been more withdrawn than usual—apparently he's a pretty quiet guy to begin with—that he's been keeping to himself even more lately, outside of visiting his brother, anyway," she explained.

Nikki's heart ached at the news. *More withdrawn? Struggling?*

Oh no...

"He needs you, girl. More than that, he loves you. I could see it in his tortured eyes that day and in the look that came over him at the mere *mention* of your name. If you love him like I think you do, you need to go to him and tell him. He needs to hear it as much as you need to say it," she said.

"What should I say?" Nikki worried her bottom lip.

Was she really considering doing this?

"Start with *I love you*, and the rest will come." Hilda came over and handed Nikki her cell phone. "Call and see if he's home and then head over there."

Nikki took a deep breath, her decision made. Of course she was going to do this. She had to. She loved Jake, and he needed to know that and to know that she'd fight for him—for *them*—until they were where they belonged: together.

Heart pounding in her chest, Nikki took the phone and went to unlock it, only to find it was dead.

Well, shit.

"It's dead, and I don't know his number by heart," she whined, her hands shaking.

"Then go over there. It's Friday night, but I bet he's home. If not, wait for him," Hilda ordered.

Nikki nodded and darted for the door. She stopped abruptly to wrap Hilda in a tight hug. "Thank you," she whispered.

Hilda returned her hug then pushed her toward the door. "Anytime, girl. Anytime."

Nikki dashed down the stairs, grabbed her purse, and bolted for the garage. She roared out of the driveway minutes later and flew down the roads of the Glenns like she'd flown around the track at Daytona.

She made good time until she hit Wood Glenn proper. Just as she darted past the high school, red and blue lights lit up behind her, followed by a siren.

Shit.

Of all the times to hit a speed trap!

Snarling to herself, she pulled over in front of the gas station where she'd first seen Jake and grabbed her license and registration. She wanted to expedite this bullshit as quickly as possible. She had a man to track down.

She rolled down her window as the officer approached. "Afternoon, officer," she said in her cheeriest, most innocent-sounding voice.

"Ma'am," he said, leaning down and peering into the car.

Nikki's eyes widened. He didn't look like any cop she'd ever seen before—at least not one that wasn't on TV or in one of those charity calendars filled with half-naked hot guys in uniform. He had a pair of large chocolate-brown eyes and golden skin that set off a bright white smile nestled beneath a neatly trimmed moustache.

Wow.

"Do you know why I pulled you over this afternoon?" he asked, a faint Spanish accent washing over her like a warm breeze.

She shrugged. "Not sure," she said, knowing it could be any number of things. She'd broken at least a dozen laws getting this far.

He smirked. "Why don't you guess?"

She arched a brow. What kind of cop was—she sought out his name tag —Officer J. Lucero? *Lucero?* Why did that sound familiar? Where had she heard it before?

Then it hit her. Jake. His friend *Johnny Lucero* was a local cop.

"You're Jake's friend," she said.

He nodded, resting an arm on the windowsill. "That's right. And you're Nikki Elliot, the girl he's crazy about," he said, face straight.

Joy trilled through her veins.

"That's right." She smiled. "How did you know?"

He smiled again, and she could have sworn her heart sighed. "Jake mentioned your unique car, among other things about you. When you flew by here, I decided to stop you—and not because you were trying to break the sound barrier in this thing."

Okay, this is weird. What's he up to?

She swallowed audibly. "All right. I'll bite. Why did you stop me?"

"To ask you to give Jake another chance. My boy's new at this. You're the first and only girl he's ever been crazy for, and he doesn't know how to deal with it. He's working on it, though. In fact, he was going to call you today. Did he, by chance?"

Crazy about her? Working on it? Going to call her?

"You with me, *cariña*?" he said when she didn't respond.

Nikki shook her head to clear it. "I don't know if he called. My phone's dead. But it doesn't matter. I'm on my way to see him. That's why I was driving like a convict on the run."

Johnny beamed at her. "You were? For real?"

"For real. I was headed over there to tell him I love him," she said, shocked at her blunt response.

"Well, all right!" he whooped. "In that case, you need to get out of here *pronto*. But I'll give you an escort so you don't get stopped again or cause an accident."

"Wow. Really?"

"Absolutely. I'd do anything for Jake. He's like a brother to me, Nikki."

Her heart warmed. "I know. He feels the same for you too."

Johnny nodded and took off for his cruiser. When he pulled out in front of her, she followed him to Restoration Way. His blue and red lights flashed and siren blared the entire trip. She could tell by the way he drove he would make a great racecar driver. She'd make sure and tell him that the next time she saw him.

When they reached the familiar cul-de-sac, he flipped a U-turn and gave her a thumbs-up as she turned onto the private road and headed for Jake's.

As Nikki got out of the Ferrari, a familiar '69 Chevelle SS pulled in behind her. She smiled broadly when Ignacio Ruiz, Nacho for short, hopped out.

"Hey there, little *mamacita*," he said, coming over and wrapping his strong arms around her.

"Hi, Nacho. What are you doing here?" she asked as he released her.

"I came by to check on Denny's place. I've been doing it ever since that thing with the Irish back in September."

"What thing with the Irish? You mean the arson and burglary attempt?" she asked, arms folded over her chest.

"Yeah, that's the one. Wait, you stopped that, didn't you?"

"I did, but what does it have to do with the *Irish*? Whatever that means."

Nacho's usually lighthearted expression turned grim. "The Irish mob, *chica*. Didn't you hear? Denny was in trouble with them. They were there to send a message that night and take enough parts to cover what he owed. You stopped them. And I have to say, you've got guts for doin' it. I wouldn't mess with those guys on my best day. They're crazy motherfuckers."

Nikki's stomach dropped, slid down her leg, and hit the ground. She'd interfered with the Irish mob? *Fuck.* That couldn't be good.

She was about to respond when Nacho held up a hand and stepped in front of her. He turned toward the street and narrowed his eyes, listening, waiting. Seconds later, the familiar black Mercedes inched by. Nikki glared at the sedan around his shoulder. She hadn't seen them since before she left for Florida back in December. She'd assumed Damon finally called them off.

Apparently she was wrong.

Nacho turned around once the car was out of sight. "You know those guys?" he asked.

"They belong to Damon." She glowered.

"No, they don't."

Her eyes snapped to his. "What? How do you know?"

"Because I know all of Damon's guys, and they don't drive top-end Mercedes sedans. That's way above even their pay grade."

Nikki's pulse jumped. "If they aren't his, do you know whose they are? Could they belong to the Irish guys?"

Nacho shook his head. "The Irish boys don't roll like that either. Whoever they are, they must be someone powerful, though. Rides like that cost a lot of coin. Why? Have you seen the car before?"

Her head spun. Damon wasn't lying when he said he'd called his surveillance guys off. All this time, it had been someone else. But who? Who would bother following *her*? And why? Who else had she pissed off besides the Irish? Better yet, what did Damon know about all of this and why did he think it was linked to her memories of Le Mans?

Nacho dropped a warm hand on her shoulder. "You okay there, Nikki? You look worried."

She needed to pull it together. She was here to see Jake and straighten out *that* situation. She would deal with this when Damon returned from South America. He was due back tonight; hopefully, she could see him tomorrow and clear things up. It would mean opening up about her flashbacks, but that was okay. Obviously it was time.

Nikki turned to Nacho. "I'm fine," she said. "I've got to go, though. I'm here to see someone."

He nodded, his expression telling her he didn't buy her story, but he didn't argue. "All right. But if you ever need anything, you give me a call. I know you and Dino are on the outs, but you and I go way back before all that shit. We're *familia*."

"Thanks, Nacho. I'll remember that," she said, hugging him.

She released him and watched him head over to Denny's. Nikki let out a heavy breath as she walked to Jake's on shaky legs. When she slipped inside the gate concealing Sean's shop, she saw Jake's Harley parked in his spot.

He was home. Good.

She steeled herself and made her way up the stairs leading to the expansive apartment that ran the length of the Den, praying that Johnny and Hilda were right.

~

JAKE GLARED DOWN AT HIS LIFELESS PHONE FOR THE HUNDREDTH TIME. HE'D left Nikki a voicemail over six hours ago. Why hadn't she called?

A sick feeling settled in his stomach. What if he was too late? It had been over two months since they'd seen each other. What if she'd moved on with someone else? Someone *without* the baggage he brought to the table?

A knock at the door yanked him from his downward spiral. He peered through the peephole and spotted the back of a honey-blond-haired head.

He straightened. Did he see that right? He bent down and took another look. *Holy shit.* He did. It was Nikki.

Jake threw the dead bolt and ripped open the door with enough force to tear it off the hinges.

"Nikki?" he asked as she spun around, startled.

"Jesus! I thought the door was going to come off," she yelped, a hand pressed to her chest. Catching her breath, she smiled up at him. "Hi, Jake."

"W-What...what are you doing here?" he stammered, gaping at her as if she were a mirage.

She inhaled deeply. "I came here to see you. Can I...come in?"

Shaking off the stupor, he nodded and stepped aside, waving her in.

She walked past him and into the apartment, stopping when she caught sight of the wall where she'd helped him hang that first set of photographs months ago. "You've added to them," she observed, her eyes roving over the dozen or so new photographs he'd added, most of her at one track or another, coming to rest on the one of her looking at him with adoration and love.

He cleared his throat. "Yeah. I, uh...I hung those after the holidays."

She stared at the photograph for several long seconds while he kept his eyes locked on her. He feared if he looked away, she'd disappear or he'd wake up and find out this was some sort of messed-up dream.

"I'm glad. You should be proud of them. You're a talented photographer," she said, turning those gorgeous sea-glass eyes on him.

He flashed her a crooked smile. "You sure you're not biased?" He felt like a dumbass the minute the words left his mouth. *What the fuck, Jake?*

Nikki bit down on her lower lip, forcing him to stifle a groan. Did she have any idea how sexy that was? How much *he* wanted to be the one biting down on that plump lower lip?

"I might be—just a little," she said.

"So...what brings you here?" he asked, moving farther into the apartment. He needed to put some space between them before he did something stupid, like jump her.

She didn't follow. She stayed rooted to the floor in front of the *wall of fame*, as Dario called it. "You," she stated.

Jake spun around, eyes wide. "*Me?*"

She nodded. "Yes, Jake. I came for you. I wanted... No, that's not right." She stopped, closed her eyes, and took a deep breath. He noticed then that she was trembling. When she'd gathered the reins of her composure, she opened her eyes and continued in a rush.

"I needed to see you so I could tell you that I missed you—missed *us*. And I know that you said we couldn't be together, but I think you're wrong. I think together is exactly what we—"

He didn't let her finish the thought. The minute he heard her say she missed him, all semblance of control fled him like a thief in the night. One second he was listening to her pour her heart out, and the next he was pulling her into the circle of his arms, kissing her.

After a few seconds, he came up for air.

"You didn't let me finish." She panted, her delicate hands gripping his forearms.

Jake smiled at her, the first real smile he'd felt in weeks. "Sorry. I sort of lost it when you said you missed me."

Her eyes went wide. "Oh. Does that mean you missed me too?" she asked, her voice like a soft caress over his soul.

He nodded. "Like crazy, angel. Not a day has gone by that I haven't thought of you, missed you—*needed* you," he confessed, the tightness in his chest easing with every admission.

She cupped his face in her hands, her fingertips running over the stubble along his jaw. "Thank God. I was afraid I'd be too late," she breathed.

A low growl rumbled through him as he leaned in and kissed her again, pouring every second they'd been apart into it. She groaned as he deepened the kiss, savoring her with every lick of his tongue, every nibble of her lush lips, every caress of his hands as they roved over her body.

She pulled away all too soon, though, driving him mad with lust. "Is that why you called me?" she asked, leaning back to look at him.

Her question hit him like a bucket of ice water, dousing the fire building inside him. "You knew I called? Why didn't you call back?" he asked, hating the hurt even he could hear in his voice.

"My phone's dead. I had no idea you called until Johnny told me when he pulled me over today," she explained.

Jake arched a brow. "Johnny pulled you over? Why?" What the hell was his friend trying to pull?

Nikki chuckled. "To convince me to come see you. When I told him I was on my way here, he gave me a police escort. We made it here in record time."

Johnny did that? *For him?* He couldn't decide if he wanted to punch the guy or hug him.

"Don't be mad. He cares about you. He was trying to help," she said, sensing his conflict.

Nikki was right. Jake couldn't be mad at Johnny—this time. But they were going to have a little talk about boundaries going forward. It was one thing to give advice, but he didn't need his friends fighting his battles for him.

"I know. I'm not mad," he said.

"Good. Now, why did you call me?"

Jake's stomach sank when he thought about the answer to that. His original plan was to lure her there to talk about the Le Mans accident. But those plans got blown to hell the minute he found her standing on the porch. Now all he could think about was getting his hands and mouth on her. He thought about lying so they could get back to that, but he couldn't do it—not to her.

"Two reasons, actually. One, I wanted to tell you that I missed you and that I was wrong to break things off," he began.

"And the other?"

He puffed out a breath. "The other has to do with some research I've been doing. Research on your accident at Le Mans."

She stiffened in his arms. "What? Why would you research that?"

"Because of this." He took her hand and led her to the office at the end of the hall, laying it out there as they went. "The day before we left for

Mid-Ohio, Dario sent me a link to a YouTube video of your accident. It was footage taken from the in-car camera."

Nikki stopped short outside the office. "That's impossible. The camera malfunctioned—nothing was recorded. Jack told me himself."

Jake's blood boiled at the thought of that bastard. "Well, he was lying or misinformed—either is a possibility in my book," he grumbled. "I've seen the footage, angel. It's of you as you hit the Mulsanne Straight before the car went off course. In it, I could hear you say that the brakes failed without warning. And then, just before you wrecked you said, 'Oh God… how did he know? How did he get to the car?'"

She stared up at him with a horrified expression. "Why didn't you show this to me before?" she demanded.

"I was going to after the championship. I didn't think telling you about it before the race was a good idea. And then everything snowballed, and I never got the chance," he said, hoping she understood he wasn't trying to hide anything from her—that he wasn't a controlling bastard like her ex.

He could almost hear the gears turning in her head as she processed that. Finally she said, "Okay. But what research did you do?"

He opened the door to the office and gestured for her to enter. "This."

She gave him a searching look before she stepped inside and gasped at the scene. "Jesus," she muttered, standing in the center of the room and moving in a slow circle to take it all in. "What is all of this?"

Jake explained his theory. When he showed her the article about the murders at the Forum, though, she leaped back from the gory images with a shout.

"Oh my God! That's what I've been dreaming about! It…it wasn't a nightmare. It was a memory, like the others," she said in a rush, stumbling back from it as if it could reach out and grab her.

Jake steadied her before she tripped over the desk chair. "What do you mean, 'others'? Have other memories come back?"

She nodded. "A few." Nikki explained about the other flashbacks, the ones of her at Le Mans before the race.

Listening to her recount the flashbacks sent Jake's warning bells into DEFCON 5 territory. His worst nightmares were playing out before his eyes. She *had* been in serious trouble at Le Mans and might still be now. The thought sent a cold blast of fear through him. If anything happened to her, he didn't know what he'd do.

"I must have seen this happen somehow. But why? What reason would I have to be associating with these guys?"

"You were seeing Marco Luccianno around this time. The men that were killed worked for his father, Gianni Luccianno—underboss of the Falco crime family. Maybe you were going to see him that night and stumbled on this by accident," he offered, hating the thought of her anywhere near this shit.

Nikki paled. "We weren't seeing each other then. I broke up with him weeks before that for cheating on me. I had no reason to be seeking him out—at least none that I can remember. Not that it matters. Obviously I saw this…" She backed away from Jake to the door. "And if that's the case, then whoever killed those men tried to kill me too. And…and I…I think they're still watching me, have been for months." She whispered the last part, her eyes darting around the room.

"What?" He moved toward her, but she backed away, putting a hand up.

"Someone's been following me since the summer. I thought it was Damon because he had his guys following me for a while too. But it wasn't just him. It was someone else—someone who wanted to keep tabs on me to see if I was a liability—which I am to you, to Hilda, to Sean…to everyone!" she cried, darting out the door.

"Nikki! Wait!" Jake called, running after her. The girl was quick on her feet, but Jake was faster. He reached her as she neared the front door. "You're not going anywhere. Not without me," he said, blocking her exit.

Her eyes were wide with panic, and her voice echoed that fear. "Don't you get it? You're in danger just being around me. I need to get as far away from here as I can before someone gets hurt!" she pleaded, trying to pull him away from the door.

Jake grabbed her by the wrists and held her there. "The only one who's at risk is you. And I won't let you face that risk alone. I'm in this with you, all the way."

She shook her head, struggling against him. "Why? Aren't you afraid for your life? What about Dario? What happens to him if you get hurt, or worse? Why would you stick around knowing it could destroy you?"

"Because, angel," he ground out, trying not to hurt her as he gripped her wrists tighter, "it's what you do when you love someone."

She froze. "What did you say?"

Jake leaned in, pressing his forehead to hers. This wasn't how he'd imagined telling her this, but then he supposed some things couldn't be planned. They just happened.

"I said, it's what you do when you love someone. I love you, Nikki. I have for—" He almost said years, but he quickly amended that since she still had no idea he'd been watching her at the cemetery. "Months…since the moment you held that shotgun to my chest."

A laugh bubbled out of her even as tears filled her eyes, spilled over, and coursed down her cheeks. "Really? Do you have a fetish for women with guns?"

He released her wrists and caught her tears with his thumbs, chuckling. "I must because not only did you capture my heart that night, you completely turned me on with your Annie Oakley swagger."

"Good." She sniffed. "Because I love you too."

Her words hit him like a bolt of lightning to the chest, and he couldn't hold himself back. Bracing his hands on either side of her head, he leaned down and took her mouth in a scorching kiss. She didn't resist. She groaned, throwing her arms around him, pressing her taut body against his.

Nikki's response scattered his thoughts, chasing away the darkness that had engulfed them moments before, leaving only the two of them and the love they felt for one another. He didn't think about the danger she was in or how he was going to help her out of it. His thoughts were centered on the beautiful girl in his arms who'd admitted that she loved *him*—a man broken down by grief, struggling every day not to break any further, and a man who, now that he was given the chance, would work even harder to be what she deserved.

Overcome with a heady blend of emotion and lust, Jake pressed himself more firmly against Nikki, letting her feel exactly how much she affected him. When she let out a sinful moan, he broke away, seconds from losing it right then and there.

"Angel, we should—"

"No. Don't stop," she cut in.

He hesitated, his mind screaming *stop* while his body roared for him to take her into his bedroom, into his bed, and ravish her until she screamed his name. To make love to her all night, until he, and he alone, filled her every fantasy.

"Nikki." He groaned, his mind winning out. "We should...damn it...I don't want this to go any further because you're trying to forget something. That's not how this should go."

She ran her hands over his chest. "That's not why I don't want to stop. I don't want to stop because I love you, and I don't want to waste any more time waiting to show you how much."

Jake searched her eyes. "Are you sure?" he asked, his voice as rough as sandpaper.

Instead of telling him her answer, she showed him. Stepping back out of his arms, she pulled off her sheepskin boots, her jacket, the tight V-neck sweater that hugged the sinful curves of her body, and finally the pink lace bra concealing a pair of breasts that drove him mad with lust.

Sweet mother of God...

All the air left his lungs in a whoosh as he stared down at her half-naked body, making him a huge fan of the whole show-versus-tell concept.

Showing fucking rocked.

"*Grazie a Dio. Ti amo, angelo—solo tu, per sempre,*" he declared, slipping into his native tongue as he swept her into his arms and carried her to his bedroom, where he planned on spending the rest of the night showing her exactly how much he loved her and always would—per sempre.

23

Nikki squeaked as Jake swept her off her feet and into his arms, kissing her deeply while he stalked back to his bedroom. What a multitasker. How he managed to kiss her senseless and make it to his bedroom without tripping and taking them both down blew her mind.

Once they were in his room, a large space dominated by a heavy four-poster bed, he kicked the door shut, insulating the two of them from the rest of the world, leaving only the passion and love they shared. Jake set her down on the bed with gentleness and caring that made her heart sigh then helped her shimmy out of her jeans. Nearly naked now, she gazed up at his face, watching his hungry eyes rake over her like a king at a feast.

"*Sei cosí bella, angelo,*" he whispered, his voice taking on an Italian accent that flowed over her like warm chocolate.

Heat singed her flesh at the blend of awe and lust behind his words, in which he referred to her as *a beautiful angel*. He bent down and placed a reverent kiss to her lips then dropped his lips to her breasts and teased them with his skillful mouth. The sensation sent shockwaves through her body, pulling a husky groan from deep within her.

At her response, Jake stood and made short work of his clothes. With his eyes locked on hers, he pulled the black Henley over his head, the muscles of his chest and abs rolling as he did. Once his shirt joined her jeans, he reached down and removed his belt, followed by his low-slung jeans and black boxer briefs.

And then he stood there before her, as naked as the day he was born. *Glorious.*

Every inch of him was a study in magnificence from the unruly dark waves that adorned his head, to the cut of his chiseled jaw and straight Roman nose, to the sculpted muscles that ran the length of his body. Everything about him screamed strength and power.

She sucked in her lower lip, feeling a pleasant hum in her veins and a gnawing hunger deep in her core.

One side of his lips curled up into the smile that made her heart melt. "Keep looking at me like that, angel, and this is going to be over before it gets started," he rumbled.

Her femme fatale purred. "Then I guess we'd better get started."

Jake swallowed. "As you wish." He grinned, leaned down and climbed on the bed, prowling toward her as she scooted up to the headboard.

Her breath whooshed out of her when he reached her and guided her onto her back, his large body hovering over hers. Nerves and excitement exploded in her tummy. This was happening. Right here. Right now. With Jake. There was no one around to stop them, no interruptions to shatter the moment. It was just the two of them and the endless hours ahead.

It was real, and suddenly, amidst the love and desire, she felt a sliver of fear snake through her. Not of Jake—he'd never hurt her—but of her lack of experience in this area. She'd never gone beyond fueled make-out sessions with guys, and even then there had only been Damon and Marco.

This...this was uncharted territory for her but not for Jake. She knew he was experienced—Angela had intimated that very clearly that night at the Ox—and she suddenly wished that she had a little more history in this department too. She wanted tonight to be incredible for both of them. She knew Jake would make this amazing for her—there was no doubt in her mind about *that*—but she wondered if she could do the same for him. She honestly didn't know.

The idea sent her femme fatale scrabbling into a dark corner.

"Hey, where'd you go?" he asked, gazing down at her.

"Nowhere. I'm right here," she replied, feigning a smile.

Jake shook his head. "I don't think so. A minute ago you were looking at me with that sexy gaze of yours, and now it's gone."

She blinked up at him. "How do you know me so well?"

He smiled. "I've had lots of practice studying you." He eased down and rested his weight on one elbow, his eyes searching hers. "You don't have to be afraid, angel. I won't hurt you. *Ti amo.*"

"I know. It's not that," she said, feeling a blush scald her cheeks.

"Then what is it?"

"It's...well..." *God, how embarrassing.* "I've never...I haven't been with anyone like this, and I'm afraid I won't—" She broke off, covering her flaming face. "Ugh, never mind. I'm being stupid."

Smooth, Nik. Real freaking smooth there. Way to kill a mood.

"Hey. Don't hide. It's okay." He plucked her hands from her face. "You're not being stupid. I get it. But you've got to know there is nothing you could do tonight that would be wrong. Tonight will be amazing for both of us, *lo prometto*. Being with you, like this, will be the most incredible, beautiful experience I've ever had, simply because it's with *you*."

Nikki peeked up at him through her lashes. When she saw the honesty in his eyes, all of her fears vanished. "Thank you," she whispered, loving him more with every second.

"No need to thank me. I'm speaking the truth." He ran gentle fingertips along her hairline. "But if you start to feel uncomfortable, we can stop any time. Okay?" he said, his voice reverberating through her. "If anything hurts or you need to stop, you tell me, and we will."

The love and tenderness that echoed in his voice rocked her to the core. She'd never known anyone like Jake before, and she knew she never would again.

"Okay," she breathed, relaxing.

He smiled softly, his lips descending on hers. The kiss started out tender and sweet but deepened to something more, something shattering. His mouth moved over hers until they were both breathless. Eventually, his lips drifted away from hers and skated across her jaw, down her neck, and over the line of her collarbone, nibbling and sucking as he went.

His mouth was incredible. Like magic, it stirred a potent desire deep within her—a desire that began to coil tighter and tighter as he continued his descent, raining kisses across her breasts. Her back arched as he took a nipple in his mouth, sucking deep, forcing a keening sound from her lips. He worried the sensitive tip as his rough fingers settled over her other breast and tugged and teased in tandem with his mouth. Every touch, every pull sent a jolt of liquid desire through her body, straight to her core, where that coil continued to wind.

Jake's mouth moved back and forth between her breasts, making every pulse point pound with pleasure. Her hips rocked against him, nudging the rock-hard length she'd gotten an eyeful of, sending more bursts of sensation through her wired system. The coil in her core tightened until it snapped, forcing a sharp cry from her lips as she came.

Jake lifted his head from her breasts, his gaze like molten lava. "Fuck, I love that sound," he all but growled.

She looked up at him through hooded eyes. "Then make me do it again."

With a devilish grin that said he'd make good on that demand, he shifted, smoothing his hand down her stomach to the lace panties she wore, and slid them off in one swift movement.

Nestling himself between her legs, he gazed intently at the most sensitive area on her body. *"Cosí bellisima,"* he murmured, dipping his head, and kissed her in the most intimate way possible.

Nikki jerked at the searing kiss, her body flooding with heat as he moved his mouth over her, working his tongue in teasing licks and tastes. Her head kicked back against the pillow as the coil tightened again, her hips rocking against his mouth, meeting the strokes of his tongue when he paid special attention to the hypersensitive bundle of nerves.

"God, Jake," she breathed, opening her eyes and angling her head so she could watch. She couldn't resist. The femme fatale she didn't know she possessed before she'd met him wanted to watch him drive her to uncharted heights. The intimacy of the act and the carnal desire it drew forth were potent. A new wave of lust crashed over her at the sight of his head between her thighs as he groaned and growled, devouring her.

Nikki gasped, the air lodging in her lungs at the primal scene.

It was too much. She went reeling over the edge once more.

She cried out, and he groaned against her as the release rushed over her in wave after wave of pleasure. Jake stayed there, pulling every bit of sensation from her until her body went lax.

He rose and moved over her, dropping more kisses to her sensitive flesh, until she was cradling him. "I love the sounds you make, angel. Especially the way you cry my name when you come. It's beautiful."

"That...God, that was incredible. I never knew *that* could be so...wow," she breathed.

Hilda was right. Non-self-induced orgasms, especially of the Jake Masercotti variety, topped everything. Her body felt boneless—like all the tension and strain had leached out of her. She could get used to this.

A look of masculine pride graced his lips as they curled up on one side. "That good?"

"Oh yeah." She nodded for emphasis.

Jake chuckled. "Well, get ready. Because it's about to get even better," he said, reaching over and patting the bed.

After a beat, he smacked the bed with a curse.

"What?" she asked, looking to where his hand gripped the comforter.

Eyes closed, he let out a slow exhale. "I just realized I don't have any condoms. Not even on the Harley."

"Oh," she said. "Wait. What do you mean, 'on the Harley'? Shouldn't you keep them in the house?"

He cleared his throat. "Yeah I, uh...I don't keep them around the apartment."

"Why not? That doesn't make sense."

He smiled contritely. "It does for me. I've never brought a girl to my place, never wanted to...until now."

"Never? Then, where did you...?" She trailed off.

"I've only hooked up outside my place—at the bar or the motel behind it, mostly. One-time things, and it's been months since I've done that," he said, a light blush tinting his cheeks.

"So, tonight is a first for you too, then," she observed.

He stared straight into her eyes. "In all the ways that matter to me, yes."

She ran her hands through his hair. "I see." She liked the sound of that. Nikki knew Jake had a past, but part of her liked that it was more distant than she'd thought and that tonight would be a first for him too. "Does that mean you've always worn condoms in the past?"

"Always," he vowed. "Why?"

She continued to play with his hair, loving its silky texture. "Because if that's the case, we don't need them. I'm on the pill. I have been since I was sixteen. And I've never been with anyone before, so we're covered."

Jake's chest froze on an inhale, his intense stare pinning her to the mattress. "Are you sure? Because we don't have to go any further, honestly."

She hooked one of her legs around him while she anchored the other to the bed. The movement shifted him, lining his hips up with hers, his hard length pushing against her damp flesh.

His eyes briefly drifted shut before blazing down at her. "Tell me you're sure, Nikki. I love the whole show-versus-tell thing you've got going on, but I need to hear you say it," he said, his body shaking as he hovered over her on his elbows.

She smiled, shifting her hips, eliciting a deep groan from him. *"Sono sicuro."*

"Grazie a Dio," he breathed, wasting no time. He shifted his weight onto one arm as he reached between them and guided himself into her. Nikki gasped sharply at the first point of pressure, tensing as she felt herself spreading. A burning sensation forced her to bite down on her lip.

He stilled. "You okay?"

She nodded. He reached up and pulled her lip free then crushed his mouth into hers as he moved his hips again, pushing in deeper. The burning increased followed by a pressure that wasn't altogether unpleasant.

"Jesus, Nikki. You're so tight," he hissed, the arm braced beside her shaking. "Still with me?"

"I'm right here," she said, exhaling slowly as she shifted her hips, taking him farther into her.

"Holy fuck," he bit out.

The guttural sound of his voice sent a shockwave through her. "I don't know if I can guarantee a religious experience, but I'll do my best," she said.

Jake chuckled, his hand cupping her face. "*Ti amo cosí tanto,*" he said then leaned down and kissed her as he thrust forward, seating him inside her fully.

His kiss swallowed her cry as a burst of pain radiated out from her center.

He froze. "Shit. You okay?"

She swallowed audibly. "Yes."

And she was. The pain was already starting to fade, as was the intense burning that had followed it.

"Good," he said, slowly pulling out and pushing back in. "Because we're both about to have that religious experience you mentioned."

A giggle bubbled up but never left her. Jake started moving again, keeping it slow and steady, chasing away any remnants of pain or other thoughts. Instead, all she could focus on was the slow simmer of pleasure stirring deep in her core, increasing with every pull, every thrust.

Groaning at the new sensations taking root in her body, Nikki slid her hands down his sides and rested them on his lean hips as she met his next thrust with one of her own.

"Damn." He groaned.

Liking the sound of that and the feel of her body falling to a rhythm with his, she met his next thrust with a stronger one of her own.

"Holy God." He exhaled, covering her mouth with his.

Nikki continued to meet his thrusts with her own, feeling the familiar —and very welcome—coil tightening again. Jake's kisses turned wild, his tongue tangling with hers as their bodies fell into a rhythm—an intimate dance—only lovers knew.

Feeling the tension continue to build, she dug her fingers into his hips, scoring the flesh there. "Harder, Jake," she whispered as her hips thrust against him.

His response was a guttural sound as he gave her what she asked for, his head dipping into the crook of her neck. Their movements became more and more frantic as the tension climbed toward a crescendo. The friction between them was electric, humming through her.

"Fuck, angel. I can feel you tightening around me. I love that—love the way your body responds to me," he whispered in her ear, panting.

Her breath caught at his words. She was close, but unlike before, this time was different. Nikki could feel something beautiful and staggering building in both of them that went far beyond the physical. His movements became more frantic, driving the two of them closer and closer to the edge until she felt it. The coil snapped, and they plummeted over the cliff, each crying the other's name like a benediction.

Minutes dragged by as they lay there, pressed together, their breaths sawing in and out of them. Jake was the first to move, lifting up and kissing her lips tenderly.

"Angel…that was…damn, if that wasn't a religious experience, I can't imagine what could be," he breathed against her damp skin.

She ran her fingertips over his backside in languid strokes. "I'd say we hit biblical proportions on the pleasure scale."

A smug look of male pride spread across his lips. "Wait here," he said, easing out of her, a hollow feeling settling in her at his sudden absence.

Her body was a boneless pile of goo as he rolled off the bed and went into the bathroom. She heard the water run for a minute before he returned holding a damp cloth. Settling down on the bed, he eased her legs apart and cleansed her body. Her eyes welled at the intimacy of such a simple—yet profound—act, flooring her all over again.

After pitching the rag into the bathroom, he lay down, pulling her into his side. "Are you really all right? I didn't hurt you, did I?" he asked as his hands drifted up and down her spine with feather-light strokes.

She ran her fingers over the lily tattooed above his heart. "It didn't hurt any more than it's supposed to. I'm fine," she said, wrapping a leg around his, drawing her closer to him.

Jake pressed a kiss to her forehead, his hands still skating over her damp flesh. Silence fell between them for several minutes. Tilting her head, she saw that he was staring up at the ceiling, his face pensive.

"What is it?" she asked, propping herself up on one elbow.

His gaze slid to hers. "I never thought sex could be like that," he said, a look of wonder rippling over his features.

"Like what?"

The hand on her back stilled, anchoring her to him. "So beautiful… and…consuming in the most staggering way. It's never been like that before."

Nikki blinked back the tears that welled in her eyes. "Never?" she whispered.

Jake shook his head. "Never. Thank you."

She arched a brow. "For what?"

"For everything you've given me, angel. Everything," he said, drawing her up and kissing her lips in a way that managed to reach down, deep inside, and touch her soul.

∼

LIGHT STREAMING THROUGH THE SKYLIGHT ABOVE THE BED ROUSED JAKE FROM a deep sleep. He peeled back his eyelids and squinted up at the ceiling with a grimace. What time was it?

Shifting carefully so he wouldn't wake the angel nestled in his arms, he looked over his shoulder at the clock on his nightstand. It was after 11:00. *Damn.* It was late—way beyond sleeping in late. Even after his worst nights partying at the Ox, he never slept in like this. But last night had been unlike any other night in his existence, so it was no surprise he'd slept like the dead until nearly midday.

He shifted back as memories of it drifted through his mind in Technicolor clarity, heating his blood. He'd spent the entire night having the most mind-blowing, earth-shattering sex he'd ever experienced, which was saying something considering how much sex he'd had in his short life. But none of what he'd done before compared to last night—to making love to Nikki time and again, until they both collapsed into a deep sleep.

Last night was a revelation for him on so many levels. He now understood the difference between sex and making love. Before Nikki, sex was a meaningless act used to numb his mind and heart. Now—now it was an awakening of emotion and thought. Making love to her flooded his body with more feeling than he ever thought possible, forging a connection between the two of them that went far beyond the physical act.

He was bound to her in ways he never imagined. They were a part of each other, and nothing—not the danger she faced or his darkest secrets, his greatest sins—could ever change that. Realizing that shattered the chains he'd wrapped around his heart so long ago, liberating him at last. He no longer feared telling her anything because he knew, deep in his soul, that it wouldn't change what existed between them.

Jake closed his eyes at the memory of when *that* realization struck him. They'd come up for air sometime around 8:30, needing to refuel. After dining on leftovers he'd scrounged up, they moved to the couch—one of many places he'd fantasized about taking her—and talked and kissed like a pair of teenagers until she ran her delicate fingers over the lily tattooed on his chest.

"Why a lily?" she'd asked.

Before last night, he would have avoided any discussion of his tattoos. They were connected to his mother and how he'd failed her—a permanent, physical reminder of his sins. But with Nikki, he didn't hesitate.

"My mother's name was Lilianna," he explained.

"You did this for her?"

He nodded. "When I was eighteen."

"It's beautiful," she whispered.

"She was a beautiful person."

"Of that, I have no doubt—not if she produced someone like you," she said, moving on to the ink snaking along his arms—intricate designs he'd drawn himself, taking years to perfect them before he committed them to his body.

"And these? What do they represent?" she'd asked, turning his arms over and reading the Latin words embedded in the designs: *Erit Auri Pretium Vitae—Life Is Precious* on the left arm and *Numquam Obliviscar— Never Forget* on the right.

Jake swallowed audibly. While he knew he could tell her anything now, it still didn't make talking about it less painful.

He ran trembling fingers over the left arm. "I inscribed *Life Is Precious* here because this is where the radial artery runs—it's a strong pulse point in the body, thrumming with life," he began. "And on this side, I did *Never Forget* because…I never wanted to forget exactly how my mother died."

Nikki's eyes darted from his arms to his face. "You mean she…" she started to say but broke off.

"Committed suicide? Yeah," he finished for her.

Tears welled in her eyes. "Oh, Jake. I'm so sorry. I can't even imagine," she said, cupping his cheeks in her hands, her eyes searching his.

Jake blinked back the flood of emotion as he watched her face fill not with pity but with empathy. He'd never seen that from anyone who knew about his mother. Everyone always pitied his situation. No one had ever tried to commiserate with him.

Until now.

Until her.

When he didn't respond—he couldn't for fear of losing the finite grasp he had on his composure—Nikki leaned forward and wrapped her arms around him. Pressing his face to her breasts, covered now by the T-shirt she'd borrowed from him, he let out a shuddering breath. He'd never told anyone what his tattoos meant, not even his own brother—though Jake was pretty sure Dario understood. He knew their mother had committed suicide; he just didn't know why.

Nikki shifted and climbed into his lap to wrap more of herself around him. Jake took her there willingly, loving the feel of the softest part of her pressed against the most sensitive part of him. Whispering words of love and solace, she ran her hands up and down his back, stopping at the tattoo of a pair of hands grasping rosary beads inked between his shoulders. He knew she'd seen them before—there wasn't an inch of him that she hadn't seen at that point—and knew what was written there.

Slowly, she had sat back, her eyes tentative as she asked, "And the hands clutching the rosary? Why the inscription, 'I despise myself and repent in dust and ashes'?"

Jake lifted his guilt-ridden eyes to hers. "It's from Job 42:6. I put it there as a reminder of my sins and as a vow to repent."

He didn't want to go into it then. It was too big, given what they could be facing with her memories. His failures and sins could wait until they straightened things out with Nikki and her accident. But when he looked into her eyes after he spoke, he realized he didn't have to say anything more than what he had. She heard what he didn't say: that he held himself responsible for his mother's death. He could see it in the pain reflected in her eyes, in the tears that trickled down her cheeks, and feel it in the way she had leaned down and kissed his lips with tenderness that shattered him. A series of shudders had rocked his body as he felt her love wash over him, eroding some of the pain and guilt embedded in his soul.

Silently, she broke the kiss, pulled the T-shirt she wore over her head, and discarded it. Her eyes never leaving his, she lifted up, freed his hard length from his boxers, and with gentleness and skill that marveled him, she took him into her, comforting and consoling him with her body. Of all the times they'd made love that night—and there were many—this one stood out in his memory the most. That moment was seared onto his heart and soul, branding him forever.

Nikki shifted in the bed, pulling Jake back to the present. He rose up on one elbow as she rolled over, and smiled when she caught sight of him.

"Hey there," she said, her voice husky from sleep.

Jake smoothed her tousled hair back, wondering how someone could look so strikingly beautiful. "*Buongiorno*, angel," he said, noticing he was speaking more and more Italian. He hadn't used it since his mother's death.

She bit down on her lower lip. "I love it when you speak Italian," she said, smiling up at him.

He chuckled. "I seem to remember you telling me that you were a sucker for Italian accents."

"I did say that, and it's true. I also remember you saying you'd 'better get yours back.' Looks like you did."

"I guess so, and I'm glad. I like having lots of ways to turn you on." He brushed her hair back from her shoulder, revealing one of her forget-me-not tattoos. He studied it for a moment, remembering her cryptic explanation of it and the others scattered across her body.

Taking her lead from last night, he traced the delicate flower and inscription, noticing the skin felt different there and not just because of the tattoo. It felt like she had a circular scar beneath the design. He moved his hands to the others, noting they felt much the same.

What kinds of scars were shaped like that?

"Why do you have these tattoos?" he finally asked.

He felt her suck in a quiet breath, her body tensing briefly. When it faded she said, "Like yours, they're there to remind me of something." When he pinned her with a look that said, 'And...,' she continued. "They cover up scars I got the night my parents were killed. We were gunned down in a drive-by shooting. I survived because they shielded me from fatal wounds. They died saving me."

Jake's stomach dropped. She'd been shot? Three times? *Jesus, Mary, and Joseph.*

He pulled her closer, his grip tightening. "Angel...Christ...I don't know what to say. I'm so sorry. That's...fuck, it's awful."

She reached up and threaded her hands through his hair. "It *was* awful. What's worse is that I blamed myself for their deaths."

"What?" He reared back. "How could you? You didn't pull the trigger."

"No. But we wouldn't have been anywhere near the area if I hadn't made us late. I was the reason we were in the wrong place at the wrong time, and for a long time, I believed that made me responsible." Her eyes bored into his as she spoke the next words, and he knew what she was trying to do. "But through counseling and the help of my close friends and family, I came to realize that it wasn't my fault—that the only people to blame for their deaths were the ones who pulled the trigger. I couldn't control that. No one could."

He heard her message loud and clear, but their circumstances were vastly different. She wasn't to blame for her parents' deaths, but he could trace the blame to him clearly and easily for his mother's. He was about to say as much when his phone went off.

"I'd better get that. It could be Dario," he said, noting her frown.

Jake glanced down at the screen. *Undisputed* appeared on the screen. Frowning, he hit the green button.

"Hello?"

"Put Nikki on the phone," a deep voice demanded.

"Excuse me?" He shot up in bed. "Who the fuck is this?"

He felt Nikki sit up behind him.

"Who the fuck do you think, Sam Crow? Now put her on."

Damon.

Son of a bitch.

He should have recognized the arrogance in his voice straight off. "What do you want, Damon?"

At the mention of Captain Douche's name, Nikki pressed her bare breasts against his back and said, "Give me the phone, Jake."

Jake put up a hand. He wasn't through. This punk needed a lesson in boundaries. "If you want to speak with her, call her phone like everyone else does. If she doesn't answer, leave a message or take a hint," he snapped, ending the call as Damon rolled off a string of curses.

"Hey! Why'd you hang up like that?" Nikki asked.

He turned to face her. "Because he needs a lesson in boundaries, babe. Not to mention manners."

"I know, but I—*we*—need to talk to him. He knows something about what's going on with my memories and the guys following me," she said, pulling the sheet up around her.

He chuckled to himself. *She's going to be modest now?*

Before he could respond, the phone went off again. Moving faster than he expected, Nikki snatched it from him and answered the call.

"Damon?"

There was a pause, during which he could hear the piece of shit yelling through the phone. She finally cut in and said, "Enough! I'm sorry my phone was dead, but you have no right to act like an asshole about it. Are you finished?"

That's right. Tell him, angel.

"Good," she continued after another pause. "Look, I need to see you. It's about Le Mans. I'm starting to remember, and what's coming back is scary. Are you free today?" She turned and mouthed, "Three o'clock," to Jake. He nodded. "That works. We'll see you at the gym at three." She ended the call and handed the phone to Jake. "We'll meet him at Undisputed—it's the gym he co-owns downtown."

Jake tossed the phone onto the bed. "You really think he knows something?"

She nodded. "I know he does."

"Okay." He glanced at the clock. It was almost noon. They had a couple of hours to kill before heading over there, and he knew exactly how he wanted to spend them.

He turned to Nikki with a wicked smile. "We've got some time to kill before we head over there. Any thoughts on what you'd like to do?"

She returned his smile with one of her own. "One or two," she said, flinging the sheet off of her.

Hell yeah.

In a flash, he was on her, kissing her as he pressed her back down to the mattress, outlining exactly what he had planned for the next few hours.

24

D amon stood under the showerhead, letting the water pound into his sore muscles. He and Tsai had sparred for almost an hour in the cage, and he could feel it. He hadn't been able to work out much while he was in Caracas outside of going for runs in the early-morning hours before the heat picked up. Today was the first time he'd been in the cage and had a real workout in six weeks. The end result: an ass kicking of epic proportions.

It was worth it, though. After trying to track Nikki down only to discover—thanks to her bitchy friend and watchdog—that she was at Masercotti's place and had been there *all night*, his temper hit DEFCON 1. He knew he needed to work out the fury and aggression the thought of her being with that tatted-up freak caused before they got there today. If not, that little meet and greet would get ugly quickly.

It worked. *Mostly.*

He shut off the water then toweled off, dressed, and headed to his office. He was nearly there when he heard Tsai's booming voice across the gym.

"There's my girl!" Tsai called, jogging over to where Nikki stood.

Damon watched as the two embraced, catching sight of Jake standing off to the side, his eyes trained on her in a way that was wholly possessive. He recognized the look. He'd worn it many times—years ago when she was his.

His blood boiled.

So much for the workout.

After doing a mental countdown, he strode over to them as Tsai jogged off to meet with his next client. "Bella," he said when he reached them.

Nikki turned and smiled up at him. Unable to resist poking the bear, Damon pulled her into his arms and lifted her clear off her feet. Douche move? Totally. Did he care? Not a fucking bit.

"*C'é la mia bella ragazza,*" he said, holding her close.

She returned his hug, whispering, "He speaks fluent Italian."

He set her down, smirking at the Hell's Angel throwback, knowing that already. "Oops."

"No worries," Jake said, coming to stand next to Nikki. "It's an astute observation."

"*Astute.* Wow. That's a big word for someone who graduated from... where? The School of Hard Knocks?" he gibed, unable to resist. It was too easy.

"Damon!" Nikki hissed.

Jake put an arm around her waist, pulling her close. "It's okay. I may not have the college degrees you do, but I have something you don't— something you'll never have again. Don't I, Damon?"

Damon's lip curled at the thought and the smug look on Tatt-Boy's face. "We'll see for how long." He smirked.

Jake's eyes flashed. "What the fuck is that supposed to mean?"

"It means," Damon said, itching to unleash some serious kick-ass on this freak, "you'll be lucky if it lasts two weeks. You'll screw it up like you have everything else."

"You son of a—" Jake ground out, coming at him.

He didn't get far.

Before either of them threw a punch, Nikki slid between them, pressing a hand against each of their chests. "Grow up, both of you! We have bigger things to worry about," she said, glaring at both of them.

If Damon weren't so pissed, he would have laughed at the sight of her five-foot-nothing frame holding back the two of them, both towering over six feet, while barking orders. She was a spitfire—always had been. He loved that about her.

"Damon, can we use your office?" she continued when it was clear no punches would be thrown.

Too bad.

He fired another glare at Jake and looked down at the little hellcat. "Of course, bella. Anything for you." He took the hand pressed against his chest and kissed it reverently.

If he couldn't punch the guy, he'd at least get his ire up again.

Jake snarled something under his breath, but Damon didn't catch it. It didn't matter.

Mission accomplished.

Damon led them over to the office, closing the door once they were inside. "All right, start talking, bella. What's going on with your memories?" he asked, dropping into his chair behind the formidable desk.

Nikki sat down next to Jake and, after a deep breath, opened up about everything she'd been keeping secret, starting with her flashbacks then going on to her chat with Nacho Ruiz—a good man and ally for the Berardi organization in the Bay Area—and finally, Masercotti's deductions about her nightmares, the YouTube video, and the research he'd done.

Damon confirmed Nikki's suspicions about the Irish situation she'd fallen into while helping Denny then helped fill in the blanks with her flashbacks by playing the voicemail she'd sent him before the Le Mans race and by showing them the email he'd received after her accident. He also explained Hilda's possible involvement through her friend with benefits, Peter, which sent Nikki into a fit of rage.

While Jake calmed Nikki down, convincing her that telling Hilda was a mistake, Damon pondered the new information. The email he'd received after the accident confirmed Jake's theory about why she was left alive, but Damon didn't like it. It didn't make sense. Guys like Gianni Luccianno and his enemies weren't the type to leave loose ends, even if they were attached to their mark. So, why did Marco leave Nikki alive?

The acid in Damon's stomach rioted during the rest of the conversation and only worsened as he went through the folder they'd brought with them containing the images of the mass slaying in Rome and the articles that accompanied it. His mind was a tempest as he mulled everything over, searching for a way out of the storm and coming up empty.

On the verge of vomiting, having an aneurism, or both, he closed the folder and looked across his desk at Nikki. She was the strongest woman he'd ever known—a powerhouse—and yet sitting there, she looked small and lost and deeply afraid.

He didn't blame her in the least. He was just as scared.

Picking up on his unspoken thoughts and feelings, as she always did, she leaned forward and said, "I've really done it, haven't I, Damon? I'm in too deep, between this and the Irish thing. There's no way to fix any of it, is there?"

Damon's heart cracked at the tremble in her voice, sending him out of his chair and over to her. He took her hands in his and knelt down, ignoring the warning growl from her overgrown pet.

"I'll be honest with you: Yeah, the thing with Le Mans is fucking awful, and I honestly don't know how to fix it. I don't have enough information, and I can't go poking around the Falco family or their associates to find out more. It would raise suspicion and risk a war between them and the

Berardis. But that doesn't mean all hope is lost. I can handle this thing with the Irish, and I know someone who can help with the Luccianno situation."

Nikki's eyes teemed with worry and sadness—not for herself but for him. "You mean your father."

Damon squeezed her hand. She knew the relationship he had with his father was difficult and that he wanted little to do with his old man. Knowing that, she'd hate for him to have to turn to his dad for anything, much less something for her. For that alone, Damon would love her until the end of days, but it wasn't *his* father he was going to this time.

"No. Not my father," he said, looking over at Jake. "His."

Silence blanketed the office. No one said a word for several tense beats.

Nikki finally broke the silence. "What?" She frowned, turning to Jake.

Jake, however, wasn't looking at her. His eyes were locked on Damon. "You work for my father?" he said, his voice flooding the office with an artic chill.

Damon released Nikki, stood, and leaned against the desk. "I'm his West Coast *capo*."

"You're kind of young for that," Jake observed.

He shrugged. "When you're as good as I am, you move up the food chain pretty quickly."

"Jesus. You're in the Mafia?" Nikki squeaked. She whirled around to Jake. "And your dad is his *boss*? Did you know this?"

Jake shook his head. "I had no idea Damon worked for my father. I have nothing to do with him or his business. I hate the man and what he does for a living. He's part of the reason my mother is dead."

Damon could feel exactly how much hate Jake felt for Carlo by his tone alone.

Nikki sucked in a breath and took Jake's hand. "I'm sorry. I should have known better."

Jake lifted her hand and placed a kiss to it. "Don't be sorry. It's a valid question. Most sons of Mafia kings follow in their fathers' footsteps. I'm an exception."

Nikki turned to Damon. "Exactly how long have *you* been perpetuating the Italian stereotype?"

Damn. What a smartass.

She had the same revulsion for the Mafia he'd seen in her father and mother though for different reasons. She was spoon-fed that doctrine from birth, while her parents' hate of it was borne from witnessing the destruction that Mafia entanglements brought firsthand.

His gaze slid to Nikki. "My whole life, though I wasn't *officially* in until I turned eighteen. But come the fuck on, bella. You're not stupid or naïve.

You knew I was involved with this shit already. You heard the stories about my dad. That's why you reached out to *me* back in France—because you knew my father's connections could help you, right?"

Her lips merged into a thin line. "I was pretty sure your father was caught up in it and that you might be by *association*, but I never thought you were in this deep. Why didn't you tell me? Why lie to me all these years?"

"To protect you," he said. "In this business, the less you know, the better. It's why I never mentioned the voicemail or the email concerning the accident at Le Mans. I knew if the memories stayed buried, you'd be safe, so I didn't do or say anything that might stir them."

She let out a heavy sigh. "Okay, fine. I get that—I guess. But how can Jake's dad help if you can't?"

Damon folded his arms across his chest. "Your confidence in me is touching. And while I am pretty fucking awesome, Carlo is the best. And that's what we need. He knows the Lucciannos; he has history with them and more contacts in Italy than I do. He may know something about the hit you witnessed or, if not, know someone who does. If anyone can help, it's him."

She nodded. "Okay. How do I do this?"

Damon frowned. "*You* don't do anything. He does." He jerked his head at Sam Crow. "You need to go see your father and ask him for his help."

Jake nodded grimly. "I thought as much. But how? He's up in Folsom. It would take us weeks to get an appointment for a visitation. We don't have that kind of time if someone's watching her. They could strike any time."

"No. No way," Nikki insisted. "You're not doing this. It'll be too upsetting for you, Jake. I'll go. Damon can arrange it."

He leaned over and placed a hand on her knee. "I have to go, angel. Damon's my father's *capo*, but he's not his son, and you aren't his daughter. Digging around in this shit is dangerous and not a risk you take for anyone less than blood. Besides, you know there is *nothing* I wouldn't do for you. *Nothing*." He turned to Damon, his gaze wary. "Though I'm not sure he'll help me. I haven't spoken to him in thirteen years."

"He will," Damon said, knowing Carlo would do anything for his boys.

Nikki pulled her hand from Jake's and stood, moving over to the wall of MMA and wrestling trophies Damon had accrued in high school.

"Angel? What's wrong?" Jake asked, his eyes darting from Damon to her.

"What's wrong?" She snorted and turned to them, tear tracks staining her cheeks. The sight drove a stake through Damon's heart. "Everything is wrong! I've gotten myself mixed up in some seriously dangerous shit, and now I'm dragging you two, Hilda, and who knows who else into it with me. And let's be honest." She held up a hand when Damon and Jake tried to interrupt. "The odds of me getting out of this alive and not taking someone I love down with me are pretty fucking slim, if not zero. I can't live with that. So forget it. I don't want Jake facing a man he hates and risking his life for me—or you, Damon, putting yourself on the line with your boss and God knows who else. It would be better for both of you if I left and took my chances on my own," she said, moving toward the door.

"No!" Jake and Damon shouted, both darting for the door and blocking her escape.

Nikki stopped short, thrusting her hands on her hips. "If you two value your balls, you'll both get the hell out of my way right now."

Jake lunged forward, blocking Damon and taking her by the shoulders. "No. No fucking way. You are *not* facing this on your own, and if that means risking my balls to do it, fine," he said, leaning down to meet her eyes. "I'm here because I love you and I'd do anything for you, regardless of the risk, and I know you'd do the same for me, right?"

"You know I would, but this is different. This is all *my* fault. You don't need to—"

"None of this is your fault," Jake cut in. "You didn't do anything wrong. In Italy, I imagine you were in the wrong place at the wrong time. In Denny's case, you were trying to help a friend. You had no idea who those guys were. And even if you did, I bet you would have gone in there anyway because it was the right thing to do. The fault lies with the assholes after you, no one else. Now, I don't want to hear any more about you doing this on your own. You got that?"

More tears trickled down Nikki's face. "But—"

Damon suppressed a snarl at the sight and Jake's declaration, wishing their roles were reversed. "No *buts*. The prospect's right," he cut in, his voice rough. "None of this is on you. It's our choice to get involved, so get that crap about going off on your own out of your head. You're not in this alone. Period. You know there is nothing I wouldn't do for you and vice versa, bella."

Nikki's eyes darted between him and Jake. When she saw that they were at a standstill, she backed down. "Fine. We do it your way —for now."

Damon glanced over at Jake, knowing what Nikki meant and that there would be no arguing with her about this—at least for the time being. Jake's expression was murderous, but he gave a sharp nod to Damon, knowing Nikki as well as he did.

Damon nodded at Jake and turned to Nikki. "Fine," he ground out.

"Good," she said, taking Jake's hand in hers.

"All right." Damon sighed, heading back to his desk. "I'll make some calls and set up a meeting with Carlo for tomorrow afternoon." He turned to Jake. "You'll have to go to your parents' place in the city and grab some cash from the safe; ten grand will do it. I'll text you the combination. In the meantime, I've put a surveillance team back on you to be safe."

"Can you put one on Hilda too? If you won't let me tell her what's going on and to watch her back, she'll need a tail. She could be in danger if this Peter guy is dirty," Nikki said.

"It's already done," Damon replied. He'd put a tail on her as a precaution right after Nino told him about the connection between Peter Navé and Marco Luccianno.

"Okay," she said, turning to leave, but not before she pulled Damon into a tight hug, whispering a thank you and a vow to string him up if he didn't stand down if the time came and let her handle things on her own in his ear.

He chuckled at her fierceness and agreed—for now.

He kept a wary eye on Jake's retreating form as they left the gym. Damon could see that visiting his parents' home *and* his father had rattled his cage—a cage that was already shaky between Nikki's problems and the guy's own personal shit. He prayed that Jake could hold it together long enough to speak with Carlo. He wasn't kidding earlier when he said they needed him. Carlo Di Silva was Nikki's last line of defense with the Italian issue. And Damon hoped like hell that *he* could make good on his promise to take care of the Irish situation before anyone got hurt.

Especially Nikki.

25

"Where do I turn from here?" Nikki asked, weaving her way through the congested streets of San Francisco. She hated driving in the city: the traffic, the cyclists, the pedestrians, Muni—it was too much, especially when her head wasn't in the right place. How could it be, given everything that had gone down in the last thirty-six hours? She was lucky she wasn't rocking in a corner somewhere—or worse, taking a dip in the Bay, sporting a pair of cement shoes.

But she'd insisted on driving after they left the gym. Jake had looked terrible since their conversation with Damon, which she knew had more to do with returning to his family's home and visiting a father he professed to hate than her situation. He was worried for her, but the look on his face as they left the gym had more to do with revulsion and anguish than it did fear for her safety.

"Go right on Ocean then hang a left on Santa Ana. It's number 1726," he directed, his grim gaze fixated on the scenery rolling by.

"Okay. Got it."

Fifteen minutes later, she pulled the Ferrari into the driveway of a classic Tudor-style home. She stared up at the grand structure with wide eyes. This was the home where Jake spent half his childhood? This whimsical palace nestled among rolling lawns and enchanting English gardens? It wasn't at all what she expected. She'd imagined something more *Scarface* and less *Cinderella*.

Jake slipped out of the car without a word, grabbing the overnight bag they'd packed. Nikki followed and found him next to a bubbling fountain, staring up at the house. The hard set of his jaw and the tension radiating from him worried her, but it was the desolate look in his eyes that nearly brought her to her knees. She'd never seen him look so lost. Something had shifted inside him since they left the gym, and it frightened her. She could feel him slipping away, and she didn't know how to stop it.

Nikki took his hand in hers, lacing their fingers together in an effort to anchor him to her. "If you want, I can run in there and grab what we need, then we can head out to a hotel for the night."

Jake shook his head. "No. I should go in and do it."

Her stomach twisted at the chill in his voice—so unlike the warmth she usually heard there. "All right."

They made their way up the sloping walkway to the wide portico and into the house. Jake didn't utter a word. A chill slithered down Nikki's spine as she stood in the foyer with him. There was something off-putting about the house despite its immaculate condition, well-appointed furnishings, and high-end art adorning the walls. The air inside was heavy with foreboding and something else...something darker—like violence. It was almost suffocating in its intensity.

Another chill ran through her. Maybe staying here wasn't such a good idea.

"Nothing's changed," Jake murmured as his eyes roved over everything.

Nikki jumped a little at his voice. She slipped off her jacket and draped it over the accent chair near the door, despite the chill in her veins. "Damon mentioned in his text that a caretaker has been looking after the place since...you all left. I guess they had directives to keep it this way for when your father is released."

Jake's expression turned to stone. "I don't think he'll ever come back here. Not after what happened." He moved toward the stairs. "I'll head up and get the money. We can stay in the guest bedroom down here."

"I'll come with you," she said, rushing up to him.

"No!" he snapped. "I'll do this myself."

Nikki reared back but didn't say anything. She could see he was barely holding it together. Arguing with him wouldn't help.

"If that's what you want," she whispered and watched as he dragged himself up the L-shaped staircase, guilt swamping her with every heavy footstep. This was all her fault. If she hadn't screwed up her life so badly, he wouldn't be here, dealing with a past he wasn't ready to face. But none of that mattered to Jake. All that mattered was being there for her, regardless of what it cost him. The idea of that made her love him even more than she already did and hate herself for it at the same time.

She stayed there until he disappeared around the corner, then began wandering through the first floor, her eyes roving over the dozens of family photos scattered throughout, mystified once more. The photographs all depicted a happy, loving family—not one led by a ruthless mobster and a woman on the brink of suicide.

Nikki stopped and smiled at a group of photos of Jake ranging from infancy to middle school. He was an adorable child—not surprising. His parents were two of the most beautiful people she'd ever seen. Carlo and Lilianna were exquisite. But beyond that, there was something else about them even more captivating—something that made it painful to look at them: love. The depth of love between them was palpable even through the paper and glass encasing their images, making the tragedy of the situation more poignant.

She wandered farther past a study, a media room, and a formal dining room and discovered a closed door off the enormous chef's kitchen. *Odd.* The rest of the doors on the first floor were open. Why was this one closed? Her curiosity piqued, she turned the knob and pushed at the door, struggling to free it from the doorframe.

After throwing her shoulder into it, the door finally broke open, giving way to a room encased in darkness. Nikki fumbled along the wall until she found the light switch and sucked in a breath as the room came to life. It wasn't a pantry or laundry room as she'd thought. It was an art studio filled with paintings and sketches of Jake and Dario and something else—the very same thing she'd felt when looking at the photographs of Carlo and Lilianna: love. The room gushed with it. She could feel it swelling around her, chasing away the foreboding and violence she'd felt in the foyer.

Nikki walked farther into the room, gazing at the hundreds of oil paintings, watercolors, and sketches of Jake and his brother, her eyes filling with tears as she took it all in. Just like the sketch she'd seen of Jake's mother, she could tell these pieces were also done with a loving hand. It was evident in the way they all captured different elements of Jake's and Dario's personalities, highlighting their inquisitive minds, their loving hearts, or their quiet strength. Only an artist who knew and loved their subject deeply could capture all of that so eloquently.

Sifting through canvas after canvas, Nikki couldn't help but wonder why someone with so much love for their children could end their life, leaving them behind to fend for themselves. She couldn't imagine a devoted mother even considering it. And looking at these paintings, she could see that Lilianna was a devoted mother. So what happened? Why did she leave the boys she loved behind?

Nikki released a heavy sigh when she reached for the final canvas in the rack, her heart aching. It was a painting of Jake with Dario next to a pond. She smiled at the devotion reflected in both their faces as they grinned at one another. It had to be one of the last portraits Lilianna did of them; Jake looked around twelve and Dario no more than four. Tears stung her eyes as she lifted the oil painting, noting how much heavier it was than the others, particularly on one side. Frowning, she turned the canvas over and discovered a leather-bound journal wedged in the bottom right-hand corner.

Nikki reached down and pulled the journal free then set the painting aside. She ran her hands over the cover, thinking how much it reminded her of Mystery Man's journal, from its worn leather cover to the initials stamped in the same ornate script. Only instead of GDS, these initials read LDS—Lilianna...DS? She thought their last name was Masercotti; it was Jake's, anyway. Were the initials DS her maiden name?

Curious, she grabbed her phone and did a search on Lilianna Masercotti. Nothing came up. Then she searched Lilianna DS. This time several listings appeared; one of them was an obituary for a Lilianna Di Silva who died October 7, 2005. There was a picture included at the bottom of the brief article; it was Jake's mother.

A frown creased her brow. Why was Jake's last name different from his parents'? Did he change it when he turned eighteen? *He might have.* He hated his father and might have changed it to avoid people connecting the two. She would have done the same thing in his shoes. Being linked to a man like that couldn't be good.

Nikki turned back to the journal. So, this journal belonged to Jake's mother. But why did she keep it here? It seemed like an odd hiding place for something like this, but then nothing about this whole situation was exactly *normal*.

She worried her bottom lip, debating whether or not to open it. Journals were private—she would know. Maybe she should save it for Jake to read first. It belonged to his mother, after all. Once he'd read it, if he felt comfortable with the idea, she could take a look at it or he could tell her about it.

His haunted eyes as he stood at the foot of the stairs earlier flashed before hers. She looked down at the journal. The pages contained therein could be extremely painful to read, especially if they chronicled Lilianna's thoughts before she took her life, and Nikki didn't know if Jake could face that yet. He already blamed himself for his mother's suicide. That became clear to her after he explained what his tattoos symbolized. They weren't just art; they were monuments of his pain and guilt. And though she knew he wasn't to blame—he was only a boy when she died—Jake didn't believe that. And what if...what if the words in these pages only helped to further solidify that idea in his mind? A shudder rocked her as she envisioned Jake's reaction to such information.

No. She needed to read through this first to make sure there was nothing in it that could hurt him any more than he already had been—then and only then would she show it to him. Right or wrong, she would do anything to protect Jake.

Anything.

Nikki opened the journal to the first page, noting the date at the top: November 5, 2004. Lilianna began the journal less than a year before her suicide. Turning the pages, Nikki scanned through the first dozen or so entries, all of which chronicled the weeks following Jake's father's conviction. Here, just as she did with her artwork, Lilianna painted a vivid image of Carlo—a good man trapped in a violent role by circumstance—and the devastation that she and her boys felt at his absence. The entries described Jake's downward spiral into an existence fueled by anger and confusion as he got into more and more trouble at school, with her, and eventually, the police. Nikki's heart ached for him and the lost little boy he'd become, as did Lilianna's. But Lilianna refused to give up on her son even when he vehemently rejected her. She did everything in her power to reach him, to make sure that he knew she would never leave and that she loved him beyond reason.

"Hypocrite," Nikki snarled, looking up from the journal. If she was as dedicated to Jake as she'd claimed, why did she do it? Why did she abandon her sons?

She took a deep breath and returned to the text, hoping the answers were there.

Nikki skimmed through more of the same, then six months in, the entries changed. A man appeared on the scene. Lilianna described him as one of Carlo's *associates*—one she'd only met once before, but once was enough. She hated him on sight, describing him as cold, calculating, and evil. Her judgment was spot on. The man wasn't there to comfort or help her but to take what he wanted: Lilianna. He threatened to have Carlo murdered in prison and her boys taken from her if she didn't do what he demanded. Knowing that someone like the nameless man could do all of that—and so much more—she surrendered to him.

Stomach roiling, Nikki read as the nameless man—Lilianna wouldn't reveal his identity in case her boys or someone else found the journal—visited multiple times a week, forcing himself into her bed each time. The horror went on for months until she couldn't take it anymore. Being with him, even though it was forced, felt like a betrayal to Carlo and the vows she'd made before him and God, and she couldn't live with it any longer. But instead of outlining her plan to kill herself, as Nikki expected, she outlined a plan to kill the nameless man. The entry for October 7, 2005, laid out the plan in detail, describing how she intended to hide a knife under the mattress, and when her attacker was adrift in his lust, she would strike and not stop until he was dead. She had to. If she didn't, he would kill her.

Nikki turned the page. It was blank, as were the others after it, save for some random sketches.

It was the last entry in the journal.

She gave her head a disdainful shake. *Of course it was, dummy. That was the day she died.*

Mind whirling, Nikki slumped against the back of the chair, her eyes roving over the artwork: a shrine dedicated to her sons—sons she never intended to leave but was forced to at the hands of a vicious animal.

Lilianna didn't kill herself. She had been murdered.

Dear God...

The sounds of breaking glass and screaming yanked her from the storm before she could process that.

Jake.

She threw the journal aside and bolted out of the studio and up the stairs, following the sounds of wood and glass breaking.

"Jake! What's wrong?" she cried, rounding a corner and coming to a screeching halt in front of what looked like the master bedroom. Clothes, framed photographs, books, and such littered the bed and floor along with broken glass and wood. In the center of the devastation stood Jake, eyes wild with a dangerous blend of rage and revulsion.

"Oh my God!" Nikki gasped, gaping from the doorway as he grabbed object after object and hurled them against the walls, shattering them.

Ignoring the danger, she charged into the room and latched onto his arm as he grabbed a photograph of his mother and prepared to throw it through the window.

"Jake! Don't!" she cried.

At the sound of his name, he whipped his head around, ripping his arm free as if her touch burned him.

"Get out of here," he ordered, his voice barely human.

She squared her shoulders and widened her stance. "No."

He jabbed a finger at the door. "I said *get! Out!*"

"No." She kept her voice calm, even as her heart rate skyrocketed. She'd never seen him so full of self-hate and disgust.

He glared at her, the veins and muscles in his neck bulging. "What the fuck is wrong with you? You don't belong here!"

"There is nothing wrong with me," she replied evenly. "And I do belong here. I love you, Jake. And nothing you say or do is going to change that."

He shook his head. "Don't be stupid. I'm poison. Take a look around!" he yelled, waving at the room. "This is me! This is the shit I do!"

"No. This isn't you. You're a good man who's hurt and upset. But I can help if you'll let me," she said, her voice wobbling at the pain radiating from him.

Jake's eyes dropped to the picture, his voice breaking as he spoke. "I killed her, Nikki. She died because I failed her in every way possible." He closed his eyes, gripping the frame with white knuckles. "I could hear her at night, crying herself to sleep over the crap I pulled day in and day out. If I hadn't been such a selfish piece of shit, hadn't driven her over the edge, she'd be alive today. That's not something you can help me with. No one can."

"You're wrong. I—"

"*Stop!* I'm not wrong. Not this time."

He turned and glared at the bed. She knew he wasn't with her now. His mind had slipped into a dark and painful memory.

"I found her here, surrounded by glass and wood, her body broken and bloody because she couldn't take it anymore—couldn't take the fact that her eldest son—her *tesorino*—took what was left of her broken heart and ground it to dust." Jake's eyes snapped to hers then, the intent in them stilling the blood in her veins. "I'm a murderer, Nikki. You can't change that. No one can. I was a fool to think otherwise—to think I could be anything else or have any amount of happiness. Men like me don't deserve that. The only thing we deserve is to rot in hell," he roared, hurling the picture of his mother at the mirror above the dresser.

When she saw him reach down and grab a shard of glass from the floor and hold it up to his wrist, she launched into action.

"*Don't!*" she screamed, rolling off a roundhouse kick to the hand holding the glass. Her booted foot hit the target with a *smack*. Jake stumbled back, stunned, but she didn't stop there. She brought him to the floor in three moves, ignoring the pain when glass imbedded itself in her knee as she pinned him.

When he struggled, she tightened her grip, choking him, sending a silent thank-you to Tsai for all of the Krav Maga lessons. "Don't even think about moving. Just listen to me, damn it," she bit out. "Your mother loved you with all her heart. She never would have killed herself because of anything *you* did. Never."

Every muscle in Jake's body tensed. "Then why did she do it?" he choked out.

"She didn't, Jake. Your mother didn't kill herself. She was murdered."

~

EVERYTHING STOPPED: THE BUZZING IN JAKE'S EARS, THE BLOOD IN HIS VEINS, the air in his lungs.

After a minute, his body rebooted, clearing the haze, and he discovered that he was on the floor, pinned there by Nikki.

How did he get on the floor like this? What happened after he left her in the foyer?

He wracked his muddled brain. It had been a long time since he'd gone into a blind rage—one where he completely checked out and had a hard time recalling what happened afterward. Whatever set him off had to be bad for this to happen.

Then it all came flooding back: walking into his parents' room, the rush of painful memories hitting him like a wrecking ball, shattering the tenuous hold he had on his rage, derailing any headway he'd made toward healing; trashing the place; Nikki coming in, trying to stop him; the cruel things he said to her; grabbing the shard of glass to gouge himself; Nikki stopping him, saving him again.

"What did you say?" he rasped around the chokehold, remembering the words that had stopped the madness.

Maintaining her grip, she said, "Your mother was murdered, Jake. She didn't kill herself."

What the fuck?

"What? That's impossible. Her wrists were *slashed*," he ground out, sickened at the memory of her bloodied, lifeless body.

"It's true. I can explain, but not like this. If I let you up, will you promise me something?" she asked, her voice softening.

Jake nodded. With his mind clear, he could never refuse her.

"Promise me—" She broke off as her voice cracked. The sound pierced his heart. "Promise me you won't try to hurt yourself."

He closed his eyes against the rush of shame. He'd never wanted her to see him like that: so far gone. "I promise, angel. I won't do anything to hurt myself *or* you," he vowed.

He felt her exhale against his back. Then with extreme care, she released her hold and stood with a sharp gasp.

His heart jumped at the sound. In a flash, he was on his feet, standing before her. "What is it? Christ. Did I hurt you?" he asked in a rush, his voice breaking at the end.

She shook her head, leaning against the footboard. "I got some glass in my knee when I took you down." She winced, looking at her knee.

Jake's eyes fell to where hers were focused. "Fucking hell," he hissed, seeing where her jeans were torn open. Blood flowed from the wound inflicted by two shards of glass still wedged there. "Shit. I'm so sorry," he croaked. "Come on." He swept her into his arms and carried her to the master bath—the one area of the suite spared his wrath.

She squeaked at the sudden movement. "Jake, I'm fine. Don't worr—"

"You're not fine. You're hurt. Let me fix this, please." He set her down on the closed lid of the toilet. When she agreed, he leaned in and examined the wound. "We need to get your pants off so we can clean and dress it properly."

"Okay," she said, unfastening her jeans. Jake worked the tight fabric over her hips and tossed the ruined clothing into the tub.

He grabbed the first aid kit from under the sink, removed the glass, and cleaned the wound. The cuts didn't look deep enough for stitches, but he'd use butterfly bandages to make sure it healed quickly and with minimal scarring.

While he worked, she told him about the art studio, the journal she found, and the startling information it contained. A hailstorm of emotions rioted inside him as she spoke, but he kept them tamped down, focusing all of his energy on tending to her knee.

She finished her story as he taped a strip of gauze over the wound. Once it was secured, he leaned down and pressed a kiss to it, thankful that this was the worst that had happened. When he thought back to what she'd walked in on and what he would have done to himself if she hadn't been there, he shuddered. Not only could she have been seriously hurt, but her final memory of him would have been of violence.

Just like him of his mother.

Leaning back, he looked into her endless eyes—eyes so honest and open and full of love...for him: a man on the brink. "Do you really think my mother was murdered trying to kill her attacker? I don't remember any man coming to the house on the regular like that," he said, his mind still reeling at the idea.

"Yes. She said in the journal that he came while you and Dario were at school, so you wouldn't have seen him. And the murder scenario makes sense, given what I read in the journal and the...condition of the room when you found her." She placed a hand on his shoulder. "As for why the police labeled it a suicide, the nameless man could have paid them off if he was as connected as your mother described."

Jake nodded, unable to speak while a new emotional storm built inside him. He tried to push back the tempest; he didn't want to lose it like he did before. But it was too much: the shame he felt for being so out of control now and as a child; the rage he felt toward the nameless man who'd murdered his mother; the regret he felt at the years of his life wasted on a guilt he didn't own.

When the first sobs broke the surface, Nikki pulled him into the circle of her arms, surrounding him with her love and strength. With his face pressed against her heart, he let the storm break, weeping until he thought his body would run dry.

Through it all, Nikki held him, whispering words of comfort and promises that she'd never let him go, that she'd always be there. He clung to those promises like a lifeline, needing her more than he ever had. Eventually, the sobs quieted. When they did, she grabbed a wet cloth and wiped away his tears, laving the wounds that ravaged his heart and soul.

His heart swelled with gratitude and love for her: his saving grace, his angel. "Thank you," he said as she set the damp rag on the edge of the tub.

She smiled warmly. "You don't have to thank me. I only did what anyone who loves you would do."

Jake's eyes roved over her as he felt the deep, all-consuming love he had for her continue to build, filling some of the empty places left from the emotional downpour. But it wasn't enough. He still didn't feel whole. He needed to connect with her on a different level, to be inside her, to feel her body wrapped around him in every way possible. Only then would he feel complete again.

"Angel, I need—" he began.

"I know. I need that too," she whispered, pulling her sweater over her head and tossing it to the floor.

A heady mix of love and lust rushed him. He pulled her into his arms and carried her out of the bathroom, into his old room down the hall. They made short work of her remaining clothing and his, their hands and mouths greedy as they went. In seconds, she was beneath him and he was sinking into her, reveling in the way she groaned his name, begging him for more. He gave her what she wanted, taking as much as he gave in return, grateful for her and the love they shared.

THEY SPENT THE REST OF THE NIGHT TANGLED TOGETHER IN VARIOUS ROOMS OF the house or talking quietly.

At one point, they ended up in the art studio. There, Jake saw the evidence of his mother's love for him—a love his twelve-year-old self believed he'd destroyed. But he hadn't. It had been there all along, waiting for him. A new wave of shame and regret hit him, but instead of breaking down, he told Nikki about his mother in great detail: how she loved all forms of art, about the deep religious faith that kept her grounded, and other things like her crazy love of American '80s movies, Italian opera, and Shakespeare. Most of the things he told her were memories he hadn't thought of, much less spoken about, in years. Before Nikki, he couldn't have done that. He wished he had, though. The more he spoke of his mother, the more he could feel her there with him, comforting and loving him as she'd done when he was a child, filling the remaining hollows of his heart.

Nikki talked of her own parents as well, of the searing pain she'd felt at their deaths and how going to therapy had saved her. He knew what she was doing, and she was right. He needed to see a therapist, a counselor, *someone* to help him deal with the toxic emotions that still lurked beneath the surface. The wounds he carried ran soul deep, and only talking to a professional who could give him the tools to further deal with everything would help him to fully heal. And he wanted that, very much.

They also talked about his father and what to do with the information regarding his mother's death. They decided, after much arguing, that Jake needed to tell him about it, no matter how little he believed his father deserved to know the truth. Nikki, on the other hand, believed Carlo had a right to know what happened. She also pointed out that there was a good chance he would have information on the nameless man and be able to help them bring him to justice. She had a point, but Jake still didn't like the idea of providing the man he blamed for his mother's demise with any kind of comfort or closure. But he would do it for one reason: justice. His mother deserved nothing less.

26

The cold concrete façade of the prison came into view as they turned onto Folsom Prison Road and made their way down the desolate stretch toward the guarded gates. Ice water trickled through Nikki's veins when a grim-faced, heavily armed guard directed them to visitor parking.

After parking in the visitor lot, they made their way through security, where Jake handed off the bag containing the money from the safe to the warden, who, like all the guards she'd seen, bore the same forbidding expression. Once they were through security, another guard led them to the public visitation area. All the tables were empty—visitations only occurred on select weekends and holidays—save one. A lone prisoner sat at a table in the farthest corner of the room, his back against the wall.

Jake's father: Carlo Di Silva, crime lord.

A shudder rippled through her. She couldn't believe the wild turn her life had taken. Never in a million years would she have pictured herself caught up in an epic shit-storm like this. It wasn't all bad, though. Something amazing *had* come out of the madness: Jake.

In him, she'd found a love she hadn't expected at this stage in her life. More than that, she'd found a partner who believed in and supported her choices when few others in her family had. And while they both came with serious baggage—his emotional, hers dangerous—they were prepared to face whatever came their way as a united front.

She had never been more grateful for anything in her life.

Or more afraid.

Jake having her back put him in danger. She couldn't reconcile that.

Nikki meant what she said in Damon's office: She'd handle this clusterfuck their way *for now*. But if things went sideways, she'd make sure that Jake and Damon were nowhere near the danger. She wouldn't let anything happen to either of them—no matter what it cost her.

The guard who led them in informed them that they had one hour before he turned and left the room. Nikki heard the door shut behind them, but they made no move toward the table where Jake's father sat. She waited, gripping Jake's trembling hand in hers, while he pulled himself together, tamping down the anger and disgust he felt for the man whose lifestyle had destroyed their family. She understood where his anger came from, and part of her didn't blame him for feeling that way. It would be hard not to. But she also knew he needed to release that anger and forgive his father if he wanted any real peace.

Nikki gave his hand another squeeze and leaned into his side. "Are you ready?"

Jake looked down at her, his eyes softening. "As long as you're with me, yes."

She smiled. "I'm here, Jake. Don't worry."

"All right. Let's do this."

They crossed the visitation room, their sneakered feet making little noise. When they reached the table, a devastatingly handsome man dressed in prison blues stood, his eyes glassy with unshed tears as he smiled at Jake.

"Son, it's...it's good to see you. It's been too long," he said, his voice hoarse with emotion as he extended a hand to Jake.

Jake didn't take his father's hand. "Dad." He nodded sharply.

Carlo dropped his hand to his side but didn't say anything; he simply nodded and turned to Nikki, smiling warmly. "Hello, Elena. It's nice to finally meet you. You are as beautiful as your father always described, and the spitting image of your mother."

Nikki blinked at him.

Nice to finally meet you? As beautiful as your father always said? What the hell?

Before she could respond, Jake said, "Elena?"

She turned to Jake, his confused expression mirroring her own, and explained what she could. "My legal name is Elena Nicole. I started going by Nikki when I began racing. My father thought Nikki went better with Elliot than Elena did. After a few years, I dropped Elena altogether." She turned back to Carlo, struck by how much he and Jake looked alike. "How did you know that or my parents?"

Carlo motioned for them to sit. "I knew your father well. We were close friends up until the day he and your mother passed. He used to show me pictures of you when you were little," he explained.

Nikki gaped at him. Her father and Carlo Di Silva were friends? Impossible.

"How can that be? He never mentioned you; we never saw you. And you...y-you're a... A-And he hated..." she stammered.

He flashed her a crooked smile that mirrored the one Jake so often used. "It's all right. I know this comes as a shock, to both of you. I can explain."

Nikki nodded. "Please."

Carlo smiled sadly and began. "Al and I grew up together in Palermo, alongside Vincent Rossi, Damon's father." He leaned forward, resting his arms on the table. "The three of us were inseparable until we turned eighteen. At that point, Vince and I were forced into following in our fathers' footsteps, joining the local family business. Al didn't go that route, though. His father, your grandfather, never liked the *lifestyle*, but he wasn't given a choice, much like the rest of us. However, he made sure that didn't happen to Al; he didn't want his only son, his only child, involved in the gruesome life of a soldier of sorts. He managed to keep his business separate from his family, so there would be no reason for Al to be forced in by the higher-ups when he came of age.

"When Al turned eighteen, his dad arranged for him to work for Dominic Gabaldini, owner of Amalfi Racing in Naples, as a mechanic. Dominic quickly discovered that Al was not only a gifted mechanic but also a gifted driver and gave him his start in racing, taking him far away from the life the rest of us were trapped in. Through it all, though, we never lost touch. After your father's accident in Germany, he came to the US, where I helped him get settled. We talked often, but I never came to the house out of respect for him and your mother and their distaste for my *work*."

Nikki slumped back in her chair. She probably would have fallen out of it, but Jake's firm grip on her hand had managed to anchor her there. Her grandfather, a man she'd never met nor had her father spoken much of, had been in the Mafia? And her father had grown up with Damon's and Jake's fathers? Jesus. She couldn't believe it.

"How come you never mentioned this friendship?" Jake asked, breaking the silence. "I don't remember you mentioning Al Eleuteri or Vincent Rossi at home."

Carlo turned to Jake. "I never mentioned Vince because we worked together, and that was something I never brought home. I didn't want our family anywhere near that part of my life. I didn't have a choice when I was forced in, but I wanted to make sure that didn't happen to you or

Dario. As for Al, I didn't mention him because I promised him that our association would remain only between us."

"I don't get it. Why would it matter if I knew about your ties to Nikki's family? You kept your work separate from us. There shouldn't have been any blowback from that," Jake said.

"Because, son, sometimes that's not enough." He turned to Nikki. "Your grandfather's connections to the business, no matter how much he tried to prevent it, followed Al across Europe and eventually caught up with him. The accident he suffered in Germany was a message for his father—a message that cost Al his career and one that eventually led to his parents' deaths. Your grandfather died going after the men who targeted your dad, as did your grandmother."

Jake swore.

Nikki blanched.

Her father's accident, the one that killed his career, was a hit? A hit that eventually led to her grandparents' deaths?

"Oh my God," she said, suppressing the urge to vomit. No wonder her parents hated the Mafia. "If that's true, why did he remain friends with you, knowing this could happen?"

"Because we were friends, not blood. While our friendship was more like a brotherhood, it was something we could keep quiet or downplay if it got out. To outsiders and enemies, we looked like casual acquaintances, which meant no one would bother with Al to get to me. Just to be safe, though, we didn't mention our friendship to our families. We didn't want anyone knowing how close we were," he said.

Nikki nodded, understanding. Carlo and Vince were the only family her father had left. And while he hated what they did, he was able to look beyond it to the men they were inside—just as Lilianna did with Carlo—men he loved and respected like brothers and didn't want to lose. Not after losing so much already.

She looked over at Jake. His gaze was fixed on the slate-gray table, but she could almost hear the gears in his head churning. Both of their families were connected to the Mafia in one way or another, and both had suffered for it. And while it would be easy to hate Carlo for his involvement in this dark, violent underworld, she realized neither of them should do that. Nikki knew from Lilianna's journal, and now from her own father's decision to remain close to him, that what lay beneath Carlo's mob-boss façade was a good man—a man Jake needed to make peace with. He needed to look beyond what his father did for a living and see the person his mother and her father had: a good man.

Nikki squeezed Jake's hand, yanking him from his thoughts. When his gaze met hers, she gave him a reassuring smile. He returned it with one of his own, gripping her hand tighter in return.

Carlo cleared his throat. "So, Damon told me you were coming today, but he didn't say why. Only that you needed my help with something."

Nikki and Jake turned back to Carlo, but it was Jake who spoke up first. "I need a favor, Dad. I wouldn't ask, but—"

"It's for me," Nikki broke in. She didn't want Jake to ask for this. She didn't want that on him—not when he still hated this man. "I fell into some trouble a couple of years ago in Italy, and that trouble has resurfaced."

"All right," Carlo said. "Tell me everything."

With a deep breath, Nikki told Carlo the whole sordid tale. He sat there listening intently, his gaze fixed on hers the entire time, just as Jake always did. He only interrupted twice to ask clarifying questions.

"We need your help to find out who's been following me and how they're connected to all of this, and if there is any way to fix the situation," she finished.

Carlo remained quiet for several minutes, his fingers steepled beneath his chin, his gaze on the table.

"Do you have any idea of what happened back then? Or can you help us find out anything, Dad?" Jake asked, breaking the silence.

Carlo's eyes darted to Jake's, softening. "I remember the hit vividly because it was so bizarre."

"*Bizarre?*" Jake asked.

Carlo nodded. "The hit took out four of Gianni Luccianno's key men, but no one ever came forward to take credit for it, which is odd. If another family puts a hit out like that, someone takes credit for the notoriety. Also, there hasn't been another move against him since. A hit like that suggests someone wanted to take over, and could have eventually. These guys clearly had the resources to infiltrate the Falco family and could have wiped the rest of them out, but they didn't. Nothing has happened since that day."

"Why not finish it? Why not come forward and take the credit?" Jake asked.

"Because of me," Nikki replied before Carlo could.

Jake turned to Nikki. "What? That doesn't make sense. Why would you stop them from taking credit or finishing the job?"

"Because," Carlo began, following Nikki's train of thought, "whoever it is doesn't want to be found out until the job is done, and if Nikki witnessed it, she can identify the men who did it. So they're staying quiet."

"Okay, fine. They stay quiet until the *Nikki issue* is resolved. So why haven't they resolved it? Why is she still alive?"

Carlo leaned back in his chair, exhaling heavily. "I'd say that whoever did this is keeping her alive because killing her has a greater consequence." He turned his dark eyes to her. "You said you were dating Marco Luccianno back then, right?"

Nikki nodded, her stomach souring. "We dated, but I broke up with him weeks before that for cheating on me." She flicked a glance at Jake, who'd tensed at the mention of her relationship with Marco. "Do you think it could be him? Why would he do that to his father's men?"

"I think it was definitely an inside job. It would explain why no one has taken credit—not with you out there as a witness who could expose them," Carlo began. "Was it Marco? I'm not sure. He's the only connection you have to the Falco family—that we know of, anyway. That's why I brought him up. Though given what you said, your connection to him doesn't explain why you're alive. If the *stronzo* cheated on you, then taking you out wouldn't have been a problem for him. It has to be someone else. Someone else connected to you and the Falco family. Is there anything you haven't told me? Anything else you can remember?"

"No," Nikki replied. "I'm sorry. I wish I had more to go on."

"Can you poke around? Tap your resources to get more info?" Jake asked.

"I will as soon as we're done here today," Carlo said.

"Thank you, Mr. Di Silva. I appreciate it." She smiled, standing as she glanced down at her watch. Their hour was nearly up. "I need to use the restroom, and there are things you and Jake need to discuss...alone."

Carlo rose from his seat and came around the table. "Please, call me Carlo," he said, pulling her into a hug.

Nikki returned it, despite the glare she caught from Jake.

"It was wonderful to meet you. Your father and mother would be very proud of the woman you've become."

"Thank you for saying that. I hope it's true. We'll talk soon." She turned to Jake. "I'll meet you out in the waiting area," she said, flashing him a sheepish grin before she turned and headed for the door, hoping he wasn't too angry for her leaving him alone with Carlo. It was the right thing to do. There were some conversations between a father and a son that had to be private—no matter how difficult or painful they were.

JAKE WATCHED NIKKI'S QUICKLY RETREATING FORM, WISHING HE WERE GOING with her for a lot of reasons. He didn't like the idea of her being anywhere alone, even within the prison's heavily guarded walls.

"She'll be safe out there, son. Don't worry."

Jake turned and met his father's gaze, still stunned that he was sitting there with him. It had been over thirteen years since they'd seen each other, and yet his father had changed very little. His hair was speckled with gray, and the lines around his eyes and mouth were more defined, but otherwise, he looked the same as he had the day the police took him away.

"I hope so. I don't know what I'd do without her," Jake replied.

His father smiled. "She's a good girl, Jake. I'm glad you have someone like that in your life. I know it's been…difficult since your mother passed."

Jake bristled. *"Difficult?* You have no fucking idea what it's been like. *Difficult* doesn't even begin to cover it."

"I know. I'm sorry. I wanted so much more for you and Dario and your mother. You didn't deserve this—any of it," he said, sounding far older than his fifty-two years.

"You're right. We didn't. But I'm not here to talk about that. I'm here because of Ma."

Carlo tilted his head to the side, an anguished expression crossing his face. "What about her?"

Jake let out a long, slow breath. "It's about the way she died." He pulled the journal out of his jacket pocket and set it on the table. "I don't think it was a suicide."

Carlo's eyes, which had been fixed on the journal from the moment it appeared, snapped to Jake's. "What makes you say that?" he asked, his voice far too calm for this news to be new.

"I have a better question," Jake said, glaring at his father. "Why don't you look or sound surprised to hear this?"

Carlo said nothing at first. He merely studied Jake from across the table. A man like Carlo Di Silva was accustomed to people doing what he wanted when he wanted it. But he wouldn't get that from Jake. He wasn't one of his father's associates or soldiers. He didn't have to do shit where his dad was concerned.

After a tense silence, Carlo spoke. When he did, his voice was thoughtful, almost reverent—not at all what Jake expected. "I was always suspicious of Lilianna's death. Your mother was a strong woman—much like your Nikki. Suicide wouldn't have been an answer for her, not with her strength and deep Catholic faith, no matter what she faced."

Anger zipped down Jake's spine. "Then why didn't you look into it? A man with your resources could have."

"Because, son." He gripped the edges of the table with white knuckles. "For years, I was lost to my grief. I couldn't think about her, let alone what had happened, without losing it. And believe me when I tell you, that's not something you can afford to do in *here*. Showing any kind of weakness only invites trouble. So I pushed it down, buried it deep, wouldn't allow myself to think about her, much less what happened that day. It was only recently that I could get to a point where I could think of any of it without falling apart and started examining her death. But I came up empty-handed. The police, the ME, all concurred that it was a suicide, and my own sources in the SFPD backed it up. So, tell me. How is it that *you* know differently?" he asked, releasing the table.

"This." Jake pushed the journal toward his father. "Nikki found it in Ma's art studio. It was hidden in the frame of one of the paintings. In it, she talks about a man who came to visit her every week. She refers to him as one of your *associates*." His stomach pitched as he outlined in detail what his mother had chronicled in the journal, his father's expression growing darker with each passing second.

"The last journal entry," he said, coming to the end, "was written the day she died. Based on all of that and the way I found her, it looks like this SOB killed her and made it *look* like a suicide."

His father said nothing for several minutes. He sat there, running his fingers over the journal with a murderous expression. It was a side of his dad Jake had never seen before. He imagined only his enemies ever saw it, and with good reason. It was as scary as hell.

Eventually, a new, softer expression appeared. "Your mother loved journaling. She said it helped her to purge her spirit of negativity and to stay positive. She was such a sensitive, introspective soul," he said, his voice tightening with emotion. "To think that her last months were spent suffering in silence at the hands of a monster, and that her last moments were filled with violence..." He broke off, his chest heaving with effort, and gripped the edges of the journal.

Jake reached over and grabbed his father's hand, stilling it before he tore the journal to pieces. "I know, Dad. I feel the same way. That's why I told you. You're the only person who can help me bring her justice."

His father looked down at Jake's hand and released a heavy breath. "I appreciate that, son. And I *will* find out who did this. I won't stop until I do." He lifted his eyes to Jake's once more.

Jake nodded as he pulled his hand away. The guard came in a moment later, letting them know their time was up.

Carlo stood along with Jake. "I'm glad you came. I've missed you."

Jake didn't know how to respond to that. Part of him hated his father for his Mafia ties and what those ties had cost their family. But another part of him loved him and missed the way things were *before*—missed the man he once looked up to and loved unconditionally.

He didn't say any of that. Instead, he extended his hand. "I'm glad I came too. Nikki and I need you, Dad. And so does Ma."

Carlo took Jake's hand in a firm grip, his eyes glassy. "I'll do whatever I can to help you and Nikki, and as soon as I know more about your mother, I'll let you know." He smiled grimly. "Look out for yourselves. These are dangerous times for you both."

"I will. Thanks, Dad." Jake released his father's hand and left, his heart heavier than when he'd arrived. But unlike earlier, Jake felt different emotions building inside there, the biggest of all being regret. Not of visiting his father today or of telling him about his mother's death, but of not having reached out sooner. While he was still angry and held his father responsible—at least in part—for his mother's death, part of Jake loved him and wanted the man he'd known as a boy in his life once more.

27

Damon gripped the steering wheel of his Mercedes with white knuckles, swearing as he barreled down the tree-lined streets, headed for home. He'd wrapped up a sit-down with David O'Brien, leader of the West Coast Irish mob an hour ago.

It hadn't gone well.

O'Brien was a stubborn SOB—always had been. He expected Nikki to pay with her life for costing him two of his soldiers and bringing potential heat down on his business. The fucker wouldn't settle for anything less. The only concession he made was to hold off on his hit as he'd heard, through rumor mills, that someone else—someone with more power and influence than he possessed—was watching her. He wanted to see how that played out first.

Damon slammed his hand against the steering wheel. O'Brien might have been backing off for now, but if things went as Damon planned, he'd have his ass to deal with eventually. And the way things looked, that situation was going to have to get bloody. Not that he minded, *entirely*. He'd love the opportunity to finally take out O'Brien. If it weren't for him, Al Eleuteri and his wife would still be alive.

Visions of O'Brien's dismembered body packed up and shipped back to the craggy rock he hailed from danced before Damon's eyes as he turned into Nikki's driveway. He pulled up to the garage in his usual spot, noting that both her car and Jake's Harley were absent. Good. He didn't feel like delivering the news of his failure right this minute. He'd promised Nikki he would solve the Irish mess, and he was nowhere near accomplishing it. It had been six weeks since she and Jake had come to him, and they weren't even close to solving either problem.

The theme from *The Godfather* sounded in his pocket.

He grabbed his phone as he hopped out of the car. "Yes, sir?" he said, his heart jumping in his chest.

"What's the word on the Irish problem?" Carlo Di Silva asked.

Damon cringed. *Here we go.* "O'Brien is standing down for the moment. His informants spotted Nikki's tail. He wants to see if whoever is behind it makes a move to kill her before he does. He doesn't want to 'waste the overhead if he doesn't have to,' as he put it."

"*Quel fottuto pezzo di merda,*" Carlo spat. "I thought he'd pull something like this. He always was a bastard."

"At least he's backing off for the time being. It's one less thing to worry about for the moment," Damon offered, hoping it calmed Carlo's temper. It could get explosive—something that seemed to run in their family.

"True. What can you tell me about Nikki's former manager, Jack Romano?"

Damon unlocked the front door and disarmed the new security system he had installed a few weeks back. "Nothing good." He kicked the door shut behind him and armed the system. "He's a greedy motherfucker, a degenerate gambler, and as shady as they come. Why?" he asked, hating the mere mention of Jack's name.

He despised Jack Romano. He'd sensed something off about him the minute he met the guy and had always wondered how Nikki's dad could have gotten involved with someone like that. While Romano wasn't employed by any of the major families, he had ties to a lot of other shady players in the crime world.

"I've been doing some digging. He's been seen meeting with Marco Luccianno off and on for the last couple of months and has connections to him going back three years. I found it curious, so I had him followed. He's been spotted in several locales in South America—like he's looking for someone," Carlo said.

Damon swore. "Did your informants say why they were meeting or who Jack might be hunting?"

"Rumor has it he's got gambling debts to the Lucciannos. That would explain his meetings with Marco. He handles the gambling side of the Falcos' business. But I don't like the fact that Jack was connected to Marco during the time of Nikki's accident. It's too coincidental. As for his South American pursuits, he's been seen asking around for a Frenchman who goes by the name of Léon Blanchet, although that's not his real name. Originally he went by Phillipe Bordeaux," Carlo explained.

Damon swore. "*Phillipe Bordeaux? Are you sure?*"

"Yes. Why? Is he connected to this somehow?"

"Bordeaux was Nikki's crew chief at Le Mans. He disappeared right after the accident and hasn't been seen since," he replied as more of the pieces of the dark puzzle fell into place.

"*Cazzo!* That must be Nikki's missing connection to the Luccianno mess —this Jack character is involved in this somehow," Carlo said.

Carlo could be right. Jack would have had access to Nikki, her car, the crew, everything back then. He could have easily orchestrated the accident and scared Phillipe off along with any evidence. But how and why was Jack connected to all of this—and Marco too? Was Marco the one trying to take down the Falco family for himself? If so, why involve Jack? More to the point: why would Jack Romano want anything to happen to Nikki? She was his meal ticket, if nothing else.

Damon shook his head to clear it. "You could be right. So, what's next? A tail on Romano? Informants?"

"All of the above and already in place," Carlo replied. "I've got men on him, and I'm quietly pressing his business associates. Whatever that stronzo is up to, we'll find out about it. What about Nikki's memory? Has anything come back?"

"No. Nothing yet," Damon said, knowing it was both a blessing and a curse. As long as it appeared she had no memory of that time, she was safe. But not having the missing information slowed their progress in solving the mystery and taking care of it once and for all.

"All right. Keep me informed. I'll be in touch as soon as I have more information."

Damon slumped against the wall. "Thank you, sir. For everything."

"No need to thank me, son. This is what we do for family: those by blood and those whom we choose," he said before ending the call.

Damon slid his phone back into his pocket with a small grin. Over the years, Carlo had become more of a father to him than Vincent Rossi had ever been. And there were plenty of times when he wished that had been the case. Damon hated his father. He always had. He was the reason Damon's mother ran off and left them when he was just a kid *and* the reason he couldn't have Nikki. If his father hadn't forced him into the life, he and Nikki would be together now—both of their lives a far cry from what they were.

NIKKI'S HANDS PRESSED AGAINST THE COOL COUNTERTOP AS SHE THREW HER head back, crying Jake's name. His hands tightened on her hips as he kept moving, kept thrusting into her, until he gave one final thrust, her name a hoarse cry on his lips.

Jake collapsed over her, his chest heaving. "God, that was—"

"Amazing," she finished.

He pressed a kiss to the center of her back before easing out of her and helping her get her panties and dress back in order. Once she was back to rights, she turned and did the same thing for him.

He reached down, cupped her face, and kissed her deeply. "It was *amazing*, but I'm afraid I took you off guard at first," he said, leaning back, his expression contrite.

Nikki arched a mischievous brow. "What? You mean when you came up behind me and growled something to the effect of *I need to be in you now* then proceeded to remove my underwear while I was trying to finish up the salad?"

Jake bit down on his lip and nodded.

She laughed. "You don't have to apologize." She ran her fingertips down his torso, loving the dips and valleys created by years of working out and wrenching on cars. "You can sneak up behind me like that anytime."

Jake's eyes flared. "Careful, angel. I might take you up on that offer," he said then leaned in and kissing her senseless.

The timer on the oven went off seconds later.

"Forget it," he ordered against her lips, pulling her closer when she tried to move away.

She managed to get her arms between them and pushed him back. "No way. I spent hours preparing your mother's famous sauce and baked manicotti. I will not just let it burn. This is your birthday dinner; it has to be special. Plus, it's the only weekend we have to celebrate between my IMSA and VAM races. So we are going to eat this food and open your gifts. Then we can practice having you sneak up on me."

Jake grinned down at her. "*Dio, ti amo...così tanto.*"

Nikki smiled. "I know. I love you too." She slipped out of his arms and grabbed a pot holder. "Now, let me get this out of the oven so we can eat."

Jake and Nikki devoured the baked manicotti and the cannoli she'd made for dessert. The conversation was light while they ate and cleaned up the kitchen. Neither of them wanted to spoil the evening with talk of the danger she faced or his father's investigation into his mother's murder. Tonight wasn't for any of that. They were celebrating Jake's twenty-fifth birthday.

Once the dishes were done, Nikki led him over to the couch, where two large boxes wrapped in checkered-flag paper waited.

"You didn't have to buy me anything, angel," he said as she presented him the first box. "Just having you in my life is gift enough. You know that, don't you?"

She dropped onto the couch next to him. "I know that, and it's sweet. But I wanted to do this for you. You earned it." She felt a constant need to remind him of all the wonderful things he deserved.

"Okay." He tore into the gift. Speechless, he lifted out the black leather portfolio nestled in the box, complete with his name engraved on a silver plaque mounted in the bottom left corner, and opened to the first page. In bold print, it read: Masercotti Photography.

He turned to Nikki. "What is this?"

She motioned to the portfolio. "Open it and take a look."

Jake turned the page, revealing a photograph he'd taken years ago of an older couple holding hands as they strolled through a park. She watched as he continued, finding the entire portfolio filled with pictures he'd taken over the last four and a half years.

The final shot was of Nikki sitting on the ground, her back leaning against her Pro-Mazda car, as she stared out across the paddock. It was one of her favorite pictures—not because she was in it or because she looked particularly good in the shot—but because it captured her love of racing. Only someone with a true gift could have captured that moment on film. Photography and art were clearly talents of Jake's, and she didn't want him to give up on them. She wanted him to pursue them as she'd pursued her talents and find the success and happiness he deserved.

"This...this is incredible, angel." He looked into her eyes. "I mean it. It's beautiful. Thank you."

Nikki reached up and cupped his cheek. "I'm glad you like it. Open the next one," she said, taking the portfolio and setting it aside.

Jake shook his head. "You did too much."

"Shh. Open it." It had taken her weeks to find the right one. She hoped he accepted it and didn't let his pride, which could be as stubborn as hers, get in the way.

Jake slid his hands beneath the seam, tore the paper from the box, and froze when the image on it came into view. "You didn't..." He turned to her, eyes wide.

"Just open it."

Jake tore his eyes from hers and removed the rest of the paper. He gasped as he opened the box and pulled out a brand-new Nikon digital camera. "Nikki... This is professional grade. How did you...? It has to cost at least—"

She pressed her fingers to his lips. "It doesn't matter. I did this for you so you could go after your dream. I know art, especially photography, is what you'd rather be pursuing instead of working on cars. I can see it whenever you're setting up a shot or looking over pictures you've taken. This is your passion; you should go after it...and now you can because you have the right tools. Do it, Jake. Go after what you want."

He didn't say anything at first. He stared at her, his pupils dilating as they roved over her face. After an intense minute, he set the camera down on the coffee table and turned back to Nikki, his eyes glassy with unshed tears.

"Thank you, angel...for this...for everything," he said, the tears breaking free as he pulled her into his arms and kissed her.

Nikki melted into him, feeling his body tremble against hers. When he pulled back, she smiled at him through her own tears. "Always, Jake. Always," she whispered before leaning in and kissing him again, pouring everything she felt for him into it, hoping like crazy he took her words to heart and followed his dreams.

JAKE MOANED AGAINST NIKKI'S LUSH MOUTH AS SHE PARTED HER LIPS, deepening the kiss. He didn't know if she understood exactly how much what she'd done tonight meant to him, but he was going to try his damnedest to show her.

He shifted, moving her beneath him, his hands easing the straps of her little black dress down so he could get to more of her. He was nearly there when someone started pounding on the door.

His head snapped up. "What the hell?"

"Are you expecting someone? Frankie? Johnny maybe?" she asked, sitting up with him and straightening her dress.

"No, but I guess it could be them," he said, running his hands over his face and through his hair.

Jake moved toward the door with deliberate steps. Whoever it was better have a damn good reason for interrupting them.

He yanked the door open and froze. It wasn't Frankie or Johnny. Dario stood there with Monica.

"Dario? What's—" Jake started to ask but stopped when he got a clear look at Dario's bruised and bloody face as he leaned heavily on Monica, who looked pretty worse for wear herself. "What the fuck happened?" he demanded, ushering them inside.

"Oh my God! Dario!" Nikki gasped, running over to him. "Are you all right? How did this happen?" she asked, dragging him and Monica into the living room.

Dario winced as he sat down on the couch. Jake darted into the kitchen and grabbed a rag and filled it with ice.

"I'm okay. I think," he ground out.

"Bullshit," Jake snapped, storming over to him, and handing him the ice. "Who did this to you? When? Start talking."

Dario and Monica exchanged wary glances. When she nodded, Dario turned to Jake. "Bruce. He and I got into it tonight when I caught him trying to—" He broke off, his face contorting into rage.

Monica spoke up then. "Dario stopped Bruce from...raping me," she said, her voice breaking.

"Jesus Christ," Nikki hissed, moving next to Monica and taking her free hand in hers. "Was tonight the first time he's tried this?" she asked gently.

Monica shook her head. "Not exactly. He...he's been touching me and forcing me to do things to him...for months," she whimpered.

Jake's temper flared as everything fell into place. This explained Dario's strange moods, the bruises and abrasions, and why he didn't like being away from the house when Monica was there. He'd been defending and protecting her all this time.

"This is why you're always banged up, isn't it?" Jake demanded, taking the chair next to Dario, clinging to the reins of his temper.

He nodded. "I caught him the first time a few months back. I stopped him, but he went after me for it and has every time I've managed to stop it."

"Why didn't you say anything? I could have helped you," Jake said.

Dario shot him a bland look. "Bro, you know why. You would have flown off in a rage and gotten yourself in trouble—maybe even sent to prison this time. I couldn't risk that, and Monica...she didn't want to say anything. We didn't have any real proof to show authorities, and Barbara wouldn't have believed us—she always sticks up for Bruce. It would have made things even worse."

Jake's gut twisted. Dario didn't say anything to him because he had been trying to protect Jake and ended up getting hurt in the process.

"Don't ever do that again. Don't worry about me. I can take care of you *and* myself. If you need help, you tell me, no matter what it is. Do you hear me?" he said, grabbing Dario's shoulder, his voice breaking.

"And if you can't find Jake, you call me. I'm here too," Nikki offered, tears streaming down her face.

Jake's heart swelled at her declaration; not only did she love him, but she loved his brother too.

Dario's eyes filled with tears. "I'm sorry. You're both right. I should have said something, even when Monica didn't want to. It's been...hell over there the last two months, especially. He's been at it more and more."

Monica buried her face in his chest, sobbing. "No. I'm sorry. This is all my fault. I never should have involved you."

"It's neither of your faults." Jake jumped to his feet. He needed to move—to do something to work off the rage pumping through his veins and the almost overwhelming urge to kill something.

"Jake's right," Nikki said, her eyes following him as he paced back and forth, offering him silent support when she knew he needed to work off the anger. "This is all on Bruce and Barbara. And it ends now. We're going to get you out of there."

"How?" Dario asked.

Jake stopped pacing. "We'll call Johnny and file a report. Then we'll get you to the hospital and get you both checked out."

"But where will we go? They'll separate us," Monica said, panic ringing in her voice.

Nikki stood and grabbed her phone from the island. "No, they won't. I'll call Sean. He was my foster father when my parents died. Since he's already in the system, he can take you both as an emergency foster placement for now. And given the circumstances, I'd say this counts as an emergency."

Jake gaped at Nikki. "You're calling Sean? Why would he help with this?"

She lifted her head, her expression softening. "Because it's what you do for family. And you're family." She looked over at Dario and Monica. "You all are."

Overwhelmed, he merely nodded and watched as she reached out to Sean, who happily agreed to take both teens in for as long as needed, proving that she was right. They were a family now—all of them.

The rest of the night flew by in a flurry of police and CPS reports, a lengthy visit to the ER, and finally, a visit to the Reynolds home, where Nikki went inside—Jake was remanded to the car for his own good—and grabbed as much of Monica and Dario's things as she could. When it was all said and done, Dario and Monica were safely ensconced in Sean's spacious home, the necessary paperwork for them to be with Sean not only for the short term, but also on a long-term basis, filed.

Jake and Nikki dragged themselves into his apartment sometime just before dawn. They dropped into Jake's bed, exhausted. He wrapped himself around her like a vine and clutched her to him, grateful for her and her unending faith and love. As his mind drifted off, he prayed that nothing ever took her away from him. She was his world, and life without her wouldn't be possible.

28

The trees rushed by in a blur of earth tones as Jake wound Nikki's Ferrari up Mountain Home Road, headed for the Cascades—the most expensive restaurant in all of Wood Glenn. She and Jake were going there to celebrate major milestones for each of them.

For Nikki, they were celebrating her team's continued success in the IMSA series, taking the podium at both the 12 Hours of Sebring and the SportsCar Grand Prix at Long Beach. For Jake, it was his enrollment in the Academy of Art's photojournalism program *and* Dario and Monica's permanent placement with Sean.

"Have I told you how gorgeous you look in that dress?" Jake asked, sliding her a glance.

She grinned. She'd picked the black halter dress especially for tonight. It highlighted her curves and was easy to get in and out of—a definite plus for later. "You have, but I don't mind hearing it again."

Jake took her hand in his and pressed a kiss to her palm. "Well, then, let me say it again: you look stunning, angel. Really."

"You look pretty hot yourself, Mr. Masercotti," she replied, eyeing him in his black sports coat, slacks, and white shirt, which he wore unbuttoned at the collar. He looked downright yummy.

Wagging his eyebrows, he said, "I aim to please, ma'am."

They arrived at the restaurant minutes later. Jake pulled into the lot and managed to find one of the few parking spots actually on pavement, not wanting to park the Modena in the mud. The Cascades was nestled in the mountains above Wood Glenn, providing patrons with a beautiful, natural setting to dine in. But that natural beauty came at a price: the parking lot was more dirt and mud than pavement.

Jake and Nikki were arguing over which version of Van Halen was better: Jake was for the Roth years, while Nikki argued for Hagar's time with the band, when Bruce Springsteen's "No Surrender" echoed from her purse.

"Shoot. I need to take that. It's Jeff," Nikki said, grabbing her phone. "Will you excuse me for a minute?"

Jake flashed her one of his infamous crooked grins. "Sure thing, angel."

With a wink, Nikki headed outside. "Hey, Jeff. What's up?" she asked, answering the call the minute she was outside.

"Hi there, Nikki. I hope I didn't catch you at a bad time. I'm calling because I need a favor."

What else is new? She appreciated Jeff. She did. But she also couldn't wait for her contract with him to be up. It was getting to be too much. He always needed *something*.

"Sure. What's going on?" She moved to the far end of the building so she was clear of the front entrance, hoping it was something small. She had very little downtime between the two racing circuits.

"The painter is finished with the repairs to the rear quarter panel from that little run-in with Dixon last month at Mazda Raceway, but he needs someone to come and inspect the car before it leaves the body shop. I can't get out to Michael Angelo's in time, so I need you to take care of it," he explained.

Nikki's stomach dropped. The Le Mans car was at Michael Angelo's Paint and Body in San Francisco. It was the best body shop in the Bay Area and the only place she ever recommended to people, but she never went there herself. She and her parents had been gunned down there five years earlier. Nikki hadn't been back since and never planned to return.

"Oh. Are you sure you can't get anyone else to go?" she asked, voice shaking.

"I don't trust anyone outside of you or me, Nik. It needs to be done tomorrow afternoon so we can get the car shipped out in time for the event coming up in Colorado. I'm afraid it's got to be you, or it won't happen."

She gripped the phone tighter, her palms sweating. "Fine. I'll go tomorrow morning and take care of it."

"Great! Let me know how it goes."

She ended the call and headed back inside the restaurant, numb. When she sat down, Jake took one look at her face and knew something was wrong.

"It's nothing, really," she said, taking a long pull from her water.

"That's crap. You're pale, and your hands are shaking. Talk to me, angel."

Setting down her water, she told him about Jeff's call. "I haven't been to the shop since the night my parents were killed. I hadn't planned on ever returning there if I could help it, but it looks like those plans have changed," she said, finishing the story.

"I'm so sorry, tesora. Is there anything I can do?" he asked.

"Go with me?"

He lifted her hand to his lips. "That was a given. Is there anything else?"

She shook her head.

"All right. What's the name of the shop?" he asked.

"Michael Angelo's Auto Body in San Francisco."

Jake blinked at her. "Really?" The color drained from his face.

"Yeah. Hey," she said, getting worried. He looked awful. "What's wrong? You don't look good." She reached across the table and took his hand in hers. It was clammy.

He grimaced. "I, um…don't feel so good. I think the sushi I had for lunch isn't settling well. Will you excuse me?" He scrambled out of his chair, and dashed for the bathroom.

"Uh, sure."

She turned around and slumped back in her chair, hoping Jake was all right. He looked almost green before he ran off.

He returned to the table a few minutes later, looking even worse. "Nikki, I hate to do this, but I need you to take me back to my place. I feel like hell," he said, leaning on the back of the chair for support.

She blinked up at him. He did look rough. "Of course." She left some money on the table then helped Jake out to the car.

The ride to his place was quiet. He sat there, head pressed up against the cool glass of the window, eyes closed the entire way.

When they reached his apartment, she moved to get out of the car.

"No, don't. I don't think you should come inside. It's going to be a long night, and if it's not food poisoning, I don't want you to catch this." He pulled himself out of the vehicle.

"Are you sure? If it's not food poisoning, I've already been exposed, so I'll probably get it anyway."

Jake nodded, grimacing like standing there was killing him. "I'm sure. I think this is best. And I hate to do this, because you shouldn't face tomorrow alone, but I don't think I'll be up to going with you to the body shop. I'm sorry, angel, really."

Nikki waved him off. "Don't worry about it. I'll be fine. Go inside and get some rest. I'll call you later to check in."

Jake smiled, but it didn't reach his eyes. "Okay." He shut the door and headed inside.

She watched him go, her heart sinking at the ruined evening. Backing down the long drive, she hoped tomorrow would go better for both of them. They had enough crap in their lives without adding to it.

Don't count on it, whispered the all-too-familiar voice she tried to ignore but couldn't—no matter how hard she tried.

～

"THANK YOU FOR COMING WITH ME, DAMON," NIKKI SAID AS THEY LEFT Michael Angelo's. "I couldn't do this on my own—not the first time, anyway."

She'd asked Damon to go with her when he got home the night before. She would have asked Hilda, but she was in Mexico with her parents at a family reunion. Hilda was far better in these instances. Damon didn't handle emotional situations well when it came to Nikki. Seeing her upset derailed him. He'd get agitated because he couldn't fix the problem, which generally made things worse. But with Hilda gone, Jake out of commission, and Sean busy with Dario and Monica, she had no one else, and she needed someone for this. So she went to Damon, who'd turned out to be amazing. He held her hand the entire time, whispering words of encouragement and solace when she cried, and stood by her side as a solid presence. It was all very un-Damon-like and exactly what she needed.

"Anytime, bella. You know that," he said to her repeated thanks, pulling her into his side as they walked out of the shop and over to his car.

Once they were on the road, she tried calling Jake. Unfortunately, like the other three tries *and* the attempts the night before, his phone went straight to voicemail. Frowning, she punched the end button and tossed the phone in her bag.

"What is it?" Damon asked, merging onto the freeway.

"It's Jake. He's not answering his phone."

Damon arched a brow. "I'm not seeing the problem."

She rolled her eyes. "He's sick, remember? I came home early last night because of it. I'm worried about him," she said, her eyes fixed to the cars whooshing by as Damon tore down the freeway. The man drove like he was on the track.

"Maybe he's sleeping. If he's sick, it would make sense," he offered.

True... *Still.* Something was off about the whole situation: the way Jake got sick right after she told him about the body shop. It was probably a coincidence, and food poisoning as he claimed, but she couldn't shake the idea that there was more to it.

"You're probably right, but would you mind taking me there so I could check on him? It won't take long," she said, chewing on her bottom lip.

Damon grumbled something nasty under his breath about not wanting to catch mad cow disease or trailer park flu but agreed to take her. Thirty minutes later, they pulled up to the Tiger's Den and parked behind a white Lexus SUV.

"Do you know who owns that?" Damon asked, motioning to the Lexus.

Nikki shook her head. "I've never seen it before." She hopped out of the car and made a beeline for the stairs leading up to Jake's. "You don't have to come up. In fact, he probably doesn't want anyone to see him like this. He looked pretty torn up last night."

"Yeah, I'm not going in. Don't worry. I don't need to catch whatever the fuck the prospect picked up at the trailer park, but I'm not letting you go alone. Not with all the shit that's going on. I'll wait on the porch and keep an eye out."

"Okay."

Nikki let herself into Jake's apartment with the key he'd given her back in January, while Damon waited out on the porch, scanning the area for any signs of suspicious activity. A rank stench struck her as she entered the apartment. It wasn't the sickly stench of someone who'd been ill but the funk of stale whiskey and cheap perfume—like he'd gone to a bar and spent the entire night there.

Her heart picked up speed.

Nikki dropped her keys on the island, where she spotted an empty bottle of Southern Comfort and two glasses—one of which had lipstick stains along the rim.

What the fuck?

"Jake?" she called, moving from the kitchen to his bedroom. "Are you okay?" she called again, marching down the hall, stopping dead in her tracks when she reached his open door. Jake was lying face down in his bed, his naked body covered by a thin sheet. And he wasn't alone.

"Well, well. Look who it is: Little Miss Stick up Her Ass," Angela O'Brien sneered from the bed next to Jake. "This feels familiar, doesn't it? Didn't we do this a few years back at Damon's place?"

Nikki didn't respond. She just stared. Angela was right, though. They had done this before. This was exactly how she found out that Damon was cheating on her with Angela. She'd walked in on them much like this.

A thousand emotions rushed her as she stood there gaping at the scene, her eyes darting from Jake's naked form to the whore next to him. Why wasn't he moving? Didn't he hear her?

"I'm guessing by the look on your face you weren't expecting this. I'm not surprised. You were clueless when it came to Damon's needs too. I mean, that's why he came to me—because you weren't cutting it in the sack. I guess things haven't changed for you in that department." Angela tilted her head to the side. "You'd think you'd learn what a man needs from a woman by *now*, though."

Nikki pulled her attention from Jake's prone form, feeling something inside her snap. She turned her fiery glare on Angela. "Get out!" she demanded, stepping into the room—the same room where she and Jake had made love countless times, where she'd given herself to him freely, willingly, because she loved him.

"Excuse me?" Angela snapped.

Nikki stalked over to the foot of the bed. "I said, *get the fuck out!*"

Angela's eyes flared. She leaped off the bed and came around and stood in front of Nikki. "I'm not going anywhere. *I'm* the one who's wanted here, not you."

Rage like she'd never known flooded her, sending all thoughts from her brain save one: she was going to kill Angela O'Brien.

DAMON READ THROUGH THE TEXT FROM NINO, SCOWLING AT THE SCREEN. Correa wanted to increase the frequency of his shipments from once to twice a month.

Jesus.

How many guns did this guy need? Was he building a fucking militia down there?

He started to fire a text back to Nino when screaming erupted from inside the apartment. Forgetting the text, he darted inside and was overwhelmed by the stench of whiskey and skank.

What the fuck?

Following the sounds of a scuffle, Damon dashed across the kitchen and down the hall to the back bedroom. He skidded to a stop and shook his head to make sure he was seeing things correctly—because honestly, he couldn't be. That couldn't be a naked Angela O'Brien he saw Nikki straddling as she repeatedly drove her fist into her face.

Could it?

"You fucking whore! Why can't you stay out of my life?" Nikki screamed as her fists pounded into Angela.

Holy shit, it is.

"I don't ask for it, bitch!" Angela snarled back, wrenching an arm free and slapping Nikki across the face. "They come to *me!*"

A howling sound erupted from Nikki. But before she could do more damage to Angela's face, Damon lunged forward, grabbed her around the waist, and dragged her from the room.

"Take your goddamn hands off me!" Nikki shrilled, beating and kicking at any part of him she could reach.

"Not going to happen, bella. Not until you calm down," he ground out, trying to avoid her feet and fists of fury, as he managed to grab her keys from the island.

After what felt like a year, he made it out to the porch, where he deposited the hissing and snarling hellcat. She glared up at him as she scrambled to her feet, trying to get around him. "Get out of my way. I've got business to finish in there," she demanded, jabbing a finger at the closed door.

"Not a chance. Take my car." He put his keys in her hands. "Clear out of here before you do something you'll regret," he said, holding up his hands, hoping she didn't try to hit him.

She stood there for several seconds, firing daggers at him with her eyes. When she realized she wasn't getting inside again, she threw a glare at the closed door.

"Fine! I'm out of here."

Once she reached the bottom of the staircase, she stopped and turned, pressing a hand to her chest, all fury vanishing. In its place, he saw something he never wanted to see in her eyes again: betrayal.

"Can you tell me one thing? Why, Damon? Why does this keep happening to me? Why do the men I love keep running to *her*?" she croaked.

Damon's heart shattered in his chest. "Bella, I—"

"No. You know what?" she cut in. "Forget it. I shouldn't have asked—it doesn't matter. Come get your car later and then make yourself scarce. I don't want to see you or anyone else connected to that bitch."

Damon watched her walk away, the shards of his heart slicing through his chest at the memory of the look on her face. He'd seen that same look when she caught him and Angela together. He'd vowed then never to see that look on her face again.

Rage like he hadn't felt in years rocketed through his veins. Nikki didn't deserve this shit. And while he couldn't do anything about what he'd done to Nikki years ago, he could do something about Sam Crow and that filthy whore. He could tear them both to shreds. They deserved nothing less.

"Angela!" he bellowed, storming inside the apartment. "You'd better hope you made confession recently because you're about to meet your fucking maker!"

He kicked open the bedroom door, his hands balled into fists. Angela, who'd thrown on one of Tatt-Boy's shirts, stood next to the bed, shaking the freak vigorously with one hand as she wiped the blood from her nose with the other. "Don't threaten me, Damon Rossi. You know who my father is!" she barked, shaking Jake. "Wake the hell up!" she yelled in his ear.

"I know exactly who your father is, which is going to make this all the more satisfying," he said, grabbing her by the hair and pulling her back. As he did, he shot a glance at Jake, noting that he hadn't moved—at all—through any of the commotion.

Damon stilled, studying his prone form. Something wasn't right about this picture. The prospect should have stirred by now—there'd been enough action in here to raise the freaking dead. He reached down and felt his pulse. It was extremely slow, even for someone sleeping off a night of binge drinking.

Shit.

"What the fuck did he take last night?" Damon demanded.

Angela froze. "How should I know?"

"I know you mess around with drugs. What did you give him?"

"I didn't give him shit," Angela hissed, grabbing the hand he had buried in her hair.

He increased his grip, eliciting a sharp cry from her. "Bullshit. Tell me what you did, Ang, or so help me God, I will do even more to fuck up that face of yours."

"Ouch! Watch it! You're going to rip out my hair!" She winced.

"You want to keep your hair? Answer the fucking question."

"Fine! I slipped a little *La Rocha* into his whiskey last night. I was trying to relax him, get him in the mood. He kept going on and on about the prude and something about his dad and how she'd never be able to look at him again. I don't know. I just wanted what I came for and thought the *La Rocha* would help. Instead, it knocked him right out," she explained.

"You slipped him Rohypnol? Are you crazy? That shit can kill a person if they use it with excessive alcohol consumption!" he roared, flinging her against the wall as he pulled out his phone and opened up the voice recording app.

"What do you care? Nikki's not your girl, and you don't run with this guy. Why do you give a shit about what happens to him?"

Damon glared at her. "Why I care is none of your business," he snapped, holding the phone up to her. "Repeat what you just said, word for word."

Angela glared at him, her lips pursed together. When Damon made another move to grab her hair, however, she put up her hands and did as he asked. When she finished, he closed the app, grabbed her purse, and dragged her out of the room.

"Take your goddamn hands off of me, Rossi! Or I swear to all that is holy, I will—"

"For once, Angela, will you shut your mouth?" He stopped at the door. In one swift move, he tore the T-shirt from her body then flung her barefoot, naked ass out of the apartment. "Now get out of here before I really get pissed."

"You can't do this! What about my clothes? I can't go out here naked!" she shrieked.

"Buy new ones. I'm sure you can afford it on the allowance your daddy gives you," he sneered, slamming the door in her bloodied and bruised face.

"You're going to pay for this, Damon! You and that little prude of yours are dead. I swear it!" she vowed.

"Yeah, yeah. Whatever." He threw the dead bolt and headed into the kitchen. He examined the glasses while he pulled out his phone and dialed Nino, noting that one of them had a blue residue coating the bottom.

"Yo! Boss! What's up?" Nino chirped.

"I need you to call Max and have him come the address I'm about to text you. Tell him to bring a drug-testing kit for Rohypnol. And bring me his fee while you're at it. Got that?"

"Sure, no problem. Everything okay?"

"Yeah, it's peachy around here." He ended the call and texted Nino the address.

Damon pulled off his jacket, dropped it on one of the barstools, then headed over to the couch to wait for Max. He didn't have to wait long— one never did when it came to Max. Somehow he managed to appear at any given location within minutes of contact. Damon had no idea how he did it.

"So," Max said as he drew blood from a still-unconscious Jake. "What's the story with the Hell's Angel? I don't usually see dudes doped up on roofies and SoCo. Was he trying to kill himself?"

Damon leaned against the wall. "No. Some bitch slipped it to him after he was good and drunk, hoping to get laid."

Max shook his head. "Idiot. All that did was solidify that she *wouldn't* be getting any."

"Yeah, well, she's not the brightest bulb in the box." It was an understatement where Angela was concerned. The girl had as much brainpower as a rock. "How do we wake him up?"

Max rummaged around in his med bag. "With this." He held a small vial beneath Jake's nose. After a few seconds, he started coughing and lurched up in bed.

"What the fuck?" He choked, bracing one arm on the bedpost and the other on the bed.

"Morning, sunshine," Damon crooned.

Jake grabbed his head with one hand. "What the hell are you doing here? And who the fuck is he?" he said, peering at him and Max through squinted eyes.

Max grinned. "I'm Max," he said, handing Jake a small cup. "Drink this."

Jake glared at the cup. "What is it?"

"It's syrup of ipecac. You need to get the shit you poured down your gullet last night out of your system. Drink it," Max ordered.

"No. Get the fuck out," Jake snapped, his head wobbling.

Max looked over at Damon. "Are you going to help me with this? He's built like the fucking Jolly Green Giant."

Damon rolled his eyes. "Fine."

Jake tried to put up a fight while Damon held him down, but he was in no condition to stop him. Once Max forced the tonic down his throat, they backed off.

"*Ugh!* What the hell, man?" Jake roared.

"You'll thank us later," Max quipped, turning to Damon. "I'll get this sample and the glass to the lab for testing. I should have the results in a couple of days. He'll be fine once he throws up. Just make sure he rehydrates afterward."

Damon nodded. "Thanks, Max."

"Sure thing. I'm always available for Di Silva's guys." Max grabbed his bag and turned to Jake. "You're going to be praying to the porcelain gods in about five minutes. After that, you'll feel better," he said then turned and left.

Damon followed him out to the door, handing him the thick envelope Nino had left on the counter while Damon was with Max and Jake. Max gave him a quick salute then disappeared down the stairs. Minutes after he left, he heard Jake bolt for the bathroom, where he spent the next half hour emptying his system.

"Make sure you brush your teeth," Damon called from the front room, where he stood studying the photographs and sketches adorning the walls. Jake snarled something at him, but Damon didn't catch it. The sound of the shower turning on drowned out his voice.

His eyes roved over the photographs and sketches, lingering on the ones of Nikki more than the others. He had to admit, Masercotti had talent. The pieces were amazing. But talent aside, the guy was a tool.

Ditching Nikki to go out and get drunk with trash like Angela? What the fuck was he thinking?

"Why are you still here?" Jake demanded, dragging himself into the kitchen, and grabbed a bottle of OJ from the fridge.

"Nikki took my car home. I haven't arranged a ride yet. I wanted to make sure you didn't die," he explained, dropping himself onto a barstool.

The bottle of OJ froze in front of Jake's mouth. "Nikki was here? When?"

"Two hours ago. I brought her here to check on you after we left the body shop."

"The *body shop*?" Jake said, pulling his brows together.

"Yeah, she had to go there to check on the Le Mans Tiger. She told you about it last night—right before you got sick. Remember?" Damon said, eyeing Jake as it started coming back to him.

"Shit. That's right." He leaned against the fridge, groaning.

"What the hell happened? Why did you get piss drunk and end up with Angela O'Brien?"

Jake dropped his head back against the fridge. After a tense minute, he said, "Nikki told me about the night her parents were killed—about how they were gunned down in front of Michael Angelo's. The body shop my father owns and uses to launder money."

Damon arched a brow. "How do you know about that?"

"Word has a way of getting around. This town isn't that big, and the community is tight. I've heard things over the years about the shop and the shit that goes down there, which means what happened to Nikki's parents was connected to Carlo. It had to be. The shootings and their connection to organized crime were all over the street," he explained. "When I realized how her parents died, I flipped. I knew she'd never look at me the same once she found out that it was *my* father and his fucked-up world that killed her parents. How could she? I'd be a constant reminder of what happened to them. So I cut our night short. After she dropped me at home, I took off. I had to go somewhere and get my head together. I ended up at the Ox and got piss drunk when I couldn't figure a way out of this without losing her. Angela was there, as usual. She must have followed me home even after I told her to fuck off; I don't know. I don't remember anything beyond leaving the bar."

Damon puffed out a breath. Under different circumstances, it would be a safe bet that Carlo's business was linked to the shooting. But that wasn't the case this time. The shootings had nothing to do with Carlo.

"Wait. How did you know I left with Angela?" Jake asked, a horrified look coming over him. "Was she here this morning when Nikki showed up?"

"Yeppers peppers." He smirked.

"Oh no... Fuck no. She must think...shit. I wouldn't. I would never sleep with Angela or anyone else. Not as long as Nikki was in my life in *any* capacity," Jake said, panic rising in his voice.

"Relax. You didn't have sex with Angela last night. You couldn't have. The whiskey dick alone would have stopped that, but she slipped you a roofie on top of it," Damon said.

"Roofies?" he choked out.

"Yeah, genius. You might want to think twice before you take drinks from sluts like Angela. That girl gets around. I would know. We hooked up when I was with Nikki."

"Are you serious? Son of a bitch!" he roared, dragging his hands through his hair. "Does Nikki know the truth about the roofies—that *I* didn't fuck Angela?"

Damon shook his head. "Not yet."

Jake pushed off the fridge and darted across the kitchen.

"Where are you going?" Damon snapped, grabbing him by the arm.

Jake glared down at Damon's hand. "To find Nikki and explain what happened."

He tightened his grip when Jake tried to wrench himself free. "You can't. She won't believe anything you say. Not right now."

Jake's eyes snapped to Damon's. "Take your hand off me, Corleone," he warned.

"That should really be your role, shouldn't it?" Damon quipped, releasing Jake and moving to stand in front of him instead. He wasn't leaving here. Not until he understood that tracking Nikki down now wouldn't solve anything.

"Ha. Very funny. I need to see her. She'll listen to me. She trusts me," he insisted.

Damon shook his head. "Sorry. Not this time—not after finding you with the same woman that destroyed our relationship. If you go to her now, you'll only make things worse."

Jake folded his arms across his chest, scowling. "Okay, so? Why stop me? Why are you so invested in what happens between Nikki and me? If she's going to dump my sorry ass, why put it off? It's what you want, isn't it? You hate me—have from the moment we met."

"I do loathe you. And I couldn't honestly give two shits about what happens to you, Carlo's son or not. But I don't hate *her*. I care about that woman more than anything. Right now she's hurting, and I will do whatever it takes to stop that. Even if it means getting the two of you back together."

"If you care about her so much, why did you cheat on her?" Jake sneered. "You could be with her now if you hadn't fucked up."

Damon's temper flared. "Because I had to!"

"You *had to*?" Jake repeated. Understanding dawned in his eyes. "You wanted Nikki to find you with Angela so she'd break up with you, didn't you? But why? It's obvious you're still in love with her. Why throw her away like that?"

"It's none of your fucking business."

Jake chuckled mirthlessly. "Whatever. I'm through wasting my time here. I'm going after her before it's too late." He moved to step around him.

When Damon grabbed him, Jake sucker punched him in the jaw, sending him crashing into the island. He struck the corner and crumpled to the floor, his head spinning from the blow. Before he could move, Jake was out the door and firing up the Harley. Damon gripped the back of his head, swearing. That idiot was going to make things worse, and he couldn't do anything to stop it.

29

"Holy shit balls! He was in bed with Angela 'I'll fuck anything with a dick' O'Brien?" Hilda gasped.

Nikki jabbed her spoon into the tub of Chunky Hubby. "Yep."

"I can't believe it. I mean, seriously, what are the odds that it would be *her*?" Hilda said, her face filling the computer screen. They were Skyping since Hilda was still in Mexico with her family.

"Tell me about it." Nikki sighed and licked the spoon clean. She really needed to stop eating the ice cream. This was her fourth tub of Ben and Jerry's in three days. If she kept going like this, she was headed for a ten-pound binge and wouldn't fit into her racing suit this weekend. "That bitch is like a bad penny: she just keeps turning up."

"More like a case of virulent herpes."

Nikki snorted. It was the closest she'd come to laughing or smiling in three days. "Absolutely."

"All right, now what? What are you going to do? What if Jake comes back again? Will you talk to him?" Hilda asked, her voice softening.

"No. I'm done with him and men in general. They're nothing but trouble," she ground out. "I leave for Texas this weekend. Between the IMSA and VAM races I have scheduled, I'll be gone for over two weeks. If Jake comes around—which I doubt he will after I had the cops haul him off the property two days ago—I won't be here. I'll be racing, which is the best medicine for me."

Hilda's face fell. "I'm so sorry, Nik. I really thought he was the one for you." She tapped her fingers on the table. "Are you sure he slept with her?" she asked, her voice skeptical.

Nikki rolled her eyes. "Uh, *yeah*. I think finding them in bed *naked* pretty much answers that question. What else could they be doing that didn't require clothing?"

Hilda was quiet for a minute. "Right... Still, it seems out of character. That's all."

She agreed. Finding Jake with Angela shocked her to her core. Why did he do it? Why would he throw away what they had together? Did it have something to do with everything going on in her life—all the danger and drama? Was it too much for him? Was that why he went to Angela—because she was uncomplicated?

Her heart sank. That had to be it. It was the only thing that made sense.

"Hey, are you still there?" Hilda said, tapping the screen.

Nikki shook her head, pulling herself from thoughts she couldn't share with Hilda. Her best friend had no idea what was happening in her life, and it needed to stay that way for her safety.

"Sorry. Lost in thought. When are you coming home?" she asked, changing to a lighter subject.

Hilda winced. "Not until the beginning of June. We haven't been back here in years, and my *abuelita* is getting on in age."

Nikki's heart fell. "That's a long time, but it sounds like it's a good thing. What does Peter think about you being gone?" she asked, trying to find out, in a roundabout way, if he was still in her life.

"Peter? I don't know. I broke things off between us right before I left."

Relief eased through her. "Really? Why? I thought you liked him."

Hilda shrugged. "I did, but..." She hesitated.

"But what?" Nikki pressed, the relief she'd felt a moment ago vanishing.

"Don't get mad," she began, "but I told him about you—your memories coming back. I needed to talk to someone about it. I was worried about you, but I didn't want to freak you out, so I went to Peter. But ever since then he's been weird. Always asking me about you, what you're doing, where you're going. At first, I thought it was because he was interested in who I was close to, but it got so frequent and he grew so insistent about asking, that it felt like there was more to it than that, so I cut him loose."

Nikki gaped at the screen, her stomach invading her chest. Damon's fears were dead on: Peter was connected to Marco. He had to be. Why else would he be taking such an interest in Nikki?

She shook off the initial shock. "I'm sorry to hear that, Hil. I know you liked him." A wave of guilt swamped her. Her best friend had been played because of the mess she was caught up in.

Damn it.

Hilda waved it off. "It's okay. He's just a guy."

"Has he bothered you at all since?" she asked.

"Not too much, no. He called a few times at first, but I blocked his number. He won't be a problem anymore," she assured her.

Nikki prayed she was right. "I'm glad he got the hint," she said, jumping when she heard the front door slam, followed by Damon's voice calling her name.

"What's wrong?" Hilda asked.

"Damon's here," she grumbled, not wanting to deal with him yet. Finding Jake with Angela stirred too many bad memories. Instead of having lived one horror show, she'd lived two of them.

"Tell him to get the hell out and then change the code on the alarm. It's time he moved," Hilda ordered.

Nikki forced a smile. "I will. Thanks, Hil."

"Anytime, girl," Hilda said and closed the connection between them.

Nikki got up and headed for the door. Like it or not, she had to deal with Damon if he was in the house. It was only so big. Before she could open it, he barged in, gripping a manila folder in one hand.

"There you are. Why didn't you come downstairs when I called?" he demanded in typical Damon fashion.

"I was busy. What do you want? I have things to do," she replied, leaning against the dresser.

"We need to talk. It's about Jake," he said, undeterred.

The muscles along her neck and back stiffened. "What about *him*?"

"He didn't sleep with Angela and never intended to."

Nikki's brows shot up. "I found them in bed. Naked. What else could they have been doing?"

Damon sat down on the bed, patting the spot in front of him. When she refused to move, he continued. "Fine. Have it your way." He opened the folder. "Jake went to a bar and got drunk. Angela followed him home, where she slipped a roofie into his drink to *relax him*, as she put it, because he was distraught over you. She intended to sleep with him, but the drugs and alcohol knocked him out. He couldn't have gotten it up for anyone. Not even you, bella."

She rolled her eyes. "Do you realize how crazy that sounds? Why would she go to all that trouble?"

Damon nodded. "I know it sounds crazy, but it's true. Angela wanted to get back at you for something. I don't know what, but I have proof that she drugged him." He pulled out his phone and played a recording of

Angela explaining what she'd done. He then showed her lab work that proved Jake had Rohypnol in his system.

She lifted her wide eyes to Damon. "Okay, so Jake didn't cheat on me. Why did he go to the bar in the first place? Why did he lie and avoid me?"

He leaned back against the bedpost. "The shop where your parents were killed is owned by Carlo. Jake assumed that the shooting was related to his father's other *business interests*. He thought—"

"I would hold it against him, and he panicked. That's why he avoided me. He assumed that I would be angry. Leave him for it. Right?" she finished as understanding dawned.

"Right."

It all made sense now. Why he'd suddenly gotten ill after her story; why he'd avoided her afterward. But...how could he assume that of her? She'd never hold what his father did against him. Didn't he know that? Didn't he trust her?

"Damn it. He should have known better. I'd never hold that against him."

"I know, but for Jake...I don't know. The dude's pretty emo if you ask me. He seems to take things to a dark place."

"He does," she agreed. "He's been through the wringer, Damon. It's no surprise he acts this way... But still. *With me?* He should know by now that I'd never judge him like that."

"You're right. Especially in this case," he said.

"What do you mean?"

Damon winced. "Your parents weren't killed in a random act of violence or because of Carlo. The Irish were targeting your father. They wanted him dead because he refused to let them use his shop as a hub for money laundering and gun smuggling. It was a hit, bella."

Nikki's jaw dropped open. "Are you serious? Why didn't I know about this?"

Her dad had been in trouble with the Irish mob? Just like her? Jesus. Was their family cursed?

Damon nodded, his expression grave. "Your dad had been having trouble with the Irish for some time. He came to me for help with strict instructions that I wasn't to say anything to you or your brothers. I tried to help; I had a security detail on him for weeks. But they got to him anyway. You can tell Jake. If anyone is to blame here, it's me and the Irish."

She blinked at him. He'd known her father was in trouble and didn't say anything? She gave herself an internal smack. Of course he didn't. Damon loved and respected her father. He never would have broken a promise to him.

She moved to the bed, sat down, and took his hands in hers, her chest tightening when she realized how long he'd been carrying this guilt. "It's not your fault, either. It's the assholes in that damn Irish mob. Don't blame yourself for what they did. I don't, and neither would my father. Thank you for trying to help him."

Damon's eyes moistened, but the tears never fell. "I'd do anything for you and your family. Anything. I'm sorry it wasn't enough."

Nikki moved closer, pulling Damon into an embrace. "I know you would, and I love you for it," she whispered.

His arms tightened around her, and he held her for several minutes, his body trembling against hers. When he broke free, he moved from the bed to the doorway, putting space between them like he typically did when things got emotional. "So, now what? Are you going to go after Jake?"

Good question. She wanted to. She loved Jake more than anything. But the bottom line was he didn't trust her. This all started because he didn't trust her enough to be honest about what he was thinking and feeling. And while she knew that Jake took things to dark places pretty easily because of everything he'd been through, she wondered how long it would take for him to trust in her love for him. Would he ever get there? Even with therapy? And if he couldn't, could she be with him knowing that?

She toyed with the folder holding the medical reports, catching a glimpse of the name on the file: Giancarlo Di Silva. "Damon, why does the report have Jake's father's name on the file?"

She handed him the folder.

He glanced down at it. "That's Jake's real name. He was named after Carlo. He changed it to Jake Masercotti when he turned eighteen. I used his birth name to keep this incident out of the system under his current identity. You didn't know that?"

Nikki shook her head, her gaze involuntarily swinging to her nightstand where the old journal sat. The journal belonged to a man with the initials *GDS*—the same initials Jake had growing up.

As she stared at the old leather volume, an idea started to form. Jake was twenty when the journal was started—long after his name had been changed. But what if the journal had been given to him years before that? What if his mother, a woman who believed in the power of journaling, gave it to him when he was a child? She had the exact same journal with her own initials engraved on it in the same lettering, in the same spot. What if she gave it to Jake before she died and he didn't use it until later?

If that was true, that could make him and the man in the book the same person, especially with all of their striking similarities.

"Nikki? What's going on in that head of yours? Are you having second thoughts about Jake?" Damon asked when she remained silent.

She whipped her head around. If this was true—and deep in her heart, she believed it was—then eventually he *could* learn to trust her and not take things to dark places. He'd done it before. He'd gone from a man on the brink of suicide to someone who wanted to live, and he could do it again. He could change.

"I need to find Jake." She grabbed her phone. Before she could dial, it rang. She didn't recognize the number, but she answered it anyway. Maybe it was Jake calling from a payphone or something.

"Hello?"

"Is this Angel?" a deep, raspy voice she recognized asked. It sounded like the guy from the bar who'd broken up her fight with Angela.

"No, this is Nikki Elliot. Who is this?"

"This is Tucker Ellis. Do you know a guy named Jake? He keeps asking for someone named Angel. This number is listed under that name in his phone," he explained.

Nikki's heart jumped. "I'm Angel—I mean, that's what he calls me. What's wrong? Is he okay?" she asked, rolling the questions off at a hare's pace.

"He's seen better days. I've got him here at the Ox. He's had a fifth of whiskey and looks pretty banged up. He may have taken a fall off his bike at some point. Is there any chance you could come get him?"

"Of course. I'll be there soon. Thank you, Tucker."

"Sure thing."

Damon walked over to her. "Who the hell is *Tucker*?"

"He's a friend of Jake's. He needs me to pick up Jake at the Ox. Apparently, he's been drinking heavily and he's hurt. I've got to go." She grabbed her purse.

"Not by yourself, you're not," he insisted. "The Ox is a rough place. We'll take my car. He can lie down in the back."

Nikki nodded and followed him out the door.

They pulled up to the bar less than thirty minutes later.

"Classy place, bella," Damon muttered, scanning the room with narrowed eyes as the door swung shut behind them. "Sure you want to be with someone who hangs out *here*?"

"Yes. And be nice," she hissed under her breath, looking around for Tucker. She spotted him coming out of the hallway at the back. "There he is."

She made a beeline for him. "Hey, Tucker. I'm Nikki," she said, extending a hand.

Tucker smiled, turning his face from hardened to charming in a flash. "It's nice to see you again and to meet you officially." He shook her hand. "And who's this? Your bodyguard?"

"Sometimes." She chuckled. "This is my friend Damon Rossi."

"It's a pleasure." Damon smirked, shaking Tucker's hand.

"Rossi? You Vince Rossi's boy?" he asked.

Damon stiffened next to Nikki. "I am. Why?"

Tucker studied him. "We've done business a time or two. It's nice to meet you."

Damon didn't say anything. He just nodded.

"Where is Jake?" Nikki asked, peering around Tucker to the hallway.

"He's in the back. You might want to have Damon here pull the car around the rear of the building so Jake doesn't have to crawl through the bar. He's not much for walking right now."

Nikki swallowed around the lump in her throat. "All right." She turned to Damon, but he was already on his way out the door.

Tucker led her down the hall to a closed door off the bathroom. When they stepped inside, she realized it was an office. On the couch lay a battered Jake.

"Oh my God!" She ran to him. "Jake? Can you hear me?" she asked, running her hands over his face and torso.

He stirred, opening unfocused eyes. "Angel? Is that you?"

She reared back. He smelled like he'd downed a gallon of SoCo then bathed in it. "Yes, it's me," she whispered as tears gathered behind her eyes. "I'm here, and I'm taking you home. Okay?"

"I wasn't lying," he slurred. "I never slept with Angela. I swear."

"Shh...I know. It's okay. We can talk about it later."

Tucker moved around her and opened a door at the rear of the office. "We can take him out here."

Damon appeared in the doorway a second later. "I'll get him," he said, stepping inside.

"It's going to take us both. It took me and a former wrestler, Tiny Rogers, to get him back here," Tucker said, pulling Jake up and slinging one of his arms around his shoulders.

Damon moved to the other side and repeated the move.

Together, he and Tucker dragged a moaning Jake from the office. "You'd better not puke on my True Religions, prospect," she heard Damon grumble.

"Don't worry," Jake slurred. "I'll save it for your car, Corleone."

"You son of a—" Damon started to say, but it got cut off when Jake turned his head and threw up all over Damon's shoes. "Fuck! Those are Giuseppe Zanotti originals!" he whined.

"For the love of God, Damon. They're just shoes," Nikki scolded, wiping Jake's face with her shirt.

"*Just shoes.* These things set me back twelve hundred dollars."

Tucker glanced down at them. "Twelve hundred dollars for sneakers? Son, you got taken."

Damon grumbled something under his breath about bikers and trailer parks as he and Tucker got Jake to the car.

Once they got Jake situated in the back of the Benz, Nikki thanked Tucker, and the three of them headed back to her place. Nikki sat in the back with Jake's head in her lap, stroking his hair and whispering comforting words in his ear. When they made it back to her place, she and Damon got him out of the car, up the stairs to her bedroom, and into the occasional chair near her bed.

"I can take it from here." She pulled off his boots and went for his pants next.

"Fuck, he reeks." Damon gagged, covering his nose and mouth. "What are you going to do with his smelly ass?"

"Get him into the shower, clean him up, and put him to bed."

"*You* are going to shower him?" Damon sneered, incredulous.

Nikki stood with her hands on her hips. "It wouldn't be the first time."

He grimaced. "All right. I'm out. That's an image I don't want in my brain."

With Damon gone, she finished stripping Jake and got him conscious enough to get in the shower. She propped him up on the built-in granite bench then made short work of her own clothes and joined him, holding the toothbrush he kept there in one hand, loaded with toothpaste.

"Jake? Are you with me?" she asked as the warm water rushed over them.

"Yeah, I'm here, angel," he said, opening his eyes. They went from unfocused to laser sharp when he caught sight of her naked form.

She handed him the toothbrush. "Here. Brush your teeth, and I'll take care of the rest."

He nodded, his eyes roving over her body as he brushed his teeth and she washed him from head to toe, careful not to be rough on the bruises and scrapes along his arms and torso. When she was finished, she stepped back to clean herself up, but she didn't get far. Jake's arm snaked out around her, pulling her into his lap.

"Wait." His deep voice rumbled through her. "Allow me?" he asked, peering up at her through his thick lashes.

She nodded, her heart swelling at the raw emotion in his eyes.

He grabbed the shampoo from the bench and lathered her hair, supporting her as she leaned back under the spray and rinsed. Then he grabbed the body wash and proceeded to wash the rest of her, his hands lingering in certain places more than others. By the time he was finished, they were both panting with need.

"Angel, I'll understand if you don't want to, but I need—"

She pressed a finger to his lips. "I need you too," she said, kissing him as she lifted up and took him into her.

They both groaned out of pleasure and relief when their bodies joined together, healing their hearts in ways only they could.

~

THE SOUND OF POTS AND PANS BANGING ROUSED JAKE FROM A DEEP, dreamless sleep. He pried his heavy eyes open and looked around, expecting to see his bedroom back at the apartment. Only it wasn't his bedroom he saw. It was Nikki's.

Was he dreaming? Had he not woken up and only dreamed that he had?

A warm, soft body shifted against him.

He looked down and saw a crown of golden hair resting on his chest and a slender arm draped across him. He ran a hand through her hair and along her side just to be sure she was real.

She was.

He closed his eyes, savoring the reality of the moment. He wasn't dreaming. But why? How did he get in Nikki's bed? He wracked his sleep-addled brain. It came back to him then: the Ox; Nikki and Damon showing up; puking on Damon; the shower—collapsing in bed together afterward with Nikki telling him not to worry, that everything would be all right.

But how could she do it? How could she look beyond what his father's connections to hers had done to her family? Did she really love him that much?

"I do. How could you ever question that?" she said, her voice husky from sleep.

His eyes snapped open. He didn't realize he'd said that aloud.

"Because...I'd be a constant reminder of what he did. How could you ever look past that?" he said.

Nikki disentangled herself from him and sat up. She wore one of the shirts he'd kept there. "That's easy: I love you, and you're not your father, Jake. You are not to blame for what happens to people because of him. Would you hold it against me if our roles were reversed?"

"Never. But you...you deserve so much, and I d—"

"Stop," she cut in. "You deserve *everything*. I don't want to hear you say otherwise anymore. Have you been discussing this with your therapist?" she asked, her eyes locked onto his.

He let out a heavy breath. "I have." He reached up and wrapped a long strand of honey-blond hair around his fingers. He'd been working on this issue, and others, with Trey for weeks now. He was making progress, but it was slow—apparently too slow. "It's going to take me a while to fully embrace all of this, but I hear you, and I'm working on it. I promise."

She smiled. "Good. But you should know that the shooting had nothing to do with your father. It was connected to *my* father and his refusal to bow to the Irish mob."

Jake's brows pulled together. "Really?"

"Yes. So *get that crap out of your head*, as Damon would say."

"I...wow...okay," he breathed. "How do you know this, though?"

"Damon told me. He told me everything, actually. About you, what happened with Angela, the Rohypnol...that girl is seriously unstable, by the way. I'm sorry I wouldn't listen to you when you tried to tell me that day at my house. I wasn't...ready to hear it. Not when it felt like it had when it happened with Damon," she explained.

Jake sat up and cupped her cheeks. "Don't apologize, angel. It looked really bad. I don't know if I would have believed it either. Not if I walked in on what you did."

She leaned in and kissed him but pulled away before it could get interesting. "There's something else," she said, pulling her bottom lip between her teeth.

He reached up and tugged it free. "What is it?"

She took a deep breath then reached around him and unearthed a book from her nightstand. It was a brown leather journal that reminded him of his mother's and the one he'd lost a couple of years back. "It's this." She handed him the journal with shaking hands.

He looked down at it, his eyes widening. It *was* his journal. The one he'd started after seeing Nikki at the cemetery—the journal that contained every thought or feeling he had about her up until the day it went missing.

Jake lifted his eyes to hers. "Where did you get this?" he asked amid beats of his racing heart.

"I found it lying in the road at the cemetery not far from my parents' grave during my first visit there after I got back from France."

His cheeks heated. "So then you know...I watched you for six months —obsessing over you then and for years after that."

"I do *now*. I didn't know the journal belonged to you until yesterday when I found out your name wasn't originally Jake Masercotti—that it was actually Giancarlo Di Silva. Before that, I had no idea who it belonged to." She glanced down at it and smiled. "I thought—several times—that you and Mystery Man, as Hilda named the owner of the journal, might be the same person. Your thoughts and experiences were so similar, but the initials didn't match, so I let it go and assumed I'd never meet the man who owned it," she said, her eyes lifting to his.

His breath stalled in his chest. "You wanted to meet him—I mean, me."

"Yes. Very much."

"You weren't creeped out that I was watching you like a stalker—obsessing over someone I'd never met?"

She shook her head. "You saved me. Your presence in that cemetery every Sunday gave me the strength and faith I needed to keep going," she began, her eyes misting over. "I felt so alone after my parents died—like there was no one out there who understood what it was like to have their soul broken. Then you appeared. Somehow I knew that you were feeling the same way, and knowing that, I didn't feel alone anymore. Having you there, knowing you were going through what I was, gave me strength and helped me heal in ways I didn't think possible. Before I knew it, I wasn't going to the cemetery to see two people; I was going there to see three."

Jake's heart pounded in his chest at her words.

"After I got back from France and was well enough to visit Our Lady of Faith again, I hoped I would see you there," she continued. "When I didn't, I was so disappointed. My life was in ruins, and I felt weak in every way imaginable. But then I found the journal. After I read the beautiful words about how strong you thought I was, how amazed you were at how far I'd come since the first time you saw me, my strength returned. I felt like I could pick myself up and move forward—put my life back together as I had once before." She took his hand in hers. "Once again, you'd saved me. I wanted to find you after that, to meet the man who'd saved me not once, but twice, to thank him, to have him in my life somehow, some way. But I had no way to find you with just a set of initials, so I gave up and resigned myself only to having you like this: in the pages of a journal," she said, brushing her fingertips over it.

He sat there for several beats, his mind reeling. All this time, he thought she'd saved him, but the truth was, they'd saved each other.

"I can't believe this," he finally said. "All this time, I was afraid to tell you who I was, to tell you that I'd loved you for years before we met, that you were the reason I was alive today, that you were the inspiration for turning my life around. And now, to hear that you felt the same all this time...I...I don't know what to say." He felt epically lame for not having a profound response.

She leaned forward and cupped his face, her tears breaking free. "That was perfect," she said and kissed him.

He didn't know how it was possible: that two people could be as deeply connected as they were, even before they'd known each other. Maybe it was fate. Maybe it was something divine. He didn't know. But he did know that he'd never take this love, this bond, for granted. And he would never, ever let her go again, no matter what.

Deepening the kiss, he rolled her onto her back, sliding his hands beneath the shirt to get to her silky skin. He groaned when she hooked a leg around him, drawing him closer.

He was pulling off the borrowed shirt she wore when the bedroom door banged open.

"Wakie, wakie, eggs and bakey!" Damon's voice chirped.

Jake yanked the shirt down as Nikki shrieked. "Jesus! Damon! What the hell?"

"Have you ever heard of knocking?" Jake bit out, making sure she was covered before he sat up and pulled her against his chest.

Damon chuckled. "Sure, but why bother? I mean, if you don't want company, try locking the door."

"What is it?" Nikki huffed.

"I need you both downstairs. I spoke with Carlo about the Italy situation. We need to talk about Jack."

Jake's grip on her tightened. "What about him?" he asked, his heart racing for a completely different reason than it had a minute before.

Damon jerked his head toward the stairs as he backed away. "I'll explain downstairs. I made breakfast—figured Sam Crow could use a healthy portion of grease this morning. I've got eggs, bacon, and sausage waiting. Don't be long. I'm starving, and you know how much I can put away, bella."

"We'll be right there," Nikki said to his retreating form.

Jake scowled at the door even as his stomach rumbled. He could use the grease after tying one on last night. "He has shitty timing."

Nikki chuckled. "Sometimes, but he means well. You can't hate him too much. He's the reason we're here now." She brushed a feathery kiss over his lips.

"I know." He admitted, hating that he essentially owed Damon. "Still. The guy needs to learn boundaries, babe. Like for real."

"He does." She scooted off the bed and slid on a pair of sweats. "But let's worry about that later. Right now there's news to go over and bacon to be eaten. I don't want to miss that. Damon cooks some awesome bacon."

"Fine. But we'll continue this later." He grabbed his boxers and T-shirt.

Nikki glanced over her shoulder with the femme fatale smile that drove him crazy. "Damn right we will," she purred and flounced out of the room with a wink.

Jake bit back a groan, wishing they could stay in bed all day—even if there was bacon waiting downstairs. He wanted to wrap himself around her, to lose himself in her and the bliss only they could create together, forgetting everything else. They had so little time together as it was, between their jobs, his therapy, and Dario. And he feared, deep down in a place he didn't like to go, that what little time they did have was running out.

PART III

"There are dark shadows on the earth, but its lights are stronger in the contrast."
—Charles Dickens

"True courage is facing danger when you are afraid."
—L. Frank Baum

30

Damon gripped the railing of the observation deck atop the tower at Circuit of the Americas raceway, his eyes fixed to the track in the last few minutes of the Lone Star Le Mans race. Nikki's team currently held the lead in both their class and overall. She and her teammates, Jose Borja and Anton Dubois, were wiping the track with their competition.

He couldn't believe it.

Damon had never attended one of her races. He'd always avoided them. He loathed situations he couldn't control, especially where Nikki was concerned. The idea of her being out on the track, traveling at ridiculously high speeds, with him unable to do anything to make sure of her safety, drove him to the brink of insanity. But he was there today, standing in the best place to watch the race, because she needed him there. He would deal with the bubbling stomach acid, the pounding heart, and the sweaty palms as he watched her hurl herself around the track if it meant she was safer when she *wasn't* racing.

He had a discreet but heavy security team on her, but neither he nor Jake felt that was enough, not with Jack and Marco as major suspects, and the rest of the players in this drama still unknown. They wanted someone with her at all times—when she wasn't racing, anyway—someone who would stay in the RV with her, in the paddock, and everywhere else that wouldn't set off any alarm bells. That left only Damon or Jake.

Jake typically held the role, but he couldn't get out of town because of a court appearance with his brother about some shady crap between the kid's foster father and foster sister. Damon didn't know the details, and frankly, he didn't care. He was where Nikki needed him, doing what he'd always done: looking out for her.

"You've got it, Nikki! Regulate your speed through turns nineteen and twenty, then flatten that accelerator once you clear the apex," Enzo Santorini squawked through the headset Damon wore so he could listen in on the race.

"Come on, bella. You've got this," he whispered to himself, his eyes locking on her Ferrari prototype as it whipped through the turns around the Grand Plaza.

He didn't follow racing, but he could tell she was heads above many of the drivers out there. Nikki had confidence and aggressiveness that he didn't see in the others—qualities that made her stand out from the pack.

Leaning against the guardrail, he held his breath as she soared out of turn twenty, an Audi prototype right on her tail, and gunned it for the finish. Whoops and hollers rang in his ears as Enzo and her team erupted into a chorus of joy when her car dashed under the checkered flag in first place. They'd done it again. They'd taken first on the podium *and* in overall for the second time this season.

Grinning from ear to ear with a blend of pride and relief, Damon pulled off the headset and made a dash for the elevator then rode the twenty-five flights down to ground level, his hands shaking from the adrenaline rush of watching Nikki and her team win.

He followed the crowd of mechanics and crew members to the podium, where he pushed, shoved, and elbowed his way to the front. He wanted to be right there, front and center, to see her face when she accepted the trophy. Seconds later, she and her team came running up onto the stage and took the center spot as the trophy girls presented them with their wins.

Cameras flashed from all sides, and the crowd roared with excitement, but Damon only had eyes for Nikki, who stood with her teammates, shining brighter than any star in the sky. As he watched her accept her win with a beautiful blend of grace, humility, and pride, it hit him. She was born for this. Racing wasn't a sport or a hobby, as he'd thought of it. It was her life. A wave of guilt crashed over him. In all the years he'd known her, he'd never treated her career choice with any amount of respect—respect she'd clearly deserved. It shamed him to know that he'd done that—that he'd belittled her gift, something she loved. It had been a huge mistake and one he wouldn't make again.

After the post-race interviews and sponsor spots were finished, Damon escorted Nikki across the paddock, still loaded with fans, back to the RV.

"You were incredible out there, bella," he said, draping an arm over her shoulders.

She leaned into him. "Thank you. I'm glad you were here. This was your first time, wasn't it?"

"Yep. You popped my racing cherry today."

"Oh my God! I can't believe you said that." She snorted.

"Are we celebrating tonight?" Jose Borja asked, running up next to them.

Damon tightened his grip on Nikki's shoulders, throwing a glare at Borja through his mirrored aviators. The guy was too much of an eager beaver around her.

"Absolutely!" She looked up at Damon. "You're up for that, right?"

"Anything you want, tesora."

"Great! Let's meet up at the roadhouse after the banquet," Anton Dubois, the team's rookie and third driver, suggested as he came up along-side Borja.

"Sounds like a plan. See you tonight," Nikki said as she stopped to take a photo with a young girl.

After several more photo and autograph stops for kids, they were nearing their RV when a twenty-something man in a Yankees baseball cap approached them.

"Can I get your picture, Miss Elliot?" he asked, his voice oddly accented.

Damon's arm tensed around her shoulders. There was something off about his voice and the way the man looked at Nikki—like he knew her.

Nikki smiled. "Of course!"

"Would you mind?" he asked Damon, holding up his phone.

"Sure, no problem." Damon grabbed the phone as he eyed the guy.

The young man smiled and stood next to Nikki, pulling his hat off for the picture.

"Okay. On three. One, two, three," Damon called, snapping the photo. "Looks good." He glanced down at the screen then handed it to Nikki. "What do you think?"

Nikki took the phone to check out the shot, her smile faltering when she saw the picture.

Before she could respond, the interloper leaned in and looked at the phone. "I think it looks great. Don't you think so, Nikki?" he asked, his accent shifting, revealing its origin.

Damon's hackles shot up.

It was a heavy Italian accent—southern Italy, to be specific. He'd recognize it anywhere. Half of Carlo's associates had the same accent.

"Yeah, it's perfect," she said, her voice shaky.

The young man studied her. "Are you all right? You don't look well," he said, sliding the phone into his pocket.

Damon watched as Nikki waved off his concern, but he knew better. Something was wrong.

"I'm fine," she said. "Just a little tired and dehydrated from the race." She turned to Damon. "I should…get into the RV for some water and…rest."

He took her hand. "Sure. Let's go."

"Thanks for the photo, *stellina*," the young man called after her.

Nikki's footing faltered at the term of endearment.

"What's wrong?" Damon whispered, picking up the pace. When they reached the RV, she dragged herself inside to the granite island and leaned against it.

"Nikki? What's wrong?" he repeated, his heart rate skyrocketing, but she didn't respond. Pressing her fingers to her forehead, she ground out a string of violent curses and collapsed to the ground.

The aroma of freshly baked bread and garlic wafted around Nikki as she and her Ferrari Rally teammates strolled past the Forum, headed for their favorite eatery. They were nearly there when Will Daniels, her navigator, tapped her arm.

"Hey, isn't that Jack?" he asked, pointing across the street.

Nikki turned and spotted Jack, her manager, and her ex, Marco Luccianno, along with several other men she didn't recognize, heading into the Roman Forum. "Yeah, it is," she said, wondering why Jack was with Marco and those other men when he was supposed to be with her. He had a dinner date at La Taverna with them tonight to celebrate their most recent win.

"Why is he going into the Forum?" Will asked. "It's closed right now for excavation and restoration. And isn't he supposed to join us for dinner tonight?"

"He is." She nodded, worry slithering through her veins as she watched two of the men shove the others ahead—like they were forcing them into the ancient ruins. She turned to Will. "You go on ahead. I want to see what Jack's up to."

"Sure. See you inside," he said then turned and headed into the tiny, rustic eatery.

Nikki darted across the street, her sundress streaming behind her. When she reached the Forum, she headed inside. The place was deserted; the restoration crews had all gone home for the day. She couldn't see Jack or the men he was with, but she heard their voices up near the Curia. Her heart rate picked up speed. Their voices sounded angry, and she could have sworn she heard one of the men threaten someone if they didn't move faster.

Afraid that Jack might be in some sort of trouble, she crept on ahead, keeping to the shadows. She didn't want anyone to see her in case there was trouble and she needed to make a break for help.

When she reached the Curia, she saw light flickering from inside. Moving as quietly as possible, she made her way around to the back of the building, hoping to find a window she could see in without being noticed. Instead of a window, one of the smaller rear doors was slightly ajar. Nikki crept up to the door, pulled out her cell phone, and opened up the camera app. If Jack was in trouble, she wanted to record it for the police.

Holding her breath, she knelt down near the door and peered inside, swallowing a gasp when she saw four of the men kneeling on the ground, while two others stood behind them with guns pointed at their heads. Panic filled her for Jack and Marco, but that vanished when she saw them standing off to the side and heard Jack say:

"When this is over, who do we hit next? Your father?"

Marco shook his head. "We'll take out his consigliere first. Then we will take out my father."

"And once that's over?" Jack pressed.

"Once that's finished," Marco said, his face twisting into an expectant grin, "I'll take over with you at my side."

"And the profit sharing? Is it as we arranged?" Jack asked, his eyes alight with greed.

Marco turned to him, blocking her view of Jack. "Of course. You'll get forty percent and all past debts forgiven, as we agreed."

Nikki blinked, unable to believe her ears and eyes. Jack Romano—a man she'd known her entire life—was helping to organize a hit. And what about Marco? She'd dated him for a time. He was in the Mafia and planned to kill his father?

Before she could entertain another thought, a third man appeared with the gunmen. Only he didn't have a gun. He had a large knife—a machete, maybe. Moving silently and with sickening precision, he moved from one man to the next, severing their heads with a single vicious sweep of the blade. Blood poured from the headless bodies, coating the floor and splattering the walls as the butcher continued to slice the bodies into pieces.

Stifling a gasp, Nikki reared back, knocking over a stone pot holding a small margarita bush. The pot shattered when it hit the ground.

"Someone's outside!" Jack shouted.

Nikki caught a glimpse of the butcher spinning around and glaring in her general direction as she scrambled into the shadows, hearing him snarl, "I'll go."

She didn't waste time. She dashed across the Forum and out onto the street. Once across, she headed up Via Baccina then tore down a narrow side street. The soles of Nikki's sandals slapped the ground, the sound of her sandal-clad feet echoing through the dark alley. She had to get out of there and find somewhere safe to hide. If she didn't, that butcher would—

Images of blood-soaked walls and dismembered bodies rushed through her mind—a gruesome reminder of exactly what would happen if he found her.

Nikki reached the end of the alleyway, and her feet lost traction as she rounded the corner. Slipping and sliding, she skidded to a halt behind a pair of dumpsters and crouched low, keeping out of sight. Her heart pounded in her chest, slamming against the cell phone wedged in her bra. She pressed a hand to the spot where the phone sat beneath her sundress, taking several deep breaths in an effort to slow her heart and nerves. Thank God she still had her phone. She'd need it to stay alive.

Heavy boots striking the cobblestone pavement, followed by a man's voice firing off directives, stilled the air in her lungs.

Damn it.

He was here, and he brought his twisted puppets.

She pulled herself into a ball, praying they passed her hiding spot without a second glance. Seconds later, two men went charging by, followed by a third a moment after that. Nikki stayed there, crouching in the shadow of the dumpsters until their footsteps faded into the distance. When she thought it was safe, she crept out from behind the dumpster and turned, letting out a blood-curdling scream.

"Dio mio! Stai bene perdere?!" shouted a middle-aged man in an apron.

Nikki reared back, landing on her derriere. "Oh, thank God!" She gasped, relief flooding her when she saw that it wasn't one of the men from the Forum. "I thought you were someone else."

The man stretched a hand out, switching to English. "Who did you think I was? The devil himself?" he asked, helping her to her feet.

"Something close," she mumbled, looking up and down the alley.

"Do you need help?" he asked.

Nikki shook her head. "No. I'll be fine, thank you," she lied. She wasn't close to fine, but she didn't want to involve this kind man or anyone else. It was too dangerous.

The man gave her a reluctant nod but didn't push it.

Nikki headed down the alley and grabbed a cab. An hour later, she sat in a small café on the outskirts of Rome, forcing a cappuccino and some biscotti down her throat. She needed something in her stomach to settle it so she could focus on coming up with a plan to keep her alive. It wasn't working. She couldn't focus. The image of Jack plotting to murder not only those four men but also others haunted her. She'd known Jack her entire life, and she'd never, in that time, pegged him as a ruthless killer.

And then there was the butcher. Did he see her in the doorway, or did she move fast enough? If he did see her, would he know who she was? Would Marco or Jack figure it out? She didn't know. He and his men had chased after her, but she'd had a good lead. There was a chance—though slim—that he hadn't seen her clearly enough to identify her.

Slumping back in her chair, she glanced out the window of the café and spotted an electronics store that advertised its late-night hours. The window display held laptops, cell phones, and other electronic equipment. As she stared at the equipment, an idea came to mind—one that might keep her alive long enough to make it home and get help from the one person she knew she could turn to: Damon. She hated the idea of dragging him or anyone else she knew and loved into this, but he was her only hope. If his father really was connected to the Mafia like the rumors suggested, he might be able to help her. It was her only chance. But first, she needed to get back to the States alive, and that was going to require a good plan, a serious amount of luck, and some kickass method acting to pull off.

~

THE SOUND OF DAMON'S VOICE CALLING HER NAME PULLED NIKKI OUT OF THE flashback and into the present.

"There you are. Jesus Christ. You scared the holy hell out of me! What happened? Why did you faint like that?" Damon demanded.

"I'm sorry. It was a flashback." She sat up and looked around. They were on the couch in the living space of the RV. "They always start with a headache, but I've never blacked out like that before. How long was I down?"

Damon ran a hand through his inky hair. "I don't know. It felt like forever, but it was probably two minutes or so. You were breathing, and your heart rate remained steady the entire time," he said, checking her pulse once more. "What did you remember this time?"

"Everything."

His crystalline eyes went wide. "Shit. Really?"

She nodded. "You and Carlo were right: Jack is at the center of it, right next to Marco Luccianno," she said, recalling everything from the time she followed Jack into the Forum, all the way up to the Le Mans wreck.

"Tell me everything, bella. Don't leave out a single detail," he ordered, lacing his fingers with hers.

Nikki did as requested, starting at the very beginning when she saw Jack and the other men go into the Forum. Damon sat listening intently, not interrupting her a single time. It was very un-Damon-like behavior, which spoke to the seriousness of the situation.

"And you've got the whole murder at the Forum on a USB stashed in a security deposit box in Modena?" he asked when she finished.

"Yes. It's at a branch of Unicredit Private Banking under my grandmother's maiden name with strict instructions that in the event of my death, it be delivered to Gianni Luccianno personally. Marco has to know this. Jack would have told him after the accident at Le Mans," she explained.

After she'd devised her plan at the café in Rome, she'd hopped a train, downloaded the file onto a laptop she'd purchased at the late-night electronics store, and transferred the file to the USB drive. Once she arrived in Modena, she contacted a friend there who helped her acquire a fake ID with her grandmother's maiden name on it and rented a security deposit box at a local bank under said name. She returned to Rome a few days later with a cover story that she'd gotten a call from a friend in need and went up there to help. No one questioned the story, not even Jack; he acted like nothing had happened. She thought she was off the hook.

Until she got to France.

While in France, she caught sight of the butcher and the gunmen from the Forum. She spotted them lurking around the paddock after she finished up the morning practice session the day of the race, wearing mechanic's coveralls; that was why she'd been so freaked out in the trailer. Worried they might tamper with the car, she confronted Jack in the paddock just before the race that day. She laid it all out there for him, hoping it would scare them off before they made a move and buy her some time until she could talk to Damon and his father.

Damon nodded. "I'm sure Jack told Marco. Your plan was a smart move. It's what's kept you alive—that and your memory loss. As long as you're breathing and your memories stay lost, that drive remains where it is," he said, rising from the couch and pacing the room.

"That must be why Jack didn't want me racing and did everything he could to sabotage my career. Racing is a risky business, and being at the track could have jogged my memory," she mused.

"Definitely," Damon agreed. "But I don't know how much longer your plan is going to work. Not if the fan you took a picture with today was the butcher from Rome. Marco and Jack must suspect that your memory is back if they sent him after you."

"But why come after me? If I die, Luccianno finds out about their plot to kill him, ruining any chance they have of getting away with it."

Damon ran a hand along his jaw. "That's true... Unless they've found a way to get to Luccianno without getting caught. According to Carlo, Luccianno's been growing more and more lax in his security, which makes this a good time for them to take him out."

"Then why bother with me? If Luccianno dies, my information means nothing to them."

"Not true," Damon corrected. "Marco won't want the notoriety for the hit. It would be viewed as betrayal by the other families and ruin him. He'll need to play the role of the grieving son and take care of any loose ends that could prove otherwise if he wants a chance in hell at filling his father's shoes."

Nikki nodded. "And that would be me." When Damon didn't respond, she continued. "Do you think I played it off well enough out there today with the butcher?"

Damon stopped pacing, his icy-blue eyes meeting hers. "I think so, but you never know with guys like that. They have a sick sense for reading people. He could be on to you, for all we know."

"Should we tell Carlo and have him alert Gianni Luccianno, then?"

"No." He went to the fridge and grabbed two bottles of water. "We can't do that. The Falco and Berardi families aren't on good terms. If Carlo or anyone associated with him approached Luccianno with accusations that his son was plotting to kill him, even with evidence of Marco's guilt, it would start a war. Luccianno has a serious hate-on for Carlo and anyone connected to him." He opened one of the bottles and handed it to her. "What we need to do is figure out a way to get the file on the USB to Luccianno *without* him knowing where it came from. Once he has the file, he'll take out Marco and his crew himself and solve the problem for us without ever knowing we were involved. But we can't do any of that until you can get the file. When do you go to Europe?"

Nikki took a long pull from her water bottle. "I leave June fifth, right after the Sports Car Classic in Detroit. Why?"

He grabbed his phone from his pocket. "Because that's when we're going to get the USB drive."

She leaned forward. "They won't suspect anything if I'm supposed to be across the pond for a race. But I'm sure they'll be following me while I'm there. If they see me go into a bank in Modena, they're going to know that's where I've got the drive stashed."

"Leave that to me, sweetheart," Damon said, punching a number into his phone.

She nodded, gripping her water with white knuckles, praying he could help her figure out a way out of this without anyone getting hurt.

Don't count on it, the insidious voice she wanted to bitch-slap into next week whispered. The problem was: the damn voice was right. The odds of any of them getting out of this unscathed were stacked against them too high to even measure.

"ARE YOU SURE YOU DON'T WANT ME TO DRIVE? YOUR HAND IS PRETTY BANGED up," Nikki said, frowning at the bruised and swollen knuckles along Damon's right hand.

He rolled his eyes. "It's fine, bella, really," he said, wincing as he threw the last suitcase into the back of the Benz that Nino had left for them in short-term parking. He and their usual tail had taken off after that. Damon didn't elaborate as to why, only that she needn't worry. As long as he was there, they'd be safe.

Nikki huffed out a breath. "Okay. I was just trying to help." She headed over to the passenger side and jumped in. If he wanted to be a stubborn ass and suffer driving with what looked like broken knuckles, fine.

Damon slid into the driver's seat a moment later, shaking the rain from his hair as he fired the engine. "And don't worry. It's not broken—just badly bruised and scraped," he reassured her.

"I hope not—though it would serve you right for clocking Dixon in the paddock," she scolded.

Ron Dixon had been in rare form at the race in Colorado yesterday. He'd been even more hell-bent on wiping Nikki off the track than usual. When that didn't work, he came after her in the paddock. Damon, of course, jumped in before she could make a move and coldcocked him. Fortunately, witnesses heard Ron threatening her before Damon hit him, so Damon escaped any assault charges, and she was still able to race in the series. Ron was also still in the series, but now he'd be racing under watchful eyes. If he pulled anything again, he would be banned from VAM.

"The fucker's had it coming for years. My only regret is he's still breathing," Damon grumbled, flicking on the windshield wipers as the rain increased. The Bay Area was getting one of its infamous late-spring rains.

"He's a dick. I get it. But he's not worth going to jail over," she pointed out.

"I wouldn't be going for him. I'd be going for—" He stopped short, his eyes narrowing on the rearview mirror.

"What?" She looked in the side mirror, spotting the familiar Mercedes sedan as they merged onto the highway that ran along the base of the mountain range where the Glenns were nestled. She quickly realized why Damon looked worried. The sedan, which usually lingered a few car lengths back, was right behind them, and it wasn't alone. An identical Mercedes was on its right.

She swore.

"Yeah, this isn't good," Damon agreed, increasing his speed. "It looks like your tail is back and wants to get aggressive."

"Oh, great."

Nikki watched as the sedan behind them accelerated, getting right up on the rear of Damon's car, while the other Mercedes moved up alongside them. She slid a glance out her window and saw the driver's-side window open and gasped.

"Oh God. It's the butcher."

"What's he doing?" Damon asked, his eyes darting between the road and the rearview mirror.

Nikki feigned reaching down for her purse while she slid another glance at the driver. He was looking over at her again, but this time he was holding a gun.

Her heart rate jumped to MACH speed. "Jesus. He's got a gun!" she hissed.

"Fuck!" Damon smashed the accelerator, cut across four lanes of traffic, and took the exit for Highway 35, the two-lane stretch of road that wound through the mountains.

"*Where are you going?*" she shrieked.

"I'm getting us off the main road. I don't want anyone else caught up in this or any witnesses if things get hairy," he said, maneuvering up the winding mountain highway toward the summit.

Nikki braced a hand on the dash. "Okay, but take it easy. This box on wheels wasn't meant for hauling ass along a mountain road, much less one that's rain-slicked," she ground out over the sounds of tires squealing as he skated along the turns at dangerous speeds.

"*Box on wheels?* Did you just diss my car? This fine example of automotive craftsmanship? Do you have any idea what this baby set me back?"

She rolled her eyes. "For God's sake, I wasn't *dissing* your precious one-hundred-forty-thousand-dollar car—just pointing out the obvious." she said, grabbing the oh-shit bar as he leaned into a hard left.

"I'll have you know—"

Gunshots sounded behind them.

"Fuck. This shit's getting real. Get down!" he shouted, shoving down her head.

Nikki shrieked as more shots rolled off, the sound of gunfire echoing in her ears as it had the night her parents were killed. For a moment, she was transported back to that awful night. Lying on the sidewalk, her parents shielding her as men fired on them from the street, the scent of gunpowder and blood hanging in the air as she trembled beneath their bodies, unable to stop the horror. She'd felt so powerless, so useless that night.

The side mirror next to her shattered when a bullet struck it, yanking her back to the present. She might have been powerless back then, but she wasn't now. She was no longer a frightened, naïve teenager. She could do something to stop this. No one was dying for her today—or ever again.

Taking a deep breath, she shoved off Damon's hand and sat up. "Where's your piece?" she snapped, ripping open the glove box.

Damon swore, flicking a glance from the rain-slicked road to her. "Under the seat. Why? I thought I told you to stay down!"

Nikki shrieked as the back window shattered, covering the back seat with glass and rainwater.

"Jesus, bella! Forget the goddamn gun. Keep your head down!" he roared, swerving the car from side to side.

"Screw that! I'm going to get these guys off our asses before they take out a tire and send us off-roading," she yelled. She reached under the seat and felt around until her fingers brushed the cool metal barrel of the gun lodged in the seat's frame.

"The hell you are! I didn't give you up all those years ago to lose you like this!" he bellowed, panic ringing in his voice now.

"What the hell is that supposed to mean?" she said, yanking the gun free and sitting up, cocking the .45.

"Forget it. Just do what you're told for once!" Damon shouted, reaching for her as she pulled off her seat belt and jumped into the back seat.

"*No!*" She dodged his hand. "I never have before, and I don't plan on starting now."

Kneeling on the back seat, she raised the gun in steady hands and fired at the Mercedes through the missing rear window, intending to scare the goons and get them to fall back. But instead of ricocheting off the hood, as she assumed the bullets would, they pierced it with shocking ease. Steam erupted from the radiator, and the car went skidding off the road and into the woods bordering the highway.

"Holy shit! Are these armor-piercing rounds?" she cried, gaping at the gun.

"Of course they are. I don't shoot to wound," Damon spat.

Before she could respond, the second sedan came up behind them, opening fire.

Nikki dove between the front and back seats to take cover as the first bullets flew, pinning herself there. Two of Damon's tires blew out, punctured by the bullets, sending them off road and speeding down the side of the mountain.

The Benz came to a jarring stop when it struck something solid, deploying the front airbags with a deafening *boom*. After several seconds, Nikki lifted her spinning head and grabbed the gun.

"Damon?" She coughed, choking on the cornstarch and talcum powder hanging in the air like a fog. "Are you okay? Please tell me you're okay."

"Yeah. Fine. Just some bumps and bruises. You?" he choked out, smacking the airbag away and turning to look at her.

Relief flooded her as she pried herself from the rear footwell and climbed onto the back seat with her good arm. "I'll live. But one of them winged me." She grimaced, clutching at her left arm.

"*You were hit?*" he roared, forcing himself out of the driver door and into the back seat with her.

"It's only a graze," she ground out, knowing that was an understatement. The bullet had definitely pierced her skin.

Damon took her arm in his hands with gentleness that was so at odds with his expression and voice. "I told you to stay down! Why don't you ever do what you're told?" he raged, looking at the wound. "That's no graze, but it looks like it's just a flesh wound. Can you move your arm?"

Nikki lifted and rotated it.

"Good." He pulled off his button-down shirt, then tore it and tied two strips around the injury. "This should stop the bleeding until we get you to a doctor." He glanced out the open door. "We need to get out of here."

"And go where? We're stuck on the side of the mountain," she said, stumbling out of the car behind him.

"I don't know. But those assholes will be here soon, and we shouldn't be when they get here."

Her eyes roved over their surroundings. If they went back up, they would hit the highway where the hunters were. If they went downhill, eventually they'd hit a stretch of road, maybe, depending on where they were, but the hike would be difficult and slow along the steep, densely wooded mountainside. Not to mention the rain making everything slick and even more difficult to navigate.

Damon went around to the back of the car and opened the rear door, unearthing two more handguns and a semiautomatic rifle from the spare tire compartment and several mags of ammo. He handed her one of the spare handguns and a second magazine then jammed the other handgun and the extra mags into the back of his jeans and shouldered the rifle.

"Good God. What are you? A one-man militia?"

"One can never be too prepared in my line of work," he replied.

She shot him a bland look. "Is that why you have armor-piercing rounds too?"

Damon smirked and started to respond but stopped when they heard footsteps and several accented voices approaching on both sides.

"How many of them are there?" she whispered as Damon dragged her around to the front of the car.

"I don't know. Seven, I think." He loaded the magazine into the rifle and turned his worried blue eyes to her. "Doesn't matter, really. This is going to get messy one way or the other. Do you understand?"

She let out a heavy breath, knowing exactly what he meant. She was going to have to help defend them however she could, even if that meant killing someone. She didn't relish the idea of killing anyone, but she'd sworn never to be a victim again—or to let anyone she loved be one either —and she meant it.

"I understand," she whispered, her voice shaking with a blend of fear and adrenaline.

His gaze softened. "Keep your head down, and as soon as it looks clear, I want you to make a run for it. You got it?"

"You mean *we* make a run for it when it's clear. I'm not leaving here without you," she corrected.

He started to argue but stopped when someone yelled, "Don't kill the girl. He wants her alive!" and opened fire.

They both dropped to a crouch. Damon motioned that he was moving to the other side of the car and for her to stay there. Nikki nodded and fired off several rounds to cover him.

There were six attackers, all of which Damon and Nikki managed to take down without getting hit themselves. It was nothing short of a miracle.

Afterward, Nikki sat in the back of the Mercedes, which now looked like it belonged on the set of an action flick, listening as Damon barked orders into his phone.

"Send the cleaner and a car to the coordinates I texted you. There are three vehicles and six bodies. Then call Max and send him to Nikki's place; we'll meet him there. She's got a flesh wound and lost some blood. Tell him to bring a pint of A positive in case she needs it. Got it? Good," he demanded, ending the call in typical Damon fashion.

"You with me, bella?" he asked, standing in front of her.

She lifted her eyes to his, feeling the adrenaline rush start to fade, and in its place, a hollow feeling settling in. "Yeah...I think so." She glanced around the woods, spotting the lifeless bodies of the men they'd killed. Bile rose in her throat. She'd known violence before but never at her own hands. Nikki wanted to scrub the memory of this day from her brain, but she knew she never would.

He peered down at her. "You don't look so good, tesora."

"Yeah, well. It's my first time killing another human being. It might take me a minute—or a lifetime—to adjust," she said, her body trembling.

"Shit. I'm sorry," he said, wrapping her in a warm embrace.

She soaked up his warmth, choosing to overlook how he could be so calm after killing people.

"Are you sure we—that they are all gone?" she asked, releasing him.

He dropped his arms, his brows drawn together. "Yeah, we got all six."

"I thought there were sev—" She stopped short when she spotted a figure emerging from the hillside with a gun pointed straight at Damon's back. "Look out!" she shrilled, shoving him to the ground as she leapt off the back of the car and fired four rounds into the attacker's chest.

Something inside her snapped.

As soon as his body crumpled to the ground, she took off into the woods, gun raised and ready. She had to make sure they were all gone, make sure she and Damon were safe. She wouldn't let what happened to her parents happen to him too.

"Bella! Stop!" she heard him yell, but she ignored him.

Nikki dashed up the hillside, slowing when the woods grew dense, forcing her to scramble over fallen logs and other forest debris. Damon was close behind and gaining ground. She could hear him cursing up a storm, threatening to lock her away once he caught her if she didn't stop.

His threats fell on deaf ears. She wouldn't stop until she knew for certain all the bad men were dead.

Her foot got caught in a hole concealed by the underbrush when she leapt over a large, mossy log, sending her crashing to the forest floor. She turned, her breath sawing in and out of her chest as she tried to free herself. What if there was another shooter nearby? What if he got to Damon before she located him? She had to get free—had to keep them safe.

Damon reached her a second later, breathless and mad as a devil in church on Sunday. "What the fuck is wrong with you? Shoving me to the ground and taking off like that? Are you crazy?" he roared, setting the rifle down and freeing her from one of Mother Nature's booby-traps.

"Nothing is wrong with me. I'm fine," she insisted, pulling herself up once her foot was free, only to be pulled back down by Damon.

"Okay. Then where the hell did you think you were going?" he demanded, gripping her shoulders. When her only response was to ignore him and continuously scan the woods for more goons, he gave her a little shake. "Bella! Look at me!"

Something in his voice made her stop and turn to him. When their gazes collided, she glimpsed something she rarely saw in Damon: fear. But it wasn't fear of more gunmen. It was fear for her and her behavior. Seeing that shook something loose inside her, and she stopped—stopped searching the woods, stopped fearing for their lives, just stopped.

"There you are," he breathed. "Where did you go?"

She blinked at him.

Damon pulled her into his arms as the sobs broke free. "Oh, bella. I get it. It's okay. It's okay, *mia cara*," he soothed, crushing her to him.

He held her there while she wept, rocking her gently as the rain continued to fall, soaking them. After what felt like hours, the tears finally stopped. "I'm sorry." She sniffed. "I shouldn't have run off like that. I just—"

"You wanted to keep me safe. I understand," he cut in.

"You do?"

He nodded. "But you have to understand that goes both ways. I want to protect you too."

"I know, Damon, but you can't. Not this time. I don't want you to."

Damon's eyes flared. "So, what? I'm just supposed to stand by and let you get killed? Is that what you're saying?" He jumped to his feet.

She glared up at him from where she still knelt on the ground, her own anger surging. "It's better me than you!" she yelled. "I don't want anyone dying for me. Not again."

"For Christ's sake, I know that! I get it," he ground out, brushing his soaked hair off his forehead. "But that doesn't mean I'm going to stop trying to keep you safe. I won't break that promise."

Promise?

Nikki jumped to her feet. "What promise? What are you talking about? Who did you promise to protect me?" she asked, moving toward him.

Damon swore under his breath. "Nothing. No one," he said, running a hand along his jaw, refusing to look at her.

"Liar!" she accused, seeing it in his body language and hearing it in his voice.

Damon held up his hand to silence her.

"Don't you dare shush—"

"Christ! Just wait!" he cut in, his gun drawn as he listened. After a beat, he called out, "Over here, Nino!"

"Who's Nino?" she asked, moving next to him, dropping her questioning—for the moment.

"He's our ride out of here," he said. "Come on." He started to lead her away. "Let's get you home and patched up."

She dug her heels in. "Wait."

He turned, his expression guarded once more. "What? We need to get you out of here. You're still bleeding." He motioned to her arm.

"Fine. But we will finish this conversation, Damon. I mean it."

The muscles along his jaw flexed. "Fine. Whatever. Let's go," he said then turned and led her back to the car, where several young men waited.

Nikki remained quiet on the ride home, her mind reeling from the attack and her unfinished business with Damon. He was hiding something, something she feared might be connected to her father—the only person in her life who would ever ask Damon to promise them anything for her sake.

31

Jake pulled his phone out of his pocket and frowned. Nikki should have called by now; her flight got in over two hours ago. Where the hell was she?

"Looking at the phone every two minutes isn't going to make her call any sooner, son," Sean chided.

"I know." He sighed, dropping the phone onto the coffee table and loosening his tie.

They'd finished up lunch at Sean's after being in court all morning for Bruce Reynolds's preliminary hearing. The hearing took the better part of the day and kept Jake from attending the Lone Star Le Mans or the VAM race with Nikki, but it was worth it. The transcripts from Dario and Monica, Jake and Nikki, *and* Dario's school regarding his injuries over the last several months were enough evidence for the courts to move forward with a trial. If they were lucky, Bruce would be headed for prison before fall.

"If you know, why do you keep checking it? Are you worried about something?" Dario asked, dropping on the couch next to him.

Part of Jake wished he could answer that question honestly, but he couldn't. He couldn't involve anyone in what was happening with Nikki off the racetrack.

He looked over at his brother and smiled. "Nah. I miss her. It's been two weeks since she left," he said, only lying a little. He did miss her like crazy when they weren't together, which thankfully wasn't very often these days. He didn't know how he'd handle it when she traveled on her own again. Or when she made it onto a Formula 1 team and would be gone even longer and possibly have to relocate altogether.

"OMG, you are so sweet, Jake," Monica gushed.

Dario pulled her into his side, grinning broadly. "Sweeter than me?" he asked and placed a loud kiss on her cheek.

She giggled. "No one is as sweet as you, *mi amor*."

Jake's chest swelled at the sight of his brother: so happy and at ease. He hadn't seen Dario like this since their mom was alive. But that was all going to change now. Now that he and Monica were with Sean, things would get better. Dario would be happy, and Jake would be able to see him whenever he wanted, scheduled or unscheduled. For the first time since their mother's death, they felt like a family again.

"All right, that's enough, you two," Sean groused at Dario and Monica, who were making goo-goo eyes at each other. He turned to Jake. "Remind me. Where's Nikki headed once she gets back?"

"She's off to Detroit in a couple of weeks and then Europe after that."

"Are you going with her for those trips?" Monica asked.

Jake started to answer when Andrea Bocelli's "Vivo Per Lei" belted out of his phone.

"Dude!" Dario laughed. "Tell me that is *not* her ringtone!"

He frowned at Dario as he swiped the phone off the table and shot to his feet. "It is, and that's our song, so watch it, *fratellino*." He darted from the room.

"Angel! Where have you been? You should have called over an hour ago," he said, stepping into the hallway.

"Aww, I missed you, too, sunshine," Damon's voice crooned.

What the fuck?

Jake's back went ramrod straight. "Why the hell are you calling me on Nikki's phone?" he ground out, his heart pounding as dark possibilities danced through his head. "Did something happen? Is she all right?"

"Relax. She's fine." Damon sighed. "She's with Max right now. We had a little accident."

"*Accident? Max?* You mean that creepy medic? What happened? You know what, never mind. Where are you?"

"We're at home. Get here, now," he demanded and ended the call.

Jake jammed the phone into his pocket. What did Damon mean by *a little accident*? Was it more than that, or was Damon being a dick? His racing heart sank. Of course it was *more*. Marco and Jack's guys were closing in on her, had been since the Lone Star race where one of them approached her.

Shit.

He dragged a shaking hand through his hair, knowing he couldn't go back in there and face Sean and Dario like this. He needed to pull himself together. He took a deep cleansing breath, imagined a serene setting, and counted slowly backward from ten. It was one of the exercises Trey taught him to use during times when things were overwhelming or he felt out of control.

When he felt calm again, Jake went back into the living room. He had to keep it together to avoid worrying the others and having to lie to them —something he hated doing but was quickly becoming second nature.

Sean looked up when he came in and lurched to his feet. "What's wrong? You're as white as a sheet!"

So much for not having to lie.

"Nothing," he said, waving off Sean's concern. "Damon had a little fender-bender on the way home from the airport. That's all. They're both fine, but I want to head up there. I don't have my bike, what with the rain and taking your car to the courthouse today. Can I borrow the Bronco?"

Sean puffed out a heavy breath. "Whew. You had me worried for a minute there." He ran a hand through his hair, glancing at Dario and Monica. "Take my Tiger instead. I have a feeling you won't be back today, and I need the Bronco to haul these two yahoos to school tomorrow."

Jake grinned, relieved. "Thanks, Sean." He hugged Dario and Monica goodbye. "You two be good. I'll see you tomorrow night for pizza."

"Sure thing, bro. Say hi to Nikki for us, and tell her congrats on the win in Texas," Dario said.

With a nod, Jake turned and headed out to the garage and fired up the Tiger. He backed down the sloped driveway then gunned the modified V8 and tore out of the neighborhood. He had a bad feeling about what happened, and he wouldn't be able to shake it until Nikki was in his arms.

JAKE ROARED THROUGH THE NEW, HEAVY-DUTY SECURITY GATE AND INTO Nikki's driveway thirty minutes later and deposited the Tiger right behind her Modena, next to a Subaru WRX he didn't recognize.

He let himself into the house using his key. "Nikki! Where are you?" he called when he didn't see her in the kitchen or the entryway.

"We're back here, prospect!" Damon called from the living room.

Prospect.

God, what a dick.

Jake strode down the hall and into the living room. Nikki sat on the large sofa near the fireplace, which Jake noted had a roaring fire going in it, with that Max guy. He was wrapping a gauze bandage around her left bicep. Damon sat across from them on the love seat, watching Nikki with rapt attention. Both of them were filthy and soaked—like they'd been running through the woods.

"Angel!" he breathed, striding into the room. "What the hell happened?"

Nikki turned and lifted her gaze to Jake's when he sat next to her and took her hand. She looked wiped, with deep shadows beneath her eyes and pallid skin that bore a green cast to it.

"Hey, Jake," she said, forcing a smile.

He smiled at her and kissed her hand. "Baby, what kind of accident were you in? Are you okay?" he asked her, cupping the back of her head.

Max finished up with the bandage and stood, fielding the question. "The accident was of the gunshot variety, Mr. Masercotti."

Jake shot up out of his seat. "You were shot?" he yelled, spinning around to Damon. "What the fuck, Corleone! I thought you were going to keep her safe!"

Damon lurched to his feet and got up in Jake's face. "Watch who you're talking to, prospect."

Jake's temper snapped. He grabbed Damon by the collar with both fists. "You know what? I've had enough of your shit. Say goodbye to your face, pretty boy."

"Go ahead and try it. See how far you get," Damon threatened, pushing Jake back.

"Stop it!" Nikki shouted, jumping between them. "It's not his fault, Jake. We can't control what these guys are going to do and when they're going to do it. We thought we were safe leaving the airport without backup. We were wrong."

He knew she was right, but that didn't suppress the urge he had to rearrange Damon's face. Fuming, he sat back down and pulled Nikki into his lap. "You're right. I...overreacted."

"Now that that's settled," Max said, handing her a glass of water and a prescription vial. "Take one of these twice a day for the next ten days and get some rest, Annie Oakley. You've got a flesh wound, and while it's not bad, you need to rest so it heals quickly." He turned to Damon. "I'll be back in a couple of days to check on the wound."

Jake stroked his fingers along the length of her spine as Damon walked Max out. "He's right. You need to get some rest." He frowned at the bandage wrapped around her bicep. "Does it hurt much?"

She shook her head. "It's not too bad," she replied, leaning on his shoulder, shuddering.

He tucked her into his chest. "Tell me what happened," he said, needing to hear it.

"It was awful. Looking back, I don't know how we survived. I really don't," she said, going into detail about the car chase, the gunfire, and how it brought back memories of the night her parents were killed, the shootout, and how deathly afraid she'd been.

"I'm so scared," she whispered. "Today was…it was awful, and I'm afraid it's only going to get worse before it has the chance to get better."

"You're right about things getting worse," Damon said, coming back into the living room and dropping onto the couch, looking haggard. It was a look Jake had never seen on him before. Generally, he was all confidence and swagger, but not now. "Now that we've taken out part of Marco's crew, he'll get more aggressive."

"Where there any witnesses?" Jake asked, praying there weren't. The last thing they needed was Nikki facing charges.

"No. We were up on a deserted stretch of 35 when things went sideways. I had a crew come out and clean the site. There'll be no trace of the shootout, us, or the accident when they're through, which"—he glanced down at his watch—"should be about now. Your dad only employs the best."

Of course he did.

"What's next? Do we make a move before they do?" Nikki asked.

Damon arched a brow. "*We*? What? No insisting you do this on your own? No *it's too dangerous for you and Jake* bullshit?"

Jake looked at Nikki. "What's he talking about?"

He watched her throw a glare at Damon before lifting her face to his. "We had an argument in the woods after the shooting. I didn't like the idea of you guys being involved in this, and I wanted you out—to keep you safe," she said, her eyes shifting to Damon's. "But I was wrong. I can't expect you two to stand down when it's not what I would do if our roles were reversed. It's selfish of me to think that I'm the only one who gets to risk themselves for the people she loves—no matter how much I hate the idea of you both being in danger."

He pressed a kiss to the top of her head. "I know it's hard, angel. It's hard for all of us." He looked at Damon. "What do we do now?"

"We lie low and stick to the original plan of going after the USB drive once Nikki's in Europe. I'll increase the security detail to round the clock."

Jake arched a brow. "What plan?"

Damon grinned. "This one," he said, leaning forward and outlining what sounded like a solid move—if everything fell into place and went accordingly, that was.

They spent the next few hours going over Damon's idea, working out the logistics and kinks where necessary. Afterward, Damon went upstairs to make phone calls to his contacts in Italy and to Carlo while Jake and Nikki ordered pizza.

The three of them were finishing up dinner when Jake's phone rang. Thinking it was Dario or Sean, he dropped his slice of combo and pulled out his phone. It wasn't either of them. The number on the screen read Unknown.

Frowning, Jake answered the call. "Masercotti."

"Hello, son."

Jake gripped the phone tighter. "Dad? How did you get this number?" he asked, glancing over at Nikki, who'd stopped bagging the leftover pizza and looked at him, her eyes wide.

"A man in my position has ways of getting ahold of people when necessary."

Duh. Crime lord. Connections.

He shook his head. "Right. Sorry. What's up?"

"Are you alone? It's about your mother, and I'd rather this stay between us for now."

"Oh, uh, no. Hold on a sec," he said, standing and motioning to Nikki he was going to take the call upstairs.

She waved him off, and he darted up to her room then closed the door behind him. "Okay. I'm alone. What's going on?"

"I've been doing some digging, and I may have a lead on the nameless man," Carlo replied.

Jake's heart kicked up. "Really? How did you get the lead?"

"I started thinking about what your mother said in the journal, about how the nameless man was one of my associates, and how impossible that would be. I never brought any of my guys or anything work-related home. Not once. She never had the opportunity to meet anyone associated with my business. And then I remembered the night your mother and I were out celebrating our anniversary. We went to Da Vinci's over on Columbus. Do you remember it?" he asked, his voice almost wistful.

"Yeah. I loved that place." Jake smiled at the memory of it and how much he and his mother both loved it. They made the best gnocchi in North Beach.

"It was good—almost as good as eating back in Palermo," Carlo began. "Anyway, while we were there, Salvatore Falco—son of Carmelo Falco, leader of the Falco family at the time—approached me with one of his father's soldiers in tow. He was in town to broker a deal between our families. I was shocked that he approached me in public. I worked hard to keep the business away from you boys and your mother, and most associates knew and respected that. But I didn't get angry about his mistake. He was still wet behind the ears. I got Falco out of there as quickly as I could, though, and arranged to meet at a later time. The thing is, he and his man were there long enough for your mother to get a good look at them and to know they were *associates* of mine—the only associates she ever came into contact with before I was incarcerated."

Jake's blood heated. "So, the nameless man is Salvatore Falco?" he asked, clenching and unclenching his fists.

"No, it's not. Salvatore was killed a few months after that in an unrelated hit back in Palermo."

"Then it's the other guy?"

"It has to be," Carlo agreed, his tone darkening. "The trouble is: I never got his name. He was Salvatore's protection when they approached us that night—meant to be there but not heard. I can't even remember what he looks like."

Jake bit back a curse. His father had a lead, but it was as weak as they came. "Okay. So how do we find him?"

"Did your mother ever describe the man in her journal? Is there anything in there—a reference to a scar, a tattoo, something distinguishing about his appearance?"

"I don't know. I haven't read much of it. It...it was too hard to read it, to hear about how much she suffered," Jake said, gripping the phone tighter.

Carlo went quiet for a moment. "I understand, son, but I need you to take a look at it. I need you to read it and see if there's anything in there we can use to track this guy down."

Jake's stomach soured. He hated the idea of reading about his mother's final, torturous months. But like it or not, he had to do it...for her. "Okay. I'll take a look tomorrow. The journal's at home, and I'm at Nikki's place tonight."

"Good man. I'll text you a safe number to call me at if you find anything," Carlo said. "How is Nikki? Damon told me about what happened to them today."

"She suffered a flesh wound, but other than that, she seems okay. She's tough—the toughest person I know," he said, glancing out the bedroom window when he heard her calling Damon's name outside. She and Damon were out front, talking.

"I'm glad to hear she's well. She reminds me a lot of your mother, actually. She was *tough* like that too. I fell in love with her for it. Strength is a beautiful and alluring thing in a woman."

Jake smiled at the thought of Nikki and his mother being so similar and how much his mother would have liked her because of that. It looked like he and his father had more in common than he realized.

"It is. I hope she stays strong through all of this. Today was bad, and it's going to get worse, isn't it?" he said, frowning as he watched the conversation between Nikki and Damon unfold on the front lawn. Judging by the looks on both their faces, he thought it was a painful one—like they were peeling open old wounds.

Carlo sighed. "I'm afraid it might, but I'll do what I can to help. I've got people watching Marco and Jack. If they make a move, I'll let Damon know. In the meantime, keep your head down and stay safe."

Jake leaned a hand against the window when he saw Nikki throw her arms around Damon. "I will, Dad. Don't worry," he said, his gut twisting for an entirely different reason now.

"It's my job to worry, son. I'm your father. It's what we do."

Jake slid his phone back into his pocket, his narrowed gaze on Nikki and Damon as she wiped tears from his eyes. He stepped back from the window to give them some privacy. The conversation had nothing to do with the situation at hand. It looked too personal for that. So what could they be talking about that would move Captain Douche to tears?

NIKKI WATCHED THE BACK OF JAKE'S HEAD AS HE RETREATED UPSTAIRS TO HER bedroom, wondering why he needed privacy to talk with his father. Did it have something to do with her mess? Was it his mother?

She shook off her curiosities when Damon stood up. "I've gotta jet. I'll see you tomorrow," he said, bolting for the door.

"Okay." She turned to put the rest of the pizza in the refrigerator but stopped when she remembered the unfinished conversation in the woods. She dropped the pizza and went after him.

"Damon! Wait!" she called, dashing out the front door and down the steps. She had to know if her father had made Damon promise to protect her and what that could have entailed. It was minor, all things considered, but Nikki couldn't let it go. She had to know the truth.

He stopped midway across the lawn and turned, folding his arms across his chest. "What is it, bella? I've got to head to the gym and take care of some paperwork."

She jogged over to him, knowing that was BS. Damon never did paperwork; he hated it. He hired people to do it for him instead.

"That's the second lie you've told me today," she said, stopping in front of him.

He rolled his eyes. "Whatever. What do you need?"

"The truth. You said you promised someone you would protect me. Was it my father?" she asked, her heart inching into her throat.

"*Dio!* This again? Why does it matter, Nikki? It's ancient history."

"It matters to me. Answer the question."

"Per l'amor di Dio! Fine," he spat, his eyes meeting hers. "I promised your father I'd keep you safe. Keep you out of all of this shit! Happy?"

"When did he do that? Why?" she pressed.

"About a year before he died. Crime rates around the shop were sky high and linked to organized groups. He feared you'd get caught up in it since you spent so much time down there," he explained, his expression guarded.

A year before he died. She thought back to that time, trying to piece together why her father would have been worried for her safety. Damon was right about the crime rates and their link to organized crime, but there was more to his story than that. Her father didn't take promises lightly. If he asked this of Damon, it was about more than protecting her from street crime.

Something Damon said in the car came back to her then: "I didn't give you up all those years ago to lose you like this." What had he meant by that? He didn't *give her up*; he threw her away.

Unless...

She stopped pacing when it hit her. Her parents knew Damon's father, knew what he did for a living, which meant they knew what Damon was involved in. And knowing that, they would never want her to be with him. But they knew they couldn't just tell her to break things off with Damon. She was too stubborn and too in love to have listened to them then, Mafia entanglements and all.

But her father could tell Damon. He revered Al Eleuteri. If Al asked him to do something, even something like breaking Nikki's heart, Damon would have done it out of respect for him.

Nikki spun around. "Did my father ask you to end things between us?"

Damon winced, but he didn't respond at first. He stood there, the muscles along his jaw popping under the strain of his teeth grinding together. But after a long minute, his hard, guarded expression shifted, revealing the Damon she'd fallen in love with all those years ago: the vulnerable boy with the biggest heart of anyone she knew.

"Yes, he did. And rightfully so," he said, his voice tight with emotion.

The words felt like taking an arrow in the chest. "What do you mean, *and rightfully so*? He had no right to do that—no matter how he felt about what you did with Carlo. Being with you was *my* decision, not his!" she roared.

"He had every right!" he roared back. "Take a look at my life. I have nothing to offer you but violence, bloodshed, and death. That's no life for you. Your father knew that, and he asked me—*begged me*—to break things off with you. He didn't want what happened to his mother and father to happen to you, to *us*. Can't you understand that?"

"Yes, I get it: he was worried about me and wanted to keep me safe. But that didn't give him the right to ask that of you or *you* the right to decide what I needed without talking to me about it first. We were together, Damon. You should have come to me. Besides, just because you were involved with Carlo didn't mean what happened to my grandparents would happen to us," she said, forcing back the tears she could feel building behind her eyes.

"Seriously? Look around: Jake's mother is dead because of Carlo's lifestyle; your grandparents died because of it; your father was targeted in Europe because of it. Being with a man in my line of work is dangerous. Admit it!"

She threw up her hands. "Fine! In those cases, it was dangerous. But look at my life. You and I aren't together, and yet I'm in danger from the same kind of people you and my dad were trying to protect me from. Our breaking up didn't keep me from any of that. So why obliterate my heart? Why make me struggle to trust men for years, huh? What was the fucking point?"

Damon shook his head. "The irony isn't lost on me. Believe me. And no one is sorrier for the way things ended between us than I am." He moved closer so they were toe to toe. "I hated hurting you—still hate myself for what I did—but it was the only way to break things off. I couldn't tell you the truth. You would have argued with me, asked things of me that were impossible. And I couldn't flat-out lie to you, either. You wouldn't have believed me if I'd said I needed a break or that my feelings for you had changed. You could always read me, still can. That meant I had to do something dramatic and irreversible, no matter how much it killed me to do it."

She wanted to scream at him that he was wrong, that he didn't have to hurt her the way he did, but that would have been a lie. He was right. She would have known he was lying and would have fought the breakup if he'd been honest with her.

"And honestly," he continued, his eyes misting over, "I always knew, deep down, that our being together was a risk to your safety—that someone could target you because of me. But I was, and still am, a selfish motherfucker. I loved you so much, so utterly and completely, that I refused to acknowledge the truth and let you go. But when Al approached me and told me about what happened to his family and to Carlo's, and what would inevitably happen to you, I couldn't deny it anymore. I knew what I had to do, and I did it because I loved you and because there was nothing I wouldn't do for you," he finished, the tears he'd been holding back breaking free at last.

A flurry of questions erupted in her head: Why didn't he quit? If he loved her so much, why didn't he choose her? Why did he choose the Mafia?

But she didn't ask them. She knew the answers: like with Carlo and her grandparents, their love had been destroyed by impossible circumstance.

Nikki's eyes flooded with tears as her heart broke all over again. She pulled him into a tight embrace and cried into his shoulder for all the pain they'd both endured and for the love they'd lost.

They stayed like that, clinging to each other like buoys in a storm, for an immeasurable time. Eventually, the tears stopped and they broke apart, both wrung out from the rollercoaster of a day.

"I'm so sorry I hurt you, bella. Please believe that," Damon said as she wiped away his tears.

Nikki nodded. "I know. I understand."

He peered down into her eyes. "Are you sure?"

She thought about that for a moment and decided she was sure. Knowing that Damon hadn't cheated on her because he was a jerk or because she wasn't *enough woman for him*, as Angela had said, lifted a weight from her shoulders.

"It hurts to know that what we had was ruined because of circumstance, but I'll be okay. It's better to know the truth, even if it's painful," she answered.

"All right. I really do need to go, but I'll see you later."

Nikki watched as he drove away, her heart aching for him and the sacrifices he'd made for her. He always said she was the strongest person he knew, but he was wrong. Damon was the strongest.

"Angel?"

She turned and found Jake standing a few feet from her. She'd been so lost in her thoughts she hadn't heard him come out. She didn't say anything at first. She simply stood there, looking at him, struck by the realization that if her father hadn't split up her and Damon, it was unlikely that Jake would be standing there today. She and Damon would have been together now, and that would have been wrong. As much as she'd loved Damon, and as good a man as he was, he wasn't the one for her.

Jake was.

In Jake's eyes, they were partners; in Damon's, she'd been a possession —a treasured one but a possession all the same. Her teenaged self hadn't seen it that way, but it was true. And eventually, years down the road, *that* would have destroyed them—not his Mafia entanglements. Damon wouldn't see it that way, but it was true.

Jake took another step toward her. "Angel? You okay?" he asked, worry flickering in his fathomless eyes.

"I'm fine," she said, closing the distance between them. "How about you? Everything okay with your dad?"

He nodded. "Yeah. He wanted to ask some questions about Ma's journal. I told him I'd call him tomorrow after I looked at it." He frowned. "Are you sure you're all right? You've been crying."

"I have been, but I'm fine. Really," she insisted.

"What happened?"

She smiled sadly. "I found out the truth about why Damon and I broke up," she said, telling him all about it. He listened intently, a myriad of emotions flowing over his face as she told him their story.

"Damn. I knew he'd done it on purpose, but I didn't know why," he said after she'd finished. "I guess he's a better man than I gave him credit for."

Nikki's brows shot up. "You knew? How?"

"He and I got into it at my apartment the morning you found Angela there. It slipped out while we were arguing, but he never said why he did it. Just that he had to," he explained. "What happens now?"

She cocked her head to the side. "What do you mean?"

He shifted his feet. "Well, you know that he didn't want to end things with you, and it's obvious that he still loves you. How do you feel about that? He was your first love, and from the looks of that conversation, that love was intense."

"Yes, it was," she agreed. "But learning what really happened hasn't changed anything in the present. I love Damon—part of me always will—but I am *in love* with you. *You* are my present and my future, Jake. Not him."

Relief washed over him, chasing away the worry. "Thank God. I don't know what I would have done if you'd said differently," he breathed. "There is no me without you, angel. You're my world."

"And you're mine."

A decadent sound rumbled through Jake as he swept her into his arms and kissed her. He carried her into the house, where they spent the rest of the night showing each other how deeply and purely their love ran, forgetting their worries and the danger while they could.

32

"Tell me again where Damon met this woman," Nikki said to Jake as she worked the brunette wig onto her head.

"She's one of his contacts—whatever that means," he called from the bathroom.

They'd only been in Italy for a little over three hours, much of which had been spent getting to the hotel from the airport and going over the plan with Damon one last time. Carlo phoned when they landed in Bologna with news that Marco and Jack were together in Rome and that several men had been dispatched to Modena after Nikki and Jake left SFO.

She knew what Damon meant by *contact*. This woman, who allegedly looked very much like Nikki, was one of his *puttanas*. Nikki scowled in the mirror, straightening the wig. She didn't like the idea of Jake hanging out with her, especially when it meant he'd be acting like she was Nikki. The thought of it made her skin crawl. But it was a necessary component to their plan. While Jake and the puttana led the surveillance tail away by touring Modena and pretending to be madly in love, she would be slipping out the back of the hotel in her disguise to retrieve the USB drive from the bank and send the file to Gianni Luccianno.

Jake came out of the bathroom, watching as she donned the wide-brimmed black hat over the wig. It was the final piece of her disguise. "Wow. You look incredible," he said, coming over to her.

She turned and smiled up at him from beneath the stylish hat. Even in pumps, she had to tilt her head back to meet his eyes. "You like the Audrey Hepburn look?"

He gave her one of his crooked smiles. "I like anything on you...or nothing at all, now that you mention it," he said, pulling her into him.

She wrapped her arms around his neck. "Funny, I feel the same way about you."

Jake leaned in and brushed a kiss over her lips, igniting swirls of heat beneath her skin. "Be careful out there today." His expression was serious as he pulled back.

"I will," she vowed. "You make sure you do the same."

He released her and grabbed his wallet. "I've got the easy part. You're the one getting the flash drive and meeting up with some dude Damon and Carlo know from the dark web."

"True, but you and What's-Her-Name will have Marco's guys following you," she replied, her stomach souring at the thought. Jake was the one in real danger today.

"I'll be fine. Don't worry. Just focus on getting that drive and meeting me at the train station for the four o'clock train to Brunate."

"I'll be there," she said, giving him a little salute, when Damon burst through the door adjoining their rooms with her lookalike in tow, whistling loudly.

"Damn, bella. You look good enough to eat!"

"She does, and I can't wait to savor her later," Jake replied for her, wrapping his arm around her waist in a gesture that was as possessive as his words.

"I'm sure you can't," Damon sneered.

"Damon, are you sure I have to wear this?" a heavily accented woman asked, appearing in the doorway. "It's so *Americano*, so uncultured. I look hideous," she whined, scowling at the tank top, jeans, and flip-flops she wore. They were Nikki's clothes.

Nikki arched a brow, letting the sting of her words go. She was doing all of them a huge favor, and from the looks of her, it might work. She really did resemble Nikki, from her height and shape to the honey-blond hair spilling over her shoulders. Add to it the outfit, and she made the perfect lookalike.

Damon smiled at her begrudgingly. "Sofia, you look beautiful—as always," he said, strolling over to her and pressing a kiss to her cheek. "And yes, you have to wear that. It's what Nikki would normally wear."

Sofia preened under Damon's attention. "All right. If you insist." She turned her gaze from Damon to Nikki and Jake, her focus zeroing in on Jake and all but skipping over Nikki.

"Ah, are you the man I'll be with today?" she asked, strutting over to Jake with a sultry little smile.

"He is," Nikki replied before Jake could utter a word.

Sofia flicked a glance at Nikki. "Well, this definitely makes up for having to wear *these* clothes," she said, placing a hand on Jake's chest.

"Take your—" Nikki started to say, but Jake cut in.

"I'm Jake. It's nice to meet you, Sofia." He took her hand from his chest and shook it while keeping the other firmly wrapped around Nikki.

"It's nice to meet you too," she purred.

"I'm Nikki, by the way. You know, the woman you're impersonating," she said, extending her hand.

"It's nice to meet you," Sofia replied, her eyes never leaving Jake's as she pressed a hand to his chest again.

Well, then.

Sensing her increasing dislike of the puttana and her roving eyes and hands, Damon stepped forward and pulled Nikki away from Jake. "All right, kids. It's time to go." He motioned for Jake to take Sofia and make their exit.

Nikki's stomach sank. This was it. There was no turning back. "Right." She turned to Jake. "Be careful out there. Watch your back."

Jake walked over to her and gave her a final kiss. "You too. I'll see you at four o'clock." He turned to Sofia. "Shall we?"

The puttana flounced over to him. "Yes, we shall. See you later, Damon," she called over her shoulder as Jake led her through the adjoining-room door.

"Everything is going to be fine," Damon said, tugging at Nikki's hand.

She turned to him, shoving the image of Sofia with her hands on Jake out of her head. "Do you really think so?" she asked, hating that her voice shook.

He ran a hand down her arm. "I do."

"Okay." She exhaled. "Let's do this."

She and Damon left the room then and took separate elevators to the ground floor. Once there, Nikki would take a taxi to the Unicredit Bank uptown, where she would access the security deposit box with the new fake ID and passport Damon had made for her, bearing her grandmother's maiden name. Once she had the USB, she would grab another taxi and meet Damon inside the cathedral at Piazza Grande. From there, they would slip out the back to a small café behind the church to meet Dominic, the guy Damon worked with when it came to sensitive online transactions and deals brokered over the dark web. Meanwhile, Jake and Sofia would be touring the Ferrari museum on the opposite side of town, only no one would ever see them leave. Once inside the museum, they would slip into disguises. Sofia would don a brunette wig and classic sundress while Jake changed into a suit, fedora, and dark glasses. They would then slip out the side door and disappear into the crowd of tourists and locals. The four were scheduled to rendezvous at the train station in Verona, where Jake, Nikki, and Damon would board a train headed for Brunate to hide out for a few days while Gianni got the file and, hopefully, put a hit out on Marco and Jack. They would then hop another train to Le Mans, France, while Sofia took a train back to Milan, where she lived.

If it all worked as planned, that was. The trouble was: things of this nature rarely did.

∾

JAKE ROLLED OVER IN BED, HIS HAND INSTINCTIVELY REACHING OUT FOR NIKKI. When he found nothing but cool sheets, he turned onto his back, his eyes scanning the moonlit room. He let out a quiet breath when he saw her standing at the windows, her gaze fixed on the silvery waters of Lake Como.

His breath caught in his chest at the sight of her. Standing there, in the incandescent light of the full moon, she looked positively ethereal—an angel come to life.

His angel.

It still shocked him, even now after so many months, that she was in his life. If someone had told him a year ago that his life was headed in this direction, he would have laughed it off, saying things like that only happened in books and movies, not in real life and certainly not to guys like him. And yet here he was: deeply, madly in love with the woman of his dreams, who loved him in return just as fiercely.

He'd never been so happy to be wrong about something.

He slipped out of the bed, walked over to where she stood and placed his hands on her delicate shoulders, feeling the warmth of her skin beneath the silk robe she wore. "Angel? What's wrong? Can't you sleep?"

She shook her head. "My mind wouldn't shut down." She leaned back against the window.

"You're worried about the plan? Why? Damon said the email went off without a hitch—that we were in the clear," he said, noting that her cell phone was clutched in one of her hands.

"I know. But...we haven't heard anything from your dad. We don't know if Luccianno saw it yet or if he's made a move against Marco and Jack. For all we know, they could still be out there, roaming free—looking for us."

"Is that why you're holding your phone? Did you think Damon would text you tonight?"

"Yes. He said he'd text when he got word, no matter what time it was."

Jake hated to see her like this. He'd do anything to ease her mind. But he knew there was little he could do, especially when he was worried too. He'd hoped they'd hear something by now; it had been four days since the email was delivered.

"I know it's been days since we sent the file, but I'm sure everything is fine. We have to be patient," he said.

Nikki puffed out a breath. "You're prob—" She stopped short when her phone chirped. "Oh my God! How did you do that?" She gasped and opened the text-messaging app, her eyes going wide. "It's from Damon."

"Well?" he asked. "What does it say?"

A giant smile lit up her face. "It says Carlo got word that a hit was put out on Marco, Jack, and anyone connected to them. And that Marco has gone to ground for now, but that it shouldn't be long before he's found. It also says the Irish are backing off—that I'm no longer of interest to them." She frowned at the screen.

"What is it, angel?"

Nikki looked up from the phone. "Not to be a Debbie Downer, but… why do you think the Irish lost interest? They were waiting to see what Marco did before deciding what to do about me. Why suddenly back off like this?"

Good question. Jake took her phone and read the text. "I don't know. But it doesn't look like Damon's worried about it. And if he's not worried, I don't think we should be, either."

She took the phone and tossed it onto the bed. "You're right. Damon would be on high-alert mode if there was something to worry about with the Irish, giving us orders to lie low." She smiled up at Jake, and he could have sworn it lit up the room. "It's over, then."

Relief washed over him, chasing away all the dark thoughts and worries in an instant.

It was over. She was free.

He pulled her into his arms. "It is, baby." He buried his face in the silky fall of her hair. "I told you everything would be all right."

Nikki wrapped her arms around him and nuzzled his neck. "I can't believe it. I'm free—at least once Marco and Jack are eliminated."

It couldn't happen soon enough. Jake wanted all of this behind them so they could move forward and work on building a life together—one free of the demons from their pasts.

"I know. I can't wait for that either." He pulled back and stared into her hypnotic eyes. "But for now, let's celebrate the victory of the day. It's only a matter of time before Marco and Jack are found and dealt with. Okay?"

She bit down on her lower lip, eliciting a deep, rumbling growl from him. "Okay," she said as he pulled that luscious lip free. "What should we do to celebrate?"

"I have a few ideas." He grinned, loosening the sash of her robe, watching as it pooled around her feet in a puddle of white silk.

She shivered as he caressed her naked body with his eyes. "I see. And what exactly do you have in mind?" she purred, her femme fatale in full swing.

Jake reached up and cupped her breasts, loving how they filled his hands as if they were made for him. "Why don't I show you?"

33

The train station in Brunate was bustling with tourists and locals alike as Nikki, Jake, and Damon worked their way through the crowd of arrivals to board the train bound for Le Mans, France. They were nearly to the doors when a young girl squealed.

"Mom! That's her! That's Nikki Elliot!"

Nikki stopped and turned, smiling. "Can I help you?" she asked the mother and daughter, American tourists by the looks and sounds of them.

The girl came rushing up to her. "I saw you race at Circuit of the Americas last month. You guys were amazing!" she gushed.

"Well, thank you," Nikki said, smiling at the girl. "Would you like an autograph?"

The girl blushed. "I don't have anything to sign, but I'd love a picture with you, if that's okay."

Damon tugged on Nikki's arm. "We really need to board the train and get into our compartments," he said, frowning as he scanned the crowd.

While Damon was relieved that Luccianno got the email and had moved forward to take out his son and accomplices, he was still concerned about Marco. As long as he was breathing, he was a threat. Nikki understood. She wouldn't feel completely safe until Marco and Jack were both dead.

"I know," she said. "But this will only take a second."

Damon muttered a string of filthy curses as she turned to the girl. "I'd be happy to take a picture with you." She moved next to the girl while her mother snapped a photo.

"This is perfect! I'm putting it up on my Instagram right now!" she squeaked. "Thank you so much!"

Nikki smiled, watching her dart off with her mother, feeling a little stab of envy at the sight of them. She'd once traveled across Italy with her mother too. In fact, she'd been around the same age as this girl. It was an amazing trip, one she'd never forget.

A warm hand slid across her shoulders. "Come on, angel. It's time to go," Jake's deep voice rumbled in her ear.

She turned and smiled up at him, grateful they were together and that things were finally falling into place. For the first time in years, her life was headed in the direction she wanted it to go, and she had this amazing man to share it with.

She made a silent vow then to savor this joy and her life with Jake going forward and to never, ever take it for granted. She would live as her father had always told her: loving those close to her and never giving up on the things that mattered.

～

Nikki sat up, careful not to disturb Jake. She glanced down at her phone—it was after midnight. The three of them had booked passage in first-class sleeper compartments for the ten-hour train ride from Brunate to Le Mans.

Her stomach rumbled. She clutched at it, as if that would quiet the starving Wolverine inside her, remembering she hadn't eaten anything for dinner. She'd pigged out on snacks much of the afternoon, her appetite revived by the news about the impending hit on Marco and Jack and word that the Irish were no longer a problem, and wasn't hungry when dinner rolled around.

But she was starving now.

She reached down and slipped on her flats, remembering there was a late-night snack service in the first-class dining car. Quietly, so as not to wake Jake, she slid out of their compartment and made her way to the dining car.

The hallways were deserted, as were the couchette compartments in the first two cars. The train was fairly empty from what she remembered when they boarded back in Brunate, with most of the passengers riding up front in the second-class cars. Her stomach continued to rumble as she made her way across the four deserted cars to the dining car, linking the first- and second-class sections together. The dining room was empty, save for the table of crackers, fruits, and a variety of cheeses and cookies laid out for travelers like her who needed a quick snack.

She grabbed a plate, nibbling on several grapes as she did, and reached for the cheese platter. She was about to grab several hunks of Swiss to go with her grapes when a tingling sensation erupted across the back of her neck.

She looked up from the food and glanced around. There was no one in the car but her. Shrugging off the eerie sensation, she turned and loaded her plate.

"You should really try the Parmesan, stellina. I hear it's very good," a familiar voice suggested from the rear of the car, near the doors.

Nikki whipped around, dropping the plate of food when she spotted the owner of the voice.

Marco.

"You look surprised to see me. Why is that, I wonder?" he said, cocking his head to the side.

"I-I..." she stammered, unable to find the words around the pounding of her heart and the blood roaring in her ears.

"Perhaps you thought my father's men would have found me by now, as they found Jack, and chopped my body into little pieces before feeding it to the crows—just like I had done to my father's men at the Forum. You remember that night, don't you?"

Her stomach roiled at the gruesome memory and the new image of Jack falling to the same fate. While she wasn't sad he was gone, she hadn't pictured him dying such a brutal death.

Karma really was a bitch.

"How...how did you find me?" she choked out, inching back toward the door.

Marco followed her, step by step. "It's funny. I knew you were in the country; my men were following you and your *Jake* while you toured the city, but then you both seemed to vanish from sight, just like that." He snapped his fingers. "One minute you were in the museum, and the next you were gone—nowhere to be found," he said, pulling his phone from his pocket. "We searched for days—a difficult task, as I, too, am in hiding—and came up empty-handed. Until today."

He held up his phone, revealing an image of her and the fan at the train station in Brunate. "You see, I follow you on Facebook and Instagram—like all of your devoted fans. When she posted the picture and tagged you in it, I got a notification." He leered down at the phone. "Social media can be such a handy tool, don't you think?"

Nikki's heart sank. They were in serious shit—all because she stopped to acknowledge a fan.

Damn it to hell.

"Marco, please. Don't hurt Jake or Damon. You've got me. I'm the one you want," she pleaded, continuing to inch toward the door until she backed into a wall of muscle. She gasped as a heavy arm wrapped around her neck, securing her there.

Marco reached into the breast pocket of his jacket and pulled out a large hunting knife. Light gleamed off the wicked blade as he admired the weapon. "Yes, I've got you, but it's not enough for me to simply kill you. I want you to suffer. I want you to watch as I take the lives of those you love, slowly, painfully. I want you to feel the agony of losing someone dear to you, knowing it was your fault. And then, once you've endured that unimaginable horror, I will take your life. It's the very least you owe me since my own days are numbered thanks to you. At least once I've done this, I can die in peace, knowing the bitch who signed my death sentence suffered before she died."

A potent blend of rage and hatred flooded her veins like a nitrous oxide boost, obliterating her fear. It would be a cold day in hell before she let this bastard hurt any of them, at least not without a fight.

"I hate to break it to you, Marco, but that isn't going to happen," she sneered.

His deep-blue eyes flared. "We'll see about that," he hissed, lunging for her.

With lightning-quick movements, Nikki fired off a snap kick to his jaw, sending Marco crumpling to the ground and the knife clattering away. Before the thug behind her could react, she thrust her head backward, and her skull collided with his nose with a sickening *crunch*. The man roared as he stumbled back, allowing her to slip from his grasp and spin around to deliver a powerful kick to his groin and a follow-up one to his head as he lurched forward.

The thug crumpled to the floor, out cold. Wasting no time, Nikki leaped over his prone form and darted down the aisle to the end of the dining car.

Just as she yanked open the door to the connecting compartment, Marco lurched to his feet and came after her, rolling off obscenities and threats.

She scrambled through the door, darted across the bogie, wrenched open the next door, and dashed into the car. She sprinted down the aisle, her mind searching for a plan. With no weapon on her, she had few options. The best one and the one she liked the least was leading him back to her compartment, where her gun was stashed. The other and more difficult plan was to find a weapon—a knife or a fire axe—*something* she could use to fight him with before she got to her bunk. But there were no weapons that she could see between here and her compartment.

Nikki charged across the empty seating area, thanking God that this part of the train was deserted. She didn't want anyone getting caught up in this and getting hurt. And they would get hurt if they stumbled upon her and Marco. He would never leave any witnesses behind.

When she reached the end of the car, Marco was fast on her heels. She'd just gotten into the next bogie and partially opened the second connecting door when he leapt at her and snagged her ankle, knocking her to the ground.

The wind rushed out of her lungs in a *whoosh* as she hit the cold metal floors of the bogie. Marco used the seconds she was stunned to his advantage. He grabbed a fistful of her hair and pulled her body into the center of the bogie, leaving the door ajar.

"You stupid puttana! Did you actually think you'd escape? Did you think Aldo was the only guy I brought? I have two more on the way up from the front of the train where they were searching," he said, forcing her onto her back. Her eyes widened in horror as he raised the knife over his head. "I guess my plans for you have changed. I'll carve you up right here and toss your parts to the crows. Then I'll go after your friends for sport."

Nikki found her bearings, reached up with her free arm, and grabbed Marco's wrist as he brought it down to her chest. The blade came to a stop inches from her heart. Marco was strong, but so was she, thanks to her workouts with Tsai. He was always pushing her to build her upper-body strength, and it paid off.

They were at a deadlock.

Holding his arm back but feeling him gain on her, she frantically tried to free her legs and flip him off her, but his position wasn't quite right, and he was too heavy to throw off completely. Even so, she managed to jar him enough to pull free the hand pinned by his left leg. With a desperate cry, she thrust her hand upward and jammed the heel of it into his nose. Marco reared back with a roar, blood pouring from his nose, soaking her shirt. The knife flew backward.

Nikki scrambled back and over to open the door, but like the not-quite-dead psycho in a classic horror flick, Marco recovered enough to grab her by the hair and fling her into the exterior door. Her head spun from the blow, giving him enough leeway to come crashing down on her and pin her to the bogie's floor.

He raised the knife once more, and she knew this was it. Her last thought as she closed her eyes and braced for the impact was of Jake and how much she loved him, wishing with all her heart that things could have been different.

$\sim$

"Dude! Wake the fuck up!" a snide voice hissed in Jake's ear while a hand clamped down on his shoulder and shook him.

Jake's eyes snapped open. "Get the hell off me, asshole," he bit out, shoving Damon's hand from his shoulder. "What the fuck are you doing in here?"

"Do you see something missing from your compartment?" Damon pointed at the bed.

He looked down at the empty spot where Nikki had been curled up against him. "What? She's probably in the bathroom." He pressed a hand to the spot where she should be. It was cold. His eyes snapped to Damon's as his stomach sank.

"It's cold. I know. I checked. If she's in the bathroom, she's taking one hell of an epic shit—something she's not prone to doing," he said.

"How the fuck would you know? Do you study her bathroom habits?" Jake snarled, grabbing his shoes, the bad feeling growing. Where could she have gone for this long?

Damon stepped out of the compartment. "I've known her for years; you've known her months. I know this kind of thing."

Jake followed him out of the compartment and down the deserted couchette car to the bogie where the restrooms were located. He shoved Damon out of the way when they reached the bathroom door.

"I've got it," he said, pulling on the door. It came flying open, revealing its emptiness.

Fuck.

Damon rolled off a string of curses as he ripped open the next compartment door and charged down the hallway. Jake followed him, his heart pounding against his ribs. Where could she have gone at this hour? Then it hit him: the dining car. She hadn't eaten dinner because she'd snacked all afternoon. She must have woken up hungry and headed down there to grab something from the late-night snack service.

"The dining car. That's where she has to be," he said to Damon's back.

"Let's hope so," Damon called over his shoulder, picking up the pace.

They dashed through another bogie and into one of the open-seating cars in first class, hearing a scream erupt from the bogie at the opposite end.

Nikki.

Jake's heart lurched into his throat as he and Damon sprinted to the end of the car, where the doors were open. Damon dove through the doors and went tumbling into the next compartment with another figure.

Jake came to a skidding halt in the bogie when he saw Nikki scrambling to her feet, her shirt soaked with blood.

NO!

"Angel? Are you all right?" he said, gaping at the blood seeping through her shirt.

"It's not my blood; it's Marco's!" she shrieked, trying to pull out of his hold. "We have to help Damon!"

Jake thrust her behind him. "Stay here!" he ordered, charging into the next compartment, where Damon was trying to wrestle the knife away from an enraged Marco.

Jake grabbed Marco by the back of the jacket, spun him around, and threw him up against the wall, sending the knife clattering away while Damon scrambled to his feet. Before they could make another move, two more men came bursting into the far end of the car.

"Gun! Where's my gun?" Damon yelled as the men rapidly approached, drawing weapons from inside their jackets.

"Here!" Jake heard Nikki shout and caught a glimpse of her throwing Damon his .45 while he pinned Marco to the wall. Thank God Damon had the foresight to bring his gun with him. Jake had forgotten his in the rush to find Nikki.

Marco lurched forward and head-butted Jake in the temple, while several muffled gunshots pierced the air. Head spinning, Jake fell backward and crashed in between a pair of seats, giving Marco enough time to pull a second knife from his jacket and plunge it toward Jake's chest.

The knife never hit him.

Nikki lunged behind Marco and drove the knife that had gone flying into the back of Marco's neck, killing him instantly.

Marco's lifeless body slumped forward and came to rest across the seats.

"Are you okay?" She panted, reaching down and grabbing Jake.

He nodded. "Thanks to you. You okay?" He stood and pulled her shaking body into his arms.

"I am. Damon, what about you? Did they hit you?" she asked, looking around Jake.

Damon turned, clutching his shoulder. "It's only a flesh wound," he grunted, dropping into one of the seats.

Nikki whimpered and darted over to him. "Are you sure?"

"Yeah. I'm familiar with them." He winced, rotating his arm to show her. "Looks like we'll have matching scars, bella."

Nikki threw her arms around him. "I guess so," she said, crushing him to her.

Damon returned the embrace. "It's okay...I'm fine. It's over, Nik. It's really over. You're safe now," he said, burying his face in her hair.

Standing, she nodded. "How are we going to explain the bodies to the authorities?"

Jake pulled Nikki into his side. He needed to feel her to remind him that she was alive and safe.

"We're not," Damon said, leaning back and pulling his phone out of his pocket.

"How is that possible? We can't hide them; someone will find them in the morning," Nikki said.

"Watch." Damon grinned, dialing a number. "Dom, it's D. I need you to intercept the train I'm on." He rolled off the train and track numbers. "I need it to stop so we can open the doors. Then I need you to get the security feeds and delete the footage in first class from midnight on, then disable the cameras altogether. Can you handle that?" He paused. "Good. Do it now." Damon ended the call and immediately dialed another number. "Nino, call Anthony and have him send the cleaner to the coordinates I'm about to text you and meet me there. Got it? Good," he clipped and ended that call.

Jake frowned. "How is Dom going to intercept the train and stop it?"

Damon leaned back, clutching his wounded arm. "By hacking into the control center and jamming the connection between the train's modem and the control center using a GSM jammer. Once the connection between the train's communication system and the control center is lost, the train will stop," he explained.

"And how long will that take?" Jake asked.

Damon glanced down at his watch. "It should stop about...now." The train shuddered and came to a screeching halt. He smiled up at Jake. "Like I said, your dad only hires the best." He motioned to the bodies littering the car. "Help me get these off the train."

The three of them heaved the lifeless bodies of Marco and his goons off the locomotive and into the pasture bordering the tracks.

"All right. That should do until my guys and the cleaner get here," Damon said, leaning against the open train door. He whipped out his phone and made another call to his dark-web contact to get the train moving again.

"Good," Nikki breathed, leaning against Jake. "Let's get back to our compartments."

Jake pushed off the wall. "I'm for that," he said. "Are you coming, Damon?"

Damon shook his head as he slid the phone back into his pocket. "Nope. This is where I get off. I need to take care of the mess outside and get my arm patched up."

"What? No. I won't leave you out in some dark pasture in BFE. You can get your arm checked out at the next stop," Nikki said, rounding on him.

"I'll be fine, bella. I need to make sure the cleaners show up, and my arm can't wait until morning. Besides, how would I explain it to the hospital? I need Italy's equivalent of a Max for this."

Nikki's shoulders slumped. "Oh, right. Still...I don't like the idea of you being out here alone. We could—"

"No. I don't want you anywhere near these guys. The less you know, the better. Remember?"

"Fine." She sighed, wrapping Damon in a tight hug. Damon returned it —a little too enthusiastically for Jake's taste—then turned to Jake.

"She's all yours, prospect. Take care of her." He smirked.

Jake bit back the sharp reply dancing on his tongue, understanding the deeper meaning behind Damon's words and how hard it was for Damon to say it. He could see that the guy was still madly in love with Nikki but that he also knew she wasn't his and never would be again. The thought humbled Jake, and while he hated to admit it, underneath that douchebag exterior was a good man.

Damon hopped down from the train as the engines roared to life. Jake and Nikki watched his form recede into the darkness as the train pulled away and continued on its journey.

"Ready?" Jake asked when Damon was out of sight.

Nikki turned to him. "Ready," she said, lacing her fingers through his.

They quickly made their way back to their compartment and collapsed onto their bed after cleaning up, weary to the core.

"Do you think he'll be okay out there?" Nikki whispered into the darkness.

Jake tightened his hold on her. "I think Damon will be fine wherever he is."

She nodded. "I hope so. I wish...I wish things could be different for him."

"I know you do." He knew Nikki wanted Damon out of the Mafia life, but that was impossible. He knew too much to ever escape.

She sighed, curling into him further. "It's really over for us, isn't it? We're finally free," she said, knowing that, unlike Damon, *their* fates weren't sealed.

He pressed a kiss to her forehead. "It is, angel. It really is," he said, closing his eyes and truly relaxing for the first time in months.

As he drifted off to sleep, he said a silent prayer of thanks that they'd survived and that Nikki was free. Marco and Jack were gone, and the rest of their crew would soon follow. He also sent a silent thank-you to Damon for all he'd done tonight and for letting Nikki go all those years ago. Like the guy or not, Jake owed him a debt of gratitude—one he wouldn't forget.

∾

DAMON STOOD IN THE SHADOWS, WATCHING THE TRAIN AS IT DISAPPEARED around the bend, taking his *bella ragazza* with it. Part of him wanted to go with her, but he knew he couldn't, and it wasn't just because of the wound on his arm. His job here was done. He'd fulfilled his promise to her father, and while he was loath to admit it, Damon knew that Masercotti was perfect for Nikki. He could and would give her all the things she needed—things Damon never could.

He turned, hearing the sounds of a car approaching from the south. The car slowed and came to a stop several yards back. Damon held up his hand to shield his eyes from the headlights.

"Yo! Boss!" he heard Nino call as the car door opened.

It was the middle of the fucking night, in the middle of Timbuk Freaking Four, and Nino *still* managed to be cheerful.

"Yeah. Turn the goddamn headlights off, will you? You're gonna blind me already," Damon ordered.

"Sorry!" Nino chirped, setting the parking lights instead. He jogged over to Damon. "The cleaner's on the way with Anthony. Did you want to wait around or go on ahead to Michael's and get that arm looked at?"

"Let's wait. I haven't met the cleaner from these parts. I want to make sure he's legit. While we wait, give me an update."

Nino shook his head. "There isn't much right now. The next shipment is ready for Correa, and the Irish are still running scared from the Nikki thing—have been for the last couple of days." He looked around Damon to where the bodies were piled up. "And it looks like the Marco-and-Jack business is over too. Yeah?"

"Yeah. That problem's been solved," he said, breathing easy for the first time in years. Something Nino said niggled at him, though. "You said the Irish are still running scared. Any idea why?"

Nino shook his head. "Nope. Just that O'Brien doesn't want to bother with Nikki—says she's not worth the hassle."

Damon nodded. It was unlike O'Brien to back down like that. Maybe it had something to do with Jake being Carlo's son. O'Brien had always feared Carlo. That had to be it. He gave himself an internal shake, letting his worries over Nikki go at last.

Turning away from Nino and the bodies behind him, Damon looked to where the train had disappeared around the bend, as pointless wishes whispered in his ear—wishes that would never come true for a man like him.

"You okay, boss?" Nino asked after a beat.

Damon let out a heavy sigh and turned to his friend. "Yeah, man. I'm fine," he said, knowing he'd lied but also knowing he couldn't do a damn thing about it. Like it or not, this was his life. It might not be the one he'd chosen—that life was on a train bound for France and greater things—but it was the one he had, and he needed to make the best of it. No matter how much he wished things could be different.

EPILOGUE

WeatherTech Raceway, August 2018

Gianni Luccianno removed his wide-brimmed hat and wiped the sweat from his brow. The California sun was a brutal bitch, especially in the grandstands overlooking turn eleven. The potential risk for heatstroke was worth it, though. Being out there, watching the Ferrari prototype kill it on the track solidified the fact that not only letting Nikki Elliot live after she'd killed his son but also hiring her to race for the Formula 1 team he now controlled had been a wise decision.

"When do you plan to approach her?" asked Salvatore Antonello, Gianni's consigliere and longtime associate.

Gianni placed the hat on his head. "Soon but not now. You said she and her team usually celebrate at a local bar after a race, correct?"

Salvatore nodded. "That's right. They usually tie one on at a local roadhouse. There's one about a mile or so from here. I imagine that's where they'll be after the race. Are you sure you don't want to approach her there?"

"No. There are too many witnesses here. I want as few people as possible to know she and I are connected," he said, his dark eyes glued to the Ferrari as it roared by the grandstands.

"Are you sure this is the right thing to do?" Salvatore asked, leaning in close. "Do you really want the woman who killed Marco working for you?"

Gianni stiffened at the mention of his traitorous son. Salvatore sounded as if he should be mourning Marco. Mourning indeed. Marco, his only child, was responsible for taking out his first consigliere and several of his top men. And as if that weren't enough of a knife to the back, he then planned to eliminate him as well, according to the video file he'd received from an anonymous source—a source he eventually traced back to Nikki Elliot. If anything, Gianni should be grateful to Miss Elliot for all she did, including taking out his traitorous son.

He cut a glance at Salvatore. "Her killing Marco is of no consequence to me. If anything, her actions on the train and delivering the evidence that condemned him shows great intelligence and backbone on her part. Couple that with the fact that the Formula 1 team I now control needs a second driver, and you have the perfect fit for my next move."

"I know she has the qualifications for everything you've got planned," Salvatore began, "but I worry about her loyalties. She didn't send the file to save you—she sent it to save herself."

Gianni cheered as he watched Nikki Elliot's car soar beneath the checkered flag, taking the win. He turned to Salvatore and motioned for him to follow him out of the grandstands.

"I know exactly why she did it, Sal. I'm not naïve." He let out a quiet sigh as they reached a shaded area. "And that's why hiring her is the right move. She's brilliant, calculating, and *wants* to live, which means she'll work for me willingly—at whatever I ask of her. She values her life and the lives of those she loves too much to do otherwise. Besides, once I've got her ensconced with her partner in Europe *and* in the business down in Brazil, she won't be able to get out, no matter what she tries. The cartel won't have it, and neither will the Russians. They're even more ruthless than I am."

Salvatore nodded. "You're right. She'll be trapped once she's in with the Friar. No one escapes him and lives to tell."

"*Perfetto*," Gianni said, leading them to the winners' circle, where Nikki and her team were receiving their trophies.

He grinned as he watched the beautiful Miss Elliot take her wins, smiling graciously for the crowd. She really made the perfect addition to his organization's expansion in South America. Her success in racing would allow him to expand the smuggling side of his business in ways he never could have before, and her intelligence and ruthlessness would pay off in dealing with the Brazilians and in keeping his South American affairs hidden from Italy.

His smile broadened. He had big plans for Nikki Elliot...big plans indeed, and he couldn't wait to begin.

GLOSSARY OF ITALIAN TERMS AND PHRASES

- **stronzo:** asshole
- **coglione:**asshole
- **principessa:**princess
- **dolcezza:**sweet/sweetness/sweetheart
- **sorellina:**sister
- **bella:**beautiful
- **angioletto:**little angel
- **angelo:**angel
- **puttana:**whore
- **sí:**yes
- **fratellino:**brother
- **capisce:**understand
- **tesoro:**treasure
- **tesroino:**darling
- **grazie:**thank you
- **colpevole:**guilty
- **perfetto:**perfect
- **ragazza:**girl
- **Lo prometto:**I promise
- **mi dispiace:**I'm sorry
- **Dio mio:**my God
- **cosí bellisima:**so beautiful
- **Sono sicuro:**I'm sure
- **ben tornato:**Welcome back

- **mi bell'angioletto:** my little angel
- **Per l'amor donna di Dio!:** For the love of God
- **Sto bene:** I'm fine
- **Stai bene perdere?:** Are you okay?
- **Ti amo angelo:** I love you, angel.
- **Solo tu per sempre:** Only you, for always
- **Sei cosí bella, angelo:** You're so beautiful, angel
- **Mio caro:** My dear

GLOSSARY OF SPANISH TERMS

- **perra:**dog
- **concha:**whore/slut
- **manito:**little man
- **hermano:**brother
- **enamorarse:**in love
- **cariña:**sweetheart
- **mamacita:**little mama
- **abuelita:**grandmother
- **mi amor:**my love

AUTHOR'S NOTE

I hope you enjoyed *Against the Odds*, the first book in the Redline Series. It's a series very near and dear to my heart and one I hope you'll enjoy reading as much as I've enjoyed writing!

Up next is *Against the Heat*: Jake and Nikki believed they were free of Mafia entanglements—free to begin their life together and pursue their dreams. They were wrong. Just as things begin to fall in place, trouble rears its ugly head, forcing Jake and Nikki apart and putting them and all they love and hold dear in danger. Will Jake and Nikki hold strong under the unbearable heat pressing down on them from all sides, or will they go up in flames?

Watch for Redline Series announcements and sneak peaks on my Facebook, Twitter, and Instagram pages, as well as my website. Until then, I wish you all the very best and, of course, happy reading!--N.L.

ACKNOWLEDGMENTS

A big thank you to all of those who helped make this book possible: my amazing beta readers—Team Cavanaugh, my editor extraordinare: Kristen Hamilton, my beautiful, loving family for their unending faith in me, and my friends who've cheered me on from the beginning.

I'd also like to thank the people who inspired characters in the story. First, to the real Frankie and Johnny: your intelligence, humor, and kind hearts inspired these characters. I hope I wrote you both well. I'd also like to thank Bill Martin of Rootes Group Depot for inspiring the character of Sean Martin and the Tiger's Den. Bill, your humor, passion for all things automotive (especially Sunbeam Tigers), keen intelligence, and kind heart inspired a loveable character with a huge heart. Thank you for that, and for Timbuk Four!

And finally, a massive thank-you goes out to my readers. None of this would be possible without any of you. Thank you, thank you, *thank you* from the bottom of my heart!!! Until next time!--N.L.